Praise for Dust
debut of his n

Deuces Wild

"When you pick up a Dusty Richards novel you'd first better pull your hat down snug because you're in for a wild ride. *Deuces Wild* is no exception. . . . And while you are enjoying a mighty fine read, Dusty is very likely to teach you a few things about the American west as well. . . . You're gonna love it."

—Frank Roderus, two-time Spur Award winner

"*Deuces Wild* is a tale of peril on the desert, of revenge extracted, and of injustice righted. Richards writes of the bloody pursuit of the infamous Apache scout, Deuces . . . with the detail and authority of a man who's walked the walk and talked the talk."

—Sheldon Russell, Spur Award finalist and author of *Requiem at Dawn*

"What a great ride! . . . With twists, turns, and tensions along the way."

—Cotton Smith, author of *The Thirteenth Bullet*

"Dusty Richards continues his long-standing tradition of pleasing his readers with Western action and historical truths. A great read."

—Robert Vaughn, author of *Clarion's Call*

DEUCES WILD

DUSTY RICHARDS

POCKET STAR BOOKS
New York London Toronto Sydney

This book is a work of fiction. Names, characters, places and incidents are products of the author's imagination or are used fictitiously. Any resemblance to actual events or locales or persons, living or dead, is entirely coincidental.

An *Original* Publication of POCKET BOOKS

A Pocket Star Book published by
POCKET BOOKS, a division of Simon & Schuster, Inc.
1230 Avenue of the Americas, New York, NY 10020

ISBN: 0-7434-7565-8

First Pocket Books printing June 2004

10 9 8 7 6 5 4 3 2 1

Interior book design by Davina Mock
Cover art design by Patrick Kang
Cover illustration by Steven Assel

Manufactured in the United States of America

For information regarding special discounts for bulk purchases, please contact Simon & Schuster Special Sales at 1-800-456-6798 or business@simonandschuster.com.

I dedicate this book to my dad, John. Together, we saw the sun come up in Bloody Basin on my first deer hunt. In the Superstition Mountains, we searched for the Lost Dutchman Gold Mine. He never knew much about a horse, but he eared down my first one. And when I got bucked off and we had to catch her again in a forty-acre field, he said, "This time, ride her." I did. Thanks, Dad. I'll keep trying to ride them.

DEUCES WILD

Prologue

A BREATH OF HOT AIR THROUGH THE SIDE WINDOW raised the sheer curtain, the first such relief in hours to the crowded military courtroom. Captain Jason Kimble used his finger to loosen the tightly buttoned collar. A woolen uniform in the heat of the Arizona summer was not only ludicrous but harsh punishment.

"Seven Forty-five is the accused's tribal number," the attorney for the defense reiterated, standing at the table beside his seated client, the Apache scout Deuces, on trial for the murder of another scout by the name of Sombrero. The deceased scout's numerical designation was Sixty-eight. Captain Kimble was familiar enough with the system used to identify the Apaches; the first number defined the tribal group, the next number was a personal ID.

Throughout the morning, the prosecutor had grilled his expert witnesses, who explained how Seven Forty-five had crushed Sixty-eight's skull with a rock tomahawk, cut off his male organ and inserted it into Sombrero's mouth, and also castrated the victim. No mention was made of the whereabouts of the man's other missing parts. A ghastly enough way to mutilate anyone, even for an aborigine.

"Excuse me!" Someone burst through the double doors. The man swept off a wide-brimmed straw hat and strode up the center aisle. On his way, he casually dropped the sombrero on the floor and continued his march.

From his center seat between the other two judges, Colonel O'Malley bolted up in surprise at the intrusion. "This is a court of military law, sir."

"I know, sir," the man said, and pushed the dark brown hair from his forehead. "But I need to say something very important to this court."

The intruder's hard gaze struck Kimble and held him. Perhaps five feet eleven and thinly built, this man standing in the aisle appeared to be all muscle. In canvas pants, galluses, and a fresh white collarless shirt, he looked like most other civilians on the frontier.

"It's the scout, Tom Horn," Captain Brokaw whispered on O'Malley's side.

"This is highly irregular," the colonel said. "We are conducting a military court of law here. Mr. Horn, is it?"

"Yes, sir. Tom Horn, sir. I've ridden all day and night from Mexico to testify in this man's behalf."

"Why didn't you present yourself for the preliminaries of this trial?"

"I've been with the U.S. Army in pursuit of the last Chiricahua hostiles in Sonora, sir."

"Your appearance this late is very irregular. Counselors, approach the bench."

Kimble leaned forward to hear them as they gathered before the judges' table. He studied the intense face of the white scout. Horn was a legend. Even at Kimble's regular post at San Carlos, he had heard much about the exploits of this man. Behind chief scout Al Sieber, Horn was the most sought-after man for scouting in the territory. For Horn to ride back from the Sierra Madres to speak at a trial should mean something.

O'Malley looked over at Kimble. "What is your opinion?"

"I would like to hear what Horn has to say. He's a man of reputation."

Horn nodded and looked at the other two judges.

"This buck is guilty as hell. I don't know what any more discussion would do. What do you say, Brokaw?" O'Malley asked.

The man looked uncomfortable; O'Malley seemed to be leaving the decision up to him. No soldier in his right mind deliberately made a colonel angry. He might have to serve under him some time. Plus, colonels had power enough to kill a future promotion. Brokaw squirmed, obviously troubled.

"What can Horn hurt?" the defense's Lieutenant Corman asked.

"Waste more damned time," the prosecutor, Captain Hampton, growled.

"That an objection, Captain Hampton?"

"No, sir."

O'Malley sat back in his chair, his arms folded over his chest. "Don't take up the whole damn afternoon, Horn. It's hotter than seven shades of hell in here. Get on with it. You may be seated, gentlemen."

When everyone had his place, O'Malley cleared his throat. "Let the record show that Tom Horn wished to speak to this court regarding the case before us today. There being no objections, we are going to listen to Mr. Horn's words regarding the defendant in this case.

"That is why you are here, sir?" O'Malley directed his question at the scout.

"Yes, Colonel."

"That's in the record. Bailiff, swear him in."

Kimble sat back, tented his fingers, and waited. The swearing in and identification complete, Horn asked O'Malley if he might stand and give his testimony.

With a sharp nod, Horn took a few steps to the right. The man's mannerisms and movements were so cat-like they intrigued Kimble. In the ways of the giant cougars, Horn's lithe, light-footed movements spoke of smooth, rippling muscles. When the scout turned, Kimble noticed the soft, deerskin squaw boots that he wore. Some said that Horn had an Apache wife. Maybe more than one. He spoke the dialect and fluent Spanish, as well.

"You call him Seven Forty-five." Horn indicated the stone-faced Apache seated with his defense lawyer. "We call him Deuces. So I shall call him Deuces when I speak of him." Then Horn spoke a few guttural words in Apache to him. The defendant nodded.

"I asked Deuces, in Apache, if he understood what this trial meant. He told me yes."

"Mr. Horn, we have a competent translator. Ramón

Hernandez has been present at all times," the colonel directed.

"Yes, sir, but I wanted to hear Deuces tell me he savvied it all."

"You may continue, but, sir—I hope this is going to be brief."

"Deuces was born up on the Gila headwaters. His mother was half Messikin. His father was a full-blood Warm Springs Apache. He came from Victorio's band in New Mexico."

Horn held up his hand to stay the colonel's unspoken warning about brevity. "Allow me to tell about this man."

O'Malley surrendered but still looked short on patience.

"Gentlemen, Deuces was raised in the traditional Apache way. He began to hunt as a boy. You may find it disgusting, but Apache boys use bows and arrows to hunt rats. His people ate them. You people eat rabbits but not rats. Same thing, only it's hard to shoot a jackrabbit with a bow and arrow. So they learned success, first killing rats. More rats than there are rabbits, anyway.

"They teach their children many things. To hunt, but since they have no laws or judges like we do, they are taught to kill the lawless. Only way that you can survive in what them professors call a Stone Age society.

"Now, you say he's a scout and has to act like we do." Horn shook his head in disapproval and continued to pace back and forth in front of the bench. Kimble wondered if this testimony was intended for himself and the other judges or for the audience of soldiers, civilians, and women. Earlier, the women had been temporarily excused from the courtroom when the doctor made his explanation of the mutilations to the deceased's body and private parts. Too indecent for any lady's tender ears.

"Let me tell you about this man called Sombrero. His record as a scout was a four-letter word. No, ladies. I ain't going to swear." Horn held up his hands. "The word was *lazy*. He wasn't worth spit. Al Sieber would not have even re-upped him, but General Crook feared it might discourage the others we wanted to hire.

"See, Apaches don't see not working as lazy. The women do all the details. A man is a warrior and hunter. He might say he was meditating. Take my word for it, Sombrero was plain lazy."

O'Malley cleared his throat loud enough that Horn stayed him with a raised hand. "That sure ain't no reason to kill him." Horn made a face and with a shrug continued, "Though twice in Sonora, I was tempted to kill him myself."

His words drew a titter of laughter from the crowd. O'Malley's displeasure at their outburst came in a hard frown that sobered them to silence.

"Sombrero was a man of forty, who married a young girl from the White Mountain Apaches. Her name was Tish." Horn shook his head as if the whole matter upset him and finally raised his face. "That ain't her real name, but her Apache name is so long I'll not waste your afternoon listening to it each time. *Tish* will do.

"Sombrero beat Tish. Every time he returned from scouting, he beat her. That's a direct violation of army orders. She came to Deuces for relief. Her own people were clear up there at Fort Apache. She had no one else she could ask for help around here." Horn dropped his head again and shook it wearily as he kept pacing back and forth.

"I hate to be a gossip, but I think Deuces and Tish must have got real acquainted in these meetings." Then, with his finger in the air, pointing at the ceiling, he continued, "Tish told Deuces that she would divorce Sombrero, and then they could marry.

"I want to tell you what kind of a soldier this Deuces is. He was with me when Captain Crawford was killed by the Messikin army. The worst day of my life." He shook his head. His eyes shone like diamonds as he stared hard over their heads and at last drew a deep breath. "Lots of you knew the captain. May he rest in peace, but there wasn't a greater man alive or a greater friend to people like Deuces.

"I took the captain's remains to Narcozi. Deuces helped me. He made sure we weren't ambushed by Apaches or Messikins on the way." Horn removed a kerchief and dabbed both eyes. "I still cry over that. Deuces cried, too. The rest of them scouts howled all night. But this boy led me to that village, where we buried the captain in the churchyard until his body could be recovered and brought back to the United States. You know the rest of that story.

"Deuces was a great scout. You should have asked Al Sieber to come here and talk for him. He would tell you that Deuces was a good worker.

"I know, I know, Colonel. He ain't on trial for being a good scout. But I told you, Sombrero was mean, and he broke the army's rules on wife treatment.

"Two months ago, when Deuces came back from Sonora with his unit, he searched for Tish. See, Apaches don't speak of the dead. But he finally learned from a friend that when Tish told Sombrero she was going to divorce him, he flew into a rage and cut off half her nose for infidelity. That's another thing that the army prohibits Apaches from doing.

"Tish was so ashamed of her disfigurement that she went up in the Chiricahuas and hurled herself off the highest bluff.

"See, learning what that no-account Sombrero did to her, all Deuces knew was what any good Apache must do to avenge pure spite."

"Approach the bench," O'Malley said to Horn. Kimble heard the colonel whisper to Horn about the other things that Deuces did to the corpse.

Horn nodded and stepped back. "Yes, those wounds look violent to us white folks. However, by him mutilating Sombrero thatta way, Deuces made certain the man would never pleasure himself in the next world." Horn shrugged his narrow shoulders. "That don't make good sense to a white man, either, I know, but I think the record also shows he killed Sombrero at night?"

O'Malley looked at the other two. Kimble nodded. He understood that the murder took place after dark.

"Well, that means that Sombrero will have to live in the between world." With a well-you-know look at them, Horn continued, "Apaches fear dying at night worse than they do smallpox. Deuces didn't aim for him to have anything when he got out of here.

"Deuces has served his new country with loyalty. He's been of great assistance on every campaign he went on. I'm saying he's a great soldier. The man he killed was not worth spit. Gentlemen, I ask for your mercy for him."

"Is that all?" the colonel asked.

"Yes, sir. I could tell you lots more about Deuces, but I think I've made my point."

"It certainly was informative, Mr. Horn. I hope on your long ride up here, you didn't fabricate this story to earn the mercy of this court for this man."

"I'd swear on my mother's grave, sir. It's the absolute truth, sir."

"Is there anything else the defense wishes to present?"

"No, sir, the defense rests."

"Does the prosecution wish to question Mr. Horn?"

"No, sir."

"We will have summation in the morning. Gentlemen, we shall resume at nine A.M. I will instruct you to be brief. I am sure we're all weary of the time already spent on this case. Court adjourned until then."

The prisoner was taken back to his cell. The crowd filed out. O'Malley made a displeased face at the other two. "How do we disprove Horn's statement?"

"I believed the man," Kimble said.

"Well—Colonel." Brokaw acted uncertain about both the colonel's wishes and what he should say.

"Dammit, man. I want your ideas, Brokaw."

"I think Horn said—I mean, told the truth."

"My God, you two are gullible as hell. That was the best cock-and-bull fairy tale I've heard since I was six years old."

"Colonel, he made lots of sense," Kimble said, wondering at that moment if his personal convictions were overshadowing his future career.

"Then we find him not guilty and turn him loose to kill another so-called bad scout?"

"No, but I would think a sentence of ten years would be adequate," Kimble said.

"This morning, we would've had him hung."

"Yes," Kimble agreed. "But that was before Tom Horn rode in."

O'Malley slammed the table with his fist. "To hell with that gawdamn Tom Horn!"

Kimble acknowledged the man's words. "Are we excused?"

"Certainly." O'Malley turned to stare at the back wall and ignored both men. "Ten years, you say." Then he gave a great exhale. "Might as well turn him loose."

Kimble was grateful to be out of the courtroom at last and into the open air. Hot as it was out of doors, it still beat the stuffy atmosphere he left. The sutler's store was across the parade grounds. Since he was on assignment at Fort Bowie for this and two other cases, he could go and find a drink before evening mess. He might have two.

A fresh morning wind swept back the curtains. Court had resumed. The three judges took their seats, and the defense quickly rested its final argument on the merits of Tom Horn's speech. The prosecutor ranted and raved, asking again for the death sentence, but Kimble felt some of the urgency of his past pleas were softened by either the colonel's constraints or Horn's plea.

In the crowd, Kimble spotted the white scout. His all-seeing eyes were like some animal on a hunt—looking, checking, and testing the whole room; clearly, he was a man who lived by his keen wits and senses.

The arguments finally completed, O'Malley indicated for the other two to move in close.

In a whisper, he began. "We find him guilty of manslaughter and then sentence him to ten years of hard labor in the prison at the Fort Leavenworth." He looked at Kimble, who nodded, and then at Brokaw, who quickly agreed.

"Have the defendant rise," O'Malley said, turned to face the courtroom.

"We, the military court, find you, Seven Forty-five, guilty of murder of the deceased Sixty-eight. And we hereby sentence you to ten years of hard labor in the prison at Fort Leavenworth." He rapped the gavel.

"Clerk, have the papers filled out for a U.S. deputy marshal to transport the prisoner to those facilities at once."

"Yes, sir."

"Gentlemen, we will hear the court-martial proceedings against Sergeant Witcom in the morning."

Both agreed.

Kimble went out the side door and noticed someone squatted and whittling. He recognized the hat, the dirt-stained, yellow straw sombrero that Horn had dropped on the floor the day before when he came into the courtroom.

"I wish you had been easier on him," Horn said, focusing on the cedar stick and his large jackknife.

"Best that we could do under the circumstances."

Horn nodded. "We asked these people to come into our world. They have to leave all they know of their past because it don't count anymore."

"Yes," Kimble said. "That must be what we did."

Horn rose and drew his shoulders back. He shook his head in disgust. "Captain, that's the biggest reason we have so damn many soldiers in Mexico right now. Nothing these people had before still counts."

Chapter 1

AN ANNOYING DRIP FROM THE CEILING ONTO THE tarp stretched over their bed awoke him. The roof leaked. A silver flash in the bedroom window, then somewhere off toward Mount Lemon, thunder grumbled in the distance. Soon a trickle ran off the shield and began to *plunk-plunk* into the tinned pots. The drum of the storm grew heavier outside, until finally the roar swept down the Santa Cruz River Valley.

Burt Green threw his legs off the bed, and his bare soles touched the cool tile floor. The outline of her shapely form, asleep on her side, was barely visible in the bedroom's darkness, then lightning illuminated the white sheet over her. *Sleep, my love.*

Quietly, he walked barefooted on the tile through the house's main portion and out the front door. As rain drilled the palm-frond porch roof, he hurried to the edge to empty his bladder. Though he preferred not to get wet, the cold drips from above felt like ice on his bare skin.

This cloudburst might postpone his leaving for the Mexican border as he had planned for in the morning. More illuminated strikes flashed back on the mountains to the east, then to the north; thunder rumbled across the desert valley like loose cannon balls in a wagon. Finally, a spidery display of white fireworks showered down on Tucson in the south.

"You'll catch a death of cold standing out here without your clothes on, Burton," she said from the doorway in a sleep-husky voice.

He turned to look toward her and nodded. "Rains so damned seldom in this country, I wanted to savor a little of it."

She finished wrapping the gown around her willowy figure and tied the belt. He hugged her and drew a deep breath of the creosote-flavored air, mixed with the smell of wet dirt and her own flowery aroma. Gently, he rocked her, blowing in her ear and savoring their closeness. Her firm body against him, he could recall their making love only hours earlier.

"Angela, Angela, you're the rain in my desert," he said, feeling a little heady over his good fortune in their marriage.

"You still plan to leave at daybreak?" she asked dreamily.

"Maybe a little later—"

His bride of six weeks pressed herself against him, and her mouth sought his. Distracted by a new sound, he turned away to listen. The hoofbeat of charging horses stole away their moment of tenderness. Upset and uncertain about the purpose of the oncoming animals, all he could think was *The raiders were coming back.* Could they be the same ones who murdered her husband, Frederick Van Dorn, the previous fall? Burt's mind, filled with the dangers they might impose, hustled her inside and reached for the Winchester.

"My gawd, Burton. You can't fight intruders naked. I'll get you some britches, anyway—" She rushed across the room for his clothes while he levered a cartridge into the chamber.

"Get their horses!" the lead rider shouted in Spanish, and sent two bullets at the house. They thudded into the plaster. Burt drew back for an instant, then quickly looked for them in the inky darkness from the safety of the doorway. A resolve filled his brain: he must stop these marauders at any price.

Ready for the next flash of lightning, Burt used the adze-hewed facing to steady the long gun barrel against it. When a raider swept into his line of sight, he took aim at a silhouette. The report of the .44/40 vibrated inside the house and made his ears ring. His marksmanship took the rider out of the saddle.

Filled with resolve to make them pay dearly for their intrusion, he rushed outside onto the porch, looking for more outlines to shoot at. His next bullet brought down a horse. Its pained scream cut the night. Burt could hear the stricken animal thrashing in the mud. He wanted their blood—not their mounts'. How dare these bastards raid her—their—ranch? The loud curses of the confused outlaws carried in the driving rain. His shooting had trapped them in the area of the corrals—their only way to escape would be to charge past his gun muzzle. From their shouts, he knew they wanted to ride out quickly, even without any stolen animals, but they feared his accuracy.

He stood in the yard gate and tried to find another target in the inky night among the milling raiders. Two more quick shots at outlines from his Winchester. A man cried out in broken Spanish that he was hit and needed help.

Someone shouted, "Vamoose!"

The raiders opened up with pistol fire at him. Their aim proved wild as their upset horses broke out and swept past him. On his knees, Burton levered cartridge upon cartridge through the repeater after them until the hammer clicked on empty.

The sulfurous stench of spent gunpowder filled his nose. His ears still rang from the gun's percussion. Cold rain ran down his bare back, causing goose bumps to form on the backs of his arms. On tender bare soles, he hurried to the porch for more ammo. Angela rushed out the door with clothes for him to wear. Sobbing, she clung to his left arm. Filled with a seething anger at the boldness of the intruders, he glared into the dark void that swallowed them.

"Here's your pants and shirt," she managed, shaken. She took the rifle from him, and he quickly pulled them on.

"Get a light," he said to her, taking back the rifle and starting inside. "I'll need my boots. Damn goat heads, sand burrs, and cactus needles all over out there," he complained, taking gingerly steps on the cool tile.

"What if they're only wounded?"

"Good. I'll squeeze out of them who they are."

"Oh, Burton. Please be careful."

He nodded as he jammed more rounds into the rifle's chamber. She brought his boots, and he sat on a chair.

Brushing off his sole, he put on the right sock and boot. Repeating the process, he pulled on the left one. His mind was on fire with plans for revenge against these bold raiders. They needed a lesson they would never forget. He stood up and stomped his heels to fit his feet into them.

"Should I light the lamp?" she asked.

"Yes."

With trembling fingers, she struck a torpedo-headed parlor match, and it flared. Then she touched it to the wick. A flame responded, and she capped it with the glass chimney. The heavy scent of burning coal oil filled the air in the rain-cooled room.

"I'll take it," he said, trying to think of a way to reassure her that things would be all right. With the rifle in his hands, he wondered what he'd find out in the darkness.

"I—I want to go, too."

"Stay right behind me, then," he said, feeling apprehensive about her safety. With the lamp in one hand, the rifle in the other, he went out onto the porch. A gust of wind blew a spray of moisture at his face and shirt, but the rain had stopped, and the storm moved off to the west. He crossed the yard, and outside the gate, he discovered the first still body on the ground.

At his back, she made a suppressed moan. "Is he alive?"

"Don't think so."

His boot toe nudged the facedown form, but it did not respond. Satisfied the outlaw was dead, he kicked a pistol away from the man's outstretched hand—in case.

"He's dead?" she asked in a small voice as they started for the corrals.

Burt nodded. That one wouldn't raid anyone else's ranch ever again.

He stopped at the moaning horse lying on the ground. She took the lamp from him; he cocked the rifle. A swift bullet to the animal's forehead silenced its suffering. What else? Taking the light back, he held it higher. As he approached the corral area, he could see someone huddled on the ground with his arms clutching his guts.

"Who're you?" Burt demanded in Spanish.

"Miguel—" the wounded man said in a pained voice.

"Where're you from?"

The man didn't answer. He handed her the lamp, then savagely kicked the outlaw in the chest and sent him sprawling on his back. Angela gasped behind him. Burt jammed the muzzle of the Winchester in the man's bearded face and cocked the hammer back.

"You ready to die, hombre?"

The man's eyes widened. "No."

"Then speak quickly. Where're you from?"

"Fronteras—Sonora—"

"Who led you here?" He used the gun's muzzle to jab him for a reply.

"Torres, Afredo Torres."

Thunder rumbled off in the distance. Burt turned the outlaw leader's name over in his mind. Alfredo Torres. At last, he had a name for the leader of these ruthless bandits from south of the border. Good. That meant one thing: he was one step closer to eliminating them.

"You know this Torres?" she whispered.

"No, but I will."

Movement beyond the corral of horses forced Burt to jerk upright to see what made it. Someone was coming around the pens. Then he recognized them. It was only the gentle farm help who worked for them—Juan Ramirez, his wife, Estrella, and their two small children.

"We heard the shots, Señor," Juan said, holding the straw hat to his chest and looking uneasy at the groaning outlaw on the ground. His family warily circled away from the prisoner. Angela stepped over and hugged Juan's wife to comfort the obviously shaken young woman under the shawl.

"The bandits are gone," she said to reassure the trembling Estrella, who was hardly more than a teen.

"What did they want, Señor?" Juan asked Burt.

"They came to rustle the ranch's horses."

Burt grasped the wounded man's collar and jerked him to his feet. From the outlaw's belt, he removed a large knife and tossed it aside. It clunked when it hit the ground. He shoved his prisoner toward the corral.

"Get some rope, Juan," he said to the hired man, and drove the bandit to the gate.

"I'm shot," the man said, crumbling to his knees.

"So? If you had killed me or my wife, would you worry about us? No. So I'm tying you up until daylight. Then, if you're still alive, I'll take you to the Pima County sheriff."

"Señor, I will die." The man sprawled himself facedown on the ground and held his stomach, moaning. "I'm dying."

"Not my concern. Where does this Torres stay in Mexico?"

No answer.

"Thanks," Burt said to Juan for the rope. He bent over to jerk the outlaw by his right arm closer to the gate to which he tied him. Then he did the same to his other arm. Tears ran down the bandit's face as he pleaded. In the predawn light, Burt could see the outlaw's blood-soaked shirt. At the moment, he felt no compassion for the man's plight.

"Tell me where Torres stays in Mexico," he demanded.

"I'm dying—"

"Good, better you than me. Where does Torres live?"

"Sonora—"

"Big place, tell me where?"

"On the Rio Verde."

"Good." Burt turned and said to Juan, "Hitch the team to the buckboard."

"Sí, patrón," Juan said, and started off to obey.

Then Burt went to where Angela stood. "Take her and the children into the house. They don't need to listen to this. And Angela—fix something for all of us to eat."

"You'll take him to Tucson?" Angela indicated the raider.

"Yes, after we eat. You can dress and go with me."

She nodded that she heard him. "We'll get some food and coffee fixed," she said, and took her wards to the house.

"Were you here last fall with them when they killed her husband?" Burt demanded from his prisoner when he was certain she was out of hearing.

The man shook his head. "No. No. I never been here before."

"You're lying."

"No, Señor, I swear on the Virgin Mary. I never been here before."

"Did Torres shoot him?"

"I don't know."

His first thought was to shake the truth from him, but in his heart he knew it would do no good. This man probably knew nothing about Van Dorn's murder. Anyone might have killed Angela's husband. He still felt a strong obligation to bring his killers to justice. Ignoring the bandit's sobbing and pleading, he considered what he must do next.

In the emerging gentle light, he went back to where the dead outlaw lay in the drive. Beside the still body, he knelt and turned him over. Holding the lantern up to see his facial features, he could make out that the dead one was hardly more than a boy. The young age of the deceased disgusted him.

His stare held hard on the boy's face as he rose to his feet. What a waste. The dead one would need to be wrapped in a blanket or wagon sheet. Still filled with biting anger over the raid, he started back for the corrals.

In front of the tack room, Juan hurried about, harnessing the matched buckskin team. Burt put a hand on his thin shoulder to slow the young man from working himself into a greater upset.

"There's no rush, mi amigo. The banditos vamoosed. They won't be back for a while, anyway."

The young man nodded and swallowed hard. "I am not so scared now."

"Good." Burt ducked, entering the tack room that smelled of barley and corn as well as leather and horse. In the candlelight that Juan had lit to see by, Burt shook the straw out of a dirty blanket. This would do for a shroud.

Outside, he tossed it onto the buckboard.

"Come to the house when you get them hitched. We'll eat something."

"Sí, patrón."

Without even a glance at the begging outlaw, Burt strode for the lighted kitchen door. After this attack, he hardly dared to leave her and the place unguarded. He needed to arrange for someone tough to move out there and stay with Angela in his absence.

Perhaps he should broach the subject of her moving back into her Tucson home until this whole bandit issue was settled? No, she hated living there. Her bountiful roses and bougainvillea grew profusely in this garden—she took such pride in all the field crops and the animals. The only way he could ever leave her would be to find some men capable enough to guard her and the ranch in his absence.

A place was set at the table for him when he came into the main room. He noticed the small children playing on the floor. So innocent, he thought to himself, taking his chair as he watched them crawling about.

"I am sorry," Estrella said, picking them both up by the waist to take them away.

"No. No. They're bueno. I'm enjoying them."

"Sí, patrón," she said and put them down.

"They are very pretty babies," he said, and reassured her with a nod. Embarrassed by his attention, she hurried back into the kitchen.

Angela brought him a steaming cup of coffee.

"Thanks," he said. "Are you all right?" With his arm, he reached to encircle her slender waist and gave her a reassuring hug. His main concern was how badly this raider business had upset her.

"I'm fine. I was afraid for a while. It was like the night they—they killed Frederick. What if you had not been awake?" The lines of a frown furrowed her smooth forehead.

"I'm going to find you some more dogs." Strange how all the curs about the place had disappeared all at once. Perhaps the coyotes ate them. Or was that more than a coincidence?

"Yes, they would bark, at least."

"We'll also need to find some men to stay here as guards when I'm gone on marshal business."

"I've been thinking—"

He frowned at her. "You wish to move back to your house in town?"

"No." The impatient look she gave him convinced him she had no such plans.

"I understand," he said, and held the steaming cup to his lips. Deliberately glancing at her for a response, he blew across the surface to cool it. "Sorry I interrupted you."

"No, it was nothing. You know I'm very happy here." She bent over and kissed him on the cheek. "I'm even more happy when you can be here with me."

"Yes. So am I." He nodded absently, engrossed in his thoughts about the intruders. The outlaw's name, Torres, kept rolling over and over in his mind. Perhaps his boss, Chief U.S Marshal Denton Downy, knew something more about this outlaw gang.

"The horses are ready," Juan announced.

"Good, come and sit down. They'll soon have food for us."

"I can eat outside." An anxious look swept the young man's face, and he tossed his head toward the doorway as if he didn't belong in there.

"No, sit here." Burt indicated for him to take a place at the table. "We need to talk about plans. Things we need to do here on the farm. Sit," he told the hesitant boy. "You're ready for the irrigation?"

"Sí, it comes mañana."

"Good. We will need to cut the alfalfa soon."

"Sí."

"Can you sharpen the sickle bar?" Burt decided from

the concerned look on the youth's face that he was uncertain about the process but afraid his patrón would be mad if he said so. To save the poor boy any more fears, he spoke up quickly. "I'll do that when I return."

Juan nodded gratefully.

"Relax, you are my *segundo* here," he said to brace the youth up.

About to laugh at Juan's obvious discomfort with being at the patrón's table, Burt concentrated on his coffee. Angela brought them plates of eggs, frijoles, and flour tortillas. She set them before both men and nodded.

"That was fixed in record time," she said.

Burt agreed, putting red sauce on his scrambled eggs.

"Something wrong?" she asked the hesitant Juan.

"Oh, no, no," he said, and began to fix his food.

She shared a private wink with Burt, then swept up the younger of the babies and headed for the kitchen with a promise to come back for his brother.

"You better eat something, too," Burt said after her.

"I will," she said from the doorway, coming after the other little one, who had crawled under the table.

He knew good and well his new bride would rather mess with little children and baby livestock than eat any time. Still, he was anxious to get the prisoner to town. He wondered what the Tucson high sheriff would say about the matter—what was he doing about the raids by Mexican bandits on ranches along the Santa Cruz River? There might even be more than one band of outlaws.

Pima County's head lawman would probably say he couldn't spare a deputy. Truth of the matter, all his men were out counting cattle to put them on the property tax rolls. Arizona sheriffs collected ten percent of all the county's property taxes. The tax business paid them much better then chasing scruffy border bandits.

After their meal, he and Juan wrapped the dead outlaw in the old blanket. Then they placed him with the wounded one, Miguel, who sat tied up in the back of the buckboard. Burt took the Winchester along in case of trouble. Once Angela, wearing a new blue dress, was on the spring seat, he handed the long gun to her to hold before he climbed up beside her.

Juan promised to drag off the dead carcass. He also had caught a loose saddle horse that came back to the ranch ones. From the Mexican saddle on the mustang, Burt decided it must have belonged to one of the outlaws. Juan unsaddled and put him in the corral. Burt doubted any nearby rancher would claim it. Still, he planned to hold the horse as some sort of payment for the inconvenience they'd suffered in the raid.

The day's heat rose from the damp dirt as they hurried southward. The towering Catalina Mountains beside them and the pristine desert sparkled from the cleansing rain as the thin iron rims cut a song on the gritty surface. In the usual dry washes, small streams of water meandered across the roadway for them to splash through.

Mid-morning, he reined up before the adobe building that housed the county sheriff's office and jail. He tied off the reins and climbed down.

"I'll wait here," Angela said from under her blue parasol.

He entered the building and let his eyes adjust to the darkness.

"Señor?" The young man wearing a star on his shirt sat up at a desk.

"Sheriff Adams here?" Burt searched around and saw no one else as his eyes adjusted to the low light.

"No. May I help you?"

"Burt Green. Bandits raided my ranch up on the Santa Cruz last night. I have one dead outlaw and a wounded one out in my buckboard. Would you remove them?"

"Oh, yes!" The deputy bolted to his feet and shouted for a swamper to come help him.

Burt followed them to the open doorway and shared a nod with Angela on the spring seat. After taking off his hat for her, the deputy helped gather the injured one. He and his helper carried Miguel through the doorway.

"He's wounded, all right," the deputy said as they took him past Burt and into the jail portion. "I better get a doc to come take a look at him." The deputy sent his helper for the physician. He turned back to Burt. "How did all this happen?"

"A gang of outlaws tried to raid Angela's—our—ranch last night. I stopped them."

"How many and what gang?"

"Must have been seven or eight. The wounded man said the leader was named Torres. He got away."

"Lots of them bandits." Warily, the deputy shook his head. "I never heard of no Torres before."

"Obviously, this wounded one is one of Torres's men. How many raids have been made on ranches around here lately?"

"Not as many as last year." The young man shrugged. "Last week, they raided a few places up at Oracle, but there aren't as many attacks happening this year."

"What's the sheriff doing about them?"

With obvious affront, the deputy suspiciously cocked

an eye at Burt. Then, very deliberately, he said, "All he can do with such limited funds and a short staff."

"Raids like this have to be stopped."

"Yeah, well, mister, you figure them out, and we'll stop 'em. These damn Messikins can ride back to Mexico quicker than a lamb can wag his tail."

"If the law won't do anything, then perhaps civilians will have to."

The young man gave a shrug as if that was all he could do.

"Tell Sheriff Adams," Burt said, "that deputy U.S. Marshal Green will check back with him on the case's progress."

The deputy only gave him a scathing look. "I'll tell him."

"You look upset. What did they say in there?" Angela asked when he climbed on the rig, undid the reins, and clucked to the team.

"They said as much as there was nothing they could do about the bandits. They had no deputies and no funds, and the bandits swooped in and ran back to Mexico before they could do a thing." He looked over his shoulder and, seeing the way was clear, put the buckskins in a trot.

"What do you plan to do?"

"Go and see my boss, Marshal Downy. Maybe he knows someone in Preskitt who can wake this sheriff up."

She looked up at the parasol. "I forget they called Prescott that. What will the governor do?"

He stared straight ahead, fighting for some control over the fiery rage inside himself. "Someone like Governor Baylor needs to make Adams do his job and put an end to such lawlessness."

"Sounds like you have work to do," she said with a broad smile.

Looking over at her, he nodded, pleased to see the attack had not depressed her this time, that this latest episode had not set her back the way the murder of her husband did. He could also see that her efforts were intended to bring him out of his own anger. Grateful for her concerns about him, he gave her a reassuring smile and clucked to the team.

His pair of horses paused for a two-wheel cart blocking the narrow street. He decided he should see Downy first, then go find some capable men to guard his new bride and ranch. The lightninglike raids coming from below the border had to be stopped. If the local law couldn't do anything, he'd have to figure out a way to end their habitual reign of terror.

Chapter 2

THE CELL WAS COOL IN THE PREDAWN DARKNESS. Seated on the iron bunk, Deuces knew from what the guards had told him that a marshal would soon come for him and take him to the place they called Fort Leavenworth, Kansas. They said this place was many days by train from Fort Bowie. He wondered if he would ever again smell the mixed aroma of creosote and juniper that filled his nose. In deep concentration, he tried to separate the outdoor fragrant air from the sweaty and fecal odors of the military jail.

The snoring of the other prisoners asleep in the adobe quarters sounded like the steam-driven sawmills that sliced up the pines in the Chiricahuas. Deserters and killers, the other prisoners were army whites and two buffalo soldiers. The blacks fascinated him the most, their kinky hair like tight wire coils and big lips, their skin not brown like Apaches but black as the polished stones called Apache tears. He could hardly understand them when they spoke, though he knew enough English to speak it and Spanish even better, as well as his own Apache. The blacks spoke in a very different tongue, but in many ways they were like Apaches. They sang their songs and danced. He did not know their meaning, but he felt more akin to them than to the cursing, grumbling white prisoners.

Looking out the small, barred window at the twinkling stars, he wished that he could once again be in Mexico as a scout with Tom Horn. That was where he belonged, not in this jail, not sentenced to years of hardship. They told him at Leavenworth he would make big rocks into small ones as punishment. He shook his head. What did rocks have to do with him killing Sombrero? Then he closed his eyes and recalled how the wet-eyed Tish told him she was sad with her husband, that Sombrero got drunk and beat her all the time.

In his heart, he knew what he did to that worthless one was what he should have done. But there was no way to explain that to white men—to officers. They had never been Apaches and lived in a wickiup. Never listened to elders tell them evil must be stopped—that you do that for your tribe. Do not shirk such duty, he'd been taught, the Apache's god, Ussen, will guide you. Pray to him, and he will give you answers.

His heart felt heavy. Never again in his life would he hear the top knotted quail whose whistles kept a man company in the desert. Would the sun dog howl there? Would the eagle soar over such a place? No antelopes to eat. No desert sheep's haunch to roast on a fire. His mouth grew thick with saliva at the thought of such a treasured meal. No hearts of the century plant to bake. No more stomp dances, where the *tiswain* flowed freely and one could pound his heels in moccasins until dawn with a dark-eyed maiden.

Instead, he would eat bitter beans, wormy salt pork, bad bread, and coffee that tasted like piss, until his spirit expired. His real heart would never die, only suffer. If only he could make his spirit fly away like a freed bird and let it live with the green-headed parrots that came in such huge flocks to the Chiricahuas each year.

"I will you to stay in these great mountains until I come back," he said in Apache. But his spirit did not fly out the bars, and he decided it, too, would go with him to this place of big rocks to little rocks.

Midday, a soldier took him from the cell. The deputy marshal stood tall and lean in his brown suit beside the jailer's desk. He wore a bushy mustache with gray hairs, his blue eyes deep set and dark when he looked Deuces over.

"Well, we've got a fur piece to go," he said as he signed the papers on the desk.

He placed handcuffs on Deuces's wrists, then with a hard squeeze made certain they were tight enough so he could not slip them off. Egan's breath smelled bad in Deuces's nostrils: tobacco, strong food, rotten teeth.

"You behave, I won't put legs irons on you?" The man looked him hard in the eye.

"I behave," Deuces said quickly. At first, he had worn leg irons in the fort's jail; only his good behavior and friendship with the soldier guards had gotten them removed. To not have to wear them on this trip would be good fortune for him; he could never escape this man with them strapped on his ankles.

"Deuces is a model prisoner," Desk Sergeant Cafferty said, handing the papers to Deputy U.S. Marshal Philip Egan.

"Yeah, that's good," the man said, stuffing them in his coat pocket. "But he tries anything, he's one dead sumbitch."

"I don't expect he will. His record as a scout was unblemished."

"Except for the murder?" Egan turned his lip up in disgust and gave an I-know-it-all glance to the sergeant.

"That's right. Tom Horn'd had his way, they'd never tried him for it."

"Well, Tom Horn ain't the gawdamn law. Just another civilian."

Cafferty shook his head. "Not just any civilian. He's a great scout."

"Way I heard it, he tells them renegade 'Paches everything the army does."

"You need anything else, Egan?" Cafferty's face grew beet red.

Deuces wanted to laugh. The marshal had better clear out of there. Things he said about Horn had made the noncom angry, and Egan did not want to see that man's wrath. Deuces knew Cafferty's reputation well.

"You damn blue bellies may like him, but I say Horn's a gawdamn spy for them Apaches." With that said, Egan roughly shoved Deuces for the doorway.

"Wait one moment!" Cafferty ordered.

Egan stopped, turned back. Deuces could see the rage pulsing in the blue veins on the side of the sergeant's red face.

"You forgot his suitcase." And he shoved the cheap valise into the lawman's gut.

The ride in the ambulance, driven by two soldiers to the Bowie station, proved to be dusty and long. Close to sundown, they reached the small community on the Southern Pacific tracks. Egan removed Deuces and both of their suitcases from the conveyance. He never said a word to the two soldiers, who drove off and left them standing in the dirt street.

"I need a damn drink," Egan said, looking around. He motioned for Deuces to head toward the saloon across the dusty street.

"Wait here," he said, and put his own bag on the ground beside Deuces's. Then he took out a small chain. At the hitch rail, he looped it over the bar and through the cuffs, then padlocked it, securing Deuces to the rack.

"Stay here. They won't let your red ass in there, anyway. I won't be long."

Deuces watched his escort disappear through the batwing doors. When Deuces decided to sit upon the edge of the boardwalk, he learned the chain was not long enough. He had to hold on to it with both hands. No matter, he squatted at the edge anyway and wondered how drunk the marshal would get before he came outside for him.

To try to escape so close to Bowie would be foolish. They had a dozen Apache scouts at the fort who could trail him down in no time. But farther on, he would find a way to slip away. Perhaps if this man Egan drank lots of whiskey, it would not be so hard to get away from him—somewhere.

Then someone spoke in Apache to him. He looked up at an old, wrinkle-faced tribesman.

"They going to hang you?" the ancient one asked.

He shook his head.

"Good. They hang you—keep you from next world."

Deuces acknowledged him before the old man shuffled on. He knew the poor devil was looking for a drink. Begging in his worn-out voice, he held out his pitiful hand to two soldiers. They ignored him and went inside the bar. Perhaps when he was released from prison, he would be as this old man was—without any pride—pleading for whiskey to forget the good times.

Egan came out, picking his teeth, then looked up and down the street. He used the side of his hand to smooth out his mustache. When he drew closer, Deuces could smell the sharpness of the liquor on his breath.

"Get up, Buck. We got to find some food. Damn train'll be here in an hour or so, if it's on time."

Deuces decided that his new name with this man would be Buck. They went behind the adobe building and drained their bladders in the dust. Then Egan took him to a café run by a Mexican. A swarthy man with a filthy white towel tied around his waist came over and took Egan's order.

Soon he delivered them plates of frijoles, some kind of stringy meat, and corn tortillas. Egan never bothered to release the cuffs, so Deuces ate with them on, forced to move them together to feed his face. The food was not fresh. He could taste the staleness, the flavor of tobacco smoke, and other bad odors in it. Still, he did not know when this man would feed him again. Life as an Apache had taught him to eat whenever he had a chance—his next meal might be days away.

"If it didn't have hot peppers in it," Egan said under his breath, being certain the cook couldn't hear him, "this food would be pure garbage."

Deuces nodded.

"Damn, hope we don't get the shits on that train from eating this slop," the lawman said, looking at the juice-dripping tortilla in his hand. "Be bad. I had them once. Had to get off the train, put the prisoner in a city jail until I got better. Whew." He took another big mouthful, then struck the prongs of his fork on the plate to get Deuces's attention. "Sure hope we don't get them eating this crap."

Deuces nodded.

After the meal, he took Deuces to the small depot. The sun was setting in the west. Red flared the sky into bloody tones that bathed the Dos Cabezas Mountains and the Chiricahuas. Deuces wanted to remember the picture of those peaks on fire, to hold the sight forever in his mind so he would recall what his land looked like during his long absence.

"The train's supposed to be on time," Egan said, returning to where he told him to sit on the bench while he went to see about the schedule. "Can't never tell about trains. They got their own schedule. Sons a bitches got all the money. Railroad moguls will own this whole country one day."

Egan's rambling words made little sense to Deuces. He spoke about dogs, trains, and mongrels and them owning the world. Maybe he meant dogs would replace white men. Like the whites had replaced the red man. How would a dog shoot a gun? No, this man was crazy. Deuces knew all about dogs—they were dumber than Pima Indians.

The distant whistle of the locomotive sank his heart. Deuces had hoped the train had been swallowed up and would never ever come for him.

"Get your bag, Buck."

Deuces obeyed and stood beside the man at the edge of the platform. He had seen the mother-of-pearl grips in his shoulder holster. Egan would not hesitate to use it, either; this he knew well.

The locomotive came to a screaming halt. A hiss of steam obscured things, then drifted away. The platform still vibrated under Deuces's soles, so close to the fire-breathing steel devil that pulled the train—he hoped its spirit had not noticed him in passing.

A black porter, in a uniform, put down a step for them, which they used to climb onto the platform between the cars. Inside the one on the right, Egan pointed to a bench and had him slide in. Then Egan pushed the other back over so they had two seats facing each other. The lawman put their cases in the rack above them. With his small chain and lock, he fastened Deuces's cuffs to the iron bar on top of the seat's back. This forced him to sit sideways with his back to the window.

"That should hold you, Buck," Egan announced, and went to digging for his passes when the frowning conductor came down the aisle.

"He a killer?" the railroad man asked when he stopped before them. The silver clicker in his hand made small pieces of paper fly out of the tickets.

"He's an Apache," Egan said.

"Where're you taking him?"

"Leavenworth."

"Need all of them savages put up there," the conductor said, and went on down the car punching tickets with a clicking sound.

While Deuces only had a short look at the other passengers, he could smell them. Strong perfume and female scents were powerful. Powder, too, he could smell it, mixed with the sour sweat of white men and the strong twang of tobacco and hard liquor. He'd better enjoy even the worst smells in his nose, for there would be no females even to sense where they would jail him.

"Don't get no ideas on running off," Egan warned. Then he slumped down in the seat, put the felt hat over his eyes, and propped his dusty boots on the other side, so he blocked the way out. Deuces nodded that he heard him.

The clack of the train's wheels on the rail joints made a song. But he did not sleep. Fear of the future did not keep him awake—his mind was set about what he must do. Somehow he needed to get away from this strange white man. The soft lamps in the car caused a low illumination of the passengers' faces, enough so he could see them when he twisted his head around to look them over. How could he escape this sleeping Egan? He heard a gagging sound. Someone up the aisle was getting sick, maybe from the swaying of the car from side to side. A young woman rushed by, holding her mouth, and the strong sourness of her vomit filled his nose. Her man followed her, looking helpless, and all heads in the car swiveled to follow their progress.

She ended up outside on the platform, and Deuces could hear her retching more in the space between the two cars. He listened to her choking sounds and how she talked desperately to her man about her illness. With the car door open, he could glimpse them standing on the swaying platform as the train steamed on.

Egan stirred and sat up. He twitched his nose in displeasure. "Someone get sick?"

"Yes. White woman get plenty sick." Deuces indicated the doorway behind him.

"Damn, you can speak English," Egan said at his discovery. "Whew. Gawd, it sure stinks bad. Someone needs to get that porter to mop it up."

In a short while, the black porter came into their car with a mop and bucket and scrubbed down the aisle, especially around where the lady sat. She apologized to him. He laughed it away, talking to her the way the buffalo soldiers did—hard for Deuces to understand him.

He looked out the window at the low brush. He could see in the starlight silhouettes of the yuccas' dry seed heads on stalks and distant mounds that must be far-off mountains. This was still part of his homeland. He knew this set of iron track would be the route back to his mountains. But this train and its speed concerned him more. Like an eternal galloping horse, the engine never quit, going away, away, away, farther from his land.

Chapter 3

BURT GREEN KNEW LOTS OF PEOPLE IN THE WALLED city: Tucson's rich, poor, tough ones, and the criminal. Prior to his marriage to Angela, he spent long hours playing poker in the local saloons to supplement his meager earnings as a deputy U.S. marshal. But meeting the lady changed that schedule, although he never missed the throat-cutting smoke that hung like a river fog over the tables and dimmed the candles' lamp power. Nor the crooked tinhorns he exposed after observing them crudely slip cards up their sleeves and into their pockets. No part about his former life as a gambler held any great emotional calling for him to return.

Some called him lucky at cards, others he knew muttered obscenities behind his back about his skills at poker, but the results never bothered him. His strapping six-feet-tall, broad frame intimidated most challengers, and the long rides after wanted fugitives gave him enough physical prowess to put the stupid ones down quickly. When he glanced over at the handsome woman on the buckboard seat beside him, he felt he'd drawn a much better hand when he married her. At thirty-seven, it was time for him to settle down. The thirty-two-year-old attractive widow made a perfect choice for this new phase in his life.

He drove the team through the narrow Tucson street cluttered with bleating milk goats and the herder-peddlers offering their production straight from the udder. Burros in trains, bristled with firewood, walked docilely to the side of the traffic. Their burdens mostly long-dead mesquite or ironwood branches, great kindling for cooking fires. Other donkeys carried water barrels, dipped fresh that morning from the Santa Cruz River. The peddlers shouted about their wares: "Tamales. Good tamales!" "Fresh milk! Fresh milk!" "Melons, ripe melons!" "Ripe corn, I pick today!"

Their voices loud in Spanish and the braying of a jackass or two added to the street sounds. Underfoot, fighting chickens scratched in the dust. Hens and chicks ran for cover at the approach of his rig. Roosters bragged in loud crows, and women shouted at one another to be heard. Burt considered the din; he had almost forgotten the town's street sounds that awoke him each morning in the boardinghouse before he married and moved to the ranch. Another reason he felt fortunate—her place north of town was such a pleasant haven for his long-stressed ears.

In the adobe office, Burt found Chief Marshal Denton Downy at his desk. The balding, bearded man looked up as if considering Burt's presence, then he leaned back in the wheelback chair, fetching a silver pocket watch from his vest. He flipped it open and checked the time, than snapped it shut.

"You here to work?" Downy leaned over and spat in the brass spittoon beside his desk.

"No. Bandits struck at her ranch again last night. I shot one, wounded another. Brought them to town."

Downy frowned with his salt-and-pepper bushy brows. "Same ones that shot her husband, Frederick Van Dorn?"

"The wounded one denied it."

"Believe him?"

Burt shrugged—made him no mind. Sooner or later, he would find that culprit and settle with him. "He said that Alfredo Torres is their leader. You ever heard of him?"

"No, but there's a zillion two-bit bandits down in Sonora."

"I need to hire some men to guard the ranch before I can go to Mexico to look for that stage robber Taylor."

"Sure, take all the time you need. I'd bet Taylor ain't going anywhere down there."

"Good. Put some feelers out for me about this Torres."

Downy spat in the spittoon beside his chair again and rose up. "I will. See you when you get the guard business all settled."

"Thanks."

Then a knowing grin parted Downy's bushy beard and mustache. "How's this married life treating you?"

"Wonderful," Burt said, not to be taken in by his sly comment.

"You won't say that in two years." Downy scowled and went back to his paperwork. "You'll be a-wishing you were single again. Mark my words."

Out in front of the building, Burt joined his wife at the buckboard, climbed onto the seat, and clucked to the horses.

"Did he know anything?" she asked.

"He says in two years, you will be tired of me."

She frowned in dismay at him. "He didn't?"

"Well, something like that." Then he grinned big. Be a damn sight longer than that before he grew tired of her. Better go see the man he planned to hire—Pedro Astanchez. If he could find Pedro at home and if he needed work, the Mexican would be his first choice for a ranch guard.

"This is where he lives?" Angela asked, looking disappointed at the sight of Pedro's run-down place. A lane from the road between two sagging barbwire fences led toward a jacal that needed to be replastered with two ramadas and a fallen-down corral.

Burt nodded and turned the team up the driveway. "We can hope he's at home." He looked at the two slab-hipped horses standing hipshot in the small irrigated pasture. The whole thing did not ring of industry, but that was by a gringo's standard.

"Ah, señor!'" a familiar young woman shouted, rushing out of the jacal. She wiped her hands on her apron. "Señora," she said with a bow when Burt reined the horses up.

"Good to see you, Juanita. You know my señora, Angela? Is your husband here?" he asked, tying off the reins.

"Nice to meet you. Pedro is taking a siesta."

He checked the sun time and agreed with a nod. "We would have been here sooner, but we had some prisoners to give the sheriff."

"No problem. He will be glad to see you. I will go wake him."

"Fine," he said, and glanced about. Then he nodded privately at his apprehensive-looking wife to reassure her things would be all right.

In a short time, Juanita returned with the sleepy-eyed Pedro Astanchez, who carried his straw sombrero in one hand at his side. His handsome features were those of Spanish aristocrats with less Indian blood than most latinos. He came with a spring in his walk, eagerness written in his look when he recognized Burt.

"Marshal Green," he said, excited. Then, as if he had discovered her, he nodded to Angela.

"Good to see you, amigo."

"I am ready for work. Do you need a posse man today, Señor?"

"No, but I have another job for you." Burt helped his wife down, and Juanita took her by the arm to take her to the ramada at the side and get her a cool drink.

Pedro had worked for him before as a posse man. The U.S. marshal paid such men a dollar a day to assist him on manhunts and to serve warrants. Pedro knew the countryside and made a good man to question latinos who might not talk to him. Brave, too, and good with a pistol, which counted in the clutches they sometimes found themselves in.

"Come, we can talk in the shade. Let's find some, or the sun will cook our brains out here." Pedro replaced his sombrero.

"Fine. There you can tell me all you know about this bandit Alfredo Torres," Burt said as they headed for the ramada. He watched Angela and Juanita go to the other palm-frond-covered shade, talking all the way. A smile formed at the corner of his mouth. Good, those two would get along fine together at the ranch.

Under the roof, Burt squatted on his boot heels. He listened while Pedro, seated on a crate, explained the little he knew about this Torres. Worthless border trash with some gun hands, who would sell his own grandmother as a puta. Listening, Burt appreciated the man's knowledge of the situation.

"This Torres is a small-time bandit," Pedro went on to explain. "He wants to be a big one. But so far, he only raids out-of-the-way ranches to steal horses."

"The dead bandit I brought in was a boy," Burt said, looking for a response.

Pedro bobbed his head. "He probably promised that boy to make him rich if he would ride with his gang."

"Yeah, I bet he did. The wounded one told me his name was Miguel."

"I am surprised he didn't say John Smith, huh?"

Both men laughed. "Yeah, I think you're right. You think he lied to me about Torres, too?"

"Who knows? But I have heard of this Alfredo Torres."

"You know him on sight?"

"No, but I could find him."

Burt considered the notion of going after Torres but had other priorities for this man at the moment. "First, I want you and Juanita to move up to the señora's ranch and see that Angela is protected. Can you get someone to watch this place?"

"Sure, but where will you—"

"First, I need to go to Nogales. I have word that a wanted American bad man is staying below the border. A man down there is supposed to know where he's hiding. Marshal Denton wants me to find him."

"And bring him back?"

Burt nodded.

"I could help you do that."

Burt shook his head. "Not this time. Worse than that, I need you to protect the señora while I am gone." He tossed his head toward the two women under the other ramada.

Pedro surrendered. "My cousin will take care of this place. But I know a man who needs work who would also help guard that place of hers with his life."

"More might be better. If I could afford the two of you. Who's he?"

"Tomás Obregón. He is married to my cousin and is a good worker as well."

"How much would he cost?"

"Fifteen pesos a month for him and his family and a place to live. He knows how to farm, too."

"Good, hire him, too, and you move him up there as well. He can assist you until I return." Shifting his weight to the other leg, he looked over hard at Pedro. "I want to be certain that she's safe."

"I savvy."

Then Burt considered his other problem. "We need some good guard dogs, too. I think the coyotes ate ours."

Pedro shook his head. "I bet that damn Torres poisoned them before he made the raid."

Burt rubbed the itch in his mustache with the tip of his index finger. If the outlaw was that organized, he wouldn't be easy to trap. Poisoned the dogs—why hadn't he considered that? They simply were gone one day when he got up. Somehow he'd been distracted from any suspicion about their disappearance, no doubt by his deep involvement with the lovely woman in his life. He closed his eyes at the thought of the passionate pleasures they shared.

"Can we get Obregón and you moved in up there in two days?" he finally asked.

"Yes," Pedro said smugly. "When do you need to leave for Mexico?"

"I was going to Mexico in the morning, but after this latest raid, I won't leave her until I'm certain the ranch's secure and she's in good hands."

With a wide grin, Pedro nodded that he was pleased. "We will all be at the señora—your hacienda in two days. Then you can go look for this bandito." They stood and shook hands on the arrangement.

His mission accomplished with Pedro, he considered the mess he must tend to in Mexico. Supposedly, this Taylor and others had robbed an army paymaster near Fort Grant and gotten away with more than fifty thousand dollars in gold. The first good lead on his location came in a letter to Marshal Downy from a man in Nogales who, for the fifty-dollar reward, said he would disclose where Taylor was hiding down there.

When Burt and Pedro stepped out in the sunlight from under the ramada, Burt watched a pair of vultures sweep low over them, circle, and come back for another look. The great, red-faced birds used little wing power but glided on the thermals.

"They know something?" he asked Pedro with a grin.

"Just hungry," he said, and shrugged it away.

"Can this Obregón drive a team and mow hay?"

"Sí, he's a good farm worker."

"Good. We have a young hired man—Juan—Obregón can show him how to do things and all of you work the place. It's a good farm."

"Ah, sí. We will make it better."

Burt agreed that would suit him and felt better that he would have two men more experienced than Juan to guard Angela as well.

"I will go into Tucson with you," Pedro said. "Then I can find Obregón to tell him the good news and also listen in the cantinas for any word about this Alfredo Torres and his banditos."

Pleased with all their plans, Burt nodded. "Angela and I better go back home tonight. Juan and his wife were upset enough over last night's raid, he'd sure be nervous if we didn't return."

The two shook hands, then Burton went to get Angela and head back for the ranch. It would be past sundown before they would reach home. The talk with his boss earlier gave him some time to get his business at the ranch in hand. But old information kept going over and over in his mind about the paymaster robbery and this man, Joseph Taylor, in Mexico. Taylor, he knew by reports, was a bishop in the Mormon church, too.

Chapter 4

DEUCES'S CELL IN THE EL PASO CITY JAIL ON THE second floor was bare, save for the iron bunk. When he stood on the narrow shelf and looked down into the street, he could see the traffic below and hear the music from the cantinas, and familiar words in Spanish reached his ears. The screams and laughter of the putas made his privates ache, reminding him of the olive-skinned women in the villages of Mexico.

If you weren't their enemy, these women sought you as a lover. Like what happened to him in the town of Narcozi after the padre spoke his words, waved the silver cross, and threw holy water at the still corpse of Captain Crawford, all wrapped in blankets and tarps, his form resting at the bottom of a fresh grave. After the three-day ride to get him there, the body had began to ripen—

a too-sweet scent of death that Deuces wanted out of his nose. Besides, the dead were not things Apaches lingered over.

"I think we need a little poon-tang," Horn announced, looking around as they led their horses and the army mule up the dusty street after the captain's burial.

"What is that?" Deuces asked, puzzled by the word.

"A little Chinese whore in Yuma once told me that's what she sold." Horn threw his head back and laughed.

Deuces loved Horn's laughter. It promised more fun things to come. The same laugh that Horn made at the San Bernardino Ranch when they were on their way south to join Captain Crawford's forces down in the Sierra Madres, Slaughter's vaqueros stopped Horn to tell him they had a horse he couldn't ride.

Obviously, John Slaughter's men had saved this bad one especially for Horn. The ranch hands all squatted in the dust, unable to hide their smug grins. These vaqueros worked for the short man, Slaughter, who owned all the Peraltas' Spanish land grant holdings up and down the San Pedro Valley on both sides of the border. They were muy tough hombres who rode wild horses themselves and loved to see them buck. This time, Slaughter's men had chosen the worst loco mustang they could find for Horn to ride. No way could he win their money in this contest the way he usually did.

Horn, with a bottle of cheap mescal in his right fist, climbed onto the corral to survey their outlaw. Deuces joined him, using his elbows on the top rail to maintain his balance. The Roman-nosed stud looked tall and powerful. Its double mane full of burrs concealed a muscular neck that Deuces knew it could snake far out, then bury its face between its feathered legs to give its rider a pitch toward the stars. No ordinary mustang, this one carried the frame and blood of great draft horses. Its blue roan hide bore the dark scars of previous combat with other stallions for possession of mares.

"By gawd, Deuces, what do you think?" Horn asked, before taking another swig from the brown bottle.

"He looks bad," Deuces said in Spanish, impressed with the stout animal.

Horn finished swallowing his mescal and began to laugh. At last, he shook his head with a twinkle in his eyes "By gawd, here, Deuces, have a snort of this piss. Why, he's just an old pony needs some dusting off."

The vaqueros might feed Horn whiskey, but Deuces knew they could as well save their liquor. They'd need a barrel of the stuff to get him too drunk to ride. Deuces tried a swallow of the fire water from Horn's bottle. It burned his tongue, then his throat, and the rest of the way down. When they were standing on the ground again, he quickly shoved the mescal back to Horn.

"Bad stuff." Deuces frowned in disapproval.

Horn laughed aloud. "Hell, son, they weren't going to feed me the good stuff. You have any money?"

"How much?"

"All you've got. I aim to ride that blue devil to hell and gone and win you a shitpot full of money." Smiling, laughing, Horn obviously intended to make the most of their one-night layover at the Slaughter ranch.

So the bets were placed, and Horn saddled the snorty roan with his double-rigged California saddle. The word had gone out up and down the valley about the competition. People hurried to see it. Deuces watched several attractive young olive-skinned women carrying their skirts so they could half run to get a place close enough around the pen for the viewing. Men, women, and children were all peering through the corral rails or seated on the rooftops of nearby sheds for a better view.

Every cent of his money was bet on Horn's ride; Deuces finally managed to get inside the large pen and squatted on the ground to see everything. Horn teased the assistants helping him. No fear in this man's veins. He would have made a great Apache brave.

The head-shaking roan snorted and strained at the rope snubbing it to the hitching post. Its great pie-shaped feet churned up dust as it stomped and kicked both heels at its unseen adversaries. A large, leather blind was fixed over its head so all it could do was squeal and grunt, plus strike with a forehoof at any unseen humans trying to touch it.

Horn wore a pair of tough bullhide batwing chaps, his special spurs with sharpened rowels to dig in and punish the outlaw, and a lightly loaded quirt with small birdshot sewed in the ends to bring pain for any resistance.

"Deuces, you want to ride this pup?" Horn shouted at him.

A quick shake of his head drew a nervous ripple of laughter from the assembled ranch people. No way Deuces wanted anything to do with this roaring, stomping, *tonto loco* horse. Then he noticed the animal had become so worked up its male organ stuck out.

Someone in the crowd shouted obscenely about what that horse would do to Horn after it threw him on the ground. Horn ducked down, saw the stud's projection, and laughed until his eyes were wet. Wiping them on his kerchief, he shook his head at the notion.

"Not to me, amigos!" he shouted, and bounded in the saddle.

They jerked off the blinds, let the tie rope loose—it was Horn and the roan. Roaring like a lion, the stud began to dive and pitch, its great hooves striking the ground and churning up the loose dirt into blinding clouds. With each explosive leap, it kicked its heels high over its back, its grunts louder than any wild boar as more dust boiled up in the pen. There, high on its back, sat the laughing Horn, shouting and whipping the big horse over the head with his quirt on every jump.

When the animal's hooves touched the ground, Horn jerked himself back in place, no daylight under his butt, the spur rowels ringing like church bells during each furious buck.

The ride went on forever, until, in final defeat, the roan stopped with a shudder, its shoulders lathered in a muddy foam that dripped on the ground. With a darker-colored body, it looked gutted. From its flared nostrils ran trickles of scarlet, its eyes were sunken in its head, the glare of anger was erased. Only the loud rasping of its hard breathing sounded as the shocked crowd realized the lanky rider, who kicked his leg over the saddle horn and jumped down, had ridden all the fire out of their roan tornado. Tom Horn had subdued their devil horse.

Quietly, they began to disperse, saying little, looking much like their done-in bucker—defeated. Their long-laid plans to have this laughing gringo mopped up in the dirt were over. They'd lost.

Deuces went over and took the saddle Tom had stripped off the horse. He could smell the roan's powerful male sweat coming from the wet pads.

"By damn, boy, we done good here," Horn said, brushing the flour like dust off his shirt sleeves and vest.

Deuces nodded. The people who lived beside the San Bernardino Springs may have learned a lesson. They'd lost plenty of money. His own share of the winnings was forty dollars in gold. This laughing cowboy was the best rider he ever knew. So Deuces was equally proud that hot afternoon when he walked up the street of the dusty Mexican village of Narcozi, and Tom Horn told him after all their hard work to bring the captain's remains there—they were entitled to a party, a fandango.

Horses and mule boarded in the stable, they headed for the cantina across the street, where guitar and trumpet music rang out. When Deuces followed Horn inside the place, the dim light blinded him for a moment. But the smoky interior of the cantina felt much cooler than outside. Soon his eyes became adjusted, and he saw several vaqueros at the bar who turned to look hard at them.

"Amigos!" Horn shouted. Then he moved into the bar among them as if he knew them and bought two bottles of rotgut.

"You brought the gringo officer's body here?" one of them asked.

Horn nodded solemnly. He stood there like a man who had lost his best friend. "We've had three days of hell to get here."

With a nod, he indicated Deuces. "Me and my compadre here need us a little Messikin whiskey now." He held up the bottles, and they nodded in their approval. Sour looks turned to smiles, and they clapped him on the back, making dust rise.

"Ah, amigos, you have a good time here," one of them said, and the others agreed.

"Gracias," Horn told them, and came over to the booth he had indicated.

Deuces slid into the seat. This man Horn could tame jaguars, the great spotted cats that sometimes stole their way this far north. Apaches never killed them, for they were sacred—el tigre. Besides, a bullet would not kill such an animal; only in hand-to-hand combat with a knife could one take such a legendary cat's life.

"Good guys," Horn said with a head toss.

The ones at the bar shared a friendly nod with him and went back to their drinking. Horn wiped his mustache with his palm before he took a large jolt from his bottle.

"That's yours," he said, shoving the other bottle over and laughing aloud as two teenage girls appeared as if by magic at the end of the table. "Deuces," Horn said aloud, "why, look who's done found us."

Horn removed his sombrero, and one of the girls took it. The other held her hand out for Deuces's straw hat, which he wore at Horn's insistence so someone wouldn't pot-shoot him for a renegade.

The string under his chin caught when he tried to remove it. He felt clumsy, but at last it came free, and she put it on the hook. Then she smiled at him. Thin and round-faced, she had little shape under her low-cut, wash-worn dress. She appeared uncomfortable but took a place on the bench seat when Deuces nodded his approval, and he moved over to make room for her to join him.

Then an older woman came and took the two girls' drink orders. Horn approved of their requests; the woman nodded and left. He spoke in English to Deuces.

"They will charge us for good liquor but bring them tea. Don't complain. It is how they play their game here, savvy?"

Deuces nodded that he understood. The girl who called herself Quana put her hand familiarly on his leg under the table. His heart stopped. He knew about women. Apache widows were generous with their bodies among the tribe's young men. With so many single females in camp after the tribe's warpath death losses, he found himself the object of attention from several such women at stomps. Always the ugly ones were the boldest at these events, and those were the ones he drew.

The mescal made Deuces laugh, and impulsively he hugged her shoulder. She scooted her hip against his and acted pleased. Horn nodded his approval.

"We're going to have a good time tonight." He reached across the table and slapped Deuces's arm to reinforce his words.

"Damn right," Deuces said, and looked into the starry eyes of the puta. Out of sight, her fingers nimbly tested his manhood through the material of his pants.

"You like big ones?" he whispered in Spanish to her.

"Sí." She grinned foolish-like up at him.

"Good," he said. "Mine is grande."

"Oh, good," she said, and, being sure no one was looking, she took a swig from his bottle. Then she wiped her mouth on the back of her hand and looked hard at him. "I like muy grande hombres."

The four of them laughed.

Then Deuces looked up in time to see a big man with a red beard start toward them from the bar. He had the small eyes of a *javelina* and looked angry about something.

"Gawdamn red sucker!" he shouted at Deuces, and his hand closed on the gun butt in the cross-draw holster. "You ain't breeding no more of them."

How Horn ever got his girl out of the way and managed to escape the booth that fast, Deuces never knew. Except María was on her butt on the floor, and Horn's right hand held the point of an Arkansas toothpick under the man's chin, forcing him to stand on his toes.

"You're mistaken, sir," Horn said through his clenched teeth. His other hand tore away the man's revolver and sent it skating across the floor.

"My friend Deuces is part of the U.S. Army forces cleaning up the last renegades in this land. Apologize, please."

"Damn, I'm sorry—mister," the man said in a high-pitched voice of urgency.

"I don't know where you belong, but obviously not in our company. Oh, you caused this little girl to get hurt. Give her a dollar." He motioned to María.

"Why, for that you could—"

Horn gave a small push on the knife, and a tiny trickle of blood ran down the polished blade. "For a man so close to his maker, it would pay to be more generous. Don't you agree?"

"Yes." The man fished out two coins and held them out. His wide-eyed stare still focused on Horn's face.

"María, for your discomfort," Horn said, and she quickly stuck out her palm to accept them.

"Now, for all my amigos at the bar. You better buy them a drink. You have disturbed them." Horn looked at the lot of them, and they nodded with new-found smiles.

"Bartender, my friend is buying each of those good

customers a glass of the best." He glared hard at his captive. "Right?"

"Oh, sí."

"Now, go pay your bar bill, and get out of here. We're having us a wake for Captain Crawford, and the next sumbitch disturbs us is going to hell on a one-way fare!"

He gave the man a hard shove toward the bar. Half staggering, the red-bearded one caught himself before he collided with it. He drew the others' nervous laughter as they showed him the glasses of liquor he'd bought for them. Several took off their sombreros and bowed to Horn.

As untouched by the event as he looked after the hard bronc ride, Horn wiped the blade on the side of his pants, slid the knife into the sheath behind his back, politely showed María the way to the seat, then laughed aloud.

"Damn, Deuces, I thought our gooses were cooked that time," Horn said, looking impressed by the whole situation.

Staring now at the few stars that Deuces could see from his El Paso cell window, he wondered what Horn was doing in the Sierra Madres. With most of the Chiricahuas sent to Florida, Horn's work for the army must be about over. Worse yet, Dueces worried he might never see his laughing friend again.

In the morning, Egan came for him, and they left on the train again. Their first train had, of course, gone on. Something that troubled Deuces the most as he climbed the iron steps to the car—was that trains never slept. He had slept little himself, but still, never before had he considered how trains had no patterns like living things.

They were like rocks and mountains, despite the smoke from the top that they belched like real breath and their driver wheels churning up the iron rails.

"My ex-wife," Egan said, "lives here. Went and saw her last night."

Deuces nodded and took the seat he indicated for him.

"Don't know what the hell for." Egan locked the chain on the seat rail and took his place across from Deuces. "She's the same old bitch I left three years ago. Asked me for five dollars to sleep with her. Said I owed her that much. Hell, she's got a job as a waitress."

"You pay her?"

"Yeah, I paid her. Hell, I was already there. Why not?"

Deuces shook his head as if it didn't matter.

"Yeah, yeah, I know I could have gone over to Juárez, and got some for fifty cents. Probably been better, too." He gave the newspaper he brought on board a big shake to get it open and immersed himself in reading it as the train rolled out of El Paso.

A different-looking desert to Deuces sped by the smudged glass. Tall mountains in the south, irrigated farmland up the valley. He looked for the tell-tale century plant but saw few of them. This plant grew all over the land where his people roamed, but now they were being forced by the whites into a smaller and smaller area. Old ones had explained to him that these great stalks with their once-in-a-lifetime blooming flowers were the symbol of his people. Not seeing any for several miles, he decided he must be past Apacheria borders at this point. But later in the day, he spotted some of the spiked plants on a desert hillside and smiled.

That evening, at a depot stop in West Texas, a woman

sold Egan a cut-up fried chicken wrapped in newspaper. Back in the car, he acted pleased with his purchase, filling his mouth with the greasy, crusty parts and tossing the bones out the open window while the train sped onward.

"Better eat some more," he indicated to Deuces with a chicken leg like a wand in his hand.

"Belly hurt," Deuces said, acting as sick to his stomach as he dared.

"Motion sickness," Egan said, leaning back with a shake of his head. He devoured the leg and, with a mouthful, went on talking about his life. Deuces answered him with nods or, if asked a pointed question, simply agreed with him.

Deuces decided that in all his talking, this man complained a lot about everything and never took any blame.

"I was the law once in Kimball, Kansas. Chief marshal there. You ever been to Kansas?"

Swaying with the train's motion, Deuces shook his head, watching the lawman suck on the snowy bone. Then, satisfied it was bare, he sailed it out the open window at the passing desert brush.

"As I was saying, I was head dog in that town. Damn, it's flat up there and hot as hell. See, I got to playing around a little with the mayor's daughter. You know," he said, searching in the grease-stained newspaper for another piece. "She was cute, kinda fat, and she was no—" he dropped his voice—"virgin, either. No, sirree. Hmm, another wing. You want some more, Buck?"

"No."

"Well, I'll eat it, then. See, this gal and I were fooling around some. Well, the mayor, her daddy, caught us and had a fit. Made the city council fire me. That wasn't fair, was it?"

"No."

"I thought the same thing. I mean, it looked awfully bad, what with her bloomers around her ankles and her dress hiked up, sitting on top of my desk."

Deuces nodded.

"Narrow-minded old goat. I told you she wasn't untouched before I got mine in her, didn't I?"

At last, Egan balled the rest up in the dark, grease-saturated newspaper and threw it all out the window. Close to the time that the sun began to set over Apacheria behind the last car on the rocking train, Egan wiped his hands on his white kerchief to clean them.

Night would soon engulf the car's interior as their train sped away from the red-orange sunset. The clack of the wheels on the rail seams and the side-to-side rock of the coach made Deuces want to shut his eyes. No sleep for him this night; he was as far from his homeland as he intended to be—he must escape and somehow find his way back. He could hide in the mountains until they gave up on him. Perhaps he would go live in Mexico. Perhaps even find that skinny puta Quana in Narcozi and take her to the mother mountains as his mate. Maybe even get a prettier one than her to go up there with him. Slumped down in the train bench seat, he worried. What would he need to do first if he could manage somehow to get away from Egan?

The train rushed on, stopping at small depots with yellow lamps in the windows. Then the chugging engine would regain speed, puff lots of bitter coal smoke into the cars as it rushed across the moonlit ground.

"Next stop in forty-five minutes, Uvalde, Texas," the conductor announced, coming through the aisle.

For the most part, the passengers were asleep. From

his appraisal, none of the men in their car seemed brave enough to assist Egan if he got into trouble. Most had stared at Deuces, and one man even gave a shudder of his shoulders when he asked Egan, "That one's a killer?"

"Big time. Why, he cut off a man's thing and stuffed it in his mouth and choked him to death on it," Egan said, throwing his arms up on the back of his bench as if he had no fear.

The ashen-faced man nodded, shaken by the words. He quickly moved on.

When the time at last came for Deuces to make his move, he would need much help from the mountain spirits to escape this man—still, he must do it!

"Mmm!" Deuces said, and held both hands over his mouth, kicking the dozing Egan in the shin. Apprehension twisted his guts over what would happen next, but the time for him to escape was now or never.

"Huh—what's wrong—my gawd, you're sick. Don't puke here." Egan fumbled with the keys, undoing the chain. "Come on. Come on." He dragged Deuces by the collar toward the platform as the Apache pretended to gag and acted ready to throw up.

"Get out there," Egan said, and shoved him through the doorway onto the deck between two cars. Headed full speed toward Uvalde, the train rocked back and forth.

Ready like a cat coiled to spring, Deuces shifted his weight and with all his force drove his elbow hard into the lawman's gut. The move pinned Egan, half bent over, against the door facing. An agonizing groan issued from the deputy's mouth. With the marshal incapacitated for a second, Deuces shoved his manacled hands inside Egan's coat and drew the pearl-handled Colt from his shoulder holster. Backing away on the swaying deck, Deuces cocked the hammer. In the half-light of the rocking platform, he could read the new fear in Egan's eyes. The revolver in his right hand, Deuces caught the iron railing with the other cuffed one for his balance and leaned out to look quickly into the direction the train was speeding through the night.

"Don't try it!" Egan shouted. "You won't survive the fall."

"Maybe I won't survive the rock place, either," he said smugly, and threw himself off the stairs backward.

He hit the ground hard and rolled. The end-over-end bruising roll never wanted to stop, until, at last, full of thorns and goat heads in his skin and face, he scampered to his knees and watched the red lantern swinging on the fast-disappearing last car. His breath came hard. The full realization of his freedom swept him despite the soreness and the stickers.

When he started to rise, several orange flashes came from someone shooting at him from the train. His head still dizzy from the fall, he knew he could not waste any more time at this place. Since nothing felt broken, he slid the Colt into his waistband and stared hard at the cuffs. They would hinder him from doing many things he might need to do to stay free. With no time to waste or worry about the bracelets, he climbed the tracks, crossed them, and looked at the dark sky to set his way by the North Star.

White men would use dogs to track him. He must find some black or red pepper to stop their noses. For the moment, he needed to get as far away from those twin iron rails as he could; they would think he would use them to find his way back toward his home. In a long gait, he soon found a dusty road barely visible under the stars and set out. Dogs barked at him from farmsteads he passed, but he ignored them. The curs stayed close to the dark outlines of shacks, not coming out to the road as he ran past their driveways. His mission for the moment was to get as many miles away from there as he could.

His breathing came easy, and his legs felt strong. They would carry him a long way. After a mile or so, he slipped up on a dark house with no dogs. His footsteps silent, he crept close enough to hear the snores of the residents. The boards in the porch made soft creaks under his Apache boot soles which only he could hear as he slipped inside the room. He drew a deep breath up his nose—white man's sweat and the sourness of piss in a jar filled the air. Then his hand closed around a square box on the table. The sharpness of a small whiff up his nose was enough. His heartbeat quickened with the box of ground black pepper in his grasp. Horn once told him that pepper spread on his tracks would stop any trailing hounds.

Tiptoeing, he eased back and out the door, grateful the occupants kept no barking watchdog. Soon he resumed his run up the road, scattering pepper in his wake. He dared to use the most direct route only until daylight, for the fields beside him were either shoulder-tall with corn stalks or half-knee-high cotton plants. Closer to dawn, he would need to find cover. He doubled his speed. How long would it take Egan to get a search party and come back to chase him?

The longer, the better, he knew, as his soles slapped the still hot dirt, and he ran even harder. The revolver in his waistband was good fortune, but he could never hold off an army with only a handgun. He'd forgotten about them; the army might come and search for him, too. Everyone would be looking for Deuces. He breathed deep and even. They would have to find him first, and that gave a burst of speed to his running.

Morning found him in a copse of cottonwoods and live oaks along a small stream. Seated on the ground, he ate some raw, green corn from the cob taken in his flight. From his vantage point, he could see any activity on the road. He had to hope the pepper he spread on his back trail the night before would deny them any more use of their bloodhounds.

With darkness, he would head north again, perhaps steal a horse. But people might recognize a horse—he would not steal one for a while. If they thought he was headed toward the setting sun, good. He would go farther north, then go west. No rush, but he felt saddened by the knowledge that he could never go back to San Carlos or Fort Apache, marry an Indian woman, and make kids. Always he would be a fugitive, a loner, cut off from the rest of his people.

He looked at the sun creasing the eastern sky. Should he pray to his god, Ussen, or the padres' god, the one with a cross and holy water to sprinkle on him, for help to get out of this land of farmers? He could never be an Apache again—never be a white man, either. He would need to find his own god. One for a man without people. The notion saddened him, but he wanted to sleep some, and then he must awaken and be aware for when Egan gave him chase.

They would come. He would be ready to avoid them. His enemies would be many. He held his hands up and looked at the chain that bound his wrists. Next, he must find a file to get them apart and then the bracelets cut off his wrists.

In the distance, a rooster crowed, and he nodded in approval. A small smile parted his lips; a chicken had set him free. The sounds of such birds must be a good omen for him.

Chapter 5

IN THE SHED, BURT USED A MILL FILE TO SHARPEN the section on the sickle bar. The low-roofed blacksmith shop was oven-hot. Streams of perspiration ran down his face as he labored. With interest, Juan watched him make passes with the file that left the finished sickle section with a new edge. Earlier, they had replaced the lost and loose rivets in the four-foot mower bar, and he had shown the man how to set and replace them. Juan proved to be a quick learner. Burt felt certain he would soon make a whiz of a hay machine mechanic out of this quiet youth.

How long ago since he had used a mower? He tried to recall. Years, perhaps. That was the main reason he didn't return to the family farm after his enlistment in the Union Army was over. Hot, hard, brainless work like this sharpening made up the days of all farmers. If it wasn't broken, it still needed repair before busting into two. Of course, new contraptions like this mowing machine saved hundreds of hours of backbreaking sickle-swinging work.

"You see?" he asked Juan, showing the man how to make the stroke by holding the file in both hands.

"Sí."

"Good. You try it."

Juan used his hands to show the angle and then shrugged.

"That's it. Go the same way as the old one." Burt used one hand over the other to demonstrate.

Satisfied, Juan began to file across the section with Burt bent over close to watch his work. Nodding in approval, he clapped the man on the shoulder. "That's how you do it."

Mopping his wet face on his kerchief, Burt blinked his sweat-stinging eyes. From there on, it would be the farm man's job to sharpen the sections. He went to the open doorway of the shed where a welcome hot wind swept his face. With a glance back, he felt satisfied the sharpening was being taken care of. He lifted his business suit coat from the nail on the door and headed for the house.

On the porch, he stopped and studied the gathering tall clouds coming in from the southwest. Probably rain again in a few hours. The monsoon season had begun. Precipitation anytime in the desert was a blessing. Even moisture falling up on the mountains was welcome.

"Did you teach him how?" Angela asked, coming out the front door.

"Yes. He learns fast."

She moved in front of him, took off his felt hat, and with a cloth blotted the beads on his forehead. "You've been sweating."

"Hot out there."

"Come in. I have some cool sun tea with fresh squeezed lemons and sugar to mix in."

"No ice?" he asked.

"No ice," she said. She stood on her toes and kissed his mouth. "You know ice in southern Arizona is rare even in winter. Besides, where would I even keep it?"

"They have it in Preskitt," he teased her.

"They have many things in Preskitt. Do you know that famous Madam Deveau up there?" she asked as he went past her to wash up and perhaps cool down some.

"No, I don't."

"She's very famous. I've heard that she knows all the legislators by their first names. Has a very large mansion."

"I've seen her place when I was up there."

"Oh, men—" she said, and went off in a huff to fix their drinks.

"Oh, men, what?" he called out from behind the wet wash cloth, scrubbing his face.

"Honestly," she said, returning with a tray and two tall glasses full of a brownish tea, lemons, and a sugar bowl on it.

"I'll be there in a minute. What is this business? I had no desire to go traipse over to some house of ill repute stocked with teenage girls." He paused as he dried his face to look hard at her over what he considered an unjust accusation.

She began to smile. "I was only teasing you."

"Good," he said, and hung the towel on a hook. "I find

your company much more pleasurable than some silly young girl anytime."

She set the tray down and stared reflectively at it for a minute before she turned to look at him. "You really mean that, don't you, Burton?"

"Bet your life I do."

Glass in her hand, she stalked over to him. "Good. I shall never mention that place again in jest or seriousness."

He took his glass of tea and nodded thanks to her. "That would be an excellent concession."

She frowned and hurried to the doorway to look at the dust boiling up from the road. "Burton, there's a rider coming hard down the road."

He joined her. Whoever it was, he was fast using up his horse. The rider was yelling and lashing at his pony when he came up the lane to the house.

"Burt Green?" he shouted, dismounting on the fly and crossing the yard on the run.

"Yes?"

The red-faced youth, out of breath, delivered a telegram on flimsy yellow paper. "It's from the governor." He gulped.

"To Burton Green—effective today, you have been appointed as a Special U.S. Marshal by order of the President of the United States—find and hire an Apache scout for a tracker—a former Apache scout—a prisoner called Deuces has escaped a U. S. Deputy Marshal—go to Uvalde, Texas, at once—and lend all your expertise and assistance to the local authorities—Judge Amos will swear you in—Governor Martin Baylor."

"You know about this?" Burt asked the red-faced youth.

"Yeah, it's the big news. That killer Deuces has escaped the deputy marshal who was taking him to prison and jumped off the train down there in Texas. They figure he'll kill a lot of folks if they don't catch him real quick, won't he, sir?"

"I don't know. Who all did this Deuces kill?"

"Some Apache scout called Sombrero. He—" The boy went silent.

Burt turned and nodded to Angela, who came out onto the porch with a dipper of water for the boy.

"Something wrong?" she asked with a frown.

"Yes, I have been made a special U.S. marshal by presidential order. Some Apache scout being sent to prison has escaped, and the governor wants me to go to Texas and assist them in finding him." He shook his head, considering the wire in his hand, still shocked by his own appointment. Without some strong political connections, the position of U.S. marshal was near to impossible to achieve. "And I need to find me a tracker and deputize him."

"Deputize an Indian?" Angela made a face of disbelief.

"Yes. Give him a U.S. deputy marshal's position, no doubt."

"You have a reply, sir?" the youth asked.

"Yes. Tell the governor I will be on my way to Texas shortly."

"Sign it Burton Green, sir?"

"Yes—and young man, don't kill that poor horse going back. He's awfully hot."

"Oh, I won't."

"Good," he said after him.

"You're a U.S. marshal now?" she said in a teasing voice. "My, you've sure moved up quick enough."

"You mean, about time. I suspect they wanted someone with authority in Texas for this search." The revelation of his new position had only begun to become a reality in his mind. Why special? He'd never heard of that before. He guessed that Judge Amos would be the man to hold the answers to his questions.

"Will this Apache tracker you hire even ride on a train?" Her raised eyebrows further questioned him as she crossed the porch to stand beside him.

He smiled at her as she clung to his arm. "Just going to have to see."

"What about Torres?"

"You'll have armed guards here the entire time I'm gone. Both Pedro and Obregón will be here."

"I know, but—"

"Don't worry, I know Pedro. These men are tough fighters and will guard this place like their own."

"And the stage robber, Taylor?"

"He'll have to go free a while longer. The governor wants me on this Deuces business."

"What happens next?"

"Hook up a buckboard, and we go back to Tucson."

"We may wear out the dirt in the road going back and forth to there," she said, and laughed softly. "Burton, we better pack you a bag." Still holding his right arm with both hands, she steered him for the front door. "I'd almost swear some power to be doesn't want us close together for very long at one time."

"You could think lots of things. This Deuces must be some kind of a devil to have the governor that upset." He glanced at the ceiling of sticks under the mud roof. It still needed to be repaired. Hay to cut. And him off to Texas. Perhaps they would have this one caught before he could get out of Tucson. One Indian in a strange land—how hard could that be to take care of?

"Can you even find a good tracker?" she asked, folding a shirt to put in his valise on the bed.

"There's many out of work. Several ex-army scouts who once worked for General Crook are hanging around Tucson."

"Oh, yes," she said. Then, as if in discovery, she posed with a look of knowing something. "I read about that Apache's trial. If he's the same one, some scout named Tom Horn came back from Mexico to testify in his behalf. This Deuces murdered another Apache scout because he cut the nose off his Apache squaw."

"Sane men have done that," Burt said, and handed her another shirt to fold. That was not a sure sign this Deuces was bloodthirsty. He went and took some underwear and socks out of the dresser drawer. Be a lot nicer to stay there with her than to go galley-flitting off to the Lone Star State—but duty called. At least, one good thing had happened; he had the full rank of a U.S. marshal. With this position came a steady monthly salary and eventual retirement—if he lived that long. No more serving warrants for a fee and making arrests for two dollars plus mileage.

Within an hour, the buckskins were hitched. Angela agreed to stay at her house in town until he returned or Pedro and Obregón were on hand to protect her at the ranch. Before they left, Burt told Juan to be careful mowing the alfalfa, as there would be more help coming.

He waited for Angela to kiss and hug the small children goodbye, then he helped her onto the spring seat. A last look around the place before he swung up and undid the reins. Work undone about the ranch was on his conscience and upset him, but the projects would have to hold until the matter of the escapee was settled.

The bright sun glinted off the quartz rocks on the sides of the Catalinas like diamonds. A strong creosote smell of the greasewood carried on the hot, stiff breeze. Somewhere off toward Mexico, a cloud bank grew taller. Monsoon moisture was coming up to wet the desert. Hard to tell if it would only be mare's tails of moisture that never reached the ground or an icy afternoon thundershower that deluged the fiery hot soil. The ovenlike wind in his face, he drove the trotting team and wondered where he would find a tracker.

The ex-scout he had in mind worked for him before, when they tracked down a white man who'd stolen five army mules. One-Eye Dick was his name. Was the half-blind Apache still loitering around Tucson? One never knew about the likes of them. He clucked to the team pulling the long grade.

"I've wondered about something," he said to her. "You and Van Dorn never had any children, did you?" At last, he pulled the sweating team down to a walk on the mesa top so they could catch their breath.

"Frederick and I wanted them, but it never happened." She shrugged and dropped her gaze to her lap. "Two miscarriages—"

When she grew silent, he glanced over at her. "I wasn't prying."

"I'm afraid I can't ever carry a child."

Feeling guilty for upsetting her, he threw his arm over her shoulder to comfort her. "No sin in that."

She dabbed at some tears with her handkerchief. "You didn't get any bargain in me."

"Who said I came for one? I was impressed with you

the day I met you. I think you're one of the bravest women I know. You stood up to those outlaws who killed your husband and even challenged me when I rode out with the deputies. I knew that first day I saw you—you were the woman for me."

She rested her forehead on his arm. "You won't be upset with me, if we can't have children?"

"No. We have each other, that's enough." He looked across the bunch grass and greasewood toward the towering bluffs looming over them. No need in upsetting her on his last day with her for some time—the matter of their having offspring wasn't that important to him. "I don't mind. Besides, when I get back from this Texas deal, why don't we have us a big shindig? You can invite all your Tucson friends out to the ranch for it."

"That a promise?" she asked, looking at him with tear drop-sparkling eyes.

" 'Course, you could always—"

"I could what, Burton Green?" She gave him a jab in the side with her elbow.

"Find a lot better fellah than me to put up with."

"Nonsense." She rose up and glanced over at him with a mischievous look. "My new party dress will be ready when you get back. Don't stay in Texas too long."

"Why?"

" 'Cause it'll be brown-colored from the dust if you wait too long."

They both laughed.

When he felt satisfied she was settled in, Burt left her at the Tucson house. He checked in a couple of bars and soon learned his former scout was still about town. One-Eye Dick supposedly was living in a wickiup somewhere out near Camp Lowell. So Burton rented a saddle horse and rode there as the sun dropped low in the west and the red blood of sunset painted the rustling cottonwoods. He looked forward to the relief sundown would bring from the day's soaring heat.

An off-duty soldier directed him to Dick's camp up the creek. When he approached, a thick-bodied Apache stood up from his place in the shade beside the grass-thatched wickiup. His obvious cloudy blind left eye glared at him.

"Green Burt," he announced, running over to take Burt's hand in both of his callused ones and pump it vigorously when Burt dismounted.

"How've you been, One-Eye?" He studied the stocky-built, shorter man in his blue army uniform shirt, breechcloth, red headband, and hair to the nape of his neck. One-Eye acted as if this meeting was a family homecoming—perhaps it was.

"Plenty damn good now you come. You got work?"

"In fact, I do have some."

"Good. Good. Not much to do here." He tossed his head in the direction of the army base.

"You ever know an Apache scout called Deuces?"

"Sí."

"He dangerous?"

One-Eye shrugged. "I have not seen him in a few years."

"He was on his way to prison and escaped."

"What must you do?" the Apache asked, with a twist of his head and his good eye narrowing with interest.

"Guess the governor wants you and me to go find him."

Neither man spoke. One-Eye bent over, took a pinch

of dirt, and slowly let it slip from his outstretched brown fingers. The trailing stream blew in the wind, and hardly a grain landed close by.

"He'll be like dust in the wind to find?" Burt asked after the demonstration.

One-Eye nodded with pursed lips. "We can go look, huh?"

"We better," he said, wondering if the Apache wasn't right about this business. Deuces might be gone like that dust. Only time would tell. He looked off toward the Rincon Mountains, where the sharp purple peaks stuck out against the darkening evening sky. Then he recalled his grandmother's old adage, "Just as well to go look for a yellow dandelion flower in a field of bloomed-out ones."

This sure might be the same case about their trying to find Deuces in Texas.

Chapter 6

MIDDAY, DEUCES CROUCHED IN THE TALL WEEDS and watched the old man and his mule cultivating the half-knee-high cotton. At the end of each long row, the farmer reined up and rested the thin mule, wiped his face on a white rag from a hind pocket, and relighted his pipe. The harsh smell of pipe tobacco smoke carried to the bushes and tall weeds concealing Deuces. He could even hear the man suck on the moisture in the bowl. Tired, the mule dropped its head and snorted wearily.

"Easy, boy," the old man said, not realizing the animal actually had scented Deuces and wasn't simply blowing hard at its own tiredness. The farmer holding up the pistol-like handles of the double-shovel cultivator, the cotton rope reins strung around his sun-brown neck, never knew the difference. A few more puffs on the pipe, and he used a small nail from his pocket to snuff out the fire. He put the pipe away in the side pocket of his bib overalls, then shook the lines and clucked to the mule. He pushed the cultivator shovel points into the ground, and it made a scuffing sound going to the east down the long row.

Deuces spotted a weathered gray board shed fifty yards away—must be where the man's tools were kept. Since the farmer never looked back, Deuces let him get halfway down the row before he chanced running low and getting alongside the shop unseen.

The night before, the pepper he'd spread on his back trail had stopped the deep-throated hounds' bawling. First time he heard them in the darkness, his blood froze, but soon they changed their bawls to yelps. Mounted posses still operated on the roads; groups of heavily armed men rode hard up and down them. Many times, they charged by only inches from where he had lain in the tall weeds before he moved on in his quest, searching for a simple file.

Deuces looked around carefully for anyone who might observe his entry to the building. Earlier, the woman had gone around to the front of the wooden frame house. He could hear her rocking and singing hymns from the front porch. She must be sewing or doing something up there. As long as she stayed there. He reached the side of the shed, opened the door, and slipped inside.

The acrid smell of a blacksmith's dead fire drew a smile to his face in the shadowy security of the shed's interior, which also reeked of a strong nicotine poison. He glanced down at the hateful chain connecting the two cuffs; he needed to be free of the restraint to continue his journey. All he wanted was one file; the old man and his mule could plow cotton till the next winter for all he cared. Plenty of tongs and hammers like the army farriers used, as well as an anvil and forge, were crowded inside. He swiftly moved in the dim-lighted space to the bench by the wall.

His fingers closed on a flat file with enough teeth left to wear through the chain. Later, he would cut the chain binding his wrists; for the moment, the freedom of his hands would be enough. With his eye on a crack in the boards, he could see the farmer and the bobbing head of the mule coming back on a new row. The man offered no threat, but he would no doubt quickly tell one of the posse men rushing about if he saw a fugitive Apache and give them a lead to his whereabouts. He must wait a while longer before he eased out of the stinking building. Quietly patting the file in his palm, he smiled for the first time in days.

In late afternoon, with the file wedged in a rotten stump, he drew a chain link held between his fingers across the edge, each time making minute filings that glistened in the shaft of sunlight penetrating the glen. The process proved tedious, but he knew eventually the link would be cut in two, and his hands would no longer be held together. The bracelets could wait to be removed later.

His ear turned, he listened. Something out there. The sound carried above the strong afternoon wind rustling through the treetops. Goats—at last, he clearly heard their bleating. His hard work finally suceeded. With the link cut through, he unhooked his restraint and sighed, letting his arms swing free. Pausing, he located the direction of the bells and bleating as the approaching herd came over the rise and down into the live-oak-choked draw where he hid.

Goats meant meat. The notion of a cooked meal made him think about all the raw corn he had consumed. For the moment, he decided to withdraw to a safer place and observe them. Among his newly gained objects was an old homemade knife in the cloth bundle where he placed the file, so he could butcher one of the kids if the opportunity came along. Fearing detection, he hurried for cover, realizing only then that he had left the cut link there on the stump. He wrinkled his nose at his own carelessness, but he decided no one would ever know who the small piece of split chain belonged to.

From atop the rock outcropping where he squatted on his heels, he observed the curious multicolored goats. Many kids in the herd hopped around, more interested in exploring than grazing. The adults reared up on trees to nibble on forage; others simply stood on their hind legs to reach low branches. Then he saw her for the first time—the white girl. Perhaps sixteen or seventeen, straight-backed, with her brown hair cut in a bob. She wore a blue checkered dress, wash-worn and perhaps too snug, which hugged her proud breasts and shapely body. She spoke sharply to the errant goats that wandered too far, and she cut some with a switch for disobeying her.

Her blue eyes shone, even at a distance. They were so deep in color they made his stomach roil. More even than the shapeliness of her body, her eyes were impossible to look away from. Who was she? Married white women did not herd goats. He curled his index finger over his mouth as if to clean it—he must have her for his own.

The threat of the posses, his return to jail, and even death were forgotten. The longer he watched her, the more obsessed he became with the way she walked about barefooted. His heart beat faster at the turn of her white ankles and the firm-looking butt encased in the cloth of the dress. He tried to shake away his hard, fast fascination with her—too late; he was smitten.

Two hours later, he cautiously stalked her back to the ranch house of stone. Smoke issued out the chimney, and two stock dogs barked a welcome to her when she drove the goat herd into a stake corral. A black-bearded man appeared, obviously her father, Deuces decided, watching them talk. He noticed with care how the man talked curtly to her and how the girl acted strangely defensive toward him. Something looked wrong between the two of them. Even from a distance, Deuces could see a void between them.

Wash hung on the lines, and two smaller children ran about making loud noises and teasing her as she went toward the house. Deuces could hear only parts of their speeches. A thin white woman came out onto the porch, threw out a pan of water with peelings for several dusty, red chickens that rushed to investigate, peck, and scratch.

Long after dark, he slipped in close to the darkened house. The two dogs snored under the porch, and he moved by them without disturbing their slumber. On silent soles, he entered the open front door and listened to the man's grumbled breathing. In the dim starlight, he could see his nightshirt-clad form on the bed, with the smaller shape of the woman in a white shift. Where was the herder girl? Then he turned an ear. Obviously sleeping in the loft with the younger ones. For a long moment, he considered climbing the ladder for another sight of her but decided that might be too much and could expose him. Disappointed that he had no access to see her, or at the least even to look at her in sleep, he began his retreat.

The floor gave small groans under his weight, but they were barely audible. On the porch at last, he skirted the slumbering dogs and soon was in the garden, picking some ripe tomatoes and then twisting off a few ears of ripe sweet corn. He planned to eat his plunder beyond the rail fences. Still intoxicated by her beauty, he schemed about how he could possibly possess her.

Stealing his way to the edge of the woods, he started at the dogs' barking. The pair at the house began to raise cain, and he tried to see what caused their alarm. Then he heard the drum of horses coming. He saw a lamp being lighted in the house, and the bearded man came outside with the flickering source held up to greet the riders.

"Hans! That Apache ain't been found yet! Better keep your eyes open, he's a killer."

"Ya, I vill. My dogs, they bark good when someone comes around. You find any signs of him?"

"No, he's gone up like smoke. But he ain't no ghost. Keep your gun handy. He might try anything."

"I vill, I vill," the man promised.

Satisfied with their warning, the posse members rushed away on their hard breathing horses into the night. Good, this information pleased him. Those men had no idea where he was. When Dueces took a large bite from the sun-ripened tomato in his hand, the warm juices ran from his chin. The sweet-acid taste filled his mouth with saliva—the first good thing he'd eaten since he left Arizona.

Mid-morning, Deuces squatted on a rock outcropping, anticipating her return. The goats were coming, and from his vantage point, he would be able to observe her unnoticed. The canyon underneath him led to a creek farther east. A place to water her wards. The night's coolness was still in the draw. Excited with the notion he would soon be seeing her again, he smiled as he watched the belled leaders begin to search for graze, followed by the others.

He could occasionally make her out through the lacy foliage. He observed her wearing the same blue-checkered dress and using a switch on the laggards, obviously wanting to head them for the water farther down. Clapping her hands made them choke up into a tighter herd and forced them to move on rather than graze. He knew by this time that wherever she went this day, he would follow her. Filled with daydreams about how he planned to ravage her ripe body, he eased himself off his perch and began to steal down the draw, using the dense, pungent-smelling cedar and live oak to shield himself.

At the creek, she chose a place to hike up her dress and waded into the half-knee-deep water. Unaware of anyone spying upon her, she flung water with kicks of her bare feet and shapely legs, then scooped up handfuls to spray in the air. The golden sunlight made rainbows in the droplets, and she threw back her arms in the splendor.

He needed to have her. But how? She would scream and be fear-filled when he abducted her. The notion disturbed him. Afterward, he would have to silence her forever—or risk them finding him. An Apache girl would submit and go with him if he kidnapped her. Most young Mexican women would do the same. But few white women ever accepted capture. He knew one white girl taken captive east of the Chiricahuas in a raid on a small wagon train; she took up with her Apache capturer. His name was Red Deer, and Deuces had always envied Deer's good fortune, for she made a good mate, but when he was killed by the Mexican soldiers, she went home to be white again. Red Deer's woman was pretty but certainly not as proud or good-looking as this one. He grinned to himself—not nearly as beautiful, either.

With the larger trees to conceal his approach and moving when her back was turned to him, he crept closer to her. Then, when he could stand it no longer, he rushed in and threw his arms around her from behind, pinning her arms to her side. She tried to break free. He soon learned that she was stronger than he thought she would be.

"Let go of me!"

Bending forward, she grunted and strained to throw him off her back. Her firm butt nestled against him, and he savored his place. Still, she did not scream.

"Let go of me!" she ordered.

"No, now you are mine," he said sharply in her ear.

"I'm no man's!"

He twisted her around, holding her arms tight in his grasp. His gaze met her deep-set blue eyes. The rage and the fury he had expected were there, but she never released a scream from her mouth. Only her defiant look bored hard at him.

"Who are you?" she demanded with a frown, and tried to shrug off his powerful hold on her limbs. Kicking his shins with her bare feet made no difference.

"White men call me Deuces." He grasped her upper arms tighter to reinforce his command.

"You must be the Apache—" She gave him a cross look.

He nodded. She stopped her struggling and stood stiff-backed before him. "Kill me."

In disbelief, he looked at her, iron defiance written in her fierce gaze. Then, in mild disbelief, he shook his head, amazed at her bold courage. She didn't understand his purpose. He let go of her arms and caught her dress front in both hands to rip it open.

She quickly caught his fingers. "Don't tear it! Don't! I will unbutton it for you. I only have this one dress to wear." She looked downcast, obedient. Was this a trick to throw him off guard? With guarded care, he watched her sun-browned fingers begin to undo the buttons.

A large rock churned in his stomach as he studied her actions. Would she go away with him? Was she like Red Deer's woman who had gone with him? Could he be so lucky? He felt his heart race faster as her white flesh began to appear between the dress parting. To see a woman undressed was nothing new for him. Apache women went naked about camp without shame. Somehow this exposure was different, spine-tinglingly different for him.

He nodded his head in approval when she finished and straightened. Her blue eyes stared hard at him when he reached out and pushed the dress off her snowy shoulders. The garment fell in a heap behind her heels. She clutched herself to hide her nakedness. Yes, she was every bit as beautiful as he thought she would be underneath the blue dress.

Chapter 7

"SPECIAL U.S. MARSHAL. WHAT'S IT MEAN?" BURT asked, seated in the chair before Judge Amos's desk.

"According to this letter sent to me, the attorney general of the United States, Robert C. Groves, has the authority from Congress to appoint up to a dozen such badge holders." Federal Judge Averal Amos, a small man wearing a brown suit two sizes too large for him, looked swallowed in the large office chair. Adjusting his gold-rim glasses, he held the letter up to the light flooding in the side window. "Due to the increased criminal activities in the territories, it has become necessary to enlist—well, you know—special U.S. marshals to combat the criminal elements and bring the lawbreakers to justice, whether they be brought to justice in local or federal courts.

"See, you have some leeway there—"

Burt nodded and sat back in the chair to listen.

"These officers shall be paid a salary of two hundred dollars a month. Plus their expenses, which they must seriously account for and submit such costs to the U.S. attorney general's office for reimbursement." Amos looked over the paper and continued reading it after Burt's nod.

"They shall file activity reports on their successes and progress directly to the AG's attention at regualr intervals.

"Oh, yes, and they may hire posse men at the rate of pay consistent with hiring competent men. Not to exceed five dollars a day. That clear?"

"Perfectly."

"It all has to do with this *posse comitatus* business. Since we can't use the army any longer to help enforce the law out here, you'll need the posse men."

Both men agreed he'd need help on many occasions. Burt crossed his left leg over his right one.

"You should carry this letter with you, since it explains your authority," Amos said. "But I think the rest is clear. Your future assignments will come from Washington, and you have no restrictions from nor obligations to any other federal officers in the field. Though it says somewhere—oh, here—special officers will, when local and federal law officials are on hand, be cooperative and show them the courtesy they deserve."

"Thanks," Burt said.

"Stand up, then, Special U.S. Marshal Burt Green, and I will administer the oath."

"Yes, sir."

"By the power vested in me . . ."

* * *

The Apache scout One-Eye Dick wore an unblocked gray felt hat to top off his new wardrobe of civilized-looking pants and shirt. He stood stiff as a ramrod on the railroad platform. Burt could see the man's obvious discomfort in the new, starched clothing and sympathized with him, though he never mentioned it. Instead, he spoke with the shorter man, Pedro, who was seeing them off at the depot, along with Angela.

"I don't know when we'll be back. Don't you try to round up this Torres by yourself," he cautioned Pedro. "But learn all you can about his whereabouts. When I get back, we'll go and find him."

"Sí, Obregón and I will guard the ranch until you return. You must be careful, too. This Apache Deuces was an army scout, but I've heard he has gone loco. Jumped off that train, they say."

Burt nodded acknowledgment. During the escape, according to the report he'd seen in print, Deuces had taken the deputy marshal's handgun, but, strangely enough, not killed him. Perhaps with his wrists in handcuffs, cocking and firing the pistol had been too hard on the rocking train. Downy showed the paper to him after Judge Amos had sworn him in as a U.S. marshal. While there, Burt also deputized his own man, One-Eye Dick.

"What happened to this Deputy Egan after Deuces escaped?" Burt asked Downy, his curiosity keyed by the absence of any word about the deputy originally involved in the case.

"Venereal disease," Downy said with a wary shake of his head. "Must have gotten himself a real bad dose of it somewhere. He's in the hospital in San Antonio. Guess that's why you got this appointment."

To save any hard feelings, Burt never mentioned the "special" part of his new job description—for all Downy knew, he was simply another equal. Best, he felt, to leave it like that for the time being.

"Ha. If you ask me, Green, it's all just a big waste of government money paying your way back there and all that," the balding man said, shaking his head. "After jumping off that fast-moving train, that damn Injun crawled off somewhere and died from his injuries. They just ain't found his carcass."

"Maybe I can find it." Determined not to get pulled into an argument with his ex-boss, Burt nodded to him as he prepared to leave.

"Waste of time and money. That buck's dead, or they'd have found him by this time. He don't know that country, and I say if he'd survived, them Texans would have already nailed his ass. Why, they've had their bloodhounds out and posses looking all over for him."

At the doorway, Burt stopped to ask Downy one more question. "This Egan ever say in his report why Deuces never shot him when he had the chance?"

"Panic, I figure." Downy shook his head to dismiss the matter. "Damn buck was shook. He had the drop on the man and probably was pissing in his pants the whole time. That's why, just plain too scared."

Burt acknowledged he heard the man's answer before he and One-Eye left the marshal's office. Standing on the platform, holding hands with Angela while her rich perfume spiraled up his nose, he still wondered why the fugitive let Egan live. There was no fear in that ex-scout. Deuces was an Apache.

"Oh, you must be careful, Burton," She dropped her gaze to the wooden flooring of the depot platform.

"Don't worry about me," he said quietly. "I only pray that you can stand to put up with being married to a lawman. I'll be on the move like this a lot. This is how I make my living."

She drew a deep breath up her slender nose and nodded. "I will be there for you when you return—so you come back to me when it's all over."

"I'll do that."

"Yes." She nodded thoughtfully, chewing on her lower lip hesitantly before she finally added, "I'm impressed with your honesty about things that are important."

"Man don't have much if he ain't at least honest."

"I agree. I've known enough liars in my life." She looked to the sky for help.

He wanted to hold her in his arms, kiss her, tell her those days were over for her—for them. Why did he wonder at times like this about her dead husband's faithfulness to her? He wanted to hug her and reassure her of his firm commitment to her. Something held him back, perhaps the publicness of the place or the onlookers ready to board. Some sort of restraint kept him from being so impulsive, until—

The train arrived in a scream of steel to steel, steam, and air brakes. He took the opportunity in all the confusion to kiss her on the mouth, and then, after holding her against him for a long moment, he smiled into her face.

"I'll be back. Then we can live our lives."

"I'll be here, Burton. You need anything, wire me."

"Good enough. Be careful and on guard. I'll feel better when I'm back."

"Me, too." She gave him a small shove toward the train. "Leave now before I cry."

From the steps, he turned back with a big smile. "Don't forget to get a party dress. We'll have that real fandango when I get back."

"I won't forget it." She beamed at him through wet lashes. "How could I?"

On the car's platform, he waved to her again, and then he followed One-Eye inside the Pullman car. From behind the dirty glass, he could see her still waving her kerchief. Pedro stood beside her, barely reaching her shoulder.

Burt recalled the first time he saw her, her dress all covered in dust and torn after her harrowing experience with the Mexican outlaws. Rifle in her hands, she cocked it and challenged him when he rode up to the ranch ahead of the posse. Even as desperate as she looked that day, he recalled the beauty he'd seen in the woman of his life.

With a jerk of the cars in a chainlike reaction, they began their two-day journey to Texas. Seated across from him, a wooden-bodied One-Eye nodded with his arms folded over his chest—prepared for departure or his death. The grim-faced Apache looked ready for his own execution. Burt knew that one peep out of anyone, and One-Eye might collapse with a deadly heart attack.

"It's okay now," he said to reassure him as the train got under way. One-Eye nodded and gave out a loud sigh of relief. They were headed full steam for Texas.

The Southern Pacific reached El Paso, then, belching ashes and smoke over its shoulder, churned its way up the Rio Grande Valley. Burt read a copy of the *El Paso Sun* newspaper and scanned the headlines. "Apache Killer Still On the Loose:"

Despite local law enforcement and the Texas Rangers, the escaped federal prisoner, a murderous Apache nicknamed Deuces, continues to evade the efforts to apprehend him. The killer, who overpowered a U.S. deputy marshal transporting him to prison and made a daring leap from the Southern Pacific passenger train last Sunday night in Uvalde County, has not been officially sighted since then. The search has been expanded to nearby Texas counties and even the international border eighty miles south. The Texas governor's office has posted a five-thousand-dollar reward for the Apache's capture dead or alive.

Rumors abound in the southern Texas hill country. Reports of raids on ranches, stolen horses and mules, and sightings of the Apache have poured into officials. Meanwhile, mounted posses continue to comb the area both north and south of the spot where the renegade escaped from the train. According to Uvalde County Sheriff Hop Grimwell, the fugitive may have been so injured in his fall from the train that he may have crawled off and died. However, Grimwell says nothing is being taken for granted. Until the corpse or the murderer is found and taken in custody, the search will continue.

Hop Grimwell—Burt rolled the name over. No doubt, Grimwell was the man he should contact at Uvalde. He and One-Eye would have a cold trail—more than a week would have passed before they would even get to examine the place where Deuces escaped. He glanced across the blood-red-bathed farmland in the last light of day—no easy thing to pick up such a cold trail. Perhaps the local authorities would get some new leads by the time they arrived at Uvalde. By his own estimations, it would be hard to kill an Apache in a fall from a train. Watching the bloody-tinted view of the towering mountains over in Mexico through the smudged window, he hoped that Angela was back at the ranch and safe.

Burt slept little through the night. He felt tired and stiff the next morning, eating some bread and butter he bought from a vendor at the last train station. Not concerned about the name of the place, after the stopover, he quizzed the conductor, who assured him they would be in Uvalde on schedule by noon.

One-Eye napped most of the time. After the first hours passed uneventfully, his first train ride had turned commonplace for his deputy, Burt decided.

"Beats riding a horse back here," One-Eye finally said, and stretched.

"Yes," Burton agreed. "It sure beats that."

"This train go to Florida?"

"I think you have to change trains somewhere and take another to get there."

The scout nodded his head.

"You weren't planning to go there?"

"No." One-Eye chuckled, then shook his head. "Must have been some ride for all those people."

"The Chiricahuas they sent there?"

"Yeah, they all rode the train."

"You miss some of those people?"

"Sometimes—not bad enough to ride the train that far." One-Eye smiled.

"I'll be glad when we get to Uvalde." Burt stretched his stiff legs under the chair ahead. All this inactivity was making him stiffer by the hour. Perhaps the train's continual swaying and clacking had him on edge.

"Me, too," One-Eye agreed.

The depot at Uvalde recently had been freshly whitewashed, and a new lettered sign gave the name. A black porter came and took their bags for deportation. One-Eye gave him a suspicious look, but Burt caught the scout's arm and reassured him that was the way such things went.

"The sheriff's office?" Burt asked the porter when they disembarked from the stairs and stood in the bright sunlight.

"Be uptown, sah, a mile that way. At the courthouse on the square."

"Very good. Get us a taxi."

"Yes, sah."

A short time later, they arrived at the courthouse. Burt paid the driver and left One-Eye with the bags in the shade while he went inside the new-looking stone building.

A man directed him down the hall, where several armed men were standing around. A shorter man with a full mustache was giving the orders. "Jesse, you take ten men and comb that creek area above the Yancy place. It's brushy enough to hide anything. Tom, you and your men scout that country west of the jumpoff place. Look hard again under every bridge and culvert. If he crawled off to die, he damn sure ain't in plain sight."

Burt waited until the man finished. Then the lawman, seeing he was obviously there for some sort of business, strode over to him.

"Sheriff Grimwell. May I help you?"

"U.S. Marshal Burt Green from Arizona."

"Good to meet you. You're—ah, yes—the one who brought the Apache scout?" Grimwell searched around the hallway as if looking for him.

"He's outside with our bags. I'm anxious to get some horses and ride out to the spot— "

Grimwell turned to an assistant. "Go catch Tom Vender before he leaves. One of his men can take the marshal out there to the place where the Apache got away."

The deputy hurried off.

"Now, I'm pleased that you came all this way; however, I doubt that there is much we haven't gone over."

"We'll not get in your way. My experience with this tracker is he has an Apache's uncanny ability to sort out tracks."

Grimwell chuckled, then shook his head wearily. "First you need to have tracks. This buck left none."

Rather than argue with him, Burt agreed and thanked the man. He'd not come a thousand miles to be talked out of looking. Obviously, Grimwell resented his presence—worried that he and One-Eye might upstage the local law by finding the escapee. For his part, Burt didn't give a big rip about the man's feelings. He had a job to do, and that was to find Deuces if the locals couldn't.

Outside, Grimwell's deputy introduced Burt to Harry Faucet. The small-framed man with gray streaks in his beard was assigned to show them the spot where Deuces left the train. Short as Pedro, the overall-clad Faucet looked to be in his late thirties. The rest of the posse rode on. They were half a block away already when Burt looked up and checked on them.

"I'm sure we could find it, if you want to ride on with them." Burton offered him a way out of guiding them.

"Naw." Faucet spit some tobacco aside. "I kinda like to see how you and him operate." He gave a head toss at One-Eye.

"Fine. We'll go see about some horses and be ready."

The man made a pained face, then he spoke. "I ain't telling you where to get your horses, but—"

"You know a better source?" Burt asked, catching the man's hesitation as a warning.

"Sure do. A block down and on the left is Pearson's. Guy's got a better rep than them folks across the street."

"Good." Burt read the sign of the livery opposite the courthouse. "Adolph Borghast's Stables." If Pearson's was a better place, then the man just proved his worth.

In thirty minutes of dickering and checking them out, Burt managed to buy two decent saddle horses and a cotton mule from Pearson to haul their gear. They rode out of Uvalde with their guide, Burton aboard a dun and One-Eye on a blue roan; the brown mule under a pack saddle came along on a loose lead. Faucet rode a long-headed bay with work collar scars on its shoulders.

By late afternoon, they reached the place that Faucet pointed out to them as the spot beside the iron rails and pine-tarred ties. "He jumped off somewhere along in here."

Burt swiveled around in the saddle. To the north of them lay hundreds of acres of farmland and crops. South of the tracks, the same—corn and cotton fields, rail fences. One-Eye gave him the reins to his horse and with a head toss went off to examine for tracks in the short weeds and grass beside the road bed. The Apache leaned over and searched the ground as he went.

Faucet pointed across the iron rails. "That side." Then he twisted around to look at Burt and tossed his head up the dirt road.

"We picked up his trail a ways north of here with dogs. Least, we thought we had. That Marshal Egan had some of that Injun's things from his suitcase. Hounds smelled them and went off bawling up the road."

"What happened?"

"They quit the trail up there, oh, about two miles, and they couldn't find a thing."

"Any reason why?"

"Guy owns them hounds was certain that he'd done peppered his back trail. But I don't figure an Injun woulda knowed how to do that." The man shook his head at the impossibility of such a thing.

Burt dismounted with all of Faucet's information going over in his mind. He decided this Deuces just might be a lot smarter than they had given him credit for being. From where Burt stood, he could see One-Eye was still busy checking the ground along the rails. His work might take forever unless they got lucky. He looked up the road.

"How many farm houses are between here and where the dogs lost him?"

"Several, why?"

"Well, Mr. Faucet, I don't figure that Apache carried that pepper or anything else to turn those hounds off in his pocket when he bailed off that train."

"So?" The farmer checked his horse and frowned at him.

"So, if he had anything at all, he stole it somewhere between here and where he fouled up those bloodhounds." Burt looked north up the dirt road, trying to decide how to learn more about the source of the substance.

Faucet's blue eyes widened in disbelief. "Nobody saw him steal any."

Burt wanted to laugh. How could he tell this dirt farmer you didn't have to see Apaches for them to have been there—most times they were like smoke. Good, after One-Eye finished, they'd ride up the road and start asking the folks along the way about missing any pepper or dried chilis.

In a few minutes, filled with impatience, Burt decided to hasten their plans. He removed his felt hat, dried the sweaty band with a kerchief, and turned to Faucet.

"If you won't mind, start up the road asking if anyone's missing a can of pepper or string of dried chili peppers."

"Missing a can of pepper?"

"Yes, or chilis. It might speed the process."

"But we were all out here with them dogs—folks was talking—no one seen hide nor hair of that buck." Faucet looked exasperated that he would even ask him to do such a thing.

Burt shook his head and grinned. "Don't mean much, but chances are that the folks lost the spices never put two and two together about an Apache stealing it out from under their noses."

"I'll go to asking, but—" He spit tobacco to the side. "Think it may be a big waste of time."

"Maybe," Burt said, and indicated for the man to go ahead and try.

Back on his horse, Faucet rode up the road. Burt tied the reins to the front leg of each of their animals to let them graze through the bits while he walked over to see what Dick was doing.

"Find anything?" he asked the scout, who was squatted on his heels by the rails.

"Plenty shoe prints."

"I sent Faucet up the road to check with the neighbors. Deuces must have stolen the material close by here that turned off those hounds."

One-Eye looked to the north, and his head bobbed as if he understood Burt's ideas. "No one saw him. They would have looked for him to be near these tracks."

"I figure he knew that they would go that way. They're still searching hard up and down the tracks for him."

"What's that country like?" One-Eye motioned to the north.

"Danged if I know, One-Eye, but if it's hills and mountains, he might be right where he wants to be."

"I can see some small peaks." The scout wiped his face on his sleeve, then nodded as if in deep thought. "Deuces not dumb."

"I think these Texans are learning that."

One-Eye grinned and motioned northward, with his copper mouth set in a straight line. "I would go that way, too."

Chapter 8

THE GRAY MARE RODE SMOOTH IN A LOPE THROUGH the dark night. Greta was in the saddle, Deuces on the back. He wanted lots of distance between her home place and where they would light again. Her closeness made his guts roil.

The hills ahead grew taller in the starlight. Less sign of people, too. The fact that they passed fewer home places made him feel easier. At times, he worried that his mind had grown so infatuated with the notion to possess her ripe body that he forgot his personal mission was to avoid discovery and arrest. He must be more careful from here on.

Sunup found them in a live oak side canyon, watered by a spring. The gray mare was hobbled and grazing nearby.

"We can stay here for a while. I must go and find

food," he said to her as she sat numblike on the ground. "If you promise not run away, I won't tie you up. Will you stay here?

"Yes," she agreed. "I will gather some dry wood for when you return."

"Don't build a fire—until I return." He didn't need a column of smoke to lead those posse men to their camp.

He felt her blue eyes studying him. The same ones that looked so hard at him the first time he had taken her. But, despite her hard staring, she had become his woman. Many things were unsaid between them, but he felt time would solve all that.

For a long moment, he wondered if she had only been acting when they made love. He watched her bend over to sweep up some sticks. Would she ride off on the gray once he left her? He chewed on his lower lip. If she did, she did, but it would mean they'd have a lead on where he had been. So far, the posses of men simply rushed about, not seeing his trail. Filled with concern about not tying her up, he started up the draw on foot to see about finding them some food.

Across a few hills, he found a small herd of unattended goats. He boxed them up and managed to grasp a small kid by a kicking hind leg while the panicked others escaped. He carried the limp carcass back and washed the body cavity in the stream below their spring.

She came and knelt beside him, looking undecided about her purpose. "It is fat," she said in approval

"Yes, it will feed us today. Tomorrow I will look for other game."

"Good." Then her hand touched the handcuff, and her eyes implored him. "I will file this one off while it cooks."

"That would be kind of you," he said, touched by her concern.

"Will they be able to track the horse?" she asked.

He shook his head to dismiss her concern. They might miss it, but they would be unable to find it. Before he took the mare from the pasture, he bound its hooves in sacking taken from the shed where he found the saddle and bridle. He'd watched them, all dressed up, drive away for church. He made sure they left no tracks for any posse member to follow until they were miles away.

The file made a grating sound as she passed it over the cuff, using both hands with a vengeance to saw away at the metal. Like sparkles in a creek, the filings trickled from his wrist with each effort she made across the deepening groove. Seated cross-legged on the ground facing her, he studied her smooth, tanned face. Not as dark a brown as most Apaches, but he liked the shade and how it blended into the snowy white of her cleavage with the dress's first top buttons undone.

"Where will you go next?" she asked.

"In time to my land."

"Where is that?" She frowned as if concerned but busied herself at the job of filing on his bracelet.

"Where the sun sets."

"Will you let me go then?"

He shook his head hard. "You are my woman now."

She nodded submissively. "I'm hungry for that goat."

"So am I."

He would need to make a bow and some arrows. The silent way to hunt would be the best. Plenty of fat deer and loose goats in these hills. To find some steel and make points would be quicker than stone ones; besides, he had not seen any flint deposits, though he felt certain they probably were about. Anyway, iron worked much easier than flint. He watched her lay down the file, take hold of the handcuff, and spring it open.

He looked in disbelief, first at his freed wrist with the reddened ring on the skin, then at her. Ussen had surely sent this woman to him. He couldn't believe his good fortune. He threw his arms around her and drew her onto his lap. His forehead pressed to hers, he considered his good fortune.

"We better eat." Her breathing quickened at their closeness. "The meat might burn."

"Then we can—"

She nodded obediently.

At sunup the next morning, they rode deeper into the rugged hill country. Midday, they found an abandoned rock adobe jacal, where he told her they would stay for a while. Acting less crestfallen about her status with the new-found place, she swept the dirt floor with a cedar bough broom and wet it by flinging droplets onto the surface until it was barely damp enough to hold down the dust. He found a hammock, rigged it between two trees in the backyard for them to sleep in, then went to making a bow of red cedar.

The first one cracked when it was halfway completed. Filled with rage, he beat the broken bow on the ground as if to teach it a lesson. Both hands gripped the shaft, and he flailed up a cloud of dust in his fury.

"Something wrong?" she asked from the doorway.

"No, only my own impatience." He felt embarrassed at his actions.

She nodded that she understood him and went back to work inside the hovel.

The job of building a bow, he knew, would not be easy, for he had used a rifle for several years and forgotten many details about bow making that his uncle had taught him. Patience would be the way. So, calmly, he selected another cedar sapling and went to carving it. Darkness set in, and the light was gone when she led him off to their new bed. They undressed to the sounds of the night insects. When they were at last in each other's arms in the throes of passionate lovemaking, the hammock unceremoniously dumped the two of them out onto the dirt and sharp sticks.

Seated on his bare butt, he shook his head. "Not a good day. First the bow broke, now the bed."

She pulled him to his feet. "We are unharmed. You must be more careful in our swing."

"I will. I will."

Chapter 9

FROM THE TOP OF THE HAYSTACK, PEDRO COULD SEE the rider coming. He took the next bunch of alfalfa off Obregón's pitchfork tines and placed it on the center on the stack he was stomping to make tight. The rich, wine-like smell of the curing alfalfa filled his nose. He paused to look hard again at the rider and recognized Guillermo Riaz on the bay horse. Good. Perhaps the man had information for him about Torres.

"Wait!" he shouted to Obregón, who stood on the wagon rack. "We have company."

"Who?" the full-mustached man in his forties asked.

"Riaz, Guillermo Riaz."

Obregón shrugged and set the fork down. He stopped to mop his face on a kerchief.

Sliding off the stack, Pedro landed on his feet and

walked out in the hot sun to greet the rider. Obregón went for a drink. The short rider in his thirties dismounted and nodded. His thin bay horse snorted wearily and dropped its head low.

"How are you this hot afternoon?" Riaz asked.

"Fine. You must have information for me," Pedro said.

"Yes, the bandit Torres and his gang are in Sonora at a place they call Diablo."

Considering the man's words, Pedro nodded. He was not familiar with the village; there were many small crossroad places in Sonora that he had never heard about.

"He's been selling some horses he stole up here. So he will be down there for a week or so."

"Is this information old you bring me?"

Riaz shook his head. "Yesterday, one of his men rode up and told my sister Consuela that Torres said that they would not make another raid up here until the next full moon."

"This man who told her?"

"Fernando Moras."

Pedro knew that worthless outfit. Moras would rather steal than work anytime. Pedro decided with this information that he had time to go down there and learn all about Torres; the patrón would be pleased when he returned if he knew all about this bandit's place. With the outlaws busy selling their stolen horses and the next full moon two weeks away, Obregón and Juan could protect the patrón's wife while he rode to Sonora and located this bandit's hideout.

"How much do I owe you?" he asked the man.

"Ten pesos you promised me for a good lead."

"I will go to the house and get your money."

"Gracias." Riaz smiled as if relieved he had agreed so easily to his price.

Pedro hurried off for the house as Obregón came over and began to talk to Riaz. The señora would have the money to pay him. Pedro planned to explain to her how the patrón needed this information. In the broiling sun, with the heat reflected in his face, he finally reached the porch and knocked on the door.

"Come in, Pedro," she said, and swished into the front room. "Is something wrong?"

"A man has brought me information about the bandits. I need to pay him for it."

"How much?" she asked.

"Ten pesos."

"Good. I'll go get the money." She paused and turned back. "Did he know much about them?"

"Yes, I will tell you when I return. But according to this man, we have no worry about a raid until the moon is full again, señora."

"Very good," she said, and smiled, pleased at his information. In minutes, she returned and gave him the coins to pay his informer.

He thanked her and went back to pay Riaz. This job working for the marshal would be a good one. Señor Green would be away much of the time and would need a man like himself to handle things. His sandals grew hot as fire as he recrossed the dusty driveway. If only he could pinpoint Torres and the rest of his gang while his boss was gone—his patrón would be pleased. Good—all he must do next is convince the señora that he should go and spy on the bandits in this place called Diablo down in Sonora.

Before he left the ranch, he promised the patrón's wife

he would only learn all he could about the man, Torres, and then return to the ranch to wait for Marshal Green's return. Obregón and Juan could guard the ranch; Pedro planned to have all the information about this bandit and his gang by the time his boss returned from Texas. After receiving the señora's permission, filled with confidence, he kissed his sweet Juanita goodbye and rode off to find his man.

Three days later, Pedro Astanchez, dressed in white cotton peon clothing and an old straw hat to arouse little attention, entered the Sonora countryside. South of Nogales, a day's ride, at the run-down village called Diablo, he dismounted his brown mustang before the adobe cantina in the square.

Siesta time. Pedro looked around, unimpressed with the place. Several men were seated on the ground in the shade of the nearby store's porch, taking their afternoon nap. They barely glanced up to see him when the village's cowardly curs barked at his arrival.

His small horse, Poco, dropped its head, snorted wearily, and blew up a cloud of dust. To its notion, the place deserved the title.

He pushed his way inside the cantina, shady and cooler inside. A bartender with a full black mustache nodded to him from behind the bar.

"Amigo, what will you have?"

"Ah, perhaps a beer."

"Ten centavos."

"I have the money," he said to reassure the man. He looked around the empty room at the deserted tables and chairs.

"The women, you look for them?" The mustached bartender indicated the curtained doorway at the back of the room. "They're in there asleep. You could go back there and pick one, but they would be very grouchy."

"I hate grouchy women," Pedro said, and indicated that beer would be enough for him.

"You're a stranger here?" the short man with the waxed mustache asked, leaning his elbow on the bar as he polished a glass.

Pedro merely nodded as if the beer interested him more than anything. Somehow he must act like a man who'd lost his way. He raised the mug and toasted the man.

"To your good health. May you never lose your job and your wife in the same week," Pedro said in a toast to him.

"Both?" The man raised his eyebrows, then shook his head in sympathy. "Did she die?"

"No, worse. She ran off with a gringo."

"Oh, that is bad. My name is Alverón, Miguel Alverón."

"Mine is Pedro."

"Pedro, welcome to Diablo. May your fortune be better here than where you came from."

"Is there work around here?"

"Can you shoot a pistol?"

"Sí. But I am not what you call a crack shot."

Alverón looked around the empty cantina, then gave a toss of his head to the rear door "Come out back. We will see how good you can shoot."

Pedro hesitated. He looked at his beer, then at the man, as if undecided if he should do this or not.

"Aw, amigo, bring your beer along. No need to let it go flat while we target practice, huh?"

A smile glued on Pedro's lips, he watched Alverón get

out a well-oiled cartridge-model Colt and a box of ammunition. He felt certain that a man who could shoot could get a job with banditos like Torres. Another sip of the lukewarm beer, and he followed the man out into the strong sunlight behind the cantina, with the mug in his left hand.

Alverón lined up brown bottles on a table at the back of the yard. Then he walked back and nodded to him. "There are the targets. Here is the pistol. How many can you hit?"

Slowly, Pedro turned the fine handgun over in his hand to examine it. A poor out-of-work vaquero needed to act as if he appreciated such a well-kept weapon. Satisfied the revolver was loaded, he pulled it up, cocked the hammer, fired, and smashed the first bottle. He looked over at the man. They shared a nod.

Then he shot again and blasted the second one to brown fragments. Alverón smiled slyly. "Shoot the last three pronto."

If he shot all three, the man would suspect he was a pistolero. He plinked number three into pieces, took the neck off number four, but let his last bullet plow up wood beside the fifth one.

"Bet I could get that one the next time," Pedro said as if disgusted, and took a swig of beer from the mug in his left hand.

"Madre de Dios, you can shoot a pistola like a real expert."

To dismiss him, Pedro shrugged. "Now, where is the gallery?"

"What gallery?" Alverón asked.

"You want to hire me to run a shooting gallery?"

"No," the man said with raised eyebrows. He tucked

the revolver into his waistband and threw his arm around Pedro's shoulders. "Mi amigo, have I got a job for you."

"A job for me?"

"Sí, a man can shoot like that should ride with real men. Tonight, I will introduce you to your new boss."

"New boss?" Pedro blinked at him.

"Sí. Tonight I will introduce you to Alfredo Torres."

"Good, I want to meet him."

"You will, mi amigo, you will. He's a muy grande hombre." Alverón threw his head back and laughed aloud. "Muy grande!"

Good, Pedro decided, that's what I rode down here for. The next thing he must do was not to act too excited about any job offer. Back inside the dark and cooler cantina, he wondered what Burt Green and the Apache tracker were doing in Texas about the escaped scout. No telling. But he would like to be there helping them—more than spying on some two-bit bandito.

He drank two more beers and then went across the street to where a woman cooked food in the open market area. She nodded when he said for her to fix him something to eat. Squatted down on his sandals, he watched her work.

The iron grill sizzled when she tossed chopped onions on it. The sweet, strong aroma wafted up his nose. Then she added some cut-up hot peppers and, last, some strips of marinated beef or goat. With that on to cook, she began to work out a flour tortilla in her brown hands. The tortilla soon became blanket-size, and she tossed it on her grill.

He could view the cantina from where he was. Torres was the main thing on his mind. If he joined the bandits, would he ever have the opportunity to leave and go back to the ranch? Things could get plenty risky being a gang member. And he would only be safe as long as Moras was in Tucson—he was the single one in the gang who knew him.

"You are new to this place?" she said, and when he nodded, she added, "Beware, there are men here who would kill you for two cents." Then she snapped her fingers to show him how fast death would be for him.

He blinked at her soft-spoken words. With a quick check to be certain they were alone, he asked, "Kill me?"

"Sí, this is not a good place for you to be."

"Why?" he asked as if pained.

She flipped over the large flour tortilla on the grill using her fingertips. Then her brown eyes met his. "I don't know why—only I know it is dangerous for you to be here. They are like mad dogs."

"I will keep my eyes open," he promised her. This woman, he was satisfied, was a *bruja,* but her warning sounded sincere. Individuals like her knew many things about spells and the future—her concern made him feel uncomfortable.

"My name is Flora. I live down by the river. If you need a place, come and find me."

"How will I know your place?" he asked, checking again to be sure no one could overhear them.

"There is a *carita* in the yard with faded red paint on it."

"Can you tell who is after me?" he asked.

She shook her head, scooping up with a metal blade the steaming browned meat and vegetables to put into the tortilla. Deftly, she wrapped it and handed it to him.

"Ten centavos."

He paid her and watched as she wiped her hands on

the apron. When she raised her gaze to meet his, she shook her head in disapproval. "Get on your horse, and ride away. Now, before they kill you."

"I can't. I promised to meet a man here tonight."

"It will cause you much pain and suffering, if not your life."

Not an unattractive woman, though her lips were too full and her hair swept back so hard it slanted her eyes. Small breasts and a belly from giving multiple births. Still, she was not hard to look at, he decided, savoring bites of her tasty food.

"You are a good cook. You have no man?"

"A widow," she said quickly. "And if you don't leave now, you are a fool."

"Yes," he agreed, and went back to eating his first food of the day. Was she a good witch or a bad one? Only time would tell, but perhaps he should more seriously consider her warning.

The sound of horses coming on the run forced him to turn and watch a half dozen men draw up and dismount across the street. Talking and laughing, they barely cast a look his way. Pounding dust off their clothing, they headed for the cantina's batwing doors and pushed inside. This would be them, Torres and his gang.

She spit in the dust after them. Then a strong curse left her lips, barely audible to him.

"You dislike those men?"

"Banditos. They took my young brother Rafael with them. He never came home."

Pedro nodded and took another bite of the wrap he held in his hands. The brother may have been the one who was killed at the patrón's ranch—he dared not mention it. Grateful she had not read his mind, he wondered about this man Torres. Had he been among the ones who rode in?

Soon a rider came on a single-footing horse, a blood-red bay stallion that shuffled in a quick gait. The big man reined up before the cantina. Once dismounted, he took off his expensive sombrero and mockingly bowed toward Flora.

She quickly turned away. The words she muttered under her breath were so fierce and with such hatred they made her face glow even in the shadows, as the sun was far down in the west.

"A friend of yours?" Pedro asked from behind his handful of food.

"He's a killer."

He nodded. That must be the outlaw leader. The reality of the moment made his stomach upset. His mission was to learn all about the leader of the gang; the goal would not be that simple. The notion sobered him.

Chapter 10

DEPUTY FAUCET STOOD BY HIS HORSE, WAITING AT A driveway for Burt and One-Eye. Burt reined up and nodded to the man. Down the lane sat a weather-gray farm house and some outbuildings. Rows of okra, green beans, and tomatoes lined the two wagon ruts leading to the house. The plants looked floured in the fine dust that horses and rigs on the road churned up.

"Learn anything?" Burt asked.

"You were right. Mrs. Henry said she's been missing a pepper can from her kitchen table ever since the time of his escape."

Burt turned to the Apache. "One-Eye, we better take a look around up there."

The scout agreed.

"You read fortunes?" Faucet asked as they rode up the lane.

"No, but pepper don't come from the sky. Prisoners don't carry it. There had to be a source."

"Well, I can tell you they never saw or heard him."

"If we don't find any tracks here, we better start checking with folks about other missing things." Burt booted his dun after the scout for the house.

"Like what?" Faucet asked.

"A missing knife or axe, for starters."

"Yeah, he would need them things. But no one's seen him."

"Faucet," Burt said with a sigh. "You don't see Apaches. They're more like a wisp of smoke, gone on the wind."

"I'm beginning to believe that."

Burt removed his hat as the slat-shaped woman in the wash-worn dress came out onto the front stoop. Her sun-darkened face looked like a dried apple with a thousand wrinkles.

"Good day."

She narrowed her eyelids against the sun. "Harry says that polecat must've stole my pepper."

"Could have. Can my man look around your place for tracks?"

"Guess so."

Burt turned to One-Eye and motioned for him to go look around. Then he dismounted.

"When did you miss it, Mrs. Henry?" he asked.

"The morning of the big commotion, when all them men was out here. At breakfast that day, Ira went to grumbling where the pepper was for his gravy, and we couldn't find it nowheres. New tin, too."

Burt nodded that he understood. "Where did you keep it?"

"On the table in there." She shook her head and then hugged her arms as if cold. "Makes the chills run up my arms to even think that crazy red devil was in my house stealing it and us'n sound asleep. Coulda killed us all."

"Anything else missing?"

She shook her head, then, as if she had discovered something, said, "Might be a knife gone. Come to think of it. There might be a butcher knife missing. You reckon he took that, too?"

"Probably."

"Oh." She shuddered.

"Mrs. Henry, I figure he's long gone," Burt said to soothe her fears.

"But my Lord, mister, what if he's got my knife and kills someone with it?" She stuck out her head to ask him the question.

Burt shook his head, seeing One-Eye come around the building. "Won't be your fault, ma'am. Thank you." He remounted, ready to go.

"Mercy sakes," she said, still upset.

The three started up the drive for the road. Burt glanced back and, satisfied the woman couldn't hear, asked his scout, "You find any sign?"

One-Eye nodded. "He went in by the back door."

"My God." Faucet swallowed hard. "And he never killed them?"

One-Eye shook his head and with typical Apache nonchalance said, "He only needed pepper."

"And a knife," Burt added, then raised his gaze. "Wonder what else he's borrowed in his flight?"

"Let me get this straight," Faucet said. "He's stealing things right off folks' tables while they're asleep. No one's seen him, and they never put two and two together?"

"That's it. I don't think this Apache is a killer. Oh, he'll kill when he has to, but so far, he's done a great job of avoiding leaving any sign." Burt turned to One-Eye as they rode up the road. "What do you think?"

"He don't want to be caught," his scout said.

Burt agreed, and they pushed on northward up the dirt road.

An hour later, they were at Sam Borger's farm. Sam, a beanpole of a man, was bent over, busy fitting a shoe on a thin saddle pony. He never stopped working, hammering the shoe on the anvil and pounding it into shape, putting it in a pail of water to sizzle, then going back and checking the fit on the horse's hoof. He spat tobacco with regularity and talked the whole time he worked like a man without enough hours in a day.

"Yeah, I been missing a good new flat file since he escaped. First I thought I misplaced it, but I tore the damn shed apart looking for it. Somehow, I never figured that crazy Injun had got it till you mentioned it. Dang thing was there that morning, 'cause I used it on a rivet in the harness to replace one; that evening, it was gone." Bent over again with the pony's hoof in hand, he spat a big brown gob out in the dust and shook his head warily.

"That red bastard had to take the file in broad daylight, and me plowing cotton right out there. And I never seed him." He dropped the hoof and straightened stiff-like. "No wonder they ain't captured him."

"Anything else missing from your shop?" Burt asked.

"Oh, a hand axe."

"By grab, Green, that's what you said he'd take," Faucet said aloud.

"What all's he got?" the farmer asked with a perplexed frown on his face.

"A can of pepper, a knife, an axe, your file, and what else?" Faucet asked, adding it all up. "That we know about."

"A pearl-handled Colt pistol he took off Marshal Egan," Burt added, recalling the conversation about Deuces being armed.

"Where do you figure he's headed?" Borger asked.

"As far away as he can get," Burt said. He thanked the man and gave a head toss. When the three were mounted, he turned to One-Eye, who had scouted around the sheds while they talked. "Was he here?"

"Came from those woods." He pointed to the back of the place where the trees started. "Then he hid in those tall weeds until that farmer's back was turned."

Borger took off his weathered straw hat and beat his leg with it. "By damn, he's slicker than a darn weasel."

"He's an Apache," Burt said, and they rode on.

"How we ever going to find the wind?" Faucet asked as they turned to ride up the road.

"Smelling for it, I guess," Burt said, looking at the low sun in the west. "We better find us some food or cook some. It won't be long till dark."

"We ain't done bad for one day," Faucet said. "We done found out more than all them posses have in a week. How far ahead you reckon he is?"

"A goodly ways," Burt said, with his thoughts more on his ranch out in Arizona than on Deuces's thin trail. Eventually, they would sort out this mess in Texas. But how were Angela and his guards at the ranch getting along?

Down the road a few miles, Faucet found a farmer's wife willing to feed them. Mrs. Vanvort was tall, with her gray hair in a bun. In her day, she had been a beautiful woman, Burt decided after he met her. Obviously Dutch; her accent remained, and they learned her husband had gone to search for a missing teenage girl.

"Been gone for four or five days." She shook her head in disapproval. "Good girl, that Greta, she took care of the family goat herd."

"No sign of her?" Burt asked, taking one of the straightback chairs she showed them.

"I never heard of no girl missing," Faucet said with a frown.

"Well, they figured she might come back."

"Come back?" Faucet asked, and looked at Burt and One-Eye with a scowl.

"Yeah, you see, Hans Schumaker, that's her stepfather—well, him and her don't get along so well."

"You saying the girl and her stepfather don't get along?" Faucet asked.

At first, Burt wondered if Mrs. Vanvort would answer him. Then, at last, she nodded as if she wasn't telling the whole story.

"So when she didn't return home, they went to searching for her?" Burt asked.

"Yes, not right away."

"You think she ran off?" Burt asked.

"Who knows about young girls?"

"How old?"

"Sixteen."

"Did she have any boyfriends?"

"No!"

Her answer came so fast Burt knew there was more to

it than that. Something was left unsaid about the girl's disappearance and why they had waited so long to take up the search for her. The whole thing did not add up for him. After all, the sheriff had posses all over that could have been looking for her while they searched for Deuces.

"Really, her stepfather was very strict with her." The woman looked up from stirring her skillet of sizzling fried potatoes before she continued, "Too strict. They say he disciplined her if she even spoke to a boy her own age."

"Maybe he was jealous—" Faucet spouted off, then he wilted at Mrs. Vanvort's disapproving look at him and tried to take it back.

Burt kept his own counsel. Outside, someone rode up on horseback, and they all tried to see who it was. She held up her hand for them to stay and went out onto the porch to talk to the visitors.

"Need to water our horses, ma'am. We're passing through," the front rider said. "If we may, ma'am?"

"Help yourself. Supper's on the stove," she said.

"No, thanks. We, ah—we better get these back to the ranch. Obliged, though." They spurred their mounts, pulling on their reluctant horses. Burt went to the back door and studied the two youthful-looking wranglers as they hurriedly brought the half dozen ponies past him and circled them around the rock-walled tank. The second rider never turned toward the house; he was either terribly bashful or too backward to look at anyone. In a few minutes, the two were ready to leave. The talker gave a loud thanks going by the house. They rode out in a stiff trot.

"Didn't take them long to skedaddle," Faucet remarked, coming to the doorway.

"You know them?" Burt asked, wondering about their haste.

"Nope, never seen them before in my life."

"Who owns the Forty-five Slash horse brand?"

"I sure don't know. Why?" Faucet paused before sipping his coffee.

"Just a hunch," Burt said. "But as nervous as those two were, I'd say those horses were stolen, and they were on the run."

"I'll be dagnapped. I don't think like a lawman. Had we better go get them?"

"Horse stealing isn't a federal law. My badge is for federal offenses."

Faucet pulled on his beard. "Guess you're right."

"Food's ready," she announced. Then she straightened from putting the big cast-iron skillet of fried potatoes and onions on the table. "You really reckon they stole them?" she asked.

"I'd bet a couple of your good meals like this that they rustled them," Burt said, taking his place.

"Terrible shame. They were such nice-looking young men." She surveyed the table. "I'll slice some bread and get butter."

Her food melted in Burt's mouth. Mrs. Vanvort hovered over them, making certain that they had everything, including a glass of buttermilk for him that tasted like dessert to his tongue. How long since he had any fresh buttermilk? Years ago, perhaps back in Missouri during the war. A dark-eyed beautiful girl named Ginny served him some as fresh as Mrs. Vanvort's. Two bushwhackers later raped and killed her. He made damn sure that they paid for their treachery with their lives. The grimness of his memory came near to spoiling his first good meal since leaving Arizona.

"Excuse me," she finally said, and broke into his thoughts. "Is Mr. One-Eye an Apache?" She indicated the Indian busy eating at Burt's elbow.

"One-Eye's a White Mountain Apache. He lives on the San Carlos reservation. He's a tracker and a deputy U.S. marshal."

"He found signs of that escapee," Faucet said, looking up from his food and shaking his head in disbelief. "I swear, you'd never seen anything if you'd looked close."

"Maybe if he had time, he could find Greta?" the woman said, looking at the three of them.

"We'll have to see," Burt said, not wanting to deny her openly, but they had an escaped federal prisoner to capture. If the girl showed up, they'd return her, of course, to her home. More than likely, she slipped off with some boy she loved, and they were miles away—things like that happened all the time.

"Marshal, Greta's mother, Hilda, is my best friend. She is beside herself over the girl's disappearance. Schumaker, he is a hard man to live with, I think, but he's a good provider. A little zealous, maybe—"

The dogs heralded a welcome for the man who rode into the driveway on a jaded horse.

"Good," she said. "My Peter is home."

When he came through the doorway, she smiled at the lean man in his forties, and before she explained about her company, she asked, "You find her today?"

"Naw." Her husband looked defeated. "She disappeared just like smoke."

Faucet shot a questioning glance at Burt, who gave

the man a mild head shake to cut off any words. If there was anything about the girl's disappearance and Deuces, they'd better check it out. But he didn't need to upset the missus—too nice a lady for them to do that to her. But there could be something to this girl's disappearance and the escapee. Perhaps they should go in the morning and check it out. More detours, probably.

Chapter 11

"WHO SENT YOU?" THE DEMAND WAS LOUD IN HIS ears, and a knotted fist hit Pedro in the gut like a mule's kick. Hanging by his wrists from the rafters, through his hazy vision Pedro studied the members of Torres's gang crowded around close, with their angry faces, hard eyes peering at him. A couple of them had jumped him when he entered the cantina, then dragged him out the back door, past a screaming half-dressed puta. They'd strung him up to the rafters on this back porch.

"Wrong man," he managed to gasp.

"No!" Torres shouted. "Your name ain't Gomez, either."

Sharp aches in Pedro's arms plus the pins and needles in his hands only added to his misery. Then his punisher slugged him again. The wiry bulldog of a man struck Pedro's midriff like a battering ram.

No one to come to his rescue. The desperateness of his position set in like a lead weight tied to his neck. Señor Green was miles away in Texas, his wife Juanita at the ranch with Angela and the others. Maybe these bastardos would soon tire of their game.

"Who are you?"

"Gomez—" he managed to gasp. "Pedro Gomez."

"Maybe he's telling the truth?" someone spouted off.

"Maybe he's part of the federales. No simple vaquero can shoot like he did for Alverón this afternoon."

"Maybe he practiced a whole lot," someone else shouted.

Pedro, with dread in his heart, saw the big man give his bulldog a nod to continue the beating, so he tried to stiffen up for the blows he knew were coming. His patrón's words echoed in his ears as the shock of the man's fist drew up the last rush of sour puke that spewed out. *Don't try anything by yourself.* How he regretted disobeying him. Too late—another hard sledgehammer blow drove the wind from him, and he went faint.

In the darkness of night, he discovered in his dizziness, someone was trying to hold him up. They had cut loose the rope on one arm. It was a female with her body pressed to him for support as she tried to reach the other rope to cut him free. All very dark—finally, he could smell her musk. She hugged him against her ripe form with one arm around him to keep him from falling and tried to reach up to slash the last rope. When at last she managed to slice it, they fell to the ground in a pile, his arms as useless as if they had been pulled from the sockets.

"Quick, we must escape," she hissed.

He blinked at her in shocked disbelief. He doubted he could even stand, let alone walk. How ridiculous; he wanted to laugh. His sea legs would never hold him. But she scrambled around to carry him with one of his numb arms draped over her shoulder.

"Come on, we must be gone," she whispered.

"Sure, sure," he agreed, not at all certain that what she expected from him would work.

Somehow she managed to half drag and carry him out into the starlight. Then she boosted him onto a cart. So grateful for his pain-filled arms to be free, he closed his eyes and hoped sleep would ease the excruciating pain in his entire upper body.

Soon the ungreased wheels began to creak so loud he feared the dead would even come alive. The carita shook and rattled as she led it away from the back of the cantina. He had no idea about her destination; as long as they made it there unscathed, he'd be satisfied.

"I can't take you home," she said to him after she paused the cart-pulling animal. "They would look for you there. I'm going to hide you down by the river until you are strong enough and can get away."

"Gracias," he managed, realizing that his lips were badly swollen when he tried to speak. A knot on his sore head, ribs probably broken, what else was torn up? Holding his aching arms tight to his side, he looked up at the stars. A good drink at the moment might be what he needed. How would he ever explain this to his patrón? He hadn't been drunk when they jumped him, hadn't been drunk in six months, and he thought for certain that his cover would work in this place. Obviously, some stool pigeon had told Torres about him. Or was it only a guess? He might never know.

In his discomfort, he tried to think of anyone who knew about him riding down there to find the bandits.

Had Riaz double-crossed him? Rocked back and forth whenever the cart wheels hit a rock or bump, he tried to imagine who the informer could be. Torres might have spies in Tucson—some lowlife people would tell on their own mothers for a quarter.

"There is some high grass and willows, they should offer you some shelter." She apologized. "I will bring you food when they aren't watching me."

"I am very grateful," he said, shocked at the weakness in his voice.

When she helped him out of the cart, he could see the silver river rushing past in the starlight. Then, with much effort, she eased him back through the reeds and weeds. At last, they decided they were deep enough to be hidden. She spread the old blanket on the ground and helped him get down on his butt.

"A weapon?" he asked her. "I have no gun, no knife."

"I have this small knife," she said, and put the wooden handle in his palm.

He nodded in gratitude. It was hardly more than a paring knife. He regretted leaving the Colt in his saddle bags; no doubt, they had discovered it. Before he ever left these weeds, he would need to feel a lot better and stronger. She helped him lie down, then told him to sleep if he could and hurried away in a rustle of the dry reeds. Soon he could hear the high-pitched screams of the carita's dry axle, and he knew that she had gone to her own place.

In teeth-gritting pain, he faded in and out of sleep the rest of the night. A red-winged blackbird awoke him. Perched precariousy on a tall reed, it rode the morning wind's swaying and sang for him to awaken, the new day had begun.

The notion of the water made him thirsty, but if he managed to crawl to it, then he would be exposed and might not have the strength to get back. Best wait for her to return. He'd been thirsty before. Lying on his back, he could look up into the cottonwood limbs overhead, the dollar-sized leaves in a constant rustle, spinning back and forth in the breeze.

Once he felt strong enough to leave, he'd need a horse or animal to ride. They, no doubt, had confiscated Poco. His pockets were empty; he realized they'd taken what little money he had on him. That wasn't so bad in Mexico because no one ever had any money, anyway, except bandits and rich hacienda owners. Everyone else would share their meager food and housing with a poor stranger.

Torres. He went over the man's name several times. No way could he forget him or the bulldog-faced man who hit him—over and over again. They would get theirs; he had many friends. Burt Green would make hash of them. First, he needed to get better so he could go and fetch him. What a mess. He had promised that he would be careful. Who even knew that he came to this place? The señora. All she knew was he went to Sonora to look for Torres. Had he mentioned Diablo to her?

Then he heard men's voices and felt for the knife handle. They spoke in Spanish, and he understood every word as they passed close by his place of hiding.

"He couldn't bite the rope in two—that's stupid."

"They said the teeth marks are on it," the other said.

"Bullshit! No one can reach that high and bite a rope. He wasn't any taller than I am."

"Any man who could walk away after such a beating can do anything."

"I don't see him around here. You go ahead. I am going to take a shit in these weeds."

"Do it. I'll meet you back at the cantina. He's not down here."

Listening close to their words, Pedro wondered how deep in the weeds the man might come. He heard the reeds being parted. The other one walked away in the direction of the square. His companion was coming in Pedro's direction to find himself a place of privacy.

If only he had the man's weapon. No doubt, the outlaw wore a gun and a knife both. Still, he wondered if he had the needed strength to take this bandit. If he could only overpower him and take his pistol . . . armed, he could hold them off if he had to. How could he hide the body? Put it in the river, and let it float downstream.

Still, he had never before been forced to murder someone. He needed to remember this hombre would shoot him like a dog in a split second. Perhaps he should wait. He sure couldn't let the man live, or he'd have the whole bunch down there on him. It was kill or be killed, and even if he had the man's weapons, he couldn't be certain of escaping this hell hole.

Seated on the ground, he flexed his sore shoulders, then tested the edge of the small knife—sharp enough. He could make out the man's outline. The bandit was squatted only a few yards away, grunting and straining. His time was at hand. Then his left hand closed on a good-size rock. With effort, he rose to a crouch and began to stalk toward his prey.

The hunkered-down bandit never knew what hit him. He spilled facedown with his pants around his ankles. Pedro dropped to his knee and tried to get his breath. No movement in the outlaw. Good. All he needed to do was pull his pants up, then get him to the stream and let them think he drowned when they found him.

Dressing him back was easy, but for Pedro to drag the body even inches was slow and hard work. The last fifty feet, the bandit, a man in his twenties, made some groans that caused Pedro to stop and reconsider. But he soon fainted. Grateful for that, Pedro resumed his efforts to pull him to the water's edge. On the gravel, Pedro removed the outlaw's holster, knife, and money. The treasures piled on the ground, he tugged on the man's booted feet and gave it his all to slide him into the shallows; then he rolled him over facedown in the water. When the bandit showed some signs he might be recovering, Pedro shoved his head down until all the struggle was gone from him. Then he jerked the limp body out into the knee-deep water and launched him in the current. For a minute, the body spun around, and he worried he might have to wade out further to get the corpse on course. Then, to his relief, it began to bobble away downstream.

"One less bandit," he said under his breath, and with effort waded out to the shore. There he secured the man's gun, holster, knife, and a few coins. He buckled the holster around his waist, and before he stuck the Colt back into it, he noticed the revolver had been converted to cartridges from a cap-and-ball version. When he finally got back into his lair in the tall reeds in his water-filled boots, he disassembled and cleaned the weapon.

Worn out from the effort, he moved deeper into the tangles to be certain they didn't discover him while he slept. So weary and sore, he knew he would be asleep in minutes. Each effort he made hurt him so deep he was forced to grit his teeth. At last, with the Colt in his fist, he passed out on his blanket.

"You moved?" she hissed, then scowled at him. "Whose gun?"

He could see her out of his slitted eyes. With her assistance, he sat up. Dazed and weaker than before, he licked his sore, cracked lips.

"A bandit came by—almost discovered me."

"Where is he?" Her round eyes flew open in shock as she searched around for him.

He held up his palm to stop her. "I put his body in the river. He's downstream."

"How?" Her smooth forehead pleated in lines of concern.

"I don't know." He shook his head. "But I had to do it and did it." He felt grateful when she never asked how the man died. He cleaned the grit from the corner of his mouth with his thumb and shook his head. "It wasn't easy."

"They'll know you are here!" Upset, she looked at him with impatience in her eyes.

"I don't think so. He's miles downriver by now."

"Did you shoot him?"

"No." He wasn't about to tell her he bashed his head in and then drowned him. "He fell in."

"I almost forgot. Here's your food." She brought out two tortilla wraps from her apron pockets.

"If I could get to a horse." He looked down at the two white flour tortillas and nodded in approval. It had been a while since he ate her last one. He took a bite and she held up a bottle of wine for him, too.

"Gracias," he said, and settled into eating.

"You need more strength if you're going to ride from this place. Promise me not to fight with any more of the bandits. They will kill you." Her face was only inches from his, demanding he agree to her terms.

"I promise."

"No, you are crazy like all men. They beat you up, and you want revenge. I have buried a husband and two brothers who were that crazy, too."

He put out a hand to stay her as she glared in disapproval at him.

"I won't do it again," he promised her between bites.

She still looked peeved at him and shook her head. "They're all crazy men."

"They hurt you?" he asked.

She never answered, simply stared toward the mother mountains in the distance. He knew the answer. That bunch took what they wanted. He suspected it that night when Torres got off his horse and bowed at her so mockingly.

"I'm not a reason for revenge." She looked over the gun harness and nodded. "My man's name was Polo. He was tough. You're very lucky even to be alive, Pedro."

He crossed himself at her words. She took the wine bottle and drank deep; some of the red juice showed at the corners of her mouth. Then she handed it back to him, and he nodded before he took a drink from it. Strong red wine, it cut the dust in his throat. He toasted her and gave her back the bottle so he could eat his food.

"I can't stay here much longer," he said.

"When they will ride out on a raid, you can escape this place."

"They are going soon?" He worried about Obregón being alone with only the boy Juan to guard Green's ranch.

She shrugged. "Who knows, but Torres likes too well

the money he makes off the raids, selling horses and treasures they take, not to go back soon for more."

"Will they miss you?"

She dismissed his concern.

"I guess I can stay here another day. I feel like some injured dog hiding under the floor."

"Better to live longer," she said, then drank some wine again from the neck.

"You want to go with me?"

She shook her head. "I have my own place here. I can make a few pennies cooking on the square and eat on that, too. I am too old to be a puta or a man's toy—what could I do up there?"

"Maybe you could work as a cook for someone."

"You are feeling guilty for me. Don't—I'm fine. And when you are stronger, you can leave this place." She handed him the bottle. "I'll be back tomorrow. Don't kill no more banditos." Then, with a wary last look at him, she put the scarf over her head and left, making her way through the tall weeds.

He stared after her until he could no longer hear the rustle of the dry stems. Turning his attention to his food, he began to eat again, washing it down with the red wine—somehow he needed to be strong, strong enough to ride, and soon, too.

Chapter 12

DEUCES BROUGHT DOWN HIS FIRST DEER WITH HIS new bow and arrow. Proudly, he came off the steep hillside on his moccasin heels to the fallen animal; the feathered shaft was deep in the young deer's chest, and from the blood, he knew it struck the animal's heart. The yearling never suffered. Good. He shouldered it and started back for their camp, holding the legs together in front.

He had not forgotten the lessons of his youth—his mentor would have been proud of his kill, swift and deadly. All the time spent with white men never erased his skills as a warrior-hunter. He climbed the last ridge in a jog. The blood of the animal was on his shirt; he would need to rinse it in the spring at camp when he finished butchering the carcass.

Freed the night before of the last handcuff by Greta's

diligent filing, he felt on his way to being a whole person again.

"Greta." He repeated her name aloud, then smiled as he crested the hill and looked down in the valley. On her knees with a knife in her hand, she fleshed a small goat hide and looked up at his approach. Struggling to her feet and with her dress tail in hand, she hurried to meet him.

"It's fat," she exclaimed, looking over the game.

"Yes," he agreed.

"Two white men rode by today. They had many horses and did not dally around here but a minute to water them. They rode west."

"They see you?" He glanced toward the setting sun but saw no sign of anyone. Were they posse members?

She shook her head.

"Good. We better move tonight."

She made a pained face, then nodded in agreement. "Let's butcher the deer. Perhaps we can jerk it tomorrow wherever we camp next."

"Yes, I have lots of pepper."

"You shot it with the bow?" She looked puzzled at the fact.

"Yes, and it worked good. We will need to make some more arrows."

"Deuces, will they chase you forever?"

"I fear so. Are you sad for your family?" He set the deer down on the ground.

"For some."

"For some?" He tied two strings of leather to a low, thick limb to hang the deer for skinning and dressing.

"My mother and the little boys—" Then she shook her head. "Not for him. Let me clean your shirt."

"Did he ever hurt you?" He wanted to know about this man and what evil things he had done to her. Waiting for her answer, he unbuttoned the shirt and slipped it off.

"Yes. Several times—he forced himself on me—" She was close to tears.

"I wondered the first time I saw you and him."

She shook her head. "I could never be alone in the barn when he was there, or he made me—"

Deuces nodded that he understood. He watched the tears run down her cheeks. He stepped in and hugged her. "He will never hurt you again."

She nodded. She had heard him and took the blood-stained garment from his hands. "I will wash it." She snuffed her nose and shook her head to escape the pain.

He watched her hurry off to the spring. How could a father do such a thing to his own? Abuse her. She left with him on her own after that first encounter—willingly. No longer strange to him why her life on that farm was not so good. Not once since they rode away had she complained to him, and she worked hard at everything they did. Now he knew the real reason why she left her family so willingly—it was all over what her stepfather had done to her. That's what she called him, stepfather, and he could hear the edge in the tone of her voice every time she mentioned him.

Deuces tried to shrug the man's wickedness from his mind and turned his attention to the deer. With the sharpened knife, he began to slit the animal open from the inside, careful not to let the knife split the hair to fall on the meat. He soon had the belly open, and the still hot guts spilled out. He cut away the liver and heart, then removed them from the body. When he looked up, he saw that buzzards already were attracted to his kill. Bad sign; the circling birds might bring white men to check it out. Nothing he could do for the moment but complete the job.

She returned on the run, out of breath, with his wet shirt. "Buzzards." She pointed at them.

He nodded. "Get the gray mare and our things. Soon as I get through, we must leave."

"Yes," she agreed, and took a deep breath, hanging the wet shirt on a bush. While she ran off the hill for the gray, he continued to work off the hide. The deer's blood dried on his fingers and stiffened them. Soon the carcass was skinned and ready to move. He hated that the sticky carcass would have to ride in her lap. Once he rolled the skin up in a bundle, he tied it with strips of leather.

He could see her toss the two large sacks they made to sling over the animal's back, and soon she came pulling on the lead to where he waited.

"Get on her," he said, and made a stirrup with his cupped hands. She stepped into them and vaulted onto the gray's back. He nodded, pleased, and untied the carcass, carried it over, and laid it across her lap. Then he put his bow on her arm and the quiver of new arrows.

"Should we leave the guts?" she asked.

"They won't know who killed it. They may think those riders shot a deer and butchered it here."

"Something strange about them," she said. "They were young. They rode good horses. But they weren't looking for us; they looked back a lot, like they'd stolen them."

"Good observation," he said, recalling Tom Horn saying the same words to him when he noticed something important about the Apaches they trailed.

She nodded and made a face at him with her lip

turned up. The set of her face was like "I can do my part." With a friendly clap on her leg, he set out up the mountain in a jog as the last bloody light of the sunset fired the tops of the ridge.

They were on the move all night, sometimes upsetting ranch dogs, going past outlying places and setting off a chorus of barking, but he turned away to avoid them. So quickly that those yard dogs yapped at the coyotes that yipped on the ridges opposite them.

Perhaps those sun dogs did not wish to share their territory with an Apache and his woman. He would not bother his brother, the sun dog. There was plenty of land in Texas for both of them. Going up a draw, they stopped at a windmill tank under the quarter-moon light and washed their faces in the warm water. Then they took drinks of the tepid liquid from the great rock tank before moving on. At the edge of the timber, he halted her and told her to wait while he went back and worked over their tracks.

"I'd forgotten," she said sheepishly when he rejoined her after sweeping their prints away with a tree branch.

"That is my job. Only an Apache could read them now," he said, and smiled.

Another mournful coyote howled at the thin moon. She stepped close, and he hugged her. "No worry, he is our brother, the sun dog."

"Brother or not, I don't like them that close," she said, then she hurried up the canyon, leading the gray, while he swept out their tracks.

Dawn came, and they had heard no dogs barking at them for hours. The broken country proved tough to cross. When he glanced up at her, she looked done in. He pointed to the small stream.

"We can stay here today. Rest before you unload the horse. I will check and be certain we are alone." He took the deer and strung it from a thick branch.

Woodenly, she nodded, seated cross-legged on the ground. Then she threw a handful of pinched grass into the air.

"Gray, we are home," she said, as if the mare could understand. The gray gave her a tired snort and began to graze the short grass beside her. With a smile at his woman, he left in a trot.

Deuces looked over the rugged country from the top of the rise. Standing on the rock outcropping and shading his eyes against the early sun, he noticed, despite his directions for her to rest, she'd already set about to unload the animal. No signs of smoke or anything else that spelled white men. He liked this live oak and cedar country, which reminded him of the mid-slopes in the Chiricahuas and Dragoons. Plenty of deer, too. He didn't eat turkey, but they were there also. An Apache could make his way here—no need for them to rush westward.

There would be time for that later. Besides, he now had a woman with him, one who continually fascinated him. He never expected a white woman to walk away with him, but he recalled her sharp order for him not to tear her dress. She did not say it from fear, but she didn't intend for him to rip it—no matter if he was a wild Apache.

Who were those two white men who rode by earlier looking back? Perhaps he and the girl were far enough away to go unnoticed in these canyons and craggy hills. Would they send an Apache to look for him? Natan Lupan, the Gray Wolf, would, but General Crook was no longer in command at Fort Bowie. General Miles would send more soldiers and put mirrors on the mountaintops; he had no use for Apache scouts. Tom Horn called him a stupid general.

Miles's buffalo soldiers would sit on every spring and water hole. Make lots of music and sing around a big campfire at night. While they danced, a renegade going to Mexico or back to San Carlos would sneak up on his belly, get himself several handsful of water, and be gone before they even knew he had been there. Most times they didn't know one of them had gotten water—or they simply didn't care.

He started down the mountainside. There would be lots of springs in this land for the buffalo soldiers to guard. Every draw had one. He reached the canyon floor, looked across the yellow grass, and saw her snowy form as she stood in the branch and washed her shapely body. His woman. The notion made him feel warm inside.

Chapter 13

"MR. FAUCET, CAN YOU TAKE US TO THIS HANS Schumaker's place. The one who's looking for that missing girl?" Burt asked the man as the three of them rode out in the early-morning light from the Vavort farm.

"You think Deuces might have killed her?" Faucet formed a puzzled look on his face and swiveled his head around to look at Burt.

"He hasn't killed anyone yet we know of, though he's had lots of chances."

"That's right, but they said he was a bloodthirsty killer."

"He killed another scout over a woman the man badly maimed. Bad enough, but not the act of a wanton murderer—even for an Apache, who thinks the life of anyone who opposes him is of little value."

"Really," Faucet said. "Well, the sheriff told us he was a killer and for us to shoot him on sight."

"He's a convicted felon, and I guess that calls for such measures. But don't get gun-happy riding with us. If we get him in range of that pistol of yours, we might take him in alive."

"I understand what you mean, Marshal. That place of Schumaker's is about twenty miles northwest of here."

"Let's push these horses, then." Burt shot a questioning glance at One-Eye, who quickly agreed with a solemn nod.

Earlier, while saddling their horses, he had discussed the matter with his scout, who figured that Deuces was somewhere miles away by this time, and all they could hope for were leads to fill in the gaps in his tracks. Perhaps the girl's disappearance wasn't related, but they'd never know until they went to their place and investigated. He hoped Governor Baylor had not promised the Texas officials that they could do miracles down here. One Apache tracker and two white men—most of the other posses he knew about if they were still out—were scouring the railroad right of way and alongside it back to the west. So far, all sign they found of Deuces went away from those rails, as if the fugitive red man knew where they'd be looking for him.

During the Apache war, scouts like One-Eye had led the army all over Arizona without a compass and never were lost for a minute. No, Deuces didn't need those rails to lead himself home; he knew the way if he really wanted to go there.

They reached Hans Schumaker's farm in late afternoon. A neat farmstead with split-rail fences and a corn crop better than most. Burt dismounted and removed his hat to introduce himself to the red-eyed woman who came out onto the porch. He told her their purpose.

"Thank God you're here. Maybe you can find her, Marshal Green."

"Where was she last seen?"

"You take that trail over there and go down that canyon, take a fork right and go over the ridge. That's where we found the goats unattended a week ago. But Hans and the others never found any tracks over there."

"Thanks," he said to reassure her. "We only want to check it out before dark."

"Come back, and I'll have supper for you men," she said, trying to act braver than she was.

"We won't impose—"

"Yes, you will, Marshal Green. Anyone looking for my Greta can sure eat here."

"We'll see," he said, and they rode east on the goat trail.

Long shadows filled the canyon when the three of them spread out. Then One-Eye shouted, and Burt came running from his side of the creek bottom. Out of wind, Faucet rushed in to peer at what the Apache held in his fingers. The scout handed it to Burt, who studied the opened link of chain.

"Handcuff chain," Burt said, looking up at One-Eye and not raising his head.

The Apache dropped to his knees and began to spread out the dirt at the base of the stump, so the silver-looking filings shone in the fading light.

"What's it all mean?" Faucet asked, looking back and forth at both men.

"Here's where Deuces filed the chain in two that held the handcuffs," Burt said.

"Did he get the girl?"

"I can't answer that," Burt said, "but it's strange that this is where she disappeared from, too."

"Oh, my gawd, has he killed her?" Faucet shrieked.

"That's speculation." Burt frowned at the man in disapproval. Still, the notion of the girl's disappearance and One-Eye's discovery so close niggled his conscience. "Let's keep news of this from Mrs. Schumaker. We'll come back here at first light and try to piece together a route that he-she-they, whoever, took from here."

Burt held the broken link up to the last light. *Damn, they'd got there a week late and a dollar short!* Must have taken hours for Deuces by himself, wearing those handcuffs, to file that link in two. He thought about the farmer who never saw Deuces slip inside his shed right under his own eyes and steal the tool. Then the fugitive carried it this far, on foot, to use the stump as a vise to wear through the link. Impressed with the Apache's patience, Burt pocketed the link and remounted. The woman's invite to eat sounded better than anything they'd fix. Except it would be pitch dark by the time they got back to the Schumakers' place.

He looked back over the dark abyss when they topped the ridge, and some twilight showed them the trail back. What had happened down there? Had she stumbled on him filing the chain in two? Perhaps they would never know. Seven days sounded awfully permanent. If she hadn't run off with some boyfriend, the chances were good she wasn't alive anymore. Then it might all be purely a coincidence, the cut link, Deuces's presence in the canyon, and her disappearance.

Burt shook his head and booted his horse after the others. At least, they had a new lead.

* * *

At dawn, they saddled their ponies as the animals ate the last of their oats from the wooden trough. Burt bought the grain from the German farmer. Their mounts needed all the strength they could get. A belly full of oats wouldn't hurt them.

"You haven't seen any sign of her?" Burt asked the smaller man, Schumaker, with the jet-black, stiff hair.

"No, ve vas looking hard for days now for her. Someone stole a gray mare from Marvel Hatfield, too. We couldn't find any tracks for it, either."

"When was it stolen?" Burt asked.

"Sunday last."

Burt frowned at the man's story. "Horses leave tracks."

Hans shook his bearded face. "By gawd, they took his saddle and his mare, and they left no damn tracks."

"Where's Hatfield live?"

"Five miles north."

"You know where he lives, Faucet?" Burt asked the man.

"Oh, yeah, I've been there before."

"We'll look for your daughter, too," Burt said.

"She's probably pregnant by now," the man said, the anger in his dark eyes showing. With vengeance in his voice, he shook his head. "I don't want her back."

"Her mother might," Burt said in a low voice, looking at the reins in his hands.

"She's a whore by now—she's never welcome back here."

"Guess that's your right," Burt said, and swung into the saddle. Disgusted with the man's manner and words, he rode to the back porch and removed his hat. "Thanks, ma'am. Wish you would take some money for our keep."

Forcing a smile on her still tear-reddened face, she nodded. "You just find my baby girl. I'll feed you lawmen anytime."

"We'll look for her. Thanks," he said, and rode off to join the other two. Schumaker's attitude toward the girl still niggled him—nothing he could do about it. The girl's return would certainly cause troubles between man and wife at this farm. Not his worry, finding Deuces was his concern, but he couldn't shake the man's bitter words, either.

"Old Hans is mad about that girl running off, ain't he?" Faucet said, glancing over his shoulder to be sure they were alone when Burt joined him and One-Eye.

"Too mad to suit me. But he's entitled to his opinion."

Faucet looked back again for something, then turned forward in time to jerk his horse around to go through the gate. "Something back there I can't put my finger on."

"He's angry."

"Don't make sense. He looked for her for four days, now he's—" Faucet shook his head and booted his horse up with them.

"He likes things his way," Burt said to silence the man. At the moment, Burt was more interested in the gray mare that disappeared. "No tracks" sounded more like an Apache trick to him.

"Reckon we should go on or look for his tracks in the canyon where you found the link?" he asked One-Eye.

"Gray mare may be the answer," the solemn-faced scout said. "I would get plenty damn tired of walking this far."

"You're right," Burt said with a small smile of agreement. "Faucet, take us to the Hatfield place."

The deputy agreed, and they set out at a trot.

Plenty to fill Burt's mind as they rode northward. How Angela was coming along with making her new dress for the fandango. And Pedro? He hoped the man hadn't done anything foolish by himself with them seven hundred miles away. He reined up his dun to let it walk going down the steep hill. Somewhere off in the live oaks, some crows called. He stood in the stirrups to stretch his tall frame and wondered some more about the people he left behind in Arizona.

Chapter 14

PEDRO CLEANED THE GRIT FROM THE CORNERS OF his mouth with the side of his thumb, bellied down and refreshed by the running water. His movements to rise shot pain through his upper body. On his feet at last, he raised his foot with much effort and stuck it in the stirrup. Grasping the horn in one hand, the cantle in his other, he stiffly pulled himself onto the burro.

His heels beat the gray donkey's sides, and the beast begrudgingly moved out. *Mucho*, she called the animal. He called him *mucho slow. Tortuga* would have been a better name. The bright desert sun blinding him, he set out northward. How far away was the border? No way to know. He must ride there, regardless. If Burt had been there, they would have already had those bandits in custody. How foolish of him to go there alone. Lightheaded, he pushed the stubborn animal onward. No time for regrets, he needed to get back to the Green ranch to rest and get his strength back—before they raided it again.

The hot day passed, but he was still in the endless, flat greasewood desert at sundown. Nothing in sight, no place to stop. He pushed Mucho onward into the night. Half awake, half asleep, dumb and sore as he had ever felt, he still looked for the North Star as a guide and didn't let the stubborn donkey circle back.

Then, in the darkness, he saw a red glow in the distance. A coyote yipped close by, but he ignored it, excited with his find. Could it be a ranch or camp? No way to know. He tried to make Mucho go faster, but the animal made a plodding step at a time.

At last, so eager to find someone, he got off and began to lead the stupid ass. Who could the camp belong to? No matter, fire meant humans, and in Mexico, travelers were generous to others.

"Greetings," he said from the edge, seeing several around the fire.

"Who are you?"

"Pedro. I wondered if I might come to your fire."

"Go on," someone said in a gruff voice. He stood up in the firelight and waved his arm to indicate he meant for Pedro to move away from them.

Unable to see their faces in the glare of the fire, Pedro wondered if they were outlaws. With only the pistol in the bandit's holster on his waist, he dropped his head and mumbled thanks. Then looked for his guiding star. *May all their colts be born cross-legged.* He drew in a deep breath and started to leave.

A fool, at last, each step was a heavy movement that sapped at him. He never looked back. Such poor manners, such—he gave a great exhalation and jerked on the lead of the stubborn Mucho. What good was the dumb animal he led? He couldn't ride it and make it go. It had stolen his energy dragging it along. Those men camped back there, he wished he had had a better look at them. Someday he would run them over.

No food, no water, no nothing. Even if he found the border, he might be miles from anything. Probably die in this stinking desert. Juanita was with the señora, probably sewing on the señora's party dress—he would miss the big fandango, too, if he died.

"Ah, you awake."

Pedro opened his eyes. Daylight, and he was on a pallet. The slanted eyes looking down at him were Asian. Overhead, he could see the sticks and mud of a ceiling. He was in a house, a jacal.

"Who are you?" he asked in a voice so hoarse he thought it was someone else.

"Sooe Sure Day."

"What they call you?" Pedro asked, from the foggy state his head was in. Strange name. Who was this little chinaman?

"Day, my name."

"How did I get here?"

"Carry you."

"You carried me?"

"You no talkee now. Sip some water." The man had a canvas bag and held the spout to Pedro's mouth as he half sat up. The liquid felt like ice going down his parched throat.

"No. No. Drink more in little while. You too thirsty. Have big belly ache."

"Where am I?" Dizzy-headed, he rested on his elbows; he felt as weak as he could ever remember.

"My place."

"Oh, good. How did I get here?"

"Burro come get drink. I follow his tracks. Find you."

"Sorry, I said bad things about him," Pedro mumbled.

"What you say?"

"He saved my life." He shook his head to try to clear it.

"Yes. Yes. Save life. Where you go?"

"Arizona."

"Big place."

"Far away?"

"No."

"Good. I better get there."

"No. No. You rest."

His head swam before he got halfway up, and he collapsed in a pile on the pallet. His concerned host spoke in Chinese a hundred words a minute to him. Pedro fainted.

When he awoke, Day was not in sight, and he rose trying to shake the fuzzy vision and dullness from his brain. Out of nowhere, a small brown-faced girl of ten came with her skirts swishing around her calves and held the water bag up for him to drink. This time, he sipped it and nodded in gratitude, before he settled back down. He must get his strength back; he closed his eyes and slept.

The next three days, he took more water and simple food like soup. His kidneys began to function, he even made a trip outside to relieve himself. The place around

Day's jacal looked like a garden, plants and flowers growing all around. Overhead, some ancient cottonwoods rustled. Then he could see the pastel tan cliffs that enclosed the canyon.

"Buenos días," someone said, and he turned to see a green-headed parrot on a perch.

"Buenos días to you, Señor Parrot." He took a seat on a bench and studied this new world. Obviously, his host, Day, and the man's Mexican wife, Bonita, were competent gardeners. Their children had been his main nurses. Bonita must have had them by another husband—they were Mexican.

His hands on his knees to brace himself, he shook his head. Too weak to do anything, he wasn't recovering fast enough. He'd heard that heat stroke could do that, but it was a new experience for him.

"Ah, Pedro, you come outside," Day said, carrying an armful of vegetables toward the ramada.

"How did you find this place?" Pedro asked, still in disbelief and half groggy.

"Several families in this canyon. Use water from the mountains for our crops."

"Chinese?"

"No."

"I just wondered. I have little money, but when I get home to Arizona, I will have money to pay you for my care."

Day shook his head. "No need to do that."

"I will do something for you, anyway. But I need a horse. That donkey—he's no answer."

"We can catch one."

Pedro considered the man. "Catch one. What is that?"

"There are horses that come to water below. We can close the gate."

"Wild horses?"

"Wild," he agreed with a bow.

Pedro closed his eyes. He needed a riding horse, not some crazy, head-slinging mustang that would fight till he died. In his condition, all he needed was to try to ride some bucking devil. Surely there was a well-broken horse in the canyon that someone would part with.

"No one would sell me a horse?"

"No one has horse. They have burros. They turn them loose and catch when they go to market. No horses."

"Do the horses come every day to water?"

Day shook his head. "Once or twice a week. It rains, they don't come."

"How do you shut the gate?"

"We must hide and them not see us. They go in. Quick, quick, put up bars."

Doing anything quick, quick, sounded impossible to him. But that would be the only way to get a horse; he'd better get started on it.

So Day took him to where he could look off the bluff and see the great pen of crooked mesquite posts planted upright in a stockade fashion. The whole area covered a couple of acres, and the stream's flow was gathered in stone-walled watering tanks. From where he sat on the rock outcropping, he could see where the river that watered their valley disappeared into the ground beyond the last tank.

"Whose pens?"

"We built them for the cattlemen who drive herds up here. Then they don't stampede our crops and fields for their herds to get water."

"Good trade-off. How will we know when the horses will come?"

"You can hear stallion scream for long ways. Children listen for him."

"Good," he said, feeling weaker than he planned and dreading the short walk back to his pallet.

The horses didn't come for two days. Pedro met the others who lived in the canyon as they came to Day's house for supper and a dance, quiet people and their children who nodded as if unsure how to talk to him, an outsider. An older woman, her face framed by a shawl, was not so shy and quickly took a place beside him and asked him about his wife. Did he have family? He explained about Juanita and how someday they planned to have children.

Then she dug in her purse and brought out a ten-centavo piece. "Buy a candle for me, and burn it at the shrine when you get to a church." Quickly, she crossed herself.

"I don't need your money to do that," he said, and tried to give it back.

"No, it will be my candle if you use that coin to buy it. I need no charity."

"I will do it when I return to Tucson."

"God bless you," she said, and patted his shoulder.

"The horses are coming," Day's bright-eyed step-daughter shouted, running into the crowded yard. "I heard the man horse."

"Stay there," Day said to him when he started to rise. "I have two young boys to bar the gates when they're inside."

Though his strength was returning, Pedro still dreaded the days ahead.

"We will help you," a short, handsome-faced man said, stepping forward. "We will help you catch one and break it."

"Somehow I will repay you," he said, feeling very emotional at all their attention.

Soon the music began, the food was spread out, and the fandango began. He watched the couples shuffling to the guitar and fiddle. *Lord, give me the strength to ride this new horse.* He looked to the stars overhead and wondered about his Juanita and Burt.

The next morning, the shrill sounds of the lead stallion shattered the predawn quiet. The horse was angry and distressed by the confinement of its harem, and its complaints carried in the early-morning light, where the men began to gather their ropes.

The village men were all there to help. Carmen, the short one with the broadest shoulders, nodded to him. Juan, with the scar above his eye. A man of thirty, Tomás, the handsome one. Rafael was the older one, and five young boys looked ready for the charge. Along with Day, they went down into the canyon to check on the captives.

The blue roan stallion, its arched neck crested, single-footed around in the first light that shone across the posts. Pedro and others looked over the mares, colts, and yearlings standing about, acting unconcerned while the fiery stud protectively paced in a circle around them, making vocal sass.

"If we can cut him out and some of the others," Carmen said, waving his brown hands to show how they must separate part of the herd.

Everyone agreed, and they quickly went inside the corral. Pedro felt as strong as he could remember. The several days of rest had helped. Men had sticks with flags to deter and separate the herd. The plan was to let the stud out and some of the mares and colts. Then they'd select a horse for him.

He wondered how these farmers would do under fire. Thundering hooves could make men lose their nerve quickly, especially when charged at by stampeding horses. The danger would be that they could lose all the horses but the crippled ones. He didn't want a crazy brood mare that had been free all of its life. It would never tame down. A three- or four-year-old horse would be fine. There would be no horses that age, or the stud would have run them off. So his choice had to be a young mare. Good enough.

"Everyone spread out," Carmen said, waving his arms to make them move apart.

The stallion had gone to the rear, watching them with caution. About the time that Pedro spotted the leggy lead mare, Pablo pointed it out.

"If we can let her and him out, we should be able to catch one," Carmen said, taking charge.

Pedro felt better. This man knew horses, and if all the horses didn't get past them in one charge, they might catch one.

"You see one you want?" Carmen asked as they eased their way across the pen.

"A line back over there. The dun mare looks okay." Pedro hurriedly tried to point it out in the bunch milling around, but dust began to boil up. Someone gave him a riata. He nodded.

"Try to rope one first," Carmen said to him and the other men with lassos. "Whoever catches one, we must all go to him and get on the rope."

Pedro moved in closer, making a loop as he went. The head of the dun was above the herd; then they whirled in mass and broke to the right. The dust blinded him. He could see nothing. He hurriedly glanced down at his loop; it was big enough.

The herd in a group collided against the corral, whirled back, split, and tore past him. At a dead run, he swung the loop over his head, threw it, and his lariat fell on the mare's back. It bolted out from under it. Men were running about. The stallion challenged them, and the dust curtain blinded them.

Amid the boiling dirt and confusion, he heard them shouting for everyone to come. A frightened mare flew past his face. Where were the others?

In a moment of clearing dust, he spotted a red roan shaking its head on the end of a rope. Good catch. He ran in to help them and grasped the rope in front of two others on the end. They had it.

A loop soon was tossed around its front legs, and they tripped it. The horse rolled and hit hard on its side. Everyone rushed to hold it down. Pedro reached it. He could read the fear in its brown eyes, but he pinned its head to the ground. Throaty snorts came as the men tied its four feet together. At last with it four-footed, the younger boys rushed to open the gates to let the upset herd out of the pen before they trampled someone.

The lead mare skirted them, racing hard along the wall. Quickly, it hit the opening, followed by the colts and others in a mad dash for freedom. Behind them, the single-footing stallion fled after the last loose one escaped. Slowly, the fog of dust began to settle, and everyone nodded in approval as they sat upon the roan mare and rolled cigarettes.

"Close the gates, boys," Carmen said, then he turned

to Pedro. "We will fashion a halter and tie a post to the end of a riata for her to drag. There is no grass here. You should feed her. Make her come to you to eat."

Pedro agreed.

"What will you call her?"

"Rojo," he said, without any imagination to help his choice.

"Today she drags a rope. Tomorrow we put a saddle on her. Then the third day you must ride her."

With a sigh, Pedro agreed. The men seated on the mare smoked their cornshuck cigarettes. He refused their offer of one. Post first to drag, saddle her, then him. He had the order of events clear in his mind.

The third day, he felt ready. Rojo had been taught to tie. He had fanned her with blankets to take her fear away, saddled and unsaddled a hundred times with one foot tied up, he'd even sat on her back several times.

So, with a long lead on her halter for a catch rope and him speaking softly to reassure her, he eased himself into the saddle. Aboard, he continued talking and petting her, and he nudged her easy-like, and she took two steps. She tried to flip away the bosal on her nose. He urged her out again. She began to walk. He relaxed. Trailing the long rope to her side, she went around the pen in a tense walk. He hauled her up, she stopped and blew. The silence of the onlookers was close to unnerving for him. In a few minutes, they began to nod in approval as he worked her around the pen again. Then he plow-reined her about, and she began going the other way.

Then she gathered up as if she had discovered someone was on her back. Her stiff-legged hops grew more intense as he held her head up as tight as he dared.

Unable to get her nose down, Rojo began to dance about under him as if ready to buck.

"What can we do?" Carmen asked, moving along beside the horse, but at enough distance to be safe.

"Take the lead off. It worries her," Pedro decided, as the mare shied from it going sideways.

"Can you stop her?"

"Yes." And he did, then patted her neck and reassured her. She blew rollers out her nose at Carmen as he quickly untied the lead rope and stepped back. The mare began to dance, and Pedro let her have some more rein. She started to trot hard. Then she lunged forward and began to buck. He hit her on both sides with the rope reins, and she broke into a run. Distracted, she set into a smooth lope around the pen. He let her run until she acted tired, and then he booted her and made her go one more lap. When he skidded her to a stop, everyone cheered.

"What will you do now?" Carmen asked, taking her by the bosal.

"Get a canteen of water and ride for Arizona," he said, and dismounted.

"God be with you," the man said.

He turned to everyone and gave them his thanks.

Day fixed him a water bag. Pedro hugged his wife, Bonita, and the children.

"I'll be back and bring candy," he promised them.

The mare buggered at the sight of the water bag, but he soon looped it over the horn and swung into the saddle. Carmen let loose of her hackamore, and she walked, trotted, and then kicked sideways with a squeal before she settled down and went through the gate. He dared not wave to them, his grip so tight on the rope reins. But the mare turned north at his pull, his stomach filled with gut-eating apprehension, and they were on their way.

Would Marshal Green be back at the ranch when he got there? The mare shied at something in the grease-wood, but he found some control and sent her on her way. He shook his head; first he must get back to the ranch.

Chapter 15

MARVEL HATFIELD QUIT HIS HORSESHOEING AND came over to greet Burt when he rode up the driveway. A tall man in overalls, he put up a suspender strap and smiled at Burt and his entourage.

"You must be the law?" he said, appraising them.

Faucet made quick introductions, and they shook hands.

"U.S. Marshal Burt Green," Burt said, releasing the man's callused hand. "Folks tell us someone stole a saddle and a horse here last Sunday?"

"Sure did, and never left a sign. She plumb vanished."

"You mind if my tracker One-Eye goes and checks things out?" Burt asked.

"No, sirree. That's the barn where they got the saddle from, and the mare was in that small pasture out back."

The scout nodded to Burt and went over to check it out.

"You got any idea who took it?" Hatfield asked, wiping his sweaty face on a rag from his pocket.

"Marshal Green and the tracker are looking for that Apache prisoner who jumped off the train," Faucet said.

"An Apache got my mare?" Hatfield made a face at the notion.

"Hard to say," Burt said, wishing Faucet wasn't so forthcoming about their purpose. "But the fugitive is definitely still somewhere in this country."

"Why, they said he probably got injured from the fall off the train and crawled away somewhere and died. There ain't been nothing about him turned up in over two weeks."

"But someone stole your mare?" Burt looked hard at the man's suntanned face.

"Right, but I figured some drifter came passing through and got her. Fact, there were a couple of cowboys herding some hosses through here a couple of days or so ago." The man shrugged. "Guess they had business, though."

One-Eye returned and nodded to Burt privately.

"You think that Apache got my mare?" Hatfield asked the threesome. The man's eyes narrowed with a serious look of concern on his face.

"Was Deuces in that barn?" Burt asked the tracker.

"Yes." One-Eye nodded solemnly.

"Well," Hatfield said with a sigh. "Glad he took her and rode off. Whew, he might have killed us all if we'd been here."

"I doubt it," Burt said, ready to remount. "He's not hurt a soul so far."

"Where did he go from here?" Hatfield asked, looking bewildered.

"We'll have to pick up his trail," Burt said, and they got on their horses. "Thanks, Hatfield."

"You could stay for lunch. Wife's got plenty of food."

"No, thanks again, we better ride."

"I wish you luck. He must be a wisp on the wind. What did you reckon that tracker of yours saw that I missed?"

"Hard to say." Burt reined his horse around to face the man. "But before I've seen other Apaches see things I'd overlooked."

They headed into the canyon country when they left Hatfield's place. One-Eye stripped down to his loincloth, going on foot, searching for signs. Burt led the scout's horse, and they made their way up the dim wagon tracks that sliced the dried brown grass carpet.

"We better make camp before it gets any darker," he finally said to Faucet.

"He finding anything?" Faucet tossed his head to where they last saw the scout disappear.

"I wouldn't bet against him."

"Strange to me how a one-eyed Injun can see signs that I can't."

"They've got their ways."

"Sure have. Hey, he's coming back."

"Water over this hill," One-Eye said, and took his reins from Burt.

"Good. What else do you know?"

"Girl not prisoner."

"What? Oh, don't tell that to Schumaker. He's been calling her a slut already. Why'd she take up with that Apache, for Christ's sake?" Faucet looked thoroughly upset by the news.

"Don't know," One-Eye said. "She not tied. He not keeping her prisoner."

"Now, how in the hell does he know that?" Faucet asked Burt.

"You never doubted him when he solved the pepper thief, the file theft, or the mare, so what's wrong with what he's saying now?" Burt asked with a shake of his head at the deputy.

"But she's a white girl." Faucet made a face.

"And he's an Indian boy."

"Yes, but that just ain't right."

"Faucet, we ain't moral judges. We're tracking down a fugitive from justice."

The man nodded his head in surrender. "Just don't seem right."

"If we don't hustle up some firewood before it's pitch dark, we'll be eating jerky."

"I'll help," Faucet said, still dismayed by the new knowledge. Dismounted, he went off talking to himself.

Been stranger things than that happen in this world, Burt decided. Still, the notion niggled at him in the growing darkness. Something about that German farmer's harsh words about the girl. Did the man already know more than he had told them back there or that he dared to say around his wife? Locusts in the night sizzled. Lots more to this Deuces deal than he ever expected to find.

A glance at the star-studded sky, and he wondered again about his new wife, Angela. Was she secure? He would be glad when this job was wound up and he could return to her. *Where are you, Deuces?*

Chapter 16

DEUCES WANTED TO MOVE DEEPER INTO THE HILL country. The deer jerky was dry enough to put in a sack. He returned from a hunting trip with a fat kid and leading a bay horse.

"Where did you steal him?" she asked, hands on her hips and walking around examining the gelding.

Deuces dropped to the ground and laughed at her words. "I found him in the hills. He has been rode before and was turned out. May have wandered away. He is very gentle."

"Good, now we have two horses. One for each of us."

"We need to find a new camp," he said.

She stopped and frowned. "You see any sign?"

He shook his head. "I am concerned they might find us."

"We can't have that." She beamed a smile and took the small carcass from him.

Her smile relieved him. Women did not like to move camp. Men did not care; but still he did not wish to displease her. Though he knew nothing wrong, the spirits sometimes gave him bad feelings, irritations he'd had all day—maybe if they moved to a new location, these notions inside would evaporate like smoke. He hoped so. They were not good signs.

So, in the first light, they loaded everything. She rode the bay and led the gray loaded with jerky and their camp supplies. He covered their tracks and signs going over places in his mind, maybe it was time for him to go to his home country. There he knew how to lose men coming on his heels. Here he could not get high enough to see the dust they made at ten miles. Still, the way west was open, and he was unsure how far away he was from it—the iron horse made many miles in a day.

If only he could lead her back to his homeland. They could live in the cool mountains in summer and the warm lowlands in winter. No man or Apache could ever catch him in Apacheria. Mexicans were easy to steal from or to trade with. They thought nothing of buying a stolen beef or horse. Yes, in Sonora they could live to be old people. She would love the mother mountains with waterfalls to take baths under and air so pure it would cure anything.

They must go west. But for now, while the white man searched so hard for him, they'd best stay hidden in these canyons amongst the live oak for a while longer.

"There's a creek ahead." She pointed to the silver ribbon.

He nodded his head. "I will search about and see that no one is here."

"Good," she said, and dropped from the gray's back. "I can wait here."

He hurried away, staying to the ridge so he could survey anything visible. Then he dropped off the steep-faced house-sized boulders, one at a time, and searched along the watercourse. Only deer and a few cow tracks. This might be the right place for them to hide for a good while. Heading back to her, he hoped this place could be home for a few moons. Then they would go west to his own land.

While this canyon and the hills around them looked secure enough, he still felt concerned. Perhaps because this was not his own land. In Apacheria, he would be home, and then he could ease his mind, for no one could find him there. He meant *them*. Him and his woman. Why would he think only *him*—she would go there; she had said so. He shook his head to clear away any doubts. And they would have children there, too.

He would teach them the ways. A smile in the corner of his mouth, he hurried uphill to hug her. Ussen had provided her for him in these troubled days. Tomorrow he would not eat any food and would meditate about what he must do next. Perhaps a sign would come to him of how he should go forth. A good one, he hoped for, as he hugged her tight to his chest.

"This is a pretty place," she said. "I will dig a hole and make a small fire."

He agreed and went to unpacking things off the horses. She would require another deer to jerk. Already her supply of food was building, but they would need a large one to cross the barren land to the west. What he saw from the train window left nothing to his imagination about the scrub country they must ride over. Still, the desert was a good place for the Apache.

"You are not angry with me?" she asked, offering him a cup of her mint tea.

"Why would I be angry with you?" He nodded in thanks for the tea.

"You have acted different the past few days. Will you have to leave me?"

He nodded for the cup and then shook his head. "I only must be careful. I have told you what they would do if they capture me."

"Put you in prison."

"Maybe shoot me—" He shook his head to show her he was uncertain of the consequences.

"We will not let them get you."

He smiled at her defiance. She would defend him if she could. The notion warmed him. He reached over and hugged her to him. Soon his fingers were unbuttoning her dress. His woman sat up on her knees and helped him.

"If you must, run away and leave me. Run away. I will always find you."

"Will they put you in jail?" he asked, his breath short at the sight of her bare flesh. Her snowy body always aroused him.

"I don't think so. I have done nothing wrong," she said, and shrugged her dress away.

He took her in his arms, and all his concerns of the future floated away like a fluffy cloud. Never had he thought he could love a woman this much, and he gently laid her on the blanket.

Days passed for him like a river flows. He wandered in great circles but saw nothing alarming, no pursuit. One day, he returned with a sack of dried corn picked from a field miles away.

She ground it with a round rock and made a gruel they enjoyed. He found honeycombs, and, despite the few stings that swelled his face so she laughed at him, they licked their fingers, gorging themselves on the luxury.

Once on Deuces's rounds, he spotted a drifter crossing the nearby country on horseback. Deuces shadowed him for half a day until he decided the white man had a purpose and was not in those hills searching for them.

She picked ripe fruit like the wild purple plums and blackberries to vary their meals. They ate venison, jerked the rest for their trip. In the long days of late summer, he helped her tan the hides so they would have enough leather soon to make new clothing for her. They both spoke together of the new dress they would sew for her. He fashioned needles from bones for the task.

They spent their leisure resting and stream bathing in the golden sunshine that saw the sumacs turn fiery red in the droughty days. He perfected his arrow making and soon could drive one through his quarry at impressive ranges. Their shelter was a ramada of poles lodged in tree forks, then covered in brush and grass.

Deuces would pray his thanks to Ussen each day. He even thought less of leaving this land. They had a good source of food, each other, and two horses. What else did they need? He sat cross-legged on a small bluff and meditated—the white men had done him a favor sending him here to her.

Unlike Marshal Egan, who cussed everyone and everything, he found good fortune in his life and raised his face so the sun could shine upon him. *Thank you, Ussen.*

Chapter 17

"NO WORD, NO SIGN OF HIM," BURT SAID ALOUD, AND rose off his log seat. "We've been here almost three weeks, and not one word has come out about any sighting of Deuces."

He walked to the fire and considered what he should do next. His hands above his head, he stretched and for the hundredth time reviewed their situation. One-Eye, with his back to the tree and his arms folded over his chest, was half asleep.

"Someone is coming," the Apache said, and sat up wide awake.

"I hear them now," Burt said, when for the first time the drum of horses approaching became evident to him. Apaches possessed keener hearing than his own. Maybe he didn't listen enough.

The riders drew up. Sheriff Grimwell stepped down, and someone held his horse's reins.

"No word on the Apache, Green. But we've got some horse rustlers working the country, and we can't seem to be able to run them down. Would you and your Indian give us a hand? I'd sure appreciate it. Harry Faucet tells us One-Eye can track a mouse."

"One-Eye?" Burt asked the reclining Apache with his face covered by a hat. "Want to help them?"

The Apache rose up and gave him a slow nod.

"That's the answer. Where do we meet?"

"If you don't mind, we'll camp here tonight and ride that way in the morning."

"Fine. If you need to cook, use the fire," Burt said, and shook Faucet's hand when the farmer stepped up.

"Can't believe that you ain't found him, Marshal," Faucet said, and began to introduce the posse members. On the last, he nodded his head to a familiar face in the outer ring of fire's light. "You know Hans?"

"Yes. Evening. How is your wife? Give her our regards."

"Yeah, I do that," the man said, and went by with a bedroll and his new .44/40 rifle to make himself a place beyond.

While the posse members waited for their food to cook, the sheriff broke out a bottle of bonded whiskey and passed it around for everyone to have some in his own tin cup.

"Faucet says that you found a link of the scout's handcuffs?" Grimwell asked.

Burt nodded his head slowly and felt in his vest pocket, then tossed the piece to the lawman.

Grimwell caught it and held it up to the firelight. Burt wanted to chuckle; the lawman no more expected him to have that than snow on the Fourth of July. With an effort, Burt rose and went over to reach in his saddle bags and toss the cut handcuffs that they'd found at the two other locations to the man.

"You found these up there and didn't find him?" Grimwell asked, shaking his head.

"Yes. One-Eye found the first one near an old home place north of here. The last one near a windmill tank, ten miles west. Took lots of filing to get them off. But I do recall with us crisscrossing this country, we've seen plenty of horse tracks up here."

"Think Deuces has been horse rustling, too?"

"Doubt it. He's more careful than that, or your boys would have found him by now."

"We've sure looked. I'm grateful that he hasn't murdered any outlying ranchers or stray cowboys so far," Grimwell said.

Burt shook his head. "Only person we know he's killed is a worthless army scout, who probably needed it, according to Tom Horn's testimony."

"Still, I've been worried sick about him doing something like that. There's been no sign of Hans's daughter since she disappeared. Faucet said you thought she was with him."

"Faucet talks a lot," Burt said, and sipped on the good whiskey.

"What do you think about her disappearance?"

"I don't know for certain. One-Eye read some of their tracks. He says she's not his prisoner."

"Well, you never know. I never believed you'd really found these," Grimwell said, rattling the cuffs in his hands. "Thought that was all made up. When I first heard they were sending you here, I figured you'd run your search from the Euphoria Hotel in town. You've been a real puzzler to me, Green."

"I came to find a fugitive. You don't do that on your butt in a hotel. But as each day goes by and we can't find a sign of him, I'd venture that Deuces has gone back home."

"Maybe, but I'm still damn impressed that you got this close to him." He handed the broken handcuffs back, then the link.

"Where do you want to start looking for these rustlers in the morning?" Burt asked.

"That cabin place where you found one of them. Faucet said there were lots of tracks up there."

"We've seen tracks of folks driving horses through up there. Fine," Burt said, and finished off his whiskey. "Good stuff. Good night, men."

A chorus of good nights went among the men, who were about to eat some hastily prepared food. Burt went past One-Eye and shook out his own bedroll.

"Why is father here?" One-Eye asked softly.

"Guess he's part of the posse. Why?"

"No one would steal his sorry horses," the Apache said, and rolled over in his blankets.

Burt smiled and shook his head at the dark mound beside him in the night. No telling what an Apache was thinking, either. He never noticed about the German's stock. Though he did have a sorry horse when he rode with them a few days. But few farmers owned good saddle stock.

At daybreak, they saddled and lit out. The smell of campfire smoke had permeated not only Burt's clothing but his nose as well. It would be a good thing to escape when this was finally over. He rode at the head of the line, with the sheriff and One-Eye trailing along. They reached the cabin site, and Burt made them all stay back while his man examined the tracks.

"Men and horses have used this way," One-Eye told Burt.

"How long ago?"

"Two days, maybe." The scout shrugged.

"You ride ahead and follow them. We will hang behind a ways. You spot them, you come barreling back to tell us."

The scout mounted his horse and left the pack mule with Faucet. Then he galloped up the sandy dry wash and disappeared.

"What next?" the sheriff asked.

"Can't charge in. Might scare them off. We'll hole up here an hour or so. He'll find them and come tell us all about them."

"Sounds easy, but all we've ever found is empty camps. This Deuces must be pretty sharp. These rustlers are, too. I've not had much luck tracking them down."

"I'd bet they've never had an Apache on their heels before."

"You and them handcuffs got me convinced." Grimwell turned his horse to drop back and talk to the eight men riding with him. "We'll wait here an hour, then take up his scout's trail."

The time went by slowly. Impatient posse members squatted on their boot heels and whittled, spit tobacco in the dust, and drew maps in the sand with sticks.

Burt checked his watch and went to cinch up the dun. "Time to go after him."

Past noontime and deep in the hills, One-Eye returned.

"They are three men. They have maybe twenty horses, and they are headed—" He pointed southwest.

"They following this watercourse?" Grimwell asked.

"Yes," One-Eye agreed.

"Good. I'll take half the posse and try to head them off. There's a pass they must go through west of here, and if you will bring up the rear, we'll have them hemmed in," the sheriff said, pleased for the first time that day.

"Good. Pick your men, and we'll ride up the trail. Good luck," Burt said.

"You know, I judged you plumb wrong, Green. I won't ever do that again."

"How's that?" Burt asked with a smile. The poor man obviously never met a real marshal was all. Lots of political appointees wanted to be big shots; he couldn't stand them, either.

"I'll tell you sometime. Hans, you ride with them, your horse ain't stout enough for this ride," Grimwell said.

"Ya," the man said, and went for his black horse.

The sheriff and his hand-picked men galloped off to the south in their long circle to head the rustlers off. Burt and his crew trotted up the dry wash after the Indian.

Long hours in the saddle had hardened Burt for the ride. The dun horse proved to have plenty of bottom. During the time in the field, he'd purchased grain from farmers and in town to keep both of their horses in good shape. Though the ride began to tell after three hours hard up the nearly dry stream bottom, it was only the farm horses that snorted wearily, while his dun and One-Eye's roan showed little effect of their efforts.

Soon fresh signs appeared where the rustlers camped—horse apples, mostly. Their flight from the posse was obvious by the dust boiling up ahead. They were on the run. Burt decided the plan could work, if the sheriff and his men made it to the pass before the rustlers.

"Ease up," Burt told them. "Things are looking good right now." He turned to his scout. "Find a high place, and see how far ahead of us they are."

One-Eye nodded, then reined the bay off through the live oak and disappeared.

"He's going to see how far ahead they are," Burt told the others. He noted that Hans carried his rifle all the time. Balanced it on one knee—poor guy didn't own a scabbard for it. Must get tiring to ride like that all day. Burt booted the dun to make it walk faster.

The muffled sounds of gunshots forced Burt to stand in the stirrups to listen. Then more popped. His hand went for his six-gun. The Colt in his grasp, he waved them on. "Hell's broke loose up there. Let's ride."

He gouged the dun in the ribs with his heels and sent him barreling down the dry side of the river. He could hear the others coming on his heels. One-Eye broke out of the brush and joined him.

"Plenty shooting!" the Apache shouted.

"Sounds like it." Burt urged the horse faster, and they broke out into the open country.

The loose horses were panicked and running in all directions to escape. Burt could see gunsmoke coming from a grove of trees. The rustlers were shooting in the other direction—obviously at Grimwell and his men. Burt tried to catch sight of the shooters and came within inches of colliding with a loose horse. Wild-eyed, the runaway bolted aside only inches from the collision.

"Look, Burt, over there." One-Eye pointed over his shoulder, then fought with his own spooked horse, which wanted to leave with the rest of the loose ones.

For an instant, Burt saw the girl look back as she ran toward the cedars. A white girl—then a curtain of boiling dust cut her from his vision.

"Go, Deuces! Run!" her shrill voice screamed over the noise of gunshots and stampeding horses.

Rustlers or not, Burt needed to catch her before she escaped. He swung the dun around and charged through the undecided loose horses and dust. Out of the fog, he saw her legs flashing less than a few yards from reaching the sanctuary of some dense cedars. This had to be the lost girl. He gave the dun the rein to charge after her.

Where was Deuces? He must be close.

The hard report of a rifle echoed over the land, and the girl broke her stride as if someone had punched her in the back.

"No!" clogged Burt's throat as he headed the dun toward her. "Don't shoot! She's only a girl!"

She spilled facedown and rolled. Burt drew his dun down on its hind legs in a skidding halt and bounded out of the saddle before it fully stopped. He could see the crimson seeping from the spot on the back of her checkered blue dress. Gently, he lifted her into his arms and turned her over. The bullet had exited below her breast, and the scarlet wound looked vast.

"Deuces—run," she mumbled, and coughed. Blood ran from the corner of her mouth. The muscles in her body gathered. She blinked her fading eyes.

"He—hear me?" she asked.

"Yes," he managed to say, holding her. Never before had he felt so helpless; he shook his head to try to clear the guilt.

"Good—" Then, as if she was satisfied, her blue eyes

turned blank, and the once strong body went limp in his arms.

Struck down by her death, he bowed his head and dropped onto his knees. "Oh, God, why her?"

With care, he placed her body on the ground, swept off his hat, and tried to organize his mind about what he should do next. His fingers trembled when he reached out and closed her eyelids.

One-Eye joined him. Squatted in his moccasins, he looked at her and nodded his head. "Bad thing."

"Real bad."

Burt turned and saw Schumaker balancing the rifle on his knee. Why had he—her own stepfather—shot her? His first urge was to blow the hard-eyed German to kingdom come.

With his anger boiling over, he rose to his feet to confront the ruthless man. "Why in the hell did you shoot her?"

"She vas a slut! Unpure!"

Out of nowhere, One-Eye was in Burt's face, blocking him from doing anything. The scout's good eye was narrowed in warning, and his strong hand was on Burt's gun arm. "Don't—not that way."

"I won't shoot the son of a bitch," Burt said in a soft voice. "The law can deal with him."

"They got the rustlers." The scout tossed his head toward the lawman approaching with three men in custody.

"Good. You have a look-see beyond those cedars. Deuces was here with her a few minutes ago. Best I can guess, they got caught in the middle of these rustlers' horse stampede and our pursuit."

One-Eye nodded and stood back. "Yes, they must have. I look around, you stay here."

The scout hesitated as if he dared not leave—not yet.

"I'll stay. I'll be fine," Burt said to reassure him.

One-Eye turned and began to wave Schumaker away. "You better ride over by the sheriff." The scout pointed for the man to leave.

"What happened here?" Grimwell asked, looking concerned about the girl on the ground.

"Schumaker shot her."

"I thought she was one of the rustlers!" the farmer shouted.

Burt shook his head in disgust and went for his dun horse. He caught the reins and led the horse back down the hillside. All he wanted was to be alone for a few minutes. This wasn't like the days before—he couldn't go around pistol-whipping people he hated—he had a marshal's badge to uphold. He noticed two of the posse men busy wrapping her body in a blanket. The short sheriff came over to where Burt stood.

"What's your side of this?"

"You're the law here. I wanted to capture her to find out where the escaped scout was—" Burt exhaled and shook his head for composure. "That madman shot her in the back. She had no weapon. Offered no armed resistance. Hell, I'd've run, too, in all the confusion of those stampeding horses and gunshots."

"What do you say it was?"

Burt looked Grimwell in the eye. "It's your call. I'm a visitor here. I'm trying to capture an escaped federal prisoner. I know what I'd do if I didn't have this badge."

"What's that?"

"I'd blow that son of a bitch to kingdom come." Burt

felt his heart surge in his chest until it hurt. "But he's lucky today. Today I've got the weight of this star holding me back."

"I would say so. I'll turn him over to the grand jury. That good enough?"

"Fine." He felt the urge to join his scout. One-Eye might have Deuces cornered up there somewhere. He shook the lawman's hand and excused himself. In the saddle, he booted the dun up the hillside, grateful to escape the situation.

He waved after he heard the lawman's loud thanks and rode for the crest. He never wanted to see Schumaker again—not ever. The dead girl's youth and beauty haunted him, and he knew they would for several days more. Her sincere concern for Deuces's safety had been so obvious. Shaken, Burt ducked a cedar bough. Next, they needed to find him.

Chapter 18

On his move to escape capture, Deuces never returned to their camp. Amidst the dust and confusion, he had seen him among the others. The rider wearing the unblocked hat. Though he did not recognize the one who wore it, he knew quite well he was an Apache. Someone to track him. He had heard the report of the rifle that struck her and felt the bullet as if it had struck his own chest. He'd also seen her stepfather sitting on the black horse with his smoking gun.

Why kill her? Running full tilt, he leaped from boulder to boulder to leave no tracks for the Apache to follow. Perhaps her stepfather shot her so she could not tell them of his incest. The images of the man and his gun only sped his flight. Her killer would pay—pay dearly for his treachery. Even if it meant his own capture, this one without a soul would pay.

He ran with the wind, keeping in the cover of the live oaks, then doubling back so he could observe any pursuit. He never feared a white man finding his tracks—but an Apache was different. How long had this cousin been after him? Everything happened so fast; the rustlers had hidden several head of horses in that basin.

He and she went there to see about stealing some fresh, powerful ones from that herd. The mare and the bay were sound enough, but for the long ride back to Apacheria, he wanted three strong ones so their flight would be swift. They left camp on foot to scout the choices.

With a riata over his shoulder to rope some great horses from the herd, he looked forward to the adventure. Her eyes sparkled with excitement as she hurried beside him. Then he heard riders coming from the west and the east. Gunshots and a herd of horses stampeding in all directions cut them off from escaping. He tried to get her to run for the cedars—in the end, it was him she worried about.

"Go, go. I will find you when this is all over," she said, and shoved him away. "They won't hurt me. Then I will escape them. Run, Deuces. Now!"

Sick in heart over abandoning her, he raced for the cover of the cedars and soon gained the ridge. A rifle shot reverberated over the land, and far below, he could see her stepfather with his smoking gun and another man rushing to see about her. No need to look anymore; he knew that she was dead. His regrets over leaving her gnawed at his stomach and brain. But more than that, his loss weighed heavy on his heart.

He would have given his life for her. Such a deed was not to be after that shot.

Deuces realized that what he heard was thundering in the south. The appearance of the tall bank of clouds struck him at first as unfortunate. Then he smiled: Ussen was going to wash away any signs of his retreat. Thunder gods were coming, and he hurried from his place on the ridge. Once again, he would need provisions, the utensils he had left in camp—knife, axe, cup, plate, even his bow and arrows which he spent so many painstaking hours making. Their food supply, blankets, the sheet of canvas—no worry, he could find more.

The pearl-handled pistol was stuck in his waistband, the large skinning knife in a scabbard behind his back. He must decide what he would do next. He stopped and smelled the rain sweeping toward him. A fishy odor filled his nostrils. Unfamiliar with the Gulf's smell in the Texas hill country, he was relieved this approaching force would obscure his tracks. Filled with a new determination, he began to circle his way eastward. One more thing to do before he left this land: settle with him over her.

"Going to rain like hell here pretty soon," Burt shouted to One-Eye. He'd gone back and recovered the mule with their packs while the Apache searched for sign. The approaching storm sounded violent enough. Burt was ready to find shelter.

The scout agreed, taking the reins to his roan.

"We can't do much more here for now. Let's find some place of shelter."

"There's a small deserted ranch house behind us a mile or so."

Burt appraised the looming cloud bank. "Let's ride for it. I don't like the sound of the thunder in this one."

The scout agreed and mounted, and they galloped for the place. Even the mule needed little encouragement to lope. Raindrops as big as goose eggs began to pelt them when they drew in sight of the adobe house with a respectable shake roof. They slid their animals to a halt at the front door just as the first pieces of pea-sized hail began to join the raindrops.

"Take him inside," Burt shouted, waving both scout and roan to go through the doorway.

Thunder rolled violently overhead, and Burt charged inside. The dun and the mule came after him as if goosed by a nearby bolt of lightning. The tumultuous hammering on the roof deafened Burt's ears. Outside, the day turned to night, and when the next bolt flashed, the accumulating hail covered the ground.

"Barely in time!" he shouted at his man.

One-Eye agreed with a nod. "He will use this storm to get away."

"Can't be helped. That hail would sure have hurt us out in the open."

One-Eye rubbed his hands together. "Plenty good to be here."

Plenty good. The same notion Burt shared. Despite the time spent, they'd never once got a glimpse of the escapee. Then that stupid Schumaker shot the girl—their only chance to find out anything at all about Deuces. Been a bad day, and the rain only made it damper.

His first case as a full-fledged marshal, and all he could do was wander around through the cedars and live oaks. Maybe his boss in Washington would understand that fugitive Indians were as elusive as ghosts. If they asked why he didn't organize a posse, he could say he saved the government money. Texas already had hundreds doing that. And he supposed the governor of Arizona expected him to have found this buck, too, by this time.

He was more concerned about Angela's well-being and the ranch. Instead of three weeks of fruitless efforts, he should've had this wrapped up. He'd been set to wire Washington and tell them it was no use—Deuces was gone from the region. But that all changed with the sighting—and the ruthless murder of the girl.

Numb-like, he loosened the girth leathers. The storm showed no signs of abating. Wave after wave assaulted the cedar shingles, and leaks began to drip down on them, forcing them to move over to escape the cold water. He lamented, thinking about the leaky roof back home at the ranch house. He closed his eyes to shut out the rain's crashing and the rest of the day's misadventures.

Daybreak, they were in the saddle, but despite One-Eye's efforts, the tracks of Deuces were long gone. Mid-morning, they squatted on their boot heels beside a gurgling, muddy branch to reorganize their plans.

"He's either going to head west—without her, this land no longer has a hold for him." Burt spoke his thoughts out loud for the scout. "Or he's going to want revenge for her death."

"Come back and kill her stepfather?" the scout asked.

"Yes. He did it once like that. This time, maybe even more so."

"So we should go see about him—the stepfather?"

Burt's hard gaze met One-Eye's, and he nodded. "Chances are good he'll try."

"Did they arrest him for shooting her?"

Burt shook his head. "I don't know. I left right after you did."

One-Eye shifted his weight to his other leg and nodded. "Maybe that farmer is already home."

"We better swing that way and check it out."

"Sometime you tell me," One-Eye, said and swung around in the saddle.

"What's that?" Burt asked, mounting the dun.

"Would you have killed him?"

"If you hadn't been there?"

The scout reined his horse around and listened.

Burt shook his head, then nodded in surrender. "But you might have saved him."

One-Eye gave him an I-thought-so look, and they rode eastward.

Deuces began to worry his own escape had been too easy. He found her stepfather by himself, busy helping a heifer on its side in the pangs of birth. His sleeves rolled up, Schumaker was on his knees with his arms inside the cow, trying to assist. The anxious heifer raised its head to cry in pain. In an instant, Deuces was behind the unsuspecting man with a hold on his collar and a knife to his throat.

"Huh. Vat you want?" The man's eyes bugged out.

"Why did you kill her?"

"She vas a slut—she deserved to die—"

"So do you!" Deuces's blade drew a small trace of blood on the knife's keen edge at the side of Schumaker's neck.

"What do you want? Money? A gun? A horse? I give you it!"

Was the white man crazy? He could easily take such things. What he wanted was revenge for him taking her life. For taking her from him—and all the bad things he had done to her.

He bound Schumaker's arms to his body and forced him to head deeper into the canyon. The day was about over, and he knew that if he did not return to the house, someone would soon come looking for him.

They walked until the moon came up and Deuces felt satisfied that no one would find them. He forced his prisoner to the ground, and, taking the riata he carried, he tied it to the mumbling man's feet. Satisfied it was secure, he straightened and tossed the tail over a stout live oak branch.

Whatever his prisoner said at this point, he ignored. Schumaker was a big enough man that hoisting him feet-first in the air proved hard work for Deuces. So he made a wrap around a tree trunk, and each time he inched the man's feet higher, he made certain he did not lose his hitch.

Soon the man grew quiet, and Deuces had him where only his shoulders and head were left touching the earth. The last pulls were the hardest, but finally Schumaker's head swung inches off the ground. Deuces tied the riata off and in the gathering darkness dropped to his hands and knees to measure the width between his scalp and the soil. Maybe the width of one hand off the ground—some of the man's hair was touching it.

"What do you plan to do to me?" Schumaker asked in a wavering voice.

Deuces never replied; he went off to gather firewood. Soon he had many large cedar knots and limbs in a pile beside his prisoner. He found matches in the man's vest and struck the first one.

A flare from the blazing boughs lighted the fear in Schumaker's eyes. He made some painful shouts as the fire grew and the air began to smell of singed hair—Schumaker's hair.

Squatted nearby, without an expression on his face, Deuces watched the fire leap at the sky, hungry flames that soon had the farmer's clothes smoldering. He wiggled in the binds behind his back and tried to swing away from the source to escape the hot tongues licking at him.

Time passed slowly. The crescent moon crossed the sky, and the victim babbled incoherently, cried, and shouted curse words at both Deuces and her. Undeterred by the man's raging threats, screams, or swearing in the night, he fed the fire more fuel until, in the early morning hours, Schumaker was reduced to mumbles behind his charred lips and half-burned-off clothing.

Deuces used a sheet of bark for a shovel and heaped the red-hot ashes all around Schumaker's head for the last step—to boil his brains. His screams of excruciating pain echoed off the canyon walls. Deuces squatted close by, so the heat of the fire reflected off his own face, and he studied Schumaker's blackened features set in the ring of glowing cherry embers. He watched until Schumaker screamed no more.

Then he rose and started for home. All his work in this place was completed. Time to return to his own land. He closed his eyes for a moment. His dreams of the two of them sharing paradise in the mother mountains of Mexico was shattered by *his* bullet. After this day, he would kill and rape whoever he wished, for his life had no meaning without her. He walked in the land of the dead.

With his back turned to the bitter smoke, he set out up the hillside.

"Hans, he never came to the house last night," the Schumaker woman said, wringing her hands fretfully. "We think we heard far-away screams all night, but they might have been coyotes."

"They weren't no coyotes," the brave-faced boy of perhaps eight said, looking up at her.

"You don't know," she said to silence him. "With her dead—" The woman sobbed into her hands, and Burt slipped off his horse to go and comfort her.

"We'll go look for him."

"He says you hate him." She never looked up when he tried to hug her shoulders to reassure her, only shook her head.

"Sorry, but his senseless killing of her upset me, Mrs. Schumaker. We'll go look for him."

"He might be in the pasture—" She pointed to the northwest. "He went to see about a heifer going to calf about dark last night."

Burt nodded and climbed back in the saddle. A head toss to One-Eye, and they headed in that direction.

"I'll open the gate for you," the boy said, and escaped his mother, racing barefooted across the yard to help them.

"Donny, you come back here," she ordered, but the youth already held the gate open.

"Paw's probably helping that heifer, huh?" he asked Burt when he rode by him.

"Probably," Burt said.

"Paw won't ever leave one."

"See you, Donny, thanks," Burt said, and pushed the dun on.

"Sure, Mr. Marshal, you tell Paw breakfast's sure getting cold, huh?"

"We will," Burt said over his shoulder, and rode off into the live oaks and up the grassy valley.

"Buzzards." One-Eye pointed to the circling black birds.

The two men trotted up the valley and found the dead heifer with the calf half out of her. One-Eye studied the rain-softened ground and soon nodded. "He took him that way."

"He's already got him?" Burt shook his head and let out a large sigh. Deuces never wasted any time getting over there, which meant they probably were too late—damn. They headed through the thick brush and at last were forced to dismount and lead their ponies as One-Eye tracked them.

At last, on top of the ridge, One-Eye wrinkled his nose. "Smoke."

"Campfire?" Burt asked.

"No, bad smell."

"I can smell it now, too. Damn, we better get down there and see. You take a look for signs of where he's gone, but have your gun ready. He might still be around here." He swung in the saddle and headed for the source of the bitter smoke.

One-Eye rode off, and Burt pushed his dun through the brush into an opening. The sight of the twisting black corpse was not pleasant. Burt rode in and cut him down into the still-smoldering ashes. Then, gathering up his strongest will, he dismounted and dragged the burned clothes and the stinking corpse out of the fire. That completed, he undid his bedroll and took off the ground cloth.

Swallowing his own sourness, he fought throwing up the whole time until the dead man was tied in his shroud. Then he looked up as One-Eye rode back in.

"See any sign?"

"Some. He's headed west. I would say he was going home."

Burt nodded that he heard him. "Give me a hand loading him on my horse."

They dug a grave for her, and in the late afternoon they buried Hans Schumaker. A few neighbors gathered for the simple ceremony.

"My mare came home with a bay horse today," Hatfield said, acting taken aback by the turn of events. "Our gray mare. She looked good. 'Course, no sign of my saddle."

"You might search around near that pass. I think they were camped up there somewhere close by and got caught up in the outlaws' capture and all those horses stampeding," Burt said.

"I'll do that. I ain't going to ask why—but that Deuces never bothered anyone before, save steal a horse. Then he comes back and does this." The man ruefully shook his head.

Burt looked around to be certain they were out of the hearing of others. "Deuces killed another man for cutting his wife's nose off and causing her to commit suicide. This time, he needed revenge for her death."

"I wasn't there, but I thought Schumaker just made a mistake. Him thinking she was one of the rustlers."

"It wasn't," Burt said, and nodded to One-Eye that he was ready to go. He spoke briefly to the widow and then tipped his hat to the ladies with her. He and the scout rode away.

Chapter 19

HOLDING HIS HAND TO HIS SIDE WHERE THE BULLET had passed through, Pedro glanced at the star-flecked sky for some heavenly intervention.

"Mother of God, Virgin Mary . . ." he muttered. His back pressed hard against the stuccoed wall in the alley's darkness, he tried to gather his wits and catch his breath. Torres must have got word to his cutthroats in Tucson to be on the lookout for him. Pedro's four-day ride over the desert from the mountain village back to Arizona on the green broke mustang had worn him out. But before he rode out to the Green ranch, he felt obligated to learn all he could about the outlaws' activities by checking with some amigos in the barrio.

The two bandits jumped him when he came outside the Mia Linda cantina. Things had happened too fast in the night. Angry men swearing at him. Red-orange flashes of gunfire in the darkness. The impact of the bullet that spun him around—then somehow he managed to run away from the would-be killers.

He turned an anxious ear to listen for sounds of their pursuit. They might be only a short ways behind him. Fear hurled him down the dark alley. The wound burned like a flaming sword in his side. Worse yet, when struck by their bullet, Pedro'd dropped the outlaw's six-gun he'd carried out of Mexico.

Filled with fears over being unarmed, he glanced back over his shoulder. No sounds of any pursuit, but he couldn't be too careful—they'd track him down to be certain he was dead. Damn, he hurt.

Not everyone in Tucson was his enemy. But he needed to get a few blocks over and not be discovered by anyone. Juanita's sister lived in a small jacal over on Frio Street. If she was home, Carla would help him. He stopped and pressed his forehead to the rough plaster on the building. Damn. His whole right side felt on fire.

Sticky blood ran through his fingers. On the move again, he'd still not heard or seen any sign of pursuit. Perhaps he had eluded them. They might fear he was still armed, too. Waves of hot lightning shot up into his chest and made him stagger.

His breathing ragged, he fought his way to Carla's place. It was long past midnight when he rapped on her door.

"Come back tomorrow!" a sleepy voice answered his knock.

"Carla, it's me, Pedro," he hissed, slumped against the wall.

"Yeah, sure," she said, and cracked the door. Then

she jerked it open and, dressed only in a skimpy night-shirt, moved underneath his arm. "What's happened to you?"

"Torres—back shooter. You've got to get dressed and go find Morales. I need to know what that ban—dit—Torres plans to do."

She helped him onto the bed.

"I'll get it all bloody," he protested.

"Quit worrying about it, and lie down before you fall over. I'll go get a doctor."

He reached out and caught her arm. "No, no, go locate Morales and find out—"

"I know, I know. You want me to learn what Torres is doing."

"Yes." He relaxed for a second, then the pain returned, and his body stiffened.

"You have any money?"

"No. But tell him—"

"Oh, damn, he won't take any credit." She shook her head as if at wit's end.

"Then do what you can. I can repay you when Burt returns."

Busy tying her skirt on at the waist in the dark room, she sighed out loud. "I am tired, and it is late. I am sorry about your wound, but I am not going to bed with that dirty old man to learn about what this Torres will do next."

"Just find out," he said, anxious about his wound and also about what he needed to know about the outlaw's plans.

"I am going now to find this Morales and what you want to know." Her voice rang with impatience. "You don't want no doctor. Well, you better not die here while I am gone."

"I'll be fine—"

"Sure, bleed all over my bed—makes no sense." She left, swearing in Spanish about him.

After the door closed, he fainted. Sunlight was coming in the open window when he awoke. The sharpness of a sword in his side made him arch his back against the fire. In the street outside, he could hear the peddlers. Why wasn't she back?

Soon he heard the front door open and Carla say, "This way. I hope he is still alive."

The man behind the glasses must be a doctor, Pedro decided. He forced a smile for him, but words were hard to speak. "You came back."

"Of course, I came back," she said impatiently. "All I learned was that Torres and his men are not in town."

"Easy," the doctor said, seated on the edge of the bed and trying to remove his shirt to see the wound.

"Where are they?" he asked.

"I guess making raids."

"Damn. Doctor, hurry and bind me up—I must ride for the ranchero."

"From the looks of you, you'd fall off a horse if you tried to ride anything."

"No! I must get to the ranch."

"In a few days, and then only if that bullet didn't perforate your intestines." The doctor stood up and removed his coat, then methodically rolled up his sleeves. "This could be a very serious wound. Bring me some water to wash it with."

"Sí," she said, and rushed off.

"Can you roll over on your side?" the physician asked.

The movement pained him, but he managed, and the medic peeled away the shirt's material. His cleansing, poking, and then at last pouring powder into the wound wearied Pedro. Carla conversed in the background with the doctor as if Pedro wasn't even present. The laudanum he gave him made him sleepy, though he fought it. If Torres was out there, he might already be raiding the ranch. Somehow he must get there and help Obregón defend the place—he had promised Burt Green. Then he lapsed off into sleep.

"You are safe—you are safe." Carla was shaking him.

"Huh?" His side felt as if a mule had kicked him. His hand flew to the bandages to press on the pain. "What about Torres?"

"I know nothing more. I have been here all day. You have been screaming his name, if that will help."

"Señora, yes, the señora has a buggy at the livery. Get it, and take me to the ranch."

"What can you do out there?"

"Help them protect the place," he managed with his teeth gritted. "Go get the buggy."

"Everyone does not love this bandit Torres. I can get some amigos to go with us."

"Hurry," he said, and, out of strength, slumped down on the bed. Dizzy-headed, he soon fell asleep.

Someone had lit a candle on the bedside table. His eyes flew open to see the giant shadows on the ceiling. The room was filled with women, and they were chattering like magpies.

"Carla?" he managed to say out loud, though the hoarseness in his voice shocked him.

"Lie down," she said, coming through the women. "A

dozen men have gone to the Green ranch to guard it. Now, you must lie down."

"Good ones?" His head swarmed, and he couldn't clear it.

"Yes, your friends Romano, Juan Rodriguez, Felipe, his cousin, I don't know all their names. Stop worrying and rest."

"Burt Green will pay them."

"They won't worry about that. That ranch is safe."

He squeezed her hand and made a smile. "You are a wonderful sister-in-law."

She shook her head as if embarrassed by his words of praise. "No, my sister has a brave husband." Then, in surrender, she bent over and kissed his forehead. "Now, sleep some more."

"I will," he said, and shut his eyes.

The second morning with no word from the ranch or the men, Pedro made Carla go after the señora's buggy and horse from Pasco's livery stable. When she returned with it, she assisted him onto the rig. With her pushing on his butt, he made the seat. Exhausted, he watched her run back for a blanket to cover him with.

She took the reins, and the fresh horse set into a long trot. They soon were north of Tucson and crossed the wide dry bed of the Rillito Creek. On the far side, she let the horse rest for a few minutes.

He huddled under the blanket despite the sun's heat. Still groggy and dazed, he wished the horse had wings despite her quick time so far.

"Where is the señor?" she asked with a frown.

"In Texas, looking for some escaped Indian scout."

"Where have you been?"

"Sonora. Looking for Torres."

"Get up," she said to the horse, and he took the bits. "Did you find him down there?"

He went on to tell her about his experiences below the border. When he finished, she shook her head. "You're lucky to even be alive."

"When I get well, I will find the back shooter who did this to me and wring his neck like a chicken."

She looked over at him and grinned. "I imagine you will."

"I will."

He felt better when he could see the ranch house in the distance. No signs that anyone had burned it or the outbuildings. Maybe he had sent help in time. He hoped so.

Felipe waved from the roof of the house when Carla pulled up.

"Any trouble yet?" Pedro shouted to him.

Felipe shook his head. By then, both Juanita and the señora rushed out of the house to greet them.

"How are you, Pedro?" the señora asked with a look of concern on her face.

"Oh, I am fine," he said, stepping off the buggy, only his sea legs would not hold him up. He collapsed on the ground to the screams of three women.

The men carried him inside and laid him on a pallet set up by the women. With his blurred vision, he shook their hands. "No bandits?" he asked in his gravel voice.

"Romano is trailing them. They struck the Anchor ranch and the Bar Nine. Stole horses and shot some people."

"They haven't left the country yet?" Pedro asked, disturbed by the news. To not run to the border after a raid was unlike Torres. Was he getting bolder?

"What does Romano think?"

They turned up their palms and gave him a blank look.

"Don't worry about those bandits. These men are staying until the danger is past," the señora said, and held out a tablespoon of laudanum for him. "Take this and rest."

He obeyed and soon felt sleepy, with his head in the lap of his lovely Juanita. Oh, how he had missed her, the quiet, efficient woman in his life whose hands petted him. Unlike her vocal sister Carla, his Juanita spoke few words, but she could always comfort him in his darkest hours, and he closed his eyes again.

Part of his strength came back by the third day. He sat up and ate at the señora's table, listening to the scouting results of Romano and Guillermo Salazar.

"They have maybe a dozen men. Some are just boys, but they are all armed and are camping with the stolen horses west of here."

"How many horses?" Pedro asked, before sipping the rich coffee.

"Maybe thirty."

"How could we take them?" he asked.

Romano looked across at him and frowned. The barrel-chested man with his handsome swarthy face was well respected in the Tucson barrio. Likewise Guillermo, the thicker-set man, was a no-nonsense hombre.

"We could take them at night. They never post good guards. They fall asleep all the time."

Romano nodded to his partner's words. "But we have to make you stronger."

"I'll be able to ride. Why have they not raided this ranch?"

"They don't know that Burt Green is gone, I would bet money," Romano said.

Guillermo agreed.

"In two nights, we raid their camp." Pedro waited for their agreement, and, satisfied, he began to eat the food before him. He would need all of his strength to ride with them.

The two men excused themselves, and the women rejoined him. Carla had taken the buggy back to Tucson and promised to listen for any news about the gang,

"Shouldn't you wait for the patrón?" Juanita asked.

"Yes, Burt could lead you," the señora agreed.

"We don't know when he will return. These bandits will take more horses in the next few days, shoot more people, and then ride off to Mexico. No, we need to capture them and give the horses back."

"You are still weak," Juanita protested.

He agreed between forks of food. "But I am healing."

"Because you are resting," the señora reminded him.

"Tomorrow night, we will get them."

Both women looked at each other and then shrugged.

"It will be your death," Juanita said, and began to gather the dishes.

"Oh, señora," Pedro said. "I will need a pistol."

"I'll get you one." Leaving the room, she shook her head in disapproval. Pedro watched the long tresses of her honey-colored hair falling to her shoulders. Burt Green had married a beautiful woman; more than that, she possessed a powerful way about her.

Already, he began to dread the hours he faced in the saddle. Never mind, he needed to bring down this bandit before he hurt any more people.

Chapter 20

REPORTS OF THE PUBLIC SIGHTINGS OF DEUCES dropped off to a trickle. Burt wired the U.S. attorney general notifying him that his services in Texas were no longer needed and he was headed home. Before he left Uvalde, he went by and spoke to Sheriff Grimwell in his office.

"Well, Green, if I ever need a real lawman in my jurisdiction, I'll have them send for you." He stood up, and they shook hands.

"I may need the work."

"I doubt it. Once again, my apology—"

"Ain't any need in that. Me and that Apache need to catch the next train west, so we'll see you again sometime."

"Yes, and I imagine you'll be glad to see home."

"I will," Burt said, and left the man's office.

An hour later, Burt and his scout were seated in the Southern Pacific's *West Coast Express*. The conductor told them when he checked their passes that they'd be in Tucson by noon the next day.

"Pretty damn fast," One-Eye said, and they both laughed.

When the train left the hill country, Burt scanned the short brush and grass desert. Deuces had a long trip to make on foot or horseback across that country.

The issue of Deuces was still far from over, Burt felt certain; the elusive Apache would be a thorn in his side for a long time.

"Señor Green! Señor Green!" Burt turned and saw the short, attractive Mexican woman running down the street. He set down his suitcase and frowned at One-Eye. What could she want with him?

"I am Juanita's sister—" Out of breath, she dropped her head.

"Is there something wrong?"

She still tried to regain her air and patted him on the arm to wait. "Pedro was shot, and he is at the ranch. There are some good men—out there—now helping him. But they say that Torres is making raids every night." She covered her mouth, coughing hard.

"Gracias. I'm headed for the ranch right now."

She bobbed her head and coughed some more. Then, fanning her face with her hand, she recovered her voice. "Pedro is still very weak, but he is so hardheaded. I am so glad you are back."

"So're we," Burt said, and smiled at her.

"I better go with you," One-Eye said to him.

"Ain't posse work," Burt warned him.

"Hey, I never saw your ranch. Besides, we been sitting around for a long time."

"That's right. You'll have to meet my wife."

"Good. Let's get the buckboard."

Pasco's livery quickly hitched up the team. In twenty minutes, they were on the seat and headed north. Burt pushed the horses hard, anxious to be with his wife and home again. They drew near the ranch, and a feeling of excitement rushed through Burt's whole body.

The thrill of expectation drove every weary muscle in his body away. He whipped the team to short-lope them the last quarter-mile. Burt could hardly wait to hug his bride.

Several men around the porch were waving their sombreros as they rode up. Then she appeared and raced to the gate, standing with arms wide open for him. He bounded off the seat and flew into her embrace.

"Oh, Burt, you're back and safe." She snuggled against him as if she couldn't get close enough to him.

"I'm fine. I saw Juanita's sister in Tucson. She said Pedro was shot."

"I'm better now," the man said from the porch, but his blanched face told another story.

"We were going to raid Torres's camp tonight," Pedro said. "Romano thinks they will be asleep and we can take them."

"Someone go saddle us two fresh horses," Burt said, and his wife's disappointed look did not escape his vision. "I need to go and help them," he said to her.

She nodded but still looked downcast over the matter.

One of the guards went off with One-Eye to saddle some ranch horses for the ride.

Romano stepped in and told him about the banditos'

camp and its location. Burt led them all inside the house while Angela went to get him some food.

Between bites, they discussed how they would need to come in from various sides and take the bandits in their sleep. Men were assigned to take charge of the horses and to be certain that no bandit could get on one and escape.

The homemade food melted in his mouth, and he hugged her around the waist when she came in range.

"You mean the food in Texas wasn't this good?" she teased him.

His "No" drew laughter from the men.

"Pedro, tell me about who shot you," Burt asked

Seated at the table, Pedro shook his head. "Some back shooter hired by Torres, I guess."

"And all of his amigos rushed out here to guard the ranch," Angela said with a large smile.

"I'm grateful," Burt said to them.

"These men with Torres are no good," Romano spoke up. "They are not only bandits, but they rape children and kidnap young women. They think they are invincible."

"Tonight, let's hope we can teach them a lesson," Burt said. "Maybe some time in Yuma prison might improve their outlook."

"Yes." They all raised their cups.

When the half moon rose over Mount Lemon and the Catalinas, they mounted their horses under the starlight and in small groups rode west through the tall saguaros and around the vast beds of prickly pear and cholla for the raid on Torres's camp.

A coyote threw its head back and yipped out of its narrow muzzle at the lunar appearance. Then another answered, and more joined in. Despite the lack of sleep and the long train ride on the hard bench seat, Burt felt relaxed to be back in his own saddle and on a powerfully built, smooth horse with a good running walk to carry him. Angela called the bay horse Bully Boy, but he shortened that to Boy.

Felipe halted his group, and they dismounted in a dry wash under the hill and out of sight. One-Eye stripped down to his loincloth and, armed with a Winchester from the ranch, waved to them and struck out on foot.

Burt watched him move through the silver desert shrubs and up the hillside. Hardly more than a ghost, he soon vanished over the ridge. Felipe went up the hilltop to be the lookout.

Pedro sat on a rock, and Burt felt concerned they couldn't talk his man out of coming along. He had no business out there in his condition—but because of Pedro's story of his trip into Mexico and all that they did to him, he couldn't deny him the opportunity to even the score. Running his tongue along his molars and considering all the eventualities that could happen, Burt decided it would be a real justice for Pedro to find the bulldog who beat him up so badly in Diablo.

A hiss in the night for their signal. Time to mount up and ride. Burt noticed that Pedro refused any assistance getting on his own horse. The riders spread out once they were on top of the rise. Each man rode with his gun drawn. In the distance, the glow of a campfire made a yellow light to center upon.

Burt could see the mass of the horse herd to the north on the flats. He wondered how that crew was doing. Romano was coming in from the west. He and his two men had the farthest to ride. Then a lighted match flashed.

"Romano is there," Felipe said in a whisper. Then he struck his and quickly blew it out.

All eyes were to the left, and soon the signal came from Bigota, and the men nodded, drawing closer to the dark camp. No signs of any guards. Then One-Eye appeared, and Burt worried for a second someone might shoot him for a bandit.

"What's happening?" Burt asked.

"The guards are taken care of. The others are all asleep in their blankets."

"Thanks," Burt said, and nodded to Felipe, who had drawn near to listen.

"You see Torres?" Pedro asked.

One-Eye shook his head. "I don't know him."

"I hope he's there."

The capture of the gang was swift. Aroused at gunpoint, they grumbled and cursed in getting up. Pedro went among them, looking at their faces in the firelight and demanding to know where Torres was.

"Where is he?" he shouted at the wide-eyed youth, and collared him for an answer.

"With some puta in Tucson," the boy managed to say.

"What is her name?"

"Carla—"

Pedro turned and frowned at Burt. They both nodded, and when the eight prisoners were tied and seated on the ground, the two men talked at the edge of the campfire.

"Could be any Carla," Pedro said.

Burt agreed.

"But I am concerned for her life."

"I understand," Burt said. "You have enough horses here to bring them in, as well as the stolen ones. Take your time, and deliver them to the sheriff. I'll ride to Tucson and try to be certain she's all right."

"I will go, too," Romano said.

"No, you all have enough to do. Where's her casa?"

Pedro explained the street location. Burt was familiar enough with the town's layout that he knew where her house was.

"You stay here and help them," he said to One-Eye.

"You sure?"

"Yes. I can handle Torres if he's there. You help them bring in these outlaws and horses. I'll have your pay for you when you get to Tucson."

The Apache nodded, and Burt grasped the saddle horn. In a bound, he was mounted and riding hard for the south. The horse's endurance would deliver him. The sun was up when he rode into Tucson. Standing in the stirrups, he made the lathered bay trot through the busy streets. When he rounded the last corner, he saw no horse at her door.

He undid the rawhide lacing holding in his Colt and stepped down. The reins dropped, the heavy breathing Boy lowered his head and blew in the dust. Burt stood beside the door and rapped with his pistol.

"Who's there?" a man's voice demanded in Spanish.

"Dónde está, Carla?" Burt remained flat against the wall of the building.

Two bullets tore through the wooden door, waist high. Burt turned with his six-gun ready and kicked in the door. A cloud of black smoke came billowing out the doorway. He heard someone at the rear tear through the house and out the open rear entrance. Seeing no one, he burst through the small house to the rear doorway.

Trapped at the backyard gate, a bulldog-faced man whirled and raised the gun in his hand.

Burt's first shot struck him high in the right shoulder and spun him half around. The second smashed into the side of his face, and the bandit's revolver went off harmlessly in the ground.

Had this one been alone in the house? Burt climbed onto a chicken coop to see over the adobe fence and survey the alley. No sign of anyone else escaping. From the description, the man on the ground was Pedro's tormentor and not Torres. Burt also noticed all the blood on the man's gun hand and sleeve—as if he'd been butchering. Burt punched out the empties, reloaded, then holstered the Colt and went back inside.

A blue haze remained in the interior; walking into the main room, he spotted a bare leg hanging over the edge of the large bed. Standing over her, he could see he had come too late. Someone had slashed her throat. Her beautiful black hair fanned out underneath her pale face—mouth open wide in pain and eyes staring forever at the ceiling, her naked body a rich coffee brown in the room's dim light.

He tossed a sheet over to cover her. Damn sonsabitches. To kill a defenseless woman was gutless. The bloody-handled knife on the floor belonged to the dead killer in back. Then he went out front to see about his horse.

"Burt Green?" The city marshal was in his thirties, wearing a black suit, and he knew Burt. Mark Vespers asked, "What's going on here, Marshal?"

"Man's dead in the backyard. He tried to kill me. Did a mean job on the girl."

"Aw, damn, going to be one of them days. How did you—I mean?"

"Law business. I thought a bandit named Torres would be here. I about got shot. See the bullet holes? Kicked in the door and took after the guy—then I came back and found her."

The marshal had lifted the sheet to look and quickly dropped it. "Bad enough, all right."

Chapter 21

THE SILVERY STARLIGHT BATHED THE UNPAINTED wood siding on the small house. To the east, the great dark hulk of the Chiricahuas hunkered down like a gigantic buffalo bull. Dueces's moccasins made only a soft scuffle on the raw flooring board crossing the porch. Night insects played a song in the yard. He slipped into the kitchen and drew out his great knife. Smells of cooked bacon, white bread, and little spicy hints tickled his nostrils.

Orienting himself to the kitchen's layout, he moved to the other room. He knew the woman was alone. Earlier, from where he bellied down under some junipers, he had watched her polygamous husband drive away in the mid-morning. The dust of his departure in the buckboard had put a smile on Deuces's face. With only the clicking windmill for her to scream to for help, he planned to pleasure himself on her ripe body.

For two days, he watched her from the cover of the pungent juniper clump on the rise above the homestead. He observed her feeding the chickens, milking the brindle cow twice a day, and carrying in split wood to fire her cookstove. A young woman with hair the color of honey in a plain calico dress. Her willowy body appealed to him. He yearned to discover her undressed and to mold her flesh with his hands. Worse yet, his loins ached to drive himself inside her.

From the doorway, he could see where she slept. The bed was in the center of the room. A shaft of milky light from the window shone on her form lying on her side under a flannel sheet. He removed his moccasins and then his shirt. His gunbelt hung over the chair. Her soft breathing filled his ears. Knife in hand, he tiptoed over to her, wearing only his loincloth. Then, like a mountain lion, he leaped upon her, pinning her under his weight and putting the blade in her face.

"Who are you?" she shrieked awake. "No!"

"Your lover," he whispered, holding her squirming form beneath him.

"No!"

"See this knife." Her struggling stopped as he waved the blade in front of her face. "You have no choice. Do as I say or die."

"Can I—"

"No! You either obey me or you die!"

He could feel her whole frame trembling underneath him. Her body's warmth and faint sweet aromas began to waft up in his nose. With the knife still ready in his hand, he rose to peel the sheet back. Every muscle tensed in his body, he pushed her flat on her back, then swept the bed covers away, settling back on her legs.

"Who—who—are you?"

He set the knife on the stand beside the bed and began to unhook the small buttons down the front of her gown. "They call me Deuces."

She shook her head.

"Never heard of me?" He wanted to laugh at her. Silly woman, married to a man who went from wife to wife. An Apache with more than one wife lived with all of them in one wickiup.

She would never do to take to Mexico with him, no fire in her eyes. He would know when he again found such a woman. He tried not to think of his lost one, for even to think about the dead could mean bad luck for him. Impatient with the buttons, he ripped her gown open, and she gave a stifled scream. Roughly he spread her legs apart, then pushed aside his breechcloth. He grinned at her growing shock as he slid down on top of her.

Later, when he had finished with her, he dressed, put on his gun belt and the knife. Seated on the floor, he listened to her sobbing into the sheet as he pulled on his Apache boots.

Ready to leave, he went over and jerked her head up by a handful of hair. "Now you are an Apache's wife. I will come back again and use your body whenever I want to. Put on that sweet-smelling stuff. I like that.

"Don't tell your husband about this. I could have cut his throat. You want him to die?"

"No," she blubbered.

"Remember what I have told you." He shoved her face

back down to the mattress. "Cry all you want. You are mine now."

At the doorway, he stopped and listened to her screaming and thrashing the bed with her legs. "No! No!"

In a slow trot, he headed for the deep wash where he last hid the fine painted horse he had stolen below the border. In a bound, he was in the saddle and riding hard for the Chiricahuas. The Mormon woman would not soon forget him.

Three days later, he abducted a woman picking flowers in a meadow. Her husband had gone off stalking a wild turkey and left her alone. Deuces carried her belly-down over his horse several miles up the creek before he raped and left her.

A week later, he visited another isolated rancher's wife who was alone, and afterward he stole two of the best saddle horses from the corral when he left.

Not satisfied with any of the white women he tried, he began to devise a new plan. Get himself an Apache woman from the reservation. He developed a new strategy for his raid up there. With fresh horses picketed along the route, he rode on the reservation. From a camp of pinyon gatherers, he abducted an attractive White Mountain Apache girl and made a wild dash using the fresh horses in relays until he and his new ward were deep in Mexico before the scouts and army patrol could even start after him.

"What is your name?" he asked her as she sulked, seated on a boulder beside the rushing stream. "Maybe I should drown you, then?" he asked when she did not answer him. He squatted down in his boots on the gravel before her.

She shook her head.

"Should I find a name for you?"

"My name is Ruth."

"Ah, you have no Apache name."

"I am Ruth." She used her thumb to jab between the proud breasts under the beaded buckskin blouse.

"I am Deuces."

"I know who you are." She refused to look at him.

"Oh, do they speak of me?"

"Yes. They say you are *tonto loco*."

"Why?"

"You live like a beast, and you are a taker of women. Why did you not take a white woman? They say they are much afraid of you raping them."

"You aren't afraid of me?"

She jumped off the rock, hands on her willowy hips. "No, but you have ruined my reputation. Now the men of my tribe will think I am a puta. They will all say she sleeps with Tonto Loco."

He shrugged. "I will keep you as my wife, then."

She drew back her arm to strike at him. He caught her wrist and glared in her face. Enough of her sass. "Prepare our wedding bed."

"No."

"Then you wish to be taken like some animal on these rocks?"

She looked at him crossly, then pried his fingers from her arm. "You will wish you had never seen me before. Where do you want to do this?" Her shoulders underneath the deerskin trembled with rage.

He grinned. "Find a soft place for your back. You will lie on it for a long time and look at the sky."

"They say around the campfires of women that men

rape because they are such poor lovers. That is why they do it. Because such women never complain."

"You won't complain," he promised her, and turned on his heel. She wasn't the German girl, but she would do. Besides, he needed to stay in the Sierra Madres for a while—too many looked for him above the border.

Chapter 22

"THE GOVERNOR OF SONORA HAS SENT YOU A LETTER?" Angela said, excited, looking through the mail Pedro brought from Tucson.

"That may be the answer I've been waiting for," Burt said.

"About him allowing you to go into Mexico and bring out Torres and Taylor?"

"Could be," Burt said, looking over the linen envelope and official wax seal on the back. He opened it and pulled out the paper.

Señor Green:

In regards to your request to arrest two citizens of Mexico, Alfredo Torres and Joseph Taylor. My captain of the rurales, Captain

Austin Malago, says the bandit Alfredo Torres is wanted for many crimes in Mexico. But if you think you can locate him, we will allow you the pleasure of trying him in the United States.

However, in the case of Señor Taylor, who is a land owner and a bishop in the Church of Jesus Christ, that is different. Only if Señor Taylor is willing to surrender and go with you willingly can you take him back to your country for trial.

I know you are sworn to uphold the law in your own country, but we cannot allow armed parties of invasionary forces through our borders. So you may not bring a posse to Mexico to secure this Torres. You and only two of your deputies are all I will allow in my state, and you will have only ten days from when you come through the custom gates to arrest him and get out.

Our country also has strong laws about murder. We expect you to arrest this man and not execute him on the spot. Anything else will make you and your men subject to the penal codes of Mexico and Sonora.

Please respond with your wishes.

Sincerely yours,
Martinez Pasco, Govenor of Sonora,
Republic of Mexico

"What does it say?"

He handed her the letter. "It says we can go down there and get Torres because he's an outlaw. But we can't have Taylor unless he surrenders. Because he's a preacher of Mormons and has money. Lots of gold money from the stage robbery of the Fort Grant army paymaster."

"What will you do?"

"Take Pedro and One-Eye and go get Torres. All of Torres's men are bound over for trial for murder and robbery. He's the only one left, as far as I can tell. He might have a new gang of thugs down there, but we'll get him and drag him back. I'm certain that he was involved in the murder of Carla, and I want to see him pay for it."

"You aren't telling me everything," she said, swinging on his arm.

"I also believe he's the one who killed your husband."

She nodded and handed him back the letter. "Then you better answer the governor of Sonora's letter, Marshal Green."

Preparation began with shoeing the horses they'd ride. Pedro, recovered from his wound, rode out to find One-Eye and bring him back to the ranch for the job. Burt was bent over, tacking on a shoe with a roan horse's hind hoof in his hand, when a man in a military officer's uniform rode up.

"Marshal Green?" he asked as he dismounted.

Burt's mouth full of horseshoe nails, he nodded. Setting the first one, he rapped the flat nail in place and then bent it over.

"Sorry to catch you at work, sir, but I'm Captain Hampton from the San Carlos post."

Burt nodded for him to continue.

"You no doubt have heard about all of the rapes and abductions of women by the renegade called Deuces?"

Burt nodded, used another nail, and bent over his work, rapping it in with the short-handled hammer. This was no place to quit, despite his company.

"Well, sir, we are considering him as a hostile. Under that heading, the army can pursue him into Mexico."

Burt took another nail out of his mouth, drove it in, bent it over on the top side, and let go of the roan's hoof. He cleared the rest of them from his mouth and sucked in a breath of air as he straightened.

"Captain, If you had a thousand good Apache scouts and went in there looking for him, I'd bet you a good-sized farm you'll never find him."

"He's not a ghost."

"Hell, man, you could find four or five ghosts easier than even a track of Deuces. I spent nearly a month in Texas looking for him with a damn good scout."

"We got Geronimo."

"He came in and surrendered."

Undisturbed by Burt's interpretation, the officer continued, "Deuces recently rode in the reservation and abducted a White Mountain Apache girl—got clean away with her."

Burt nodded; he had heard about the incident. "Way the story went, he stole some damn fast horses out of Sulphur Springs Valley to relay on, too."

"I believe that was the same report I received. But you know how fragile our situation is up there at San Carlos. What I mean is the difference between keeping those hot-blooded young bucks on the reservation and them wanting to join the likes of this Deuces in Mexico?"

"To tell you the truth, I don't blame them. If I had to sit under a greasewood bush in that hell hole you call an agency and wait for the next delivery of stringy beef, I might want to join Deuces, too."

"I understand, Marshal, that you are planning on going into Mexico after some criminals."

"I'm going after a bandit by the name of Torres. The governor of Sonora has denied my other request to arrest the army payroll robbery suspect Taylor."

"A shame. Some good soldiers were killed in that robbery. But about this hostile—Deuces. Do you have any idea where he is down there?"

"One-Eye, an Apache scout who's also a deputy U.S. marshal, says Deuces, no doubt, is up in the Sierra Madres. However, in the short time span the Sonora governor has allowed me to capture Torres and get out of Sonora, I have no time to go search for a needle in a haystack in the Madres, if that's what you're angling at." He stretched his aching back muscles and waited for the officer's reply.

"My superiors certainly want some sort of reassurance that a sortie down there would have a chance of being successful."

"Why not sent Tom Horn, then? I understand he and this Deuces worked together as scouts in those mountains."

"You, of course, know that Tom Horn and General Miles had some strong words at Geronimo's surrender."

"Words or not, Tom Horn is your man. Not me."

"I doubt I could—"

"Depends on how bad you want Deuces. Horn's the man. Miles can like it or not. And maybe after all that's happened, even Horn couldn't get him to come in." Burt looked off through the heat waves that distorted Mount Lemon's towering height to watch a lone buzzard ride on the up drafts. "I was Deuces, I wouldn't come in, either."

"Thank you, sir." The officer turned to leave.

"Hold up, Hampton My wife would skin me alive if I don't invite you in for a cool drink and some food."

"Very good. I accept."

Burt gave a head toss toward the house and untied the roan to put it in the corral until later. Angela loved to fuss over company, and a nice-looking officer like him would make her day. He undid the lead and slapped the roan on the butt, then closed the gate after him. He needed a break, anyhow.

That evening, Pedro and Burt's Apache deputy arrived at the ranch after dark. Angela fed them, and the three men talked around the table after they ate.

"We only have ten days to get in there, find Torres, and get out."

"Why a time schedule?" Pedro asked with a frown.

"Number one, the governor don't like armed Americans tromping all over his countryside. Secondly, he said only two deputies, then stipulated that we not murder Torres."

Pedro laughed, and One-Eye smiled.

"We can ride to this place Diablo in two days," Pedro said.

"Then if he hasn't been warned by that time, we can surprise him." Burt shook his head. This job looked a lot tougher than it seemed when he first received the letter.

"What if I put out the word, we're going to Mexico after—" Pedro scratched his sideburns.

"Deuces." Burt smiled at the notion.

"Yes, at least put that out around Tucson. The word would get to Torres that's who we're after, and he wouldn't worry about us."

"Might work," Burt agreed. "We still have two horses left to shoe. Get that done tomorrow while you take the buckboard back into Tucson, and tell everyone we're going after Deuces."

One-Eye leaned back in the chair and laughed. "You know, among the Apaches, Deuces is becoming a big legend."

"Yes. Captain Hampton from San Carlos was here today wanting me to go look for him. He says at the rate they're going, Deuces will soon have the young bucks following him down there if they don't stop him." Burt looked across at the expectant-looking scout. "I said no, we couldn't."

"Good deal. He's hard to track." One-Eye shook his head.

"We better get some sleep," Burt said.

He showed the two outside, then returned.

"You will be careful in Mexico?" she asked.

"I'm always careful." And he buried his face in her sweet-smelling hair. The roof still wasn't fixed, and he was riding out again. Most of all, he hated to leave her and the warm, sensuous body he hugged. Whew, she had become addictive to him. Two nights left to share the bed with her, and he'd be gone again.

The three left the ranch before daybreak, leading two pack horses. Skirting Tucson to keep the gossip down aside from the word that Pedro left while securing supplies, they made the Tubac by sundown. The Santa Cruz River offered their weary horse stock running water and lots of curly grass to fill their hollow bellies. Burt planned to rest at the old fort until noon the next day, so their border crossing in the village of Nogales would be after midnight. Less for gossiping tongues to tell about.

Firewood was gathered, a fire built, and beans boiled. Earlier, Burt had bought tortillas from an old woman making them outside a small store. So they ate beans in flour tortillas and some with honey from their supplies for their trip.

A day later, with the acrid slick taste of desert dust on Burt's tongue, they rode the greasewood flats headed southeasterly from Nogales for Diablo. Pedro promised they would be there by dark, and he would check with a woman who knew all about the bandit's movement. Pedro's effort to find Torres had Burt impressed: all the man's hard work and the risks he took for his sake. He also felt concern over how close Pedro came to losing his life—and the bloody bed scene at Carla's never left his thoughts for long. The threesome gnawed on jerky, dry cheese, and crackers for substance as they rode.

"What did you eat in Texas?" Pedro asked.

One-Eye shook his head warily as the three men rode abreast through the stirrup-tall greasewood. "Sometimes people would feed us. Sometimes we ate jerky, and sometimes he would cook."

"He a good cook?" Pedro asked with a head toss at Burt.

"Sometimes," the Apache said, and grinned.

Pedro and One-Eye scouted the village of Diablo. The consensus between them was the sight of a *gringo* might forewarn Torres and send him off in flight. So the two slipped into the town under the cover of night, leaving Burt with a rifle across his lap and his back against a warm rock to guard the horses in a dry wash.

Somewhere a coyote yapped at the rising moon and made its cowardly way along the ridge above to check out the invaders in its land. At discovery of the horses, it tucked its bushy tail to its rectum and fled off into the desert, no doubt counting its good fortune for surviving the encounter. Noisy insects filled the night with sounds. Burt considered the work he needed done at the ranch when this was over.

He turned an ear and heard the soft steps of someone in the sand. He raised the rifle with both hands to be ready.

"It is me, Señor." Pedro came and squatted on the ground beside him. "Torres is in the saloon. One-Eye is guarding the back way. You want to take him?"

"That's what we came for. How about a horse for him to ride?"

"He rode a big horse in. It is hitched outside the cantina."

"What's he look like?"

"He is a big man. Like you. Has a beard and mustache and wears a big black sombrero."

"Anything else?" Burt rose and brushed off the seat of his pants.

"There are some hombres in the bar." Pedro made a face. "But they are not pistoleros. The bartender—I will watch him."

"We don't want to have to stand any murder trial." Burt chuckled and tightened the cinch on the roan horse. "Let's go get him."

"You know I owe him for that beating?"

"I've been thinking on that." Grasping on the horn, Burt pulled himself into the saddle. "Let's make sure we have him and are on our way home first."

"Sí, Señor."

"Burt," he reminded him for the hundredth time.

Slowly, they rode up the starlit street past the dark jacals. A few cur dogs barked, but all else was silent, except for the insects' sizzle. At the hitch rack stood hipshot horses. Soft candlelight filtered out the front door of the cantina.

Burt dismounted. His thumb pushed the rawhide thong guard off the hammer of his Colt, and, out of habit, he shifted it to be exactly where he wanted it. Then he shared a nod with Pedro to go ahead.

Sounds of a guitar filled the night. Burt came on the right, Pedro on the left of the hitch rail. Burt paused for moment to allow his eyes to adjust to the light, then pushed through the doorway.

All heads swiveled in his direction, and even the music stopped. Burt's gaze fell on the big man's back and black hat just as he twisted half around to see him.

"Alfredo Torres?"

The man started up out of the chair, but not quickly enough. Burt's .45 muzzle was jammed in his back.

"You're under arrest. You savvy dying?" Burt asked, and swept the big hat away.

"Sí."

"Raise your hands slow-like, and tell all your compañeros to sit tight."

"Don't try anything—" Torres said sharply to the other hard-eyed men at the table.

"You wish to die, hombre? You just try to bring out that shotgun," Pedro said to the bartender. "Get out from behind there. You already know how good I can shoot."

The shorter man raised his hands high, his face blanched and his anxious stare directed at Burt's posse man

"You can't get me out of Mexico, you stupid gringo." Torres laughed.

"Oh, you don't know. The governor—he don't like you," Burt said, and ripped the pistol out of the outlaw's holster. He jammed it in his waistband, then tossed the large knife on the floor. No doubt, the man had more weapons than that on him, but Burt had removed the obvious ones. He cuffed Torres's hands, then looked over the half dozen frowning faces and the two skinny putas. No signs of resistance in any of them.

"Pedro, march your friend the bartender out back, and get One-Eye. I'm ready to leave."

"Get going, hombre," Pedro said, using his pistol to poke him in the back. He marched the man out through the back door.

Burt, satisfied, shoved Torres toward the front one.

"You will never live to see the border," Torres said through his teeth.

"If your men try anything, you'll be the first to die. Want to tell them that now?" Burt asked, loudly enough that everyone could hear him.

"You won't—"

"The hell I won't shoot you." And he shoved the bandit for the batwing doors. Outside on the boardwalk, he nodded to his deputies.

"The bartender?" he asked.

"Sleeping," Pedro said, and untied the reins of the horses at the hitching rail. "We can borrow one of these for One-Eye, huh?"

Burt nodded. He kept a close eye on the bandit and the lighted doorway for any sign of resistance. With Torres in the saddle on the horse Pedro selected and One-Eye's rifle held on the outlaw, Burt mounted the roan.

"Let's ride," he said, and they hurried out of Diablo.

While they paused to gather the pack horses from the dry wash, Burt made certain the cuffs would contain

Torres by using a second pair to lock him to the saddle horn. One-Eye abandoned the borrowed horse for his own, and they set out northward.

"How far to the border?" he asked.

"Maybe seventy miles," Pedro said.

"All desert?"

"There are some springs," One-Eye said.

"I'll trust you," Burt said, checking over his shoulder. He knew that the former scout had been across this land many times chasing the hostiles. If anyone knew where to find water, he did. The real question was how many friends the big outlaw had—they might learn that number before they reached the border.

They rode in the silver night for the invisible line, save for a few survey stakes that showed the division between Mexican law and the United States.

Besides cursing them under his breath, Torres remained the unblown volcano. The arrest went too easy. Burt twisted in the saddle. No sign in the night so far of any pursuit. Didn't mean that wheels weren't grinding out behind them to recover their boss.

They used their horses hard to make plenty of distance between them and any pursuit. Pedro led the outlaw's horse. Rifle in hand, the Apache brought on the pack string. Burt rode with them, lashing the laggard pack animals to keep up. He wanted them to be close enough to the line, so the following day they'd be over the border.

Close to two A.M., they drew up at a spring that One-Eye guided them to. Torres was cuffed to a mesquite tree for safekeeping. Burt walked four of the horses to cool them so they didn't stiffen, while his men watered the others. Leading the snorting horses, Burt studied the constellations and felt satisfied their route was as direct as one could find.

"Trade you," Pedro said, and they exchanged animals. He led the other two, though they were breathing easy, and he thanked himself for selecting the right ones.

Somewhere out in this star-cast silver country, Deuces must be, he decided. Someplace, the man cut off from his people slept under a rimrock. But Burt could see how such a rebel would attract the eager young Apaches like honey bees to wildflowers. He shook his head. Then there was the sullen bandit Torres. The farther they rode, the less Burt worried about his allies trying to take him back. The only thing nagging him: had he killed Angela's husband? Lots could be put to rest if he knew the truth.

Taylor would have to wait. When he got back home, he needed to talk personally with Governor Baylor. Thank him for the marshal commission; no doubt his political influence had gotten that accomplished. Weary from all the riding and no sleep, he yawned. When Torres was behind bars, he could sleep for twenty-four hours.

"Ready to ride, Señor?" Pedro asked.

"I guess. You two all right?" Both of his posse men nodded.

"I'll get Torres," Burt said, and took the keys for the cuffs out of his pocket.

"Torres, I heard you had some fancy claybank horses for sale," he said, undoing the handcuffs and keeping an eye on the sullen outlaw seated on the ground. "Who did you sell them to?"

"How should I know?"

"I think you'd remember. Two big palominos," Burt

said, recalling Angela saying her husband's best yellow horses were taken in that raid.

Torres shrugged, getting to his feet. "I sold them in Guaymas."

Burt slugged him with his backhand in the face and staggered Torres until he fell down. His rage under control, Burt jerked Torres to his knees. "You killed her husband in that raid."

"I didn't kill anyone."

Burt pulled him over beside the horse and clamped the cuff on the horn. "Try anything, and you're dead."

Pedro rode in and took the rein to the prisoner's horse. "What did he say?"

"He sold her husband's yellow horses in Guaymas."

"Then he did kill him?"

"He was there," Burt said, and climbed onto the roan, the anger still evaporating like steam from a kettle. He knew the answer at last.

"Arizona's that way," he said, and booted the roan for the border.

"Damn good thing, too," One-Eye said.

"Why's that?" Burt asked.

"I be able to sleep a long time when we get there."

All three lawmen laughed. Burt twisted in the saddle and searched the desert. No sign of any pursuit. He put the roan in a trot. *I'm coming home, Angela, and I feel a lot better.*

Chapter 23

"YOU SEE ANYTHING FROM UP THERE?" DEUCES asked the girl as she hurried down the steep slope.

"Nothing."

He nodded and motioned to the coffee boiling on the small fire. Above them, the pine timber clung to the steep slopes, and the eroded reddish-orange bluffs rose up to the granite peaks.

"Why are you so nervous?" she asked, pouring him coffee in a tin cup he held out.

"I feel someone is coming."

She gave him an impatient head shake. "No one knows where we are. I doubt Ussen even knows. This place is so far away we may meet ghosts here. Maybe you are seeing ghosts."

"No. When I have such feelings, someone is coming—

good or bad. When the lawmen came for the rustlers in Texas, I had that same feeling."

"Then why did you stay there?"

"I didn't know what the feelings meant."

She nodded, pouring herself some coffee.

"Who would be coming? Mexican army? This white man and one-eyed Indian you spoke of?"

"He is a White Mountain Apache."

"Yes, his name is One-Eye. He is married to a woman called Kettles. I think she may be part Chiricahua. Maybe she is daughter of one of their Mexican captives. My mother speaks of her."

"This One-Eye, you say he was a scout once?"

"For Crook."

Deuces had been over this story before with her. He could recall being hidden in a cedar bush when the two rode by him in Texas. The scout had almost discovered him. Close enough to them that he could hear their breathing and a few words. Who was the white man? Deep in his thoughts, Deuces looked across the vast jumbled canyons and pine-clad slopes beneath them. The Madres were a good home. His woman, whom he called by her Apache name, Deer Runs Away—not Ruth—only wanted to have some squaws around her to gossip with. She missed her mother and her relatives was all.

They had plenty of coffee and flour, lots of canned goods he found in the packs of the pack train that he brought back, supplies headed for some mine. He jumped the three packers at daybreak, firing the Winchester from his hip, spraying death and gunsmoke at the three shocked, half-awake men. One who survived, he bashed in his head with a large rock and left them for the magpies, ravens, and buzzards. He brought the supplies to their cave and turned the mules loose, though he seriously considered eating one of them. Mule meat was superior to anything but mountain sheep.

They had plenty of deer to eat.

Still upset by the feelings of dread inside him, he shook his head, finished off the coffee, then rose to his feet. He stared into the cup as if in the grounds remaining there would be a simple answer for his concerns. "I am going to look around and be certain. You stay here and listen. You hear something wrong, you slip away."

"Yes."

"Mexicans would treat you badly."

She nodded obediently.

Deer Runs made him a good woman. But he knew she would always complain about his taking her from her family. Tradition said the man should join her group, not estrange her from them. No way for him to do that. He skirted the patch of mountain mahogany with the polished red branches and made his way along the rimrock, the oily rifle in his hand. He even slept with the new weapon. He took the rifle from a ranch house in Arizona.

He recalled how the honey-haired woman screamed at him: "I don't want your little red bastard in me!" Too bad—at least he never killed her. He never killed any of the white women. He smiled at the pleasure he took from them. But none of them was that satisfying in her bed. He never found another white female like *her*. That was what he sought. So he went to San Carlos and took

Deer Runs to Mexico as his real woman—his wife. He paused to watch the blue jays flitting in a scrub pine; far below, he spotted a color for a second not like the rest of the broken country.

Two Apaches were making their way up the mountain. His heart stopped. Were they two scouts hired by the army—that white man? He had seen them twice in the timber. Leading their horses. Who were they?

He drew the Winchester to his shoulder. Through the iron sights, he drew down on the one on the right. At the distance, the shot would be a long one. If he missed, it might only scatter them. Why did they wear white headbands? Scouts wore red ones to tell each other apart—both of these wore white ones.

He decided to shoot close enough to spook them. They were near enough he could still get away and ambush them later. But who was behind them? Buffalo soldiers? Mexican soldiers or the big white man? He aimed the Winchester at the pine to their left. The rifle kicked in his arm, and the black smoke drifted.

His shot caused the black horse to rear and go backward. The other Apache waved his arm. "Friends! Amigos! Don't shoot!"

"Who is with you?" he shouted back.

"Only us. We come to talk."

Still not satisfied, he moved to the left for a better check. The black horse had calmed down. Both men were armed with pistols, he could see, but were not carrying rifles, as scouts usually did when close to their enemy.

"Come up here!" he shouted. "My squaw will kill you if you try anything." They should be aware he had backup, even if she might be miles away after the shot. Deer Runs had no desire to be raped by twenty Mexican soldiers with the clap. Deuces smiled at the notion of her fears.

"Deuces! Deuces" the Apache called to him. "I am Chako and with me is Mica. We want to talk to you."

"About what?" he said, looking down on the two young men.

"We want to join you."

Join him? What for? He shook his head in dismay, still looking for dust or any sign of a posse coming behind them. Why had they come this far?

"We want to be Apaches, not dogs on the reservation," Chako shouted through his hands, and the echo came back twice . . . *dogs on the reservation.*

"Come up here, but no tricks."

"We are alone. Believe us."

He waved his arm impatiently at the two. Crazy young bucks. Want to join him. Made no sense. Then he whirled with his rifle at his hip at the sound of someone coming downhill. He saw her.

"Who are they?" she asked, out of breath, peering off the steep side.

"Two crazy boys. Chako and Mica."

"What do they want?"

"To join us."

"Why?"

"Because we're exciting."

She frowned at him.

"Yes. We are exciting to two boys who hate the reservation."

"They came a long ways."

"For nothing." He shook his head, eagerly trying to

get a better look at them as they made their way up the steep mountain.

"They don't look younger than you."

Deuces never answered her.

"We hate the reservation," Chako said, sitting cross-legged on the ground as she served them tin plates of venison, beans, and her flour tortillas.

The smoke from the small fire ran up Deuces's nose. Seated on the Navajo blanket, he considered the two loincloth-clad Apaches. Chako bore a bad scar on his left cheek. Both of them were short. Deuces stood at least a head taller than either, but he towered that much taller than most of the men in the tribe. Mica, he noticed, had blue eyes. Listening to the two speak, he wondered how many more Apaches had blue eyes? Mica, perhaps, had a white ancestor. For years, his tribesmen took white captives and made them either wives or slaves. But there was no doubt from his nose or the high cheekbones—Mica was an Apache.

"There are many who would like to come here and join you," Mica said, then went to eating, using the tortilla for a spoon.

Deuces shook his head. "I can't lead many. Besides, they would track us down. The Mexicans. The army. But if there were eight or ten—"

"Would they bring their women?" she asked, pouring more coffee.

He frowned at Deer Runs, displeased that she had entered a man's conversation unasked. But his displeasure with her showed no signs of wilting her insistence on an answer. She stood firm, holding the coffee pot.

"We can talk of that later," he said to dismiss her.

"They better bring wives," she said, in a swirl of her fringed deerskin skirt. "I don't intend to feed that many myself."

Mica and Chako first smiled at her outburst until Deuces began to laugh. Then they, too, slapped their legs and joined him.

"Yes," Deuces said, loudly enough for her to hear. "Women, too."

Chapter 24

Governor Baylor, a portly man in a striped business suit, sat behind the large desk. Above him on the wall was the seal of the Arizona Territory behind framed glass. On the side wall were several books in a walnut case, and the other side of the room displayed a large map of the territory. Burt sat back in the leather chair, a glass of whiskey in his hand, anxious to hear what the governor had to say.

"There's some items left on my list I'd like you to handle. I'm pleased, of course, you brought in that Mexican bandit Torres."

"I feel quite certain he's the one who killed Van Dorn last fall. Torres admitted he sold those two fancy claybank horses in Guaymas last year. That, to me, is enough link to say he was in on the raid, anyway."

"Yes, and your wife, she's such a gracious lady. Give my regards to her, sir."

"I shall, Governor. She's very busy at home preparing for a party, or she'd have come to Preskitt with me."

"Oh, yes, my list. That Joseph Taylor. You know, he had the gall to pay off the note on several of those Mormon farmers with the fresh-minted money from that army payroll robbery."

"I know that. But the governor of Sonora said he was too politico to allow me to arrest him down there. And Taylor won't ever give himself up."

"You watch. He'll make a slip."

"I will, sir."

"What else? Oh, yes, I know you tried hard to capture this Deuces in Texas. I have a letter from the sheriff of that Texas county bragging on your efforts there and how you helped him. Now the wild savage is raping women and rustling horses in this territory."

"The army wants him, too. They're afraid he may lure some young bucks off into his band down there in Mexico." Burt sat back in the chair and took a sip of the fine whiskey. Not bad-tasting, must be expensive; if all whiskey was this good, he'd drink more of it.

"Any ideas?"

"I told the captain that Tom Horn might capture him. Heaven's sakes, Horn might even find him."

"What did he say to that?"

"Horn and General Miles had words at Geronimo's surrender."

"Lots of folks have words with that damn Miles. They should never make an enlisted man a general. They have no give to them. We all know he hates Apache scouts, but he ought to hug them. He'd never got those last

Chiricahuas out of Mexico without them. Couldn't you deputize Horn?"

"If I can find him, and you told my boss in Washington we needed him. I'm not certain he would okay my vouchers for Horn's pay and expenses otherwise."

"I understand." Baylor shook his head. "This damn country would be a lot safer if we simply could do what we thought was right and went from there."

"I thank you for this commission. I know that I'd never have gotten it without you."

"Oh, I really think you are the sort of man they needed. The rest of these marshals all have businesses and big ranches to support them. They set up courts, send people out to serve warrants. Have a secretary to run their office and only show up once a week, if then. The U.S. Marshal Service needed some special full-time ones, to handle the things they couldn't. Solve some of the crimes, too."

"I appreciate it, anyway. You think of anything else, wire me," Burt said, putting the empty glass on the desk and thanking the man again.

"Good talking to you. You're going back tonight?"

"Yes, my wife is making some preparations for a large party at the ranch, and I need to get back there and help her. I'll try to find Horn and see what he says about becoming a deputy."

"I'll damn sure get it approved for you."

"You know he may turn us down?"

Baylor showed him to the front door of the large log cabin and shook his hand. "I know, but we need to try. Heavens, I get tired of reading in the territorial papers how one dumb ex-scout has this territory treed."

Burt left the governor and walked the three blocks

back to the Brown Hotel on the square. The afternoon was sunny and nice; he enjoyed the relaxation of the moment. In the lobby, the clerk waved him over and handed him a yellow sheet of paper.

> Burt Green
>
> Joseph Taylor is supposed to leave Mexico and go to Salt Lake City for a bishops' meeting with Brigham Young. To leave on the 10th. Understand he's taking a stagecoach there.
>
> Downy

Three days—one to get home on. Whew, he'd better wire for Pedro and One-Eye to meet him Tucson.

"Where's the telegraph office?"

"Fort Whipple."

"Will someone take a communication out there?"

"This afternoon?"

"Yes."

"Good. Get them, and I'll write a wire."

"Yes, sir."

He could only hope the telegram got through. The stage ride took twenty-four hours. That would leave him less than a day to find the one Taylor was on and arrest him. Made sense, but it was all too close.

"Oh, Marshal," the clerk said. "I also have another letter in the box for you."

"Fine," he said, in deep thought about the Taylor issue and how it was unfolding. Absently, he accepted the mail and started for the staircase.

He noticed a small smile on the clerk's face and could smell perfume on the letter but ignored it. Later, in his room, he could open it. The outside carried no return address or postage stamp.

In his room at last, he lighted a strong lamp and tore open the end of the envelope. A strong perfume appeared to come from inside, and he shook the letter open.

Dear Marshal Green,

Allow me to introduce myself. My name is Lucinda Deveau, and any time you are in town, my house is at your disposal, sir. I have a lovely suite for your comfort, five-course meals that rival Paris, and, of course, beautiful courtesans to rub your aches and pains away. So feel free to drop in any time and relax in the company of the most beautiful women in the territory.

And it is all absolutely free, my dear.

Lucinda Deveau

Wouldn't Angela have a fit about that letter? Well, he had no use or time for that business. Interesting, when he was a lowly deputy, she never offered him anything. Must be on the cusp of being there with his new commission. He laughed as he sprawled himself on the bed. He'd not trade his wife for the fanciest one in her circus of ill repute. Now, how would he work out the capture of Taylor?

He sat up and went through his knowledge of the man's description. Taylor might come through disguised as someone else. The man had to know by this time he was wanted and was taking a big risk.

One thing Taylor could count on. He'd be there to greet him.

* * *

The twenty-four-hour stagecoach ride back to Tucson proved bad enough. Indigestion over some stop-off food plagued him, and he got no sleep. Both Pedro and Angela met him at the stage office.

"You look wrung out, Marshal Green," his wife said with a warm smile. "We better get you over to the house in town. Some food, a bath, and a few hours' sleep, huh?"

He held his hand up. "No food. What do we know about Taylor?"

"If he gets on the stage in Nogales, we will get a telegram," Pedro said.

"From who?"

"Oh, a cousin, Alandro. I promised him five dollars." Pedro gave him a questioning look as they started for the buckboard.

"That's wonderful. I'll pay him. Where's One-Eye?"

"He rode to the border. There is word about Deuces coming back."

"All we need. Taylor and Deuces at the same time." Then he stopped and looked her in the eye. "Your party?"

"Oh, well, if worst comes to worst, then I'll have it without my very busy husband. Let's get you some rest," she said, heading him for the rig.

"I'll stay and watch for a telegram and look out for him," Pedro said.

"Good. What was the word on Deuces again?"

"One-Eye heard something about him taking Geronimo's place and leading off all the young hotbloods from the reservation."

Burt shook his head, wishing his upset stomach was

in hell. He heard his deputy. "Be careful with Taylor. I don't know how he'll act when we arrest him."

"I will, señor—ah, Burt." Then a smile stole across Pedro's face. "I'll watch things here."

Burt agreed, then helped Angela up onto the spring seat, climbed on himself, and undid the lines. "I'll check back in a few hours."

He realized Angela was making signs to his deputy behind his back. When he turned to look at her, she had stopped and looked very demure.

"I can't sleep all day."

"Part of it, anyway."

He clucked to the team and set out up the narrow street. Only two deputies, and both were spread way too thin. Taylor's arrest had to be his primary goal. If he had him behind bars, then he could show something for more than a month's expenses. They might get tired up there in Washington of putting out money without results.

"Nice that Pedro had a relative in Nogales," he said to her, reining up for a goat herd to divide and let him by.

Angela chuckled and shook her head.

"Sorry," he said. The way clear, he clucked for the team to go on. "What's so funny?"

"He sent that boy down there for the five dollars to watch and wire you."

"I see," he said, and more unpleasant roiling in his stomach took his mind off his worries for a second. "I'm lucky, I guess, to have all three of you. Pedro knows how to handle the Mexican side, One-Eye the Indian problem, and you, my love, know how to handle me."

She hugged his arm and pressed her forehead to his

shoulder. "Oh, Burt, I must say my life with you is no end of variety."

"That ain't all bad."

"No, I rather enjoy it. Most of all when I have you to myself."

He looked off toward the Catalinas and nodded. Should be more of that time, too.

Chapter 25

DEUCES SQUATTED IN THE DARKNESS AND STUDIED the picket line of mules outlined by the red light of the packers' campfire. The .44/40 balanced across his bare legs, he wondered how many bucks Chako and Mica would bring to the meeting they planned. He wanted no more than fifteen. That might be more than he could successfully lead around and stay out of both the armies' way. His mind should be more on the packers, the three men he'd seen in the distance earlier. Actually, he saw their dust and wondered about their business. Were they taking supplies to some remote mining operation? They took valuable items to such destinations, made for easy pickings.

If he decided to lead a band—he would always need lots of supplies. Deer Runs and he could hardly eat all they had stashed in the cave. Still, there would be times of need. Also, he could use a few mules to pack what they might need. He promised Deer Runs that she could visit her family when they went up there.

He closed his eyes; better to agree to such a concession than hear her complain for six moons. They said Cochise, whom he'd never met, had several wives. How did he please all of them, or did he not try?

The packers' low voices talking in Spanish carried on the night's breath. He caught small parts of the conversation. One was about some redhaired puta in Cannonia. Another spoke of someone's sister, and that drew some loud laughter. In a few hours, he would have to slice their throats and then load the mules by himself—be better if they had them loaded, but he could not fight three of them awake with their rifles.

Satisfied, Deuces turned and went back to the draw, where Deer Runs waited.

Squatted down in the wash, he nodded to her in the starlight. "Much food and supplies. We will have the cave full after tonight."

Seated on a Navajo blanket with her back to a large rock, she nodded. Deuces knew the boulder still gave off the sun's warmth, why she was seated so close as the night wind turned the day's heat to cool. Dressed in her new buckskin skirt and blouse, she looked very attractive to him. No wife of a chief-to-be should look like a poor Mexican's wife. He smiled, reached out, and squeezed her knee. She nodded with a sly grin; she knew his meaning. He thought about making love to her muscular body underneath the leather clothing. Time for that later—even doing that with Deer Runs, he thought of *her,* and that was bad medicine all the time gnawing at him. To think of the dead anytime was bad, but he could not clear his mind of *her.* They had planned on such a garment for *her* too.

"When I finish with them, we will load the mules," he said.

She nodded.

"You may sleep now. They have no idea we are here."

She scooted down the blanket, then curled in a ball on her side, and he left her.

In the wash, he picked up a smooth rock as big as a tomahawk head. During the last ambush, he bashed in two of the packers' heads with such a weapon, then cut the third one's throat.

He crept back to listen to them. Their fire's flames licked the black sky.

"Holy cow—"

Listening, Deuces's heart stopped.

"You boys got enough damn fire going to signal the whole damn world to come down here!"

He recognized Horn's voice. When did he join them? A frown and growing anger rose in his thoughts. Horn must have ridden in while he went back to see her. What was he doing there?

"You boys want them bandits or renegades that got the last train to get our asses, then keep building these gawdamn big fires!"

No doubt, Horn was there to guard the dumb packers—from themselves, maybe. To hear his old friend ranting at them made him feel warm. But what should he do? No questions. He must ride back to their camp. No mules. No raid this night.

Deuces hurried back to the wash. He jerked her roughly by the arm. "Come on, we must go. Now!"

"But—"

He pulled her to her feet by the arm, swiped up the blanket, and towed her to the horses.

"But I thought—"

His open-handed slap across her face silenced her. Then he jerked her face close to his with a fistful of hair. "Get on the horse!" He saw her shrink back from him, and he knew she understood.

They rode in silence back up the mountain. He paused several times and listened for any pursuit. When there was none, he tossed his head for her to go on, and he followed. To be so close to his old friend left him thinking many bad thoughts. Should he have killed him, too? If he started a new band of Apaches, would Horn lead the army to his camp?

He knew the answer. Horn would bring them. He should have killed him back there when he was unaware. When he did not have his guard up. To kill Horn would have been hard. With those packers, he could have done it swiftly and never flinched.

They dismounted as the first spears of sun shone on the peaks. Deep in thought, he bumped into her.

"Why did you take me all that way, and you did nothing—"

Her words struck him like lightning does a dead snag. Anger raged through his body. He tore the riata from his saddle and began to beat her to the ground with it. His arms raised high each time, he smashed her with the coils. *She must learn respect*—he said it over and over in his mind as he swung the rope. When he was through with her, she would never question his command. The sharp slap of the rawhide strands lashed her leather dress and her flesh and echoed like a shot across the canyon.

He beat her until his arm grew numb. Then he tossed aside the rope and stared at her huddled in a ball on the ground with her hands covering her face, expecting more of the same treatment, but not crying, not whimpering. Numb to the core, he dropped to his knees, roughly jerked apart her legs, and raised the skirt. Then he tore aside his breechcloth. He was not through with her yet.

Chapter 26

"WAKE UP, BURTON. PEDRO SENT WORD HE'S ON THE stage." Angela was on her knees, and her face shone above him in the shadowy bedroom.

"Taylor?" he asked in a sleep-crusted voice, trying to open his heavy lids. Damn, he could have slept two more days at best.

He sat up, threw the covers back, and ran his fingers through his hair. Needed a haircut, too. The yawn came close to unhinging his jaws and made his eyes water. He might never wake up. His arms went out and hugged her.

"When's the stage arrive?" he asked with her in his arms.

"In one hour."

"How long have you known he was coming?"

"A while. I tried to let you sleep."

"I appreciate that, but I better dress. No time for—"

"Right." She used her index finger to push on his nose. "Not this time."

Another yawn about incapacitated him, and he scooted off the bed. "You have some coffee?"

"And food, if you want it. You feeling any better?"

"Too damn sleepy to know. Yes, I'm much better," he said, buttoning his shirt.

In an hour, Taylor would arrive in Tucson. In an hour and a half, he'd have him before U.S. Commissioner Henry Lacey, charged with robbery and murder. After that, the *mayordomo* could rot in jail until they had his trial. His ex-boss would be responsible for the jurors, the courtroom, and the rest. The more he thought about his place as special marshal, the more he liked it. Let the locals handle it—they probably would do as good a job—but this case was federal, army paymaster robbed, several buffalo soldiers shot and wounded, and more than a hundred thousand dollars in gold coin taken.

"You ready to eat?" she asked as he pulled on his boots.

"Yes, ma'am."

"Good. It's on the table in the kitchen."

"Coming."

"You look nice in a suit," she remarked about his clothing when he came into the kitchen smelling her rich cooking.

"Depends. Out in the desert, I don't. But in this case, it probably looks more official to wear a suit."

"Will that count when you arrest him?"

He slid into a chair at the table. "No, but this guy somehow has been high-handing the law. He used a portion of the money to pay off mortgages for several Mormons. I mean, where would he get, say, forty thousand dollars in newly minted gold?"

"That much?"

"Only a fraction of the total. Then he hightails it to Mexico. Some say because he's polygamous, but it's damn funny he waits till after the robbery and after the bank payoff to do that."

He began to fill his plate with the smoked chicken and beans. "This looks wonderful," he bragged.

"Those people are very clannish."

"I know. But crime is crime, and being a preacher don't leave you out of the law."

"They don't have preachers, the laymen do that."

"Well, a bishop, then."

"Head of the ward, you mean. The church's business is his job."

"Angela, I could care less. If he stole that gold and killed those men, he needs to be locked up."

She put her hands on her hips and smiled at him. "I agree, Marshal Green."

"Good. Food's good, too. Pedro send any word about One-Eye?"

She shook her head and filled his coffee cup. "You think he's all right?"

"One-Eye can handle himself. He's learning something about Deuces, or he'd been back by now."

"The party is set for two weeks from now—"

"That should work," he said, busy eating and planning his strategy for Taylor's arrest.

"I know you'll try to be there, but—"

"Angela, I'll do my damnedest. Taylor in jail is one less obligation I have to fulfill."

"There's still Deuces."

"Maybe we'll get lucky before then."

She rushed over and hugged his head to her apron. "I'm not complaining, Marshal Green, but I sure like it when you're around."

His arm encircled her waist, and he returned her hug. "I agree, but right now, I have a job."

Burt found a captain's chair in the back of the stage office. He placed it a few feet from the passageway where the passengers coming off the Nogales stage would go by to get into the station's food service. Pedro sat on a crate of freight in the center of the room and nodded at his boss. If Taylor offered any resistance, he would be behind him.

The telegram said, "Taylor on the 8:10 stage." That was good enough not to let even Jack or Joe know much more information. Burt checked his pocket watch, comparing it to the one on the wall. The stage was due in Tucson four hours later, if it encountered no problems.

Eleven-thirty on both timepieces. He snapped the lid shut and replaced it in his vest pocket. It would not be long. Two rather matronly women with several parcels beside them on the bench were obviously waiting to take the northbound one. Both were talking rapidly and reminded him of old hens clucking.

Pedro came over and squatted down on his heels. "What will you do about One-Eye if he doesn't return soon?"

"I'm not concerned he hasn't returned yet. But if we have to, we can go down on the border and try to find him."

Pedro nodded and rose to his feet. He sauntered out

onto the porch and looked up and down the street. The bright light outside about blinded anyone who looked that way. On the other hand, coming inside might do the same to Taylor.

The thirty minutes passed slowly. At last, the trumpet of the guard could be heard to signal they were coming. Burt put away the jackknife he'd been cleaning his fingernails with.

The stage arrived in a clatter of wooden brake pads on iron-rimmed wheels and the driver's "Whoa" to the double team. Lathered and breathing hard, the horses stomped about as the puff of their dust swept inside the office.

"Tucson, folks," the driver said. "Be here thirty minutes and I'm leaving. You ain't ready to go with me, catch the next one. Be careful there, ma'am, that's a big step." The driver wearing a buckskin shirt helped a nice-looking woman down first.

Next came a grandmother, a wary-eyed man under a bowler hat, and a businessman in a brown suit. Around thirty, near six foot tall, he had broad shoulders and blond hair. That was Taylor. His man was coming off at the rear of the others, looking around as if he expected to meet someone. The notion made Burt feel more on edge—did he have henchmen to meet him?

Taylor came inside and followed the others. When he was ten steps away, Burt stood up.

"Joseph Taylor?"

"Yes—" The man blinked his blue eyes and frowned.

"Put your hands out. You are under arrest for robbery and murder."

"What—"

"Get those hands out!" Burt clamped the bracelet on Taylor's left hand and reached for the right.

Pedro guided Taylor's arm forward from behind, and the bracelets were locked in place. Burt removed a short-nosed .45 from Taylor's shoulder holster and brushed him down for any other weapons.

"You're making a big mistake, Marshal. I'm a man of God."

"I can't help it. I have a grand jury indictment for your arrest." With Pedro on the prisoner's left and him on his right, they headed for the front door.

"My wife—"

Burt wanted to say, "Which one?" but caught himself. "You will be at the U.S. commissioner's office. Then the Pima County jail."

"No," Taylor said with authority. "My wife, Jane, is in the restaurant. She needs to know what's happening."

"No tricks," Burt warned. The notion Taylor might have allies going to meet him concerned him—he knew the LDS church would try to bail him out immediately, but in the case of a murder warrant, they couldn't. "Pedro, go tell Mrs. Taylor in there that her husband has been arrested."

Pedro nodded and looked at Taylor.

"She's wearing a blue dress."

Burt watched Pedro disappear. Anxious to get this over with as smoothly as possible, he begrudged the seconds ticking away.

"Robber?" she said in a shrill voice, and ran over to him, looking in disbelief at the handcuffs on her husband's wrists.

"This is all some big mistake," Taylor said. "Contact Bishop Monroe here and tell him. He'll know what to do."

She nodded in agreement. Then she looked with concern at Burt. "What are the charges?"

"Murder," Burt said. "Excuse us, ma'am." He directed Taylor to the front door.

"Tell him to bring a lawyer, too," Taylor said over his shoulder. "You know, in an hour I'll be bonded out and on my way. You have nothing to charge me with."

"Grand jury felt there was. They don't bond out people on murder charges."

"All a waste of your time."

"Get on the buckboard seat. I will warn you one more time, should you attempt to escape, my deputy and I will shoot to kill."

Taylor laughed aloud. "Try to escape? No need. I'll be free in less time than you can snap your fingers."

Burt never gave him the satisfaction of an answer. He drove the team for the commissioner's office, and when they reached there, he directed the swaggering man into Lacey's office.

Marshal Downy and his new deputy, Tadd Higgins, both rose from their chairs.

"Well, is this Joseph Taylor?" Downy asked.

"Fresh off the Nogales stage," Burt said. "And he's all yours, Marshal."

"Guess your men are entitled to the reward. Drop by, and I'll see that they get it. Well, Taylor, nice of you to drop by."

"You men may not have jobs when this is over."

Downy shook his head and undid the cuffs. "Here, Burt. Well, Taylor, you'll be looking at snow out that Detroit prison window if they don't hang you."

Burt nodded to both men and gave a head toss to Pedro. The job of Taylor's incarceration belonged to Marshal Downy henceforth.

Burt and Pedro were outside and ready to get on the

buckboard, when a rig came racing down the street in a cloud of dust. Two red-faced men bounded out, and Burt could see Mrs. Taylor trying to recover her hat and get her clothing in place after the wild ride.

"You arrest Bishop Taylor?" the fattest one shouted.

"Yes," Burt said, ready to face the windbag. "I delivered him to U.S. Marshal Downy and the U.S. commissioner as per the federal grand jury instructions."

"This is a slap in the face of justice—"

Burt stepped up on the seat and shook his head warily. "Not in my book."

"Giddup," Burt said, and drove off with the smiling Pedro on the spring seat beside him. They left Red Face, the other blustering man, and the indignant Mrs. Taylor standing on the curb, as she fought with both hands to get her dress into place.

Chapter 27

THEY SPOKE OF OLD DAYS AND NEW ONES AT THE campfire. Chako and Mica had returned with word from San Carlos. Thirty to forty bucks wanted to join them. They did not know how many more in the far corners of the reservation wanted to ride with him, too.

Deuces looked into the blue flames eating at the pieces of oak. Too many. No way could he lead that many and stay away from officials. No way to provide food. No way to keep them in arms and ammo. No, they would need to be secret—and small numbers. He had managed to avoid all white men in Texas, even an Apache scout. But so many would leave too many tracks.

"Ten is all." He shook his head over any more. "There are hundreds of buffalo soldiers. They would track us down if we had so many."

"Fill my cup," he said to Deer Runs, who sat aside from the three men.

She rose and brought the enamel coffee pot, poured for him and the others. In the fire's light, the dark stripes where the riata struck her cheek showed. She said nothing, put the pot back, and resumed her place at the edge of the light.

"Come and talk to them," Chako said. "They want to eat and drink with you. And hear your stories. No one will tell a word about you coming, or they will cut their throats."

"Death," Mica said, and then nodded in solemn agreement.

"Why should I go up there?" Deuces asked, feeling they must make the reason good.

"Geronimo is gone, and all the real ones with him. We have old leaders who drink whiskey all the time and agree with the tribal police, who are bullies and would never be warriors in an Apache society. They swagger around in their uniforms and use rifle butts on anyone who challenges them."

Mica agreed.

"So," Chako said. "Come and tell them what it is like to be free."

"I will come, then, but we must act quickly, or someone else will know about it."

"We can be ready."

"In a week, then, I will meet one of you on the Gila. Be sure that no one knows. I will look for an eagle feather at the old outpost. It will be tied on a cottonwood limb. I see no feather, I will not come to the Gila."

"Good, you won't come by Fort Grant," Chako said, as if relieved to hear he would go east of Mount Graham and come in from that direction.

"What day counts?" Chako asked.

"Tomorrow is the first one."

"We must leave tonight, then." Both men jumped to their feet.

"The old place where we used to stomp on the Gila. It has many ways to escape from there," Chako said.

Deuces agreed. "Get them some food," he said to her. She rushed off in the night.

Both bucks were on their feet. They clapped each other on the arms. The deal was made, and he would come to talk to the ones who hated the white eyes and their resurrection.

In minutes, they were gone into the night. Deuces turned to look for her. She stood apart, wrapped in her blanket.

"We will go there in three days."

"Wear your best clothes," she said.

"Why?"

"So Ussen will know you when you meet him."

He studied her form for a long moment. She knew nothing. He smiled to himself. It would be good to speak with old friends—his exploits must be reviewed in his mind to have stories ready for them.

She bent over and put another log on the fire. "Better be sure to wear them."

Chapter 28

THE FRESH CANVAS SHEETING WAS LAID ACROSS THE roof. Obregón was hauling up buckets of mud from Juan to plaster it down with. On the ground, Burt operated the hoe, mixing the next batch, and Angela poured more water in the boat for him. The job was arduous, but Burt felt satisfied the effort would solve the roof's leak problem.

"Well, see what you end up doing when you marry a woman with a ranch?" Angela teased him.

He laughed and winked at Juan. "She thinks this is hard work."

"Plenty hard for me," Pedro said from the roof, where he and Obregón were spreading the sealer over the material with trowels and floats. Juanita brought them fresh water from the well at breaks.

Juanita and Estrella were also barbecuing a fat calf.

The smell of the mesquite smoke caught Burt's nose every once and a while.

"Rider coming," Pedro said. "He's not wearing a hat. I bet it's One-Eye. He have your good roan horse?"

"Yes," Burt said, trying to see.

"Not quitting work," Angela said. "We have to finish this job."

"Boy," Pedro said. "She's a worse slave driver than my own wife."

Everyone laughed.

Burt laid down the hoe and went to the front gate when the Apache dismounted. The dried salt on the roan's chest and the dust caked on his legs told lots about the distance the roan had covered.

"How have you been?" he asked One-Eye, as the weary scout dropped to his haunches and shook his head.

"Good. Got big news for you."

"What's that?"

"Deuces is coming to big meeting on San Carlos."

"What for?"

"They say he will lead the Apaches who want him as their chief."

"When?" Burt asked as he undid the cinch on the roan.

"Soon."

"Where's he now?" Burt gave the roan's reins to Juan. "Put him up, and feed him some grain after he cools down."

"Sierra Madres."

"When will he come north?"

One-Eye shrugged. "Soon, maybe."

"We need to notify the army." Burt looked off to the south and chewed on his lower lip. Whom should he report this information to?

"He sees the army, he won't come."

Pedro nodded, standing with his arms folded over his chest. "He gets any sign of detection, he'll flee back down there. Army units would spook him. Besides, by himself, he could sneak around most of them."

"How could we intercept him, then, if he's coming from Mexico?" Burt said, looking at the Apache for an idea.

"If he comes down the Sulphur Valley, someone might see him, and on the east side of the Chiricahuas the same thing. But there is an ancient trail on the spine he might use—or he could stick close to the base and make better time."

"Which one is he most likely to use?"

"If we watch the spring at Erickson's ranch and the ancient trail on top, we maybe catch him."

"When's he supposed to come north?" Pedro asked.

"Soon."

"He could already be up there?" Burt asked.

One-Eye shook his head to dismiss the notion. "They need time to get those young bucks word of the meeting."

"You think he'll try it?"

"They went to offer him to be chief of all the Apaches. He can't turn that down."

Burt agreed. No way Deuces was likely to deny such an honor or the obligation. Three men to guard thousands of acres of tough terrain for the passage of one man. They'd have to get very lucky. Worse than that, they had no time to waste.

"What can I do to get you ready?" Angela asked.

"Pack some jerky, dried apples, food that won't perish. We better get some horses ready. This roan won't make it."

"We going to ride there?" Pedro asked.

"No. We'll load our horses on the train at Tucson, jump them out at Wilcox, and we can be there by nightfall."

Pedro nodded his approval with a smile. "What should I do?"

"Well, get provisions. One-Eye may need some rest—"

"No, me plenty good." The solemn-faced scout dismissed his concern.

"Pedro, you ride ahead and have the depot master get us a car on an eastbound to load the horses into. We'll be coming on your heels. Tell him this is an emergency."

"What if—"

"Tell him it's for the safety of the entire territory."

"What if he—"

"Show him your badge. But don't mention Deuces's name; that will only stir up a hornet's nest."

Pedro took off at a lope for the corrals and a horse. Burt watched him, thinking of all they would need. Three rifles, ammunition, spy glasses. He would have to pick up some items in Tucson.

"You had any food lately?" he asked the scout.

"Some."

"Come on. Angela will have something." Burt turned and shouted to Obregón on the roof. "Can you finish that without us?"

The man's brown face appeared, and he smiled. "Oh yes, Señor. I already figured on that."

"You're a good man, Obregón."

"Gracias, and God be with you, Señor." Then the man disappeared behind the wall.

Burt hurried for the house, waving his scout on. Get One-Eye some food, pack a few personal items. He wouldn't bother wearing his suit. Canvas pants, a thick shirt. It could get cool up there in the higher elevations of the Chiricahuas, especially at night. No telling where he'd end up waiting. A hurried-up plan that might work. He still had doubts about their final success. Mostly the insurmountable area the three must cover. And the time factor.

"Be careful," Angela said privately to him in the hallway.

"Yes. I should be back for your party. I'm sorry—"

"If you aren't here, I'll tell everyone they'll have to wait a while longer to meet my busy husband."

"I'll be back here." He bent over and kissed her on the lips. A quick hug, and he sighed, listening to the sounds of the men working on the roof. "Good thing you have Obregón and Juan," he said, and kissed her lightly.

"And you." Her smile warmed him to his heart.

Five hours later, the rock and sway of the express car made the horses restless. But not nearly as restless as the fidgety mail clerk armed with a scoop shovel, keeping a watchful eye on the horses and any effort they made toward releasing their bowels.

Burt was amused. Obviously, that depot master took Pedro at his word. The fastest way to get to Wilcox was the afternoon passenger train. Without time to hitch to anything else, he slid back the car door, issued the mail clerk a shovel, and waved the three men and their horses into the yellow-sided car.

"No time for arguments, these men are federal marshals, and they are only going as far as Wilcox."

It would be close to dark by the time they reached

there. Burt kept wondering if this was a fool's chase or if they would be successful. Deuces proved to be such a ghostlike figure in Texas. He didn't want to recall that senseless shooting of the girl and all the confusion of the stampede of the horses. The girl dying in his arms, still trying to save Deuces from capture. No one would probably ever know the whole story. Her devotion impressed him the most.

"We coming to Wilcox?" he asked the shovel-bearing clerk.

"I think so." The man had a look of despair on his perspiring face.

"We need to unload on the platform. Will this car be close to it? I don't want these horses having to make a big leap out of here and get hurt. We need them."

"I'll signal the conductor."

"And we need to unload quickly."

"Yes. I want that, too."

The engine whistle blew for the first crossing west of town, and the clerk put down the shovel, slid the door back, and went to waving.

"Get ready," Burt said to Pedro, who held the reins.

One-Eye, who had slept most of the way on some mail sacks, stood up and stretched.

"First time I ever took a shortcut with horses on a train," the Apache said, amused about it.

"May not be the last," Burt said, taking the reins to Brown, a powerful bay horse from the ranch string. Angela's late husband kept several good horses—for that, he was grateful.

"I sure hope so," the clerk said. "You guys after bank robbers?"

"Yeah," Burt said as the train's wheels screeched steel

on steel and the train stopped. He could see they were beside the platform.

"Sorry, folks," he said, and led Brown out of the car parting the wide-eyed onlookers and people ready to board, so he and his posse could pass through them.

Mounted, they headed south, leaving the train depot, curious onlookers, and the shovel bearer behind.

"Good thing your horse was the only one crapped in his car," One-Eye said as they loped past the adobe jacals and wide-eyed naked children for the desert beyond. To their right, the playas shined like oceans. Barely inches deep, the large shallow lakes without any outlet made the arid land look blessed with water.

"What will we guard?" Burt asked.

"One watch the big spring. The other the ancient trail. I will scout for any signs."

"Good," Burt said, and they hurried southward. Across the valley, the bloody Dragoon Mountains looked afire in the blazing sunset.

Long past dark, they made camp in a live oak and cottonwood grove a few miles from the mouth of the canyon.

"If we leave Pedro to watch the spring, how do I get up to the ancient trail?" Burt asked.

"I can go up there," Pedro offered as they chewed on their jerky supper.

Burt shook his head. "If One-Eye learns anything, you'll be easier to get hold of down here. Besides, I want to see that crest again. Been a few years."

"You know the trail up there?" One-Eye asked.

"Just follow the canyon above the spring, that will lead you up the canyon?"

"You will need to leave your horse."

"Why don't you ride up there with me and bring him back? Then he won't be in the way, nor will Deuces spot him."

"What if you need a horse?" Pedro asked, concerned.

"I'll have to walk, or one of you can bring me one."

"Be a good way," One-Eye grunted. "If he comes to the spring, he will expect some extra horses. Everyone uses it."

"Sounds dangerous. Up there alone and no horse." Pedro shook his head in disapproval.

"It'll work," Burt promised him. "A few hours' sleep, and we need to get in place."

Before dawn, they rode past the dark ranch house and entered the canyon. Stiff live oak brushed Burt's legs, and the ride up the tortuous trail in the starlight made for slow travel, but by the time the sun came up over New Mexico and the Panatello Mountains, he would be in place.

He yawned big and picked Brown's head up when he stumbled on a rock in the trail. The pathway presented close quarters through thick pines and house-size boulders. Many times, save for the rush of the small watercourse below them, he had the feeling of being in a cave. Then they emerged into the silver light that shone on the towering eroded upright pipes across the canyon. This was a pretty place in the daytime. He looked after the rump of One-Eye's horse and shook his head at the night wind—getting cooler up there, too.

Despite Burt's view of the golden rays reaching across the land, little warmth came with sunup. Left alone on the crest in a grove of young pines, he scoped the country. One-Eye had suggested they not take their horses up to the crown and leave any tracks to spook Deuces. Before he left, the scout had checked the small trail that came from the south.

"He has not passed here."

"If he's using this way," Burt said, and grinned at the Apache.

"I would come this way," One-Eye said.

"Good. I'll watch out and be sure not to shoot you."

They both laughed.

Then Burt was left alone. One-Eye took the horses back. Under a blanket for warmth and facing belly-down, he scoped the ridge line with his new glasses. He gave his old telescope to One-Eye to use. Some small birds frittered in the limbs above his head. A doe and her spotted fawn crossed the top and grazed around undisturbed on various shrubs. At last, they went off the east side toward the San Pedro drainage.

His canteen water tasted cold. Mid-morning, he saw something coming from the south. A paint horse, bobbing its head. Good-looking animal. The binoculars in his hand, his heart stopped.

He spotted the familiar face from the posters of the handsome Deuces. A grim set in his eyes, he rode the paint. Burt watched him turn in the saddle and speak to someone following him. A woman. He focused the glasses better and saw two mules under packs come into view. He needed Deuces to get much closer. At the range of one-fourth mile, his Winchester would only raise some dust and spook him away.

Burt dried his right hand on the side of his pants and then took up the rifle. He checked the chamber and found it loaded. Then, taking a rest for his elbow to support the long gun, he looked through the iron sights. Something wrong? Deuces had ridden to the west among some great boulders. To get a good shot was impossible with all the mountain mahogany and juniper between them.

His heart rate sped up. He wanted to get on his feet and rush the deal. But that would only spook Deuces. The sensible thing was to wait. No way Deuces could suspect he was up there hiding. He tried to space his breathing. A new headache pierced the top of his head with a drumlike pattern. Must be the elevation doing that to him.

His mouth dry, he tried to draw some saliva. A case of heartburn hit his chest, and he held on to his patience. Then he saw the dish face of the paint coming out of the evergreen boughs, and he knew to get ready.

Deuces, hatless, with an eagle feather twisting and rapping the side of his head in the wind, held a rifle in the crook of his arm. He wore a new-looking white blouse, and his brown legs were bare. Some gold coins hung in a necklace around his neck.

Not his style to take a prisoner like this—from ambush—not his at all, but if he issued a command or showed himself, Deuces would either run off or start shooting. This was the only option left. The territory couldn't afford another Apache uprising with the loss of lives and property it would incur. Nor could the rest of Deuces's people stand to be in prisons like those where Geronimo and the others were held in Florida.

His aim in place, he drew a breath and held it. Steady. He squeezed the trigger off. The black gunsmoke blinded him for a second, before the wind swept it away. He rose to his knees, levering in another round. But Deuces was hit hard with his arms in the air, his rifle flew away, and the paint spooked out from underneath him.

In an instant, Burt was on his feet. He raced across the rocky ground between them. For a moment, he wondered if she would take up arms against him, but the young Apache woman on horseback looked too fear-stricken to shoot him or even ride away with the two pack mules.

Out of breath, Burt viewed the crumpled body, thirty feet down the steep mountainside. His arms flung wide, blood covered his chest, and his mouth was open. "He's dead," Burt said finally, and sat down the rifle. Then, at the snort of a mule, he whirled to look at her.

Bugeyed and her white knuckles grasping the mule lead ropes, she nodded in agreement.

"I'll need one of those mules," he said, satisfied the man that he'd sought so hard and long lay dead under the rim.

"I'll buy this mule," he said to her, taking the lead away from her when she didn't answer him.

Woodenly, she agreed.

"You want this gear?" he asked, looking over the panniers filled with clothing and cooking pans. In seconds, he set the heavy canvas bags off the cross bucks and on the ground.

She sat frozen on her horse.

"I'll leave them for you," he said, and took the mule over to the edge. Deuces's crumpled body lay sprawled on his back. His head pointed downhill. From the look in his open eyes, there was little doubt in Burt's mind the Apache was dead. He hitched the mule to a sapling to save him wandering off, then took cautious side steps down the steep slope until he could see the bloody wound in the scout's chest. Death came swiftly, he decided, and looked up to see if there was any threat. Nothing but the mule's face against the brilliant azure sky. He shivered—it was finally over.

He labored to drag the limp form up the hillside. He needed to take the body in, get it positively identified and then buried. Finally, after a tug-and-pull war, he had Deuces's corpse strapped across the pack saddle. He led the mule over to where the woman sat on a rock, moaning a death song.

Numb-acting, she stared off to the east.

"Can I help you?" he asked, counting out twenty dollars for the mule.

She never looked at him, not even when he forced the money into her hand. She only sat there, shaking her head and moaning in sorrow over her loss. Burt felt sorry for her, but he still had a long hike down the mountain ahead. She'd have to find her own way back—a shame the paint horse ran away.

Taking a deep breath and a sigh, he looked a last time across the yellow grassy valley far below and turned to gaze downhill from the trailhead. Long ways down to the ranch, he'd better get going. Still had to round up his two deputies. He looked out through the pines at the far-off red Dragoon Mountains. He'd better get back in time for that party she had planned on for so long.

The music of the Mexican band carried outside along with the laughter and noise of the large gathering in the house. Burt stepped out onto the porch. Estrella told him that a stranger was out there who wished to talk to him.

"Burt Green." He stuck out his hand to the man dressed in cowboy gear standing on the porch

"Tom Horn, Marshal," the man said. His grasp was firm, and he met Burt's look.

"Good to finally meet you. What can I do for you, sir? We're having a party. Could I invite you in?"

"No, I was just passing through. I needed a little information."

"Certainly. What's that?"

"Where did they bury Deuces? He meant a lot to me. We worked as scouts together, but I guess you knew all about that."

"Yes, I'm sorry it didn't work out better. He's buried in the Methodist church cemetery in Wilcox."

"Thanks. Good to meet you."

They shook hands again, and Horn was gone.

"Burton, who was that?" Angela asked, standing in the lighted doorway.

"Tom Horn." He looked into the inky night where the man had disappeared.

"Did you invite him in?"

"I did, but he said he was only passing through."

"What did he want?"

"Wanted to know where they had buried Deuces."

"Why?"

"Guess he meant a lot to Horn, is all I can say." He shook his head to try to dismiss the whole thing.

"Come back inside. You're missing all the fun."

He smiled at his lovely wife and agreed. No sense missing any more.

Three months later, he was reading the latest issue of the *Tucson Times*'s front-page headlines: "Mormon Bishop Taylor Found Not Guilty." Burt already knew the partial jury made up of Mormons had turned Taylor loose. The notion left him worked up until another article caught his eye. Body of a renegade Apache scout strangely dug up and the corpse removed. The grave of the notorious army scout Deuces was found open and empty by a church official when he arrived to prepare for services.

Burt dropped the paper in his lap and looked off toward Mount Lemon and the Catalinas, knowing full well that somewhere out there, Tom Horn had replanted Deuces's body with his ancestors.

One year later they were in the divorce courts, and his wife ungraciously informed a reporter that her soon-to-be ex-husband had brought a buddy along on their honeymoon and spent more time playing Ping-Pong with him than he did in his wife's company.

Clearly, she was impugning his masculinity in the eyes of the public, who probably believed there was something seriously wrong with him. After all, a "real man" would have been solely occupied with and jealously guarding his wife and would have had an ecstatic time spending hours in bed making love, interspersed only with sips of champagne and elegant meals, a few brief shopping sprees and moments in the sun or on the streets posturing for the envious world.

How many countless other "macho warrior" males have been hauntingly obsessed by feelings of inadequacy and self-doubt in similar situations because they did not experience with their women the kind of ecstasy and satisfaction they had expected on their honeymoon?

Because of their different psychological makeups, in the moment-to-moment process of being together the "macho warrior" man and his "earth mother" woman have precious little besides their fantasies of what ought to be to sustain an interesting, stimulating or pleasurable interaction. Many of these couples, in fact, could hardly make it through an afternoon alone together without feeling bored, yet they expect to maintain a lifetime of stimulating, enjoyable interaction.

The more gender polarized they are, in fact, in terms of his being "all man" and her being "all woman," the less of a psychological basis they have for relating to each other, because *they are opposite sides of a coin.* She is everything he is not, and vice versa. Consequently, they can only drive themselves into self-hating, hurtful and angry tailspins because they do not experience what they anticipated and were told by others they were going to. If indeed they remain together as a couple, the high-energy bursts of their initial romantic feelings will inevitably be transformed into deliberate, often painful efforts to be "nice" and "understanding" with each other. The relationship becomes a kind of stalemate, a painful, passionless compromise, as these couples try and force into existence what cannot exist authentically and naturally under their gender orientations and rigid role-playing interactions.

What is really often happening behind their closed doors was suggested in the following account written by a woman working in a model middle-class area of Los Angeles.

> For the past several years I have worked as a technician in a pharmacy in the San Fernando Valley. The neighborhood is middle-class and the customers are smiling, polite, clean-scrubbed professionals. Most of them visually fit the clean-cut American stereotype of USC graduates with season tickets to the Dodger games. In short, they are some of the "nicest" families in the Valley.
>
> When I first began working at the pharmacy, I was struck by the fact that although the volume of work was heavy (filling about 150 prescriptions a day), there were only half a dozen prescriptions a day for antibiotics, antihistamines, or oral contraceptives. The remainder were for mild tranquilizers, antidepressants, codeine with aspirin, sleeping pills, muscle relaxers, amphetamines, and codeine cough syrup. The amount of codeine cough syrup dispensed was staggering and the only real rival to Valium and Librium; however, the customer rarely appeared to have colds or to be ill in any way.
>
> I then began to notice that the heaviest work days were invariably Mondays, especially the Mondays after a long three or four day weekend. The refill business on Mondays often tripled our new business. Customers, both men and women, would begin calling as soon as we opened for Valium refills that they could pick up on their way to work; or with requests to call their doctor to ask for double the amount of their last prescription. When I mentioned this to the attending pharmacist, he laughed and said that the Monday "emergencies" were nothing compared to summer vacations.
>
> When vacations began in June, the Friday business picked up to the Monday level as families prepared to go camping, to Mexico, or to Europe for three weeks.

ble interaction. His energy will be sapped by his unconscious resentment, boredom and sense of futility about changing this pattern. Her "femininity," once a delight, will become instead a heavy weight.

Likewise, his dominant, performance-oriented, emotionally unexpressive, rational and hyperactive orientation will become an annoyance and an irritation to her, and she, too, will begin to feel resentment over the very qualities that drew her to him initially. She will begin to feel pushed around, invisible, taken for granted and exasperated by his inability to communicate.

The lethal aspect of this relationship for the male is that, because of his dominant, performance orientation, which makes him feel responsible for what goes on, he will probably see himself as the "heavy" when the communication and relationship break down. She, in turn, may be only too willing to corroborate this image of himself as being the responsible party when things go wrong. This interplay was well expressed by a recently divorced woman who was looking back on her marriage in a mood of warped sentimentality. She commented, "It's a little like the battered child syndrome. You never find a battered child that does not want to be back with its parents, because they are the only parents it has. I just have very much this feeling."[20]

It is easy to see how the "macho warrior" in these relationships, married to a traditional "earth mother," would be both chronically guilt-ridden and driven to distraction by his restlessness, boredom and a chronic sense of being inadequate. The higher the pedestal he has chosen to put his "earth mother" on, the more vulnerable he will be to self-hate in comparison with her and to shock, confusion and panic when she emerges as a person different from what he had imagined her to be when she no longer colludes with his fantasy image of her.

These relationships are also lethal for him because, in the end, he can only emerge as the pathetic one, feeling himself a failure, unworthy of love. The relationship that began with him as the dominant, influential force and with her as the submissive, helpless and childlike person will see her grow into strength and independence, while he progressively crumbles.

The greatest tragedy here is that many of her growth changes may come at a time when he is least capable of benefiting from them—or at a time when he is feeling most vulnerable in terms of his career and self-confidence. Consequently, when his wife announces she wants out, the impact on this man, in his forties, perhaps, and fearing a life decline, will be devastating.

Consider the woman who informed her husband that she wanted out after twenty-five years of marriage and five children.

> "She told him she had played the game by all the rules for long enough," her attorney said. "She figured that at the age of 46 she wanted out of her \$200,000 house, out of the business–cocktail party circuit and out of a life-style that looked like nothing more than a well-oiled treadmill toward death. She was very determined about it, very much together. She gave custody of the children to her husband and moved to a commune in Arizona."[21]

The "macho warrior"–"earth mother" interaction only serves to reinforce and exaggerate the most self-hating and self-destructive aspects of his style. Her "purity" and "sub-servience" will intensify his sense of guilt and animalism. Her unwillingness to confront, assert and engage will make her look like the peaceful, self-denying one and make him appear to be the "heavy." In his desperate attempt to prove himself worthy, he will give vent to the most regressive, irrational and self-destructive parts of himself as he overworks, overeats, constantly competes to prove himself superior, isolates himself and develops a compulsively active style to keep himself busy and to prove himself ambitious and productive. It will be a relationship composed of extreme mood swings, denial of feelings, boredom, self-numbing through alcohol and excess food consumption leading to weight problems, nervousness and tension. The feelings between him and her will swing from sentimentality ("Aren't we lucky to have each other?") to hateful and murderous recrimination ("Why don't you drop dead!"), with very little that is real or pleasurable in between.

In abandoning this model of the "macho warrior"–"earth mother" relationship, a man will have nothing to lose but his fantasies and his guilt. His "earth mother" image of her, while temporarily reassuring, comforting and even exhilarating, ultimately dwarfs him and brings out his most self-destructive tendencies. "Earth mother" is a powerful, seductive fantasy, and the process of becoming unhooked from its grip is the greatest challenge he faces in the man-woman relationship. His potential, however, once he is unhooked, is incredible, for in the "macho warrior"–"earth mother" relationship he is a pathetically vulnerable, out-of-touch creature, functioning at the bottom of his human potential. Once released from it, he could move toward full expressiveness, and the honest struggle for growth, mutual relationships, joyful sexuality and a self-caring, fluid style.

As a released person with recognized feelings and needs and with an attitude of guiltless self-care, he will come to the male-female relationship expecting to be stretched by it, not to hide behind it. He will expect to learn from his partner, to share responsibility equally so that he avoids being sucked into the debilitating trap of constantly being the strong man—provider—protector—decision maker.

As a self-caring person, he will not be able to tolerate a relationship with a woman who lets herself be a trophy which he can show off to the world, a tagalong companion to his activities or a person who is not in touch with and expressive of her own autonomously originated sexuality, aggression and need for independence.

The acid test of any future relationship will be whether it frees him to be more creative and expressive than before, rather than constricting him and smothering him under the pressures of performance, lopsided responsibility and guilt. He will see through the romantic stereotype of the "macho warrior"–"earth mother" relationship that he has been taught is the sanctified one but which is, in reality, an involvement based on each gender's incompleteness. As a "macho warrior," he is psychologically but an unborn fetus who must see through the fantasies and stereotypes that have seduced, dwarfed and chained him in order to be born, lest he be destroyed in their devitalizing grip.

10. Sex Distortions, Misinterpretations, Myths and Stereotypes About Men

The seemingly unending quest for new information on sex, sex techniques, the physiology of sex and the latest "secrets" of sex appeal, arousal, control and performance testifies to a sub-liminal awareness that there is something missing, something elusive, something more or something wrong. Or it reflects the existence of some critical evasion, conscious or unconscious, that requires constant covering over and deflection by the illusion of search for the great aphrodisiac or sex liberator that will send us all to orgasmic heaven.

Books written on the subject of sex tend to fall into four major categories:

1) *Permission-giving books* that inform the reader that anything that feels good is O.K. as long as no one innocent is hurt.

2) *Technique manuals* that inform about the "latest and best ways to do it."

3) *"Plumbing" manuals* that blueprint the physiology of the sex organs and how the various parts of the body react and are affected during sexual intercourse.

4) *Clinical books* that describe and offer solutions for "sex problems."

As with hypochondriacs, whose restless, continual and obsessive preoccupation with their health drives them from doctor to doctor and from nostrum to latest "cure," all in order to maintain their belief that, indeed, they have a unique, mysterious ailment—a belief that allows them to evade other more threatening emotional issues—it seems that the eternal obsession with sex information facilitates the evasion of some very powerful and threatening psychological awareness. I believe that the awareness being evaded is this:

Every sexual response, no matter how seemingly insignificant, or under what circumstance, is a true statement of feeling and reaction toward one's partner, as well as being a revealing reflection of oneself as a person. Indeed, it is perhaps the most uncontrollable, powerful, clear and uncontaminated reflection of the overall feeling tone and quality of that relationship and of one's true self. It therefore always threatens to expose truths that one or both people would rather avoid.

Most "sex problems," I believe, arise from a situation in which at least one of the two people who are having sex is resisting or not totally involved but is unwilling or unable to get in touch with and communicate these reservations, resistances and negative feelings because it would risk uncovering issues and emotions that might upset the balance of the relationship or jeopardize the person's desired image. Unless one has totally depersonalized sexual encounters and transformed them into impersonal, mechanical ones in which the partner is simply an interchangeable object or outlet for sexual desire or tension, *each sexual response must be seen as pair-specific*. That means that each response is a unique and personal reaction toward one's partner. Just as one does not have the identical reactions toward any two people, neither are sexual responses the same from person to person. Rather, each is unique to one's partner at the time.

Specifically, the man who is impotent with his wife may be a premature ejaculator with a prostitute, be very slow in ejaculating in a new love affair, in which he feels insecure and needs to "stay inside" as long as possible for reassurance, and be in perfect control with a partner where the relationship is comfortable, mutual, caring, pleasurable and open.

Furthermore, with one woman a man might be detached and basically cold, while with another he will be aggressive, rough and urgent. With a third he might be clinging and insecure, while with another still he might be delicate and exquisitely sensitive in his touch and timing. Likewise, with his wife he might turn away and fall asleep almost immediately after intercourse, while with a new lover he may continue to reach out and touch and have the high energy provided by the adrenaline racing through his body.

For the alive man, aware of women as people rather than objects, *each* reaction will be seen by him as a unique reflection and expression of himself that is making a clear-cut statement about his feelings toward her and himself in the relationship and is at the same time a response to whatever *she* is communicating to him.

Evasion of the profound truths that one's sexual response conveys and the inability and fear of confronting the emotional and interpersonal issues that exist in a relationship has, I believe, resulted in a situation and cultural climate in which most people have focused on and become obsessed with "sexual problems" and "symptoms" rather than emphasizing the underlying interpersonal meanings and truths being expressed by each response.

The medical and psychiatric professions have been given the role of interpersonal and emotional launderers, and they stand ready with a host of diagnostic labels and syndromes to provide people sanctioned shelter from their inner experience. These medical rationalizations allow individuals to avoid the painful and disruptive process of confronting their psychological and emotional selves and avoid dealing authentically with their relationships by giving the threatening response an "illness" label. This label allows its owner psychological immunity, the special privileged and protected status and even the concern and deference one gets for being sick and "working on" one's problem.

Medicine, for example, by attributing the major or primary cause of the "problem" to a vitamin or hormone deficiency, fatigue, performance pressure, alcohol or even early trauma, provides permission for the evasion of what most people wish to evade, which is a here-and-now encounter with their deepest feelings and responses toward their partner.

A woman, for example, whose vagina is tight and resistant to opening up for her husband, even when there is no physical disorder, might be given the diagnostic label of "vaginismus." By turning over the "problem" to a physician, she removes the threat of having to take responsibility for the statement her body is making toward her husband, which is a powerful NO! One such woman, known to the writer, had been "tight" from her honeymoon on with her husband and had even submitted to surgical procedures, which still didn't completely alleviate her "problem." Toward the end of her marriage, when she began engaging in affairs, she was pleasantly surprised to discover how wide open and welcoming her vagina was to her new lovers.

Along with contemporary sexual liberation has come an ever-increasing incidence of "sexual disorders" such as impotence and non-orgasmic response in women. This is *not,* I believe, because sex has resulted in increased pressure to perform, but rather because it has become more difficult to evade the sexual encounter in a relationship and the truths it reveals. With increased sexual awareness and focus, underlying psychological and emotional truths threaten to surface. Consequently, medical rationalizations are welcomed as sanctioned evasions, and we hear of "impotence plagues," or the large numbers of non-orgasmic women who continue to be so during intercourse in spite of a more permissive climate.

THE MALE "NOT ME" PHENOMENON IN SEX

The traditionally conditioned male is so disconnected from the emotions attached to his sexual response that when he is not performing sexually as he believes he should be, he disclaims his response by denying responsibility. Specifically, he curses his penis for not performing, as he sweats and strains and informs his partner that *he* really wants to, even though something seems to be wrong with *it.* He is relating to his penis as if it were a piece of machinery that has become faulty but that has no connection with his feelings about or desire for his partner.

Because he does not perceive his penis as an expression of his feelings but rather as a separate mechanism with a will of its own, when it "malfunctions," his inclination is to get "it" fixed as quickly as possible. During those times of "impotence," in which a man has been described by Dr. Helen Singer Kaplan, author of the acclaimed book *The*

New Sex Therapy, as "almost unbearably anxious, frustrated and humiliated,"[1] he is open to any kind of advice or "cure," so long as it offers the hope or promise of *instant* recovery, be it vitamins, injections, hypnosis, sexual "secrets" from the East, pornography, sex paraphernalia or special medications. His masculinity is at stake, and he cannot afford the luxury of any process that will not immediately allow him to recoup his threatened image. He would probably even submit himself to surgical procedures if the physician promised to "cure" his rebellious penis. In general, he will be receptive to any remedy that allows him to avoid probing his inner experience and which might yield immediate results of the kind he feels he must have in order to reinforce his belief that he is the victim of a foreign malady. In that way he does not have to confront the possibility that his penis's reaction is *his* reaction, and that when it malfunctions, it is making statements that he does not want to or cannot explore and deal with. He will therefore experience a great sense of urgency for a rapid resolution of the difficulty.

The traditional male-female sexual interaction, in which the male has taken primary responsibility for the initiation and success of the sexual experience, has also meant that he will carry the burden of the so-called problems to a significantly greater extent.

This was the conclusion of three researchers reporting in the *American Journal of Psychiatry* on the distinctions between male and female invested partners in sexual disorders. Because the male has the greater responsibility in the role of lover, he also carries a greater burden of failure. Thus, it seems that men suffer as much psychologically from their partner's sexual difficulties as from their own. Women, on the other hand, appear not to "experience significant levels of conflict arising from feelings of responsibility for their partner's dysfunctional status," the researchers reported.[2]

At the suggestion that his "problem" might have some connection with his feelings rather than being physically caused (which only about 10 percent are, according to Masters and Johnson), he is liable to feel threatened, impatient and even enraged and to search for a doctor who will confirm his belief that, indeed, it is a medical problem.[3]

A thirty-five-year-old, recently divorced scientist came to my office for help because he had not been able to have an erection with his last two girl friends. He wanted me to "fix it." When I told him that I would be doing him a disservice by just helping him get his erection back quickly without his understanding and coming to terms with the feelings that were producing his reaction, he agreed to try psychotherapy. After three sessions and with still no erection, he became impatient and announced that he would see a physician instead, because he felt sure that he was suffering from an organic disorder. His whole orientation, life attitude and stance of being in control, approaching every problem cerebrally, not depending on others or acknowledging vulnerability or helplessness were being threatened. His anxiety was so great, in fact, and he felt so terrorized by his non-cooperating penis, which put his masculine image in jeopardy, that he could not afford the luxury of looking at himself as a person. Bizarre as it seems, he would have felt greatly relieved if he could have even linked his "impotence" to a serious disease. At least then it would not have been his "fault" or a reflection on his masculine image and he would not have had to take responsibility for his reaction or go about the painful process of becoming self-aware in order to deal with it.

"NORMAL" MALE FUNCTIONING

In light of the traditional processes of male conditioning, it is senseless, misleading and even destructive to speak of such a thing as normal male functioning, much less the super-stud image many men would like to have and believe they could live up to. The "normal" male on whom statistics are based, struggling to live up to the image and standards he has introjected, is a master of camouflage and evasion and also probably has a female partner who, out of love, conditioning or the desire to "build up his ego," has disowned her own sexual needs and rhythms to confirm his fantasies of sexual prowess by telling him what he wants to hear. So long as he provides her with security, she will provide him with sex and all the expressions of ecstasy he needs to affirm his masculinity. His being out of touch with his own feelings and sensibilities, coupled with a great need to believe, will make it possible for her to tell him anything he needs to hear. He doesn't want to know differently.

It is also interesting to speculate on the extent to which the sexual-superman image has been *unconsciously* reinforced by the woman. That is, by supporting his fantasies of being a wonderful lover, he will become uncomfortable, embarrassed, fearful of rejection and eager to redeem himself when inevitably he is no longer able to live up to the sexual-superman image, be it one month or several years later. Then, when she responds gently and lovingly to "his" problem, he'll become more attached and grateful for her "understanding." In effect she has become the powerful partner, able to control him by being "nice" when his self-hate and inability to live up to the superman image are causing him to anticipate ridicule.

THE MALE IN SEXUAL JEOPARDY

The traditionally conditioned male must be sexually in jeopardy because his entire early conditioning process creates the basis for him to become a psychological stranger to himself and his sexual responses.

1) His emotions are largely repressed. He is unable to read or express his feelings, much less act on them. This emotional estrangement makes it equally impossible for him to read his partner accurately. For example, there are many men who have lived under the illusion that their women were highly satisfied and orgasmic when, in fact, they were faking their responses to please the man. Often, even when the relationship was over, he harbored the delusion that she would return because "nobody can satisfy her like I can, and as soon as she finds that out she'll come crawling back."

2) From early boyhood on, his sensuality is repressed. Hugging, kissing, touching, stroking, being close and en-

gaging in body play were not considered masculine. Indulgence in them, in fact, made him suspect of being a "sissy." Consequently, as an adult he approaches sex as a goal-oriented activity, rather than a playful, sensual interchange in which the process of lovemaking is the major source of pleasure and satisfaction.

3) He is pressured by the continual compulsion to prove his masculinity through performance, and the proving *never* ends. It is final-exam time every time.

When he describes what for him was a great sexual experience, he tends to talk about how many orgasms he was able "to give" the woman and "how long" he was able to maintain his erection. The degree of his satisfaction is correlated to the success of his performance more than anything else. Sooner or later the performance compulsion will push him to participate or "try" even when he's not turned on, because, in his mind, a man is ready whenever a woman is. When his performance falters, the anxiety begins and a downward performance cycle is set in motion. Performers are winners or losers, heroes or bums, and "a miss is as good as a mile." Losing is inevitable sooner or later, and then he will be flooded with self-doubt and self-hate.

4) The more traditional the man, the greater will be his tendency to put "his" woman on a pedestal when he "falls in love," to attribute Madonna-like qualities and virtues to her and to perceive her as fragile, sensitive and to an extent an untouchable being. She is, in his eyes, beyond the bounds of the "animallike" impulses that he feels. He will greatly subdue any aggressive or even assertive impulse on his part, and he will be careful not to confront her specifically with information about what turns him on or turns him off for fear of offending or hurting her. He will also have great difficulty saying no if he thinks she desires him, even when he is not excited. In general, he will tend to paralyze himself with his self-conscious protectiveness of her and his overreaction to his own "animalism."

On the other side of the coin, he will unconsciously inhibit *her* sexual expressiveness by his indirect messages that convey his fantasy of her as pure, angelic and unlike all other women. Her own tendency to be sexually passive, based on her conditioning, will thus be reinforced, and she will be highly reluctant to be expressive, active and assertively sexual for fear of disturbing and disillusioning him in regard to this fantasy of her as ethereal.

When resentment or disappointment arises on either side, neither he nor she will be prone to talk about it. Rather, these feelings will tend to be suppressed and denied, and therefore matters will get worse.

5) He tends to choose a wife or long-term lover on the basis of "shoulds." The "right" woman for him is one whom his mother and his friends and business associates will approve of as being an appropriate partner who is "worthy" of being his lifelong partner. The choice is primarily a cerebral one, the woman who best fits the traditional image, and he will then try and force his body to respond with equal enthusiasm. However, his body may resist the non-sensually satisfying choice. This will be manifested by an uncooperative penis, which ejaculates too fast or does not stay hard.

He will not hear or understand the body messages. Instead, he will strive to overcome them. Soon thereafter he may be labeling himself according to some sexual diagnosis and begin a search for cures—magical stimulants, aphrodisiacs or a "treatment" to overcome his resistance. He may find the quality of his sexual experience rapidly deteriorating to bottom-line expectations, meaning being able to perform just often enough and well enough to save masculine face, no matter what artificial methods it takes to arouse him. He has once again sold out his inner self in order to accommodate role and image demands.

In summary, when masculine conditioning results in his:

a) Not being able to experience, express and deal with his emotions;

b) Not being able to confront "his" woman with his turn-ons and turn-offs, or clearly define his limits by saying yes or no according to his desire;

c) Feeling responsible for performance and the success of the lovemaking;

d) Being uncomfortable with prolonged sensual play;

e) Being unable to accurately read and act on his own emotional and interpersonal responses or to decipher hers;

f) Striving to live up to images and statistics of "normal" male sexual functioning set up by others;

g) Making love to a partner who reacts in a passive-submissive-receptive way and who will not be open and honest in sharing her inner experience because she sees it as her responsibility to build up his ego;

h) Being terrorized by underlying fears of "not being a man" or being a "latent homosexual";

i) Emotional isolation from others to the point that he will tend to develop an unconsciously inordinate dependency on the woman, thus transforming her into a mothering figure;

j) Needing to prove himself constantly in every way, *how can we even begin to speak about the "normal" or "healthy" male sexual response?*

NEGATIVE STEREOTYPING OF THE MALE

Owing to the traditional male-female interaction, in which he has assumed the role of *actor* while she has played the part of the *reactor*, the male has developed a built-in guilt reflex toward the woman, which manifests itself particularly strongly in sex. Since he sees himself as having to be dominant, in control and the sexual initiator, he will also tend to view himself as the responsible one and the insensitive "animal" whenever there are problems, while viewing her as the injured, though patient, understanding and forgiving party.

This built-in guilt reflex creates a bottomless-well potential for self-hating, "bad boy" feelings, which the militant feminists have played upon in their portrayal of the male as a sexual exploiter and chauvinist pig. He has, in fact, been accused of every heinous sexual crime and motive. Men may very well be the last remaining subgroup in our society that can be blatantly, negatively and vilely stereotyped with little objection or resistance.

Examples of such stereotyping by writers who, I am sure, would otherwise see themselves as liberals and humanists abound.

Gloria Steinem, for example, in a cover editorial for *Ms.* magazine, which discussed child pornography, wrote:

Children being undressed and sexually fondled by adult males. Men performing sexual acts on children. "Fathers" having intercourse with "daughters." These widely available, very profitable films and photographs are the subject of Congressional hearings and TV documentaries as America discovers child pornography, and condemns it as a sexual perversion. In fact, it is neither sexual nor a perversion. It is one logical, inevitable result of raising boys to believe they must control or conquer others as a measure of manhood, and producing men who may continue to believe that success or even functioning—in sex as in other areas of life—depends on subservience, surrender, or some clear tribute to their superiority. If that sounds farfetched, consider the facts of child pornography. And consider their echoes in our own observations, perhaps even in our own lives.

Who are the purchasers who feed their sexual needs and a nationwide, lucrative industry by buying books, films and magazines of the humiliation, the brutalization of children? *They are of course, men.** That fact is so taken for granted that it's rarely specified, nor is it a surprise that investigations have yet to turn up even a significant few female buyers. (Yes, there have been some women who help produce such pornography, but their need seems to be money or the approval of men they're dependent on, not the personal need for intimate, obscene power that creates the pornography market in the first place.) *. . . But how different are those obsessed, power-hungry purchasers of child pornography from the many "normal" men who are convinced of the need and permission to be violent, to conquer sexually?*† Once the belief in a false superiority is inflicted on men in order to perpetuate a male-dominant system, surely the question is only one of degree; of how far the individual has to or will go in order to get the drug of male superiority to which society has addicted him.

And how different are the child victims of pornog-

* Italics not in original.
† Italics not in original.

> raphy from the millions who have been sexually approached or molested or continually brutalized as children, sometimes by men in or close to their own families? How many readers of these words have had one such childhood experience themselves?"[4]

With a mixture of facts, half-truths, hyperbole, sweeping generalizations and the fiery adjectives of an old-time preacher or charismatic crowd manipulator, Gloria Steinem castigates, in wholesale fashion, the *entire* male sex.

Similarly, Susan Brownmiller, in her successful and widely discussed book, *Against Our Will: Men, Women and Rape*, stereotypes and indicts the entire male sex for being rapists, or latent rapists who get vicarious satisfaction and pleasure from the exploits of the actual perpetrators of rape. Never mind that men have literally killed each other over as slight a matter as an uncalled-for or derogatory comment toward a woman, or that convicted rapists in prison often are in grave jeopardy in relation to other prisoners.

Brownmiller goes so far as to assert that men perceive rapists as "heroes." In a chapter titled "The Myth of the Heroic Rapist," she first quotes Genghis Khan: " 'A man's highest job in life,' said the man who practiced what he preached, 'is to break his enemies, to drive them before him, to take from them all the things that have been theirs, to hear the weeping of those who cherished them, to take their horses between his knees, and to press in his arms the most desirable of their women.' "[5]

From this statement Brownmiller generalizes as follows: "This remains, I think, the definitive statement of heroic rape: woman as warrior's booty, taken like *their* proud horses. We owe a debt to Genghis for expressing so eloquently the direct connection between manhood, achievement, conquest and rape."[6]

Later in her book she writes, "Hero is the surprising word that men employ when they speak of Jack the Ripper. . . . Jack the Ripper became an important murderer and mythic figure precisely because his identity remained unknown. In other words, he got away with it."[7]

Articles have been written attacking the male sex for exploiting women in every sexual manner, from harassment on the job to forcing them into lives of prostitution on the streets. All employ a common stereotype. Men are exploitative, insensitive, destructive abusers of women.

There has been little protest because these hostile stereotypes coincide with male self-hate. This is even perpetuated by well-intentioned men. I attended a film program sponsored by a major men's collective ("men's lib" organization). The films dealt with the issues of masculinity. One particular movie stands out in my memory as a vivid example of subtle, insidious negative male stereotyping. It depicted a group of men together in a private men's club. All of the men were caricatured in cartoon form as penises and were engaged in various repulsive behaviors such as loud farting, belching, snorting and so on. In a word, they were portrayed as disgusting boors.

The audience, which was, I am sure, composed of "liberal" and "enlightened" men and women, roared with laughter and delight. Had any other subgroup been stereotyped in such a negative, hostile fashion, the outcry would have caused the film to be shut down.

Negative sexual stereotyping is even perpetuated in the form of psychiatric interpretation. For example, a recent article in a major magazine discussed men's responses to the emerging sexual assertiveness of women. One prominent California psychiatrist interpreted male resistance as meaning the following: "If I cannot dominate you sexually with my erect penis, then I will not be involved with you at all. I will control you by withholding that which you wish."[8]

The fact that men have traditionally expressed their sexuality actively while women have expressed theirs in passive-receptive ways has given men a psychological heritage of viewing themselves as the lusting, demanding and aggressive animal. Consequently, any negative label or interpretation which is pinned on the male is introjected and accepted as being valid. This self-hating propensity makes it that much harder for him to function in an assertively self-caring, growth-oriented way rather than in a defensive, self-accusing and destructive one.

For example, the man who is having a "problem" with his erections tends to interpret the underlying reasons in a negative way. Perhaps the "problem" is seen as an expression of his unconscious hostility toward women in general, his desire to punish his wife or a manifestation of his latent homosexuality.

Again, these accusatory, one-sided interpretations sometimes come from society's appointed authority figures in these matters. A professor of psychiatry at New York University School of Medicine coined the term the "new impotence" in describing the so-called contemporary male sexual plague. According to a published account, he and several of his colleagues "attribute impotence in these men to the changing and more aggressive sexual roles of women . . . they are already likely to be *hostile** toward women, have castration fears, or be latent homosexuals."[9]

In light of these negative interpretations he gives himself and also tends to get from the experts, it is not surprising that sexual "problems" would fill him with self-contempt and motivate him to "repair" his uncooperative penis as quickly as possible without allowing himself sufficient breathing space in order to listen and come to terms with the voice of his body.

To project the necessary image and to keep his penis functioning at its best in spite of anything else, some men even resort to self-abusive, outrageous "tricks" in order to maintain performance. For example, a man who claimed to have an excellent sex life and to have sustained it for over thirty years explained to a writer on male sexuality how he did it:

> The man's "trick" is to take a shower before having sex and before leaving the shower to rub adhesive cream for dental plates on his penis. It seems that this cream has anesthetic properties, for deadening sensitive gums, that also works to deaden the sensations of the sensitive penis. There is presumably a multimillion-dollar business in products such as Detain and Prolong that partially anesthetize the penis. I have even heard that cocaine on the penis deadens the sensations.[10]

* Italics not in original.

"IMPOTENCE" AND SEXISM

The word "impotence," aside from its intimidating impact in the way it implies a "sickness" or deficit in masculinity is also a *sexist and destructive* concept. It is destructive because it automatically suggests a medical or psychological disorder, and one that also contains an implicitly negative value judgment, despite assertions of professionals to the contrary. A man who labels himself "impotent" feels himself to have a serious problem, and it becomes impossible for him to perceive his response as a concrete expression of his emotions.

As I suggested earlier in this chapter, it is my belief that one reason why men have passively accepted the onus of such labels is that unconsciously it would be even more threatening for them to see their sexual response as a manifestation of their true feelings and to examine them and take responsibility for the messages being communicated.

In its widest ramifications, the causes of "impotence," when pursued to their root, might reveal that the nonfunctioning or resistant penis is merely the tip of the iceberg, a manifestation of a whole life on the verge of collapse because it was built on the psychological and emotional lies of compulsive masculinity. "Impotence" might be an unavoidable, visible announcement of the collapse of these defenses. Clearly, since men tend to base life decisions on their compulsion to prove themselves rather than on true personal needs, it is very likely that they have stayed in "good" marriages out of guilt, remained in an onerous job in order to be "responsible," fathered children to prove their potency and please their wives and society and in the process of all of this have built up considerable hidden resentment and frustration. Once they have committed themselves both economically and psychologically to the emotional lies of their lives, a resistant penis that threatens to expose and even topple this sand castle by precipitating a confrontation with frustration, anger and unhappiness would constitute a powerful threat. At the same time, a medical interpretation of "impotence" as being caused by vitamin or hormone deficiency, fatigue, alcohol, latent homosexuality or even "unconscious hostility" toward women would be far less threatening than the trauma of having to explore and reassess the psychological structure of one's life. The men are between a rock and a hard place, and the self-hate and torment associated with labeling oneself "impotent" is actually less threatening than inner exploration.

Were I to write slogans for a men's movement, one bumper sticker would read, "Your penis is years ahead of your brain." While I say this in a humorous way, I do believe that many men would have saved themselves the anguish of a decimated life in middle age had they learned to listen to, trust and act upon their body statements rather than denying and trying to transcend them. *The male who is in touch with his inner experience will come to realize that he doesn't "have sex," but rather that he "is sex," which simply means that his so-called sexual response is "his" response and as such is one of the deepest, least consciously controllable, most powerful, truth-telling expressions of who he is and what he feels.* It is not an encapsulated, emotionally unrelated experience, or the result of faulty plumbing.

Beyond just his penis response, he would need to read and trust his total body response in relation to the woman. That is, is he inclined spontaneously to move toward the woman and to cuddle after sex, to freely express emotions, to feel focused and interested in her as a person, or is he inclined to resist touching and other sensual contact as he finds himself wanting to turn away, while his mind wanders or he falls asleep almost immediately after intercourse?

FAKING ORGASMS

Furthermore, it is meaningless to try and assess the scope of "male sexual problems," as eminent researchers have done, when, according to recent reports on women's sexual response, the majority of women are nonorgasmic during intercourse and may even fake orgasm to "please" their men. One eminent psychologist who writes on feminine psychology reported that the majority of college women she interviewed perceived sexual intercourse as a way of either securing love or ensuring they would not lose it. Very few of the women interviewed reported obtaining orgasm. It is mind-boggling to surmise what the subliminal impact of all of this has been on men's responses. Surely, on some level they picked up the cues of a non-orgasmic response, and it is safe to say that a reaction, possibly "impotence," became inevitable.

It is therefore both paradoxical and sadistic to establish standards of male sexual functioning when the female partner has traditionally come to bed in a passive-submissive manner, resistant to verbalizing her real reactions, feeling obliged to massage his ego by feigning greater excitement than she actually experienced, while suppressing her own desires.

Indeed, a man who functioned from a motive of self-care, who could correctly read and then act upon his body's responses, could totally transform his consciousness, life-orientation and relationships. His body responses, rather than being viewed as symptomatic because they were not as they "should" be, would be seen as statements of resistance and would be welcomed as cues and clues to his inner world. He would choose lovers toward whom he felt spontaneously and naturally sensual and playful, awake, eager to touch and be touched, unpreoccupied with performance, open with his responses and feelings, comfortably able to set limits and toward whom his penis responded in congruence with the way he felt. In other words, he would choose a partner toward whom his organism was communicating a clear YES!!

THE DANGERS OF SEX THERAPY

In light of the above, some of what is called "sex therapy" today can be seen as perpetuating the mind/body split by treating the symptom, which is his uncooperating penis, without sufficiently exploring the statement of feeling it is making.

For example, a widely used technique by reputable, well-trained sex therapists for the "treatment" of "premature ejaculation" is the "squeeze technique." This involves teaching the woman to manipulate the penis in such a way as to control the man's ejaculation. The approach, which clearly implies that the "problem" is a mechanical one, is rationalized by interpretations such as the following one offered by the Masters and Johnson team. Dr. Masters expressed it this way:

> In the old days of the cat house it was hurry up, hurry up. The faster the girls worked, the more money they made. The males hardly had a chance to get their pants off. If a young man learned that way—and at one time most of them did—it carried over to his marriage.
>
> Today it often begins in the back seat of a parked car. Again, it's hurry up and get the job done. The back seat of a car hardly provides an opportunity for the expression of personality.[11]

A clinical professor of psychiatry at Mount Sinai School of Medicine, explained it in a similar vein. "Premature ejaculation is just a failure of reflex, like a child not toilet-trained."[12]

These interpretations, which do have a positive impact in that they remove the guilt, sense of responsibility and failure and the depiction of the man as a "bad guy" who is unconsciously seeking to deprive his woman, nevertheless reinforce the tendency of the man to disown the immediate statement being made by his body. For example, in this instance he would say to himself, "When I come fast it's because I learned it in the back of a parked car or was just never properly trained," rather than focusing on the feeling being reflected by his too rapid ejaculation.

As a rule, so long as a man's sexual response is different from time to time, and from partner to partner, it must be viewed as a statement of feeling and reaction. Only men who repeatedly and over long periods of time have the same sexual response, with different partners, can be viewed simply in terms of expressing learned habits and symptoms resulting from problems which are basically unrelated to the relationship.

Viewed in this light, even the most benign therapeutic orientation which communicates to the man that it's O.K. not to have an erection and that he's still as much of a man even when he is "dysfunctional" misses the critical point, which is that every sexual response is an expression and reflection of how a man really feels toward his partner and himself. In addition, he will be done the disservice of being deflected from an ideal opportunity for self-exploration and change, because when he is having "sexual problems," his motivation for help is usually at its highest, and once he is made to "feel better" and told that his "problem" is a learning flaw rather than an expression of himself, a fine opportunity for growth will have been lost.

One man, who had become aware that indeed his penis was an expression of himself and not a disconnected piece of plumbing, expressed the meaning to him of this awareness as follows:

> The faster I come, the less I care for the woman as a person. When I can barely come at all, it's usually because I'm clinging. For some reason I'm sensing that I care for her or am hooked into her much more than she is to me and I'm feeling insecure. In a way, I don't want to get out because I may never get in again. When I turn over and go to sleep right after I make love, it's not my chauvinist insensitivity. It's that I really don't want to be close to her because I don't feel involved in a happy, sensual way. Perhaps I'm bored, made love out of guilt or was just horny and I used her. I'd probably rather leave but don't have the guts to say so, so I escape by falling asleep. Once in a while, when I don't get an erection at all, or when the erection seems to come and go, that's no accident either. When I examine my feelings closely in these instances, I realize that I want to avoid that woman for some reason. Maybe I don't trust her or maybe it's because she's cold and cutting or even using me. If I were really in touch and honest, I wouldn't even be there.

In fact, it is a reflection on how depersonalized and how compulsively performance oriented the traditional man has been that he has always expected himself to be potent and a good performer, regardless of how he felt toward the woman he was with.

SEXUAL STEREOTYPES AND MYTHS

1. *Men have a "fragile ego."*

The stereotype that says that men have a "fragile ego" when it comes to sex and that consequently women shouldn't own up to their real feelings and should even fake their orgasms in order to protect his self-esteem is destructive to the man and could also be seen as self-serving for the woman. By attributing their reluctance to be honest in their responses to the fragility of the man's ego, women can avoid facing an at least equally basic fact—that in many instances the man is a source of security or hoped-for security and that if she were honest it might, to her mind, put the relationship in jeopardy.

Indeed, many men might feel hurt or threatened by a woman's honest statement of frustration, disappointment or resentment. However, if there is a loving attachment and genuine caring, the short-term discomfort and threat created by the confrontation would translate into long-term growth. Avoiding an honest encounter locks the man into his misperceptions and delusions and makes him more vulnerable to the sudden ending of the relationship later on, because he was never even told anything was wrong. Worse still, long before that contingency the phony statements of satisfaction will contradict the woman's nonverbal and body messages. This creates a crazy-making, double-bind situation resulting from the multilevel, conflicting communications. He may even become "dysfunctional" as a result and blame himself because his partner seems to be so sexually responsive while he is the one with the visible problem.

In general, the woman who fakes or withholds honest negative feedback, allegedly to preserve the man's ego, contributes to his emotional and interpersonal stagnation, reinforces his tendency to feel guilty and responsible when things go wrong and intensifies his tendency to withdraw emotionally as he unconsciously seeks to protect himself from the impact of confusing, contradictory messages that tell him verbally how wonderful he is while simultaneously giving him messages of rejection and anger on nonverbal levels.

2. *Men are threatened by and dislike sexually assertive women.*

In a time in our culture when individuals are increasingly striving to take charge of their lives and to assert themselves constructively, it is important to differentiate between assertion and hostility, demandingness, the need to control and threats and put-downs which may come disguised as innocent self-assertion.

Many recently liberated women in the process of change are also experiencing the breakthrough of long repressed rage and resentment. What they perceive as being simple, new-found assertion may actually be a mixture of assertion with hostility, challenge and threat. On the other hand, assertive caring, which is an honest statement of personal feeling and need, is motivated by the desire to increase intimacy. It will be revitalizing to the relationship because it adds new person-to-person dimensions and moves the relationship away from role-rigid, *actor-reactor* interactions.

As to women who are experiencing a new, increased sexual appetite, this is only threatening to men who still see a woman's desire as a mandate to perform. In fact, were he comfortable in allowing himself to be made love to when he was less turned on than she, with no feeling of *having* to get turned on, new dimensions of physical play could be experienced.

3. *Men use women as sex objects.*

Many women express concern over being used by men sexually and wonder whether they should wait a certain length of time after they enter a dating relationship before having sex in order to protect themselves against such "exploitation." *To my mind, there is only one valid reason for a woman to go to bed with a man at any time, and that is that she is turned on and doing it for herself, with her pleasure and satisfaction in mind.* Perhaps she might go to bed with him on occasion simply because he desires it and she wants to satisfy him, but in that case she will indicate that to him rather than pretending desire she doesn't experience.

Women who, in a new or ongoing relationship, feel used need to ask themselves whether, in fact, they are not themselves using sex manipulatively, as a ploy to get or hold on to a man or for bargaining purposes. If a woman is in bed for herself, it will not matter to her whether it is the fifth date or the first, or even whether the man is "using" her, for even if she never sees him again, she will have satisfied *her* desire and had the pleasure of an experience she engaged in for *her own satisfaction.*

The traditionally sexually reactive woman who does not recognize or take responsibility for her own appetites is the one most likely to feel she is being treated like an object, because, in reality, by not defining her needs, desires, likes and dislikes and by simply reacting to the man she *is* denying her personhood and, in fact, behaving like an object. Indeed, the self-caring, in-touch man would not continue a relationship with a woman who allowed herself to be used, because, aside from its being essentially a boring, degrading, and dehumanizing experience, it reinforces his guilt, his self-hate, his sense of being responsible for her satisfaction, of being a lusting "animal" and of owing her something in return for her "gift" or "service."

4. *Men are insensitive to women sexually. They only want to satisfy themselves.*

If I were to write a book on female psychology, I would include a chapter on the "wisdom of the vagina" as a counterpart to a chapter I wrote in my book *The Hazards of Being Male* entitled " The Wisdom of the Penis."[13] In it I would encourage women to read and act upon their own body messages and the ones they receive from the man. A self-caring, secure woman would then choose as partners only those men whose body language and responses signaled their genuine interest, and she would reject the insensitive, selfish man outright rather than complain or try to change him. His chronically insensitive behavior is making a clear and powerful statement of rejection. It is my belief that a man who is turned on, involved and experiencing genuinely loving feelings toward a woman will not react in insensitive ways except occasionally, when that insensitivity stems from innocent ignorance of her needs. In that case, remedy would come quickly as a result of an honest exchange of feeling.

In many instances in the past, a woman chose a man for his potential as a provider and security source and then was resentful because she did not get the sensual response that she desired. My interpretation of a man's cold, "insensitive" response in these instances is that he may be unconsciously reacting to and resenting the fact that he is being seen primarily as a success symbol and security source rather than as a person, even though he may have consciously invited this himself.

In a future time when men and women come together sexually to give each other pleasure rather than to complete or rescue each other, they will make love only for the joy of the process and will choose a person who excites them on that level primarily.

5. *Men reach their sexual peak in their late teens.*

This often repeated notion about men I believe to be primarily an artifact of conditioning rather than a biological phenomenon. Men begin to enter firmly into harness in their late teens and begin to deny feelings and drown out impulses. They also strive to live up to models of responsible husband-father-provider and to assume the posture of chronic proving while taking the role of *actor* to the female *reactor*, at the same time relating progressively more dishonestly to their inner life.

The decline in sexual capacity, therefore, seems to me to be a reflection of the enormous repression of emotion and self, coupled with the smothering effects of guilt, unconscious anger over their suffocation and the compulsion to accommodate their female partner while denying themselves.

6. *Men are not basically monogamous.*

I believe that the conditioning of the male creates in him a powerful ambivalence toward monogamy. On the one hand, he has a deep craving for a special female partner based on his early experience of mother as his lifeline and source of nourishment and comfort. This is coupled with other factors that cause him to hunger for one special partner, such as his intense emotional isolation from other men because of his competitive stance toward them, his fear of being open and vulnerable in front of them, his homosexual anxiety and the fact that men are not usually sources of nourishment and comfort to each other. Finally, his orientation toward "his" woman is usually a possessive, protective and guilt-laden one. All of these factors would tend to make him lean *toward* monogamy.

His push *away* from monogamy would result from early conditioning in which he learned to view sex as a game of challenge and conquest. His masculinity was validated by the number of women who would go to bed with him. Second, his emotional and sensual repression and a concomitant tendency to relate to sex in terms of goal (ejaculation) rather than process (the pleasure of sensual play) would tend to create boredom and rigidity with any partner. Third, if his wife or lover is the traditional reactive-passive-submissive woman sexually, she will be a monotonous, highly predictable partner and will also trigger his tendency to feel guilty and self-hating for feelings of imposing himself on her. Finally, unconscious resentment over the strictures of his role may reflect itself in sexual resistance. All of this would tend to pull him *away* from monogamy.

In general, powerful ambivalence rather than a clear-cut positive or negative feeling would seem to be the logical experience of the traditional man.

7. *Middle-aged men in sexual pursuit of younger women are unconsciously expressing panic over growing old and are trying to deny their age and prove their virility.*

I perceive the craving of some middle-aged or older men for younger partners to be, at least in part, an expression of an underlying awareness that they have lived an unauthentic, emotionally self-denying life based on guilt and the need to prove themselves and that they are on the verge of having thrown their lives away. They see in the young woman the fantasy and possibility of rebirth, a fresh start and an opportunity to experience the spontaneous, sensual and expressive excitement they have not permitted themselves in their compulsive pursuit of the masculine role and ideal. It is, in effect, a last-ditch attempt, albeit unconscious, to reclaim their lives.

8. *Men are———(Fill in the stereotype of your choosing).*

The male sex is heavily encumbered with negative stereotypes that remain unexamined and unchallenged. The time has come for him to reject the role of all-purpose whipping boy and to reclaim his right to function as a self-caring, growth-oriented human being rather than a mechanical robot.

The only generalization that seems to be valid is that male sexuality has been so encumbered by a conditioning process that destroys the potential for joyful, authentic, spontaneous sexual responsiveness that one can only speculate and create visions of what might someday be if the male freed himself of these powerful and destructive role bindings. In the meantime, it only adds insult to injury to speak of norms of healthy sexual behavior, since he is an organism motivated by guilt, performance compulsion, emotional repression, denial of dependency and a resistance to passivity, plus a tendency to put the woman he "loves" on a pedestal and not to communicate with her or even see her as a person.

The potential for men who can read, trust and act upon their organismic responses is mind-boggling considering the present orientation. A caring cultural climate would place its emphasis on growth and exploration rather than on the cataloguing, describing and treatment of symptoms and the establishment of misleading, destructive norms.

11. Filters That Distort His Communication and the Impossible Binds He Puts Her In

It is a relatively simple thing for a man to be non-possessive, non-sexist, non-judgmental and liberal when he doesn't care, when he hasn't hooked into the woman on a deeper emotional level—the hungry, lonely, love-craving part. However, something entirely different seems to emerge when he believes he's found the "only person on earth for me," the special partner he fantasizes will put his whole life in balance and will offset the struggle, the pain and the depressing aspects of his day-to-day survival rituals. That "something entirely different" that comes out often means that he regresses and does many of the posturing, manipulative, corny things he may have always despised when he's seen them played out in other people when they thought they were "in love." It all seemed so transparent then.

For many men this regression might simply involve washing the car before he picks her up on a date in order to impress her; spending half a week debating the pros and cons of various restaurants he might take her to; worrying about the clothes he'll wear, the color combination and even his hairstyle; thinking of ways to make more money so that he can buy her the things he thinks will "make her happy," so that she'll "love him" more; becoming suspicious even of his long-standing, close male friends who he believes might come on to her and try to take her away if he's not vigilant; watching her all the time and even wanting to "protect her" if another man looks at her in the wrong way or makes an offensive remark, or uses "dirty" language in front of her. With other women words such as "cunt" and "cock" come out casually and unselfconsciously. Around her he says "vagina" and "penis" or maybe even "down there." Even with these cleaned-up words, he feels a little "dirty" using them around her.

When he's feeling insecure about her, which is most of the time, he uses manipulative strategies, such as being deliberate about when he telephones, calculating how many times she's called him since he last called her. He goes to concerts and museums he has little or no interest in because he thinks it impresses her, and he even wears a suit and tie on occasion, which he otherwise would never do except for work and ceremonial situations when he absolutely has to.

It is amazing how even the more avant-garde life-stylist seems to regress and transform from an enlightened, "you do your own thing—I'll do mine," "let's give each other lots of space," "no laying of trips on each other" into a clinging, jealous, mendacious, moralistic, irrational person who embodies all the regressive, conservative characteristics that he previously rejected as being stifling, destructive and archaic when he becomes emotionally involved, *particularly when he has attibuted to the woman all of the properties of specialness and of being* the *important person in his life.*

Often he even recognizes the regression in himself, hates himself for it and struggles to overcome it. He tells himself, "I don't own her. She can talk to, sleep with or go where she pleases." But the urgency and anxiety and possessiveness are still there, along with the discomfort and guilt for being that way and the great effort to deny, control and suppress these feelings. In the process, he drives himself crazy trying to put it all into balance, to see clearly, to make sense of the communication and to get a handle on the contradictions, conflicts, extremes and impossible binds that are generated.

The usually complex process of male-female communication is made even more complicated in today's age of liberation, of changing consciousness, role transitions and growth, particularly where breakthroughs in intellectual awareness have not been emotionally assimilated and integrated. This liberated orientation, then, all too often only adds one more warring level of contradiction, confusion and inconsistency to the already manifold levels of man-woman communication.

Traditionally, there are at least four levels of experience and communication, two of which are largely unconscious, one of which is partly conscious and one which is conscious and operates when a man becomes emotionally involved with a woman; when his usual defensive, distancing barriers and protection have been broken through and he feels magnetized and fixated by her and desires to have her as a soul mate, *the* woman to be close and intimate with and committed to.

1) THE FANTASY LEVEL

Most, if not all, men, before they get attached to "their" woman, have a fantasy of what that woman should be like. The most common stereotype includes her being very "feminine," meaning she should be "soft," tender, gentle, selfless, loyal, sexy, sensual (but only to *him*), uncompetitive, charming, beautiful, adoring, fragile, nurturing, sensitive and giving.

For the "hipper," contemporary man who sees himself as having transcended gender-role stereotypes, the "ideal" woman fantasy he looks for is even more complex. Unbeknownst to him, he may actually be searching for psychologically impossible combinations in one woman and may become very frustrated and despairing looking for her.

I asked a group of sophisticated single men, many of whom had been looking for the "right" woman for a long time or who had periodically thought they'd found her only to have become disappointed and disillusioned as the realities emerged and the relationship crumbled, to write out a description of their "ideal" woman, the woman they would be willing to "give up" their freedom for if they found her. The most striking thing about most of these descriptions was their unreal and contradictory quality. One man in his mid-thirties wrote a description which classically embodied this "impossible dream" quality of many of the men's fantasies.

She should be autonomous in such a way that she won't be the dependent, clinging type who is an emotional drain. Of course, she shouldn't be so autonomous or independent that she wouldn't need me or could do without me, because then I'd feel too insecure.

She should be in touch and comfortable with her sexuality so that she is sensually expressive and free and comfortable with experimenting and exploring so that we can have fun acting out our fantasies. That doesn't mean I want her to be an animal, some insatiable nymph, one of those demanding "give me my orgasm" liberated type women or even one who gets easily turned on to other men and might screw around on me.

I guess I wouldn't mind if she got turned on to other men, so long as she told me about it in a nonthreatening way and didn't act on it unless we had discussed it first. Even then, I would hope that if we agreed it would be all right that she still wouldn't ever feel the need to actually go to bed with another man, because our sex life would be satisfying enough.

If I desired other women, I'd want her to be the kind of woman I could tell that to and she'd accept that in me without feeling threatened or without needing to retaliate. If I had a transient affair or a one-night stand, I'd hope she'd understand that it had nothing to do with her and that it did not reflect on our relationship or my love for her.

I want her to be a woman of strength, able to deal with the real world, successful at getting what she wants, but without being a competitive, driven type or a "ball breaker," the way some women are getting to be. She'd be able to get what she needed and wanted using the velvet touch and the strength of her talents and abilities. And no matter how successful she'd become, I'd want her to retain that softness, vulnerability and emotional quality.

If her ambitions jeopardized our relationship—I mean if it required her to be away a lot—my ideal woman would put our love and our relationship first. I'm being honest about it even though it comes out sounding like a double standard, but I'd want her to be old-fashioned enough to be loyal, devoted and selfless to the point that our relationship came first.

In the same vein, she'd be compassionate, warm, sympathetic and supportive, but not in a mothering, smothering way. She would just have a deep, natural capacity to care.

In terms of her interests, I'd want her to be an outdoor type person, able to rough it, to participate in athletic things. She'd be a woman who was not spoiled, hooked on luxury, comfort and the good life, who could withstand some physical strain and even some deprivation, a "man's woman," so to speak, but definitely not a masculine woman.

It sounds like I want everything, but why shouldn't I hold out for the best in a lifetime partner—a woman who's soft and strong, sexy but still faithful, competent and successful at what she does but not competitive, needing me but not overly dependent, nurturing and compassionate but not smothering or even mothering—a complete person, and if I find her I'll *never* let her go.

Much like the woman looking for the impossible "dream man"—one who is ambitious, successful, dominant, powerful, brilliant, while also sensitive, artistic, sensual, domestic, emotional, gentle, faithful, who loves children and is understanding, patient and warm—the man in search of his "ideal woman," like the man who wrote the above description, is leading from his head and imagining a composite woman who is actually full of psychological contradictions and probably could not authentically exist. He may on occasion believe that he has found "the only one" when, in the throes of an adrenaline high of romantic energy, both he and she become for each other what the other wants, acting out the ideal part. This posture, however, will be impossible to maintain, and disillusionment and disappointment will inevitably replace the euphoria of the temporarily fulfilled fantasy.

2) THE PROJECTION LEVEL

Perhaps the most elusive and difficult aspect of intimate male-female relationships, when the emotional investment is high, is to be able to see the other person as he or she *is*, rather than as one would like him or her to be. For example, it is a fairly common phenomenon that the last one to know that a spouse is having an affair is the other spouse, and the last one to fully recognize that a child is mentally retarded or drug addicted is the parent. Denial of what one doesn't want to see is very common when one is emotionally involved. Consequently, the last one to see one's lover as he or she really is is the person who is "in love" with the other and whose vision is blurred by the power of his need and hunger. Anything that threatens the required perception will be blocked out.

In fact, the process of becoming attached romantically, and that high and magical euphoria which accompanies it, seem to involve a temporary unconscious suspension of aggression, meaning an inability to see the negative, the flaws, the bad habits, the distasteful characteristics, or to acknowledge boredom, anger and resistance when they come up and to maintain honest personal boundaries and limits. Instead, there is a strong propensity to fuse identities, to be increasingly unable to identify autonomous desire ("I want" as opposed to "we want") and to constantly rationalize incongruities and negative awarenesses in order to preserve the romantic projection.

This process of romantic projection (seeing in the other person what doesn't exist) and denial of reality often results in the positive interpretation of a behavior or characteristic at the beginning of the relationship that is viewed with repulsion or anger toward the end. For example, what is seen as fetching naïveté and charming innocence at the beginning may be seen as narrowness, ignorance and a boring provinciality at the end. Similarly, a bold, brash manner that is romantically perceived as daring and healthy assertiveness initially is transformed by the absence of the romantic vision into abrasive pushiness, insensitivity and egotistical self-obsession. Emotionality and carelessness about detail may be seen as "femininity," vulnerability and fragility at the start only to become irrational hysteria and irresponsibility at the end. Likewise, a woman's willingness to have sex soon after first meeting may be interpreted as her spontaneity, powerful attraction and freedom at the beginning, while in a turned-off frame of mind it may be seen as shallowness, cheapness, "something she does with everybody" or a reflection of her inability to say no. Smells, voice inflections, movements, idiosyncrasies that were found to be endearingly human at the beginning may also become unattractive and even repellent by the end.

Therefore, projection and the tendency to deny and distort perceptions in order to make them congruent with one's required romantic fantasy add a second level of potential distortion or unreality to the intimate male-female communication process.

3) THE REPRESSED, REJECTED AND UNEXPERIENCED CORE LEVEL

Involved in the conditioning process of becoming a "man" and behaving in an acceptable masculine way is the repression of important core psychological aspects of the male, which are therefore not experienced consciously. This core is encapsulated and denied, though it continues to operate in indirect, sublimated or covert ways, and searches for safe outlets for expression and satisfaction.

This repressed core is composed of the man's "forbidden" parts; his dependency craving, his vulnerability, fear and other emotions, his desire to let go and be taken care of and anything else inside him that might be equated with femininity or unmasculine behavior. The more powerful and threatening this core is, the more rigid the defenses against it will be and the more he will need constantly to prove his autonomy, ability to perform, rationality, unemotionality, lack of dependency hunger and other human needs.

When he gets romantically involved, much of this

repressed core may be unconsciously manifested in hidden and deliberately denied ways. That means he may become possessive, jealous, clinging, demanding of attention, dependent and emotionally volatile, all the while denying that it's happening.

In the instance of one couple whom I counsel in therapy, the man played the macho who repeatedly protested his need for freedom and independence. When she, in response to his protests against *her* dependency, encouraged him to take a vacation, weekend trips or even evenings out by himself, he refused. He told her that he knew that she didn't *really* mean it, and that he also *knew* that she wouldn't be able to handle it if he went off without her. When she insisted that her motives were selfish and that she really wanted also to go off by herself, be became visibly upset. It was clear that it was *his* dependency on *her* that he was protesting and denying, and that in reality she would have been more than happy to have time to go off by herself.

This denied, consciously unexperienced core plays a large role in the communication distortions, ambivalences, conflicting expectations and impossible binds he will create for her in the course of the relationship. The struggle is between the underlying needs hungering for expression in the face of a psychological defensive system that works constantly to deny expression to the core and, for the sake of his masculine image, to prove that the core doesn't exist.

4) THE MASCULINE SELF-IMAGE LEVEL

This level represents the conscious self-image, or the way he needs to see himself. When he behaves in a way that is contrary to it, he will rationalize or even deny that he's doing it. For example, he needs to see himself as independent, patient and in control of his emotions. When he is confronted, after an outburst over a meal served late, for example, with the fact that he is behaving like an irritable, demanding child, he will deny this with vigor. He might even scream out in fury, "I'M NOT ANGRY!!"

The culturally dictated role image calls for him to be rational, self-contained, controlled, independent, strong, fearless, productive and dominant. This, then, is the way he needs to see himself and wants others to see him also.

Because we live in a "polite," "nice" society, which means that honest encountering and confrontations seldom, if ever, take place between people, most individuals can continue to see themselves as they believe themselves to be even though others don't see them that way. Or they may actually succeed in projecting the image they wish to. Still, the masculine self-image is just another defensive layer filtering his communication in order that he can affirm his image. It continually grates against the repressed core.

5) THE "LIBERATED" LEVEL

For some men who are working to free themselves from sexist behaviors and orientations, another level may be added to the already highly complex, often "crazy-making" business of man-woman communications. I call this level the *denial of the role-image level*, or the "liberated" level, because, for the man who is idealistically aspiring to liberate himself, there may very well be a rigid and defensive denial of the "typical masculine orientation" within him. In other words, his is a psychologically defensive liberalism that can be recognized as such because of its rigidity, its "protesteth too much" flavor and extreme hostility toward those men who behave in any other way. These men acknowledge the validity of the accusations and victim-philosophy of militant feminism, and proceed to echo these man-hating strains themselves in the name of "male liberation." It is not an authentically humanistic, flowing, freeing up of role behavior, but rather a militant, rigid, holier-than-thou attitude, and it is noted that these men tend to relate primarily on a cerebral and ideological level to each other rather than on a playful, spontaneous, warm, and accepting one that they claim to espouse.

Their defensive sermonizing was the attitude that caused a female writer, Karen Durbin, to write, in an article for a national women's magazine entitled "How to Spot a Liberated Man":

> A woman I know . . . startled me the other day by suggesting that she found it less irritating to be with a male chauvinist than with many of the supposedly liberated men she meets. "I find these self-consciously liberated men slippery," she said, "and I don't like slippery people. Conversations with them always seem to end up with them telling me how to liberate myself. The hell with that. Maybe I'm feeling the way some black people did in the mid-sixties toward white liberals—'No thanks, I'd rather do it myself.' "[11]

What these women who find themselves more comfortable with the traditional "chauvinistic" male (whom they find philosophically abhorrent) than with the "liberated" man may be reacting to is that the latter may very well be engaged in psychologically defensive behavior that is emotionally unauthentic and therefore unpleasant to be around. The behavior is brittle, rigid, predictable, boring, bloated with pretension and "born-again" religiosity rather than pleasurable, spontaneous humanness.

In this sense, the defensively "liberated" man communicates through five filters or levels rather than four. Although this filter is a relatively new defense of the kind a religious convert might communicate through, it is as powerful as the masculine self-image level, because this type of man sees himself as a rescuer, a savior of the downtrodden female and the righteous opponent of society's male chauvinist pigs.

All of these levels which filter a man's communications tend to cause him to send out contradictory and confusing messages and also to create impossible binds in the form of either-way-you-lose demands. In the following pages I describe the classic binds which manifest the conflict between the way he needs to see himself and the periodic eruption of repressed needs and feelings.

THE ASSERTION-SUBMISSION BIND

If she's direct in defining her needs, her likes and dislikes and her limits, he sees her as demanding, pushy, shrewish and possibly even castrating.

If she's reluctant to define her needs and to express her likes and dislikes and tries to avoid conflict by giving in, he sees her as being passive and unexciting and tells her that they will get along much better if she would only tell him how she *really* feels, what she *really* wants and what she *really* likes and dislikes.

Either way she loses. If she's assertive, she's a demanding shrew. If she's submissive and conflict-avoiding, she's a passive bore.

THE INTRUSION-NEGLECT BIND

If she shows considerable interest in what he does, who he's with and where he's going—wanting to join him in his activities, to help with his work and so on—he perceives her as intrusive, suffocating and distrustful.

If she leaves him alone, steers clear of his activities, never questions him about who he's with, where he's been or what he's doing, he feels neglected and tells himself she doesn't really care about him, his work or his feelings about his life.

Either way she loses. If she tries to be an integral part of his activities, he feels intruded upon. If she keeps her distance, he feels neglected.

THE CAREER-HOMEMAKER BIND

If she has a career or job that she finds satisfying and pleasurable and is therefore emotionally involved with, he views it as competition for her energies and concerns, feels neglected, and may accuse her of being selfish, uncaring, rejecting and unfeminine.

If she commits herself and her primary energies to homemaking, he sees her as a drudge, a compulsive cleaner, a dull companion and a guilt-maker because she's always at home waiting for him and "makes him" feel self-conscious and guilty for being late and for not paying enough attention to her. He then accuses her of insulating herself from the "real world," of not developing herself, and encourages her to get involved in outside activities.

Either way she loses. If her primary energies go into her career, he sees her as neglectful, uncaring, rejecting and says she loves him less than her outside endeavors. If she devotes herself to homemaking, he resents having to shoulder all of the financial burdens and complains that she is a compulsive, nagging, demanding, boring drudge who's always making him feel guilty.

THE MOTHERING BIND

A variation of the "career-homemaker bind" occurs once the woman has children. If she makes the mothering role her primary one, she may become increasingly desexed in his eyes as he relates to her increasingly as a mothering figure and his sexual passions go into his fantasies, or perhaps even outside flings and lovers. Furthermore, the consuming nature of the maternal role cuts her off to a great extent from outside input, and in his eyes she becomes less interesting and stimulating to be with.

On the other hand, if she involves herself in a career that takes up a significant amount of time, she may be made to feel guilty for being a rejecting, neglectful mother.

Either way she loses. If her focus is on mothering, she becomes a less interesting, less sexually attractive partner. If she pursues her career interests after she has children, she is blamed for being an unconcerned, rejecting and uncaring mother.

THE SEXUALLY ACTIVE–SEXUALLY PASSIVE BIND

He complains if she responds in a sexually passive-receptive-submissive way and chides her for lacking passion, being uninteresting in bed, and tells her that she is not really excited by him or that she is frigid for not participating more. He encourages her to liberate herself sexually and to become more exploratory and experimental.

If, however, she's sexually active, comfortable in initiating sex, expressing her needs and turn-ons, assuming a dominant as well as passive posture and, in general, being sexually assertive, he may read that as a demand and be intimidated and repelled by what he perceives to be her insatiable appetite and her "masculine" and aggressive ways. If she is assertive to the point that she complains about his need to control and his insensitivity to her, he may even accuse her of being castrating.

Either way she loses. If she is sexually hesitant, he reacts negatively to her conservative, puritanical attitude. If she is sexually direct, he feels pressured and defensive about her "demanding," unsatisfied and complaining attitude.

THE AUTONOMY-DEPENDENCY BIND

In everyday language this bind may be expressed as the "set me free—don't leave me" conflict. If she encourages him to have an autonomous life outside of the relationship, his own friends, occasional evenings, weekends and vacations alone, and if she also indicates her desire for the same, he becomes insecure, suspicious that she doesn't really care for him, does not really want to be with him, is preparing to leave him or is involved with somebody else.

If she builds her life around his, wants to be with him evenings, weekends, and holidays, refrains from developing a separate set of friends and desires an exclusive sexual relationship, he complains that she is possessive and dependent and that he feels smothered and engulfed.

Either way she loses. Supportive of maintaining their own identities and separate interests, she gets an insecure, suspicious and resentful reaction from him. If she wants them to share friends, activities and free time as a couple, he sees her as dependent, engulfing and possessive.

THE "YOU'RE LETTING YOURSELF GO"– VANITY BIND

If she downplays concern for her physical appearance, mutes her sexual attractiveness, spends minimal time and money on "vanity" aspects, he resents her for letting herself go, tells her that she's not as attractive as she used to be and wonders if this means that she's losing interest in being attractive to him or in how he sees and reacts to her.

If, however, she *is* attentive to her appearance and spends time attending to grooming, clothing, hairstyle, cosmetics, dieting, beauty sleep and so on, he reacts negatively to her emphasis on the superficial, her self-preoccupation and her "narcissism." In his darker moments he may even wonder why she's so concerned about the way she looks. Is she trying to make herself attractive to other men?

Either way she loses. If she is casual about her physical appearance, he accuses her of "letting herself go." If she is attentive to it, he interprets this as her superficiality and vanity or her interest in attracting other men.

THE "TELL ME HOW YOU REALLY FEEL"– "YOU'RE REALLY HOSTILE" BIND

In intimate relationships with men, women have been taught to avoid fighting, conflict or saying things that would hurt the male ego. He complains, therefore, that she won't fight, won't tell him what she's thinking or how she really feels, and that he never knows what's bothering her or what's going on inside of her. He encourages her to level with him.

If, however, she is out front with her reactions, shares her negative feelings, expresses her anger openly and refuses to falsify her responses in order to pamper him, he complains that she is hostile, undermining, rejecting, unsupportive, "unfeminine" and "a bitch."

This bind was clearly evidenced in a man of thirty-three who came for marriage counseling with his thirty-one-year-old wife of nine years. At the beginning of counseling he complained that she was too passive, did not stand up for what she really believed and that as a result he found her boring. After seveal months of counseling she became significantly more assertive, and as her long repressed anger began to emerge, he told her, "Now that you're feeling more secure, you jump on me all the time!"

Either way she loses. If she resists sharing negative feelings or expressing anger, he complains that they can never resolve any issues and that he doesn't really ever know where he stands because she won't tell him what she feels. If she is open in expressing the full range of her feelings and reactions, he becomes defensive, resents her "bitchiness" and accuses her of not really caring for him and putting him down.

THE "WAIT ON ME"–"DON'T FUSS OVER ME" BIND

If she is very attentive to him, anticipates his needs, looks after him and is doting and concerned in her manner, he complains that he is being "mothered" to death. He tells her she is being overprotective, and that he needs more "space."

If she treats him like an adult who must assert his needs, ask for whatever he wants, take care of himself, and if she keeps a comfortable distance and relates to him on an adult-adult, friend-friend level rather than mothering him, he sees her as thoughtless, unnurturing, unloving and insensitive.

Either way she loses. If her attitude is nurturing, he

feels he is being treated like a little boy. If she relates to him on an adult-adult level, he feels unattended to and unloved.

WALKING THE TIGHTROPE OF MAN-WOMAN INTIMATE COMMUNICATION

The man-woman communication process is fraught with "damned-if-you-do, damned-if-you-don't" binds, hazards, impasses and breakdowns whose roots are the following:

1) The traditional romantic approach to courtship, which is usually the original basis for permanent relationships. This means that initially, in the getting-together process, aggression and negative feelings are repressed and denied. In the urgency to be "nice," conflict is skirted, and an artificial emphasis is placed on "fairness" and "equality," which later erodes into undealt-with dominance-submission issues, denied turn-offs and fundamental man-woman rage. That is, in the early romantic phase the other person is magically transformed into a unique being who is of a different mold from the rest of that gender, and consequently the usual resistances, resentments and distrustful feelings that are initially inherent in intimate heterosexual interactions, because of the woman's learned anticipation that she will be exploited and dominated and the man's fear that he will be manipulated, trapped, engulfed and smothered, are repressed and denied in the desire to "make it work."

It is a relationship whose foundation to a significant degree is in mutual fantasy and image creation rather than in the reality of two people rooted in the same culture and with similarly learned value systems of everybody else. The aggression that is temporarily suspended, the assertiveness that is muted or denied, seep through continuously in elusive, indirect ways and generate the push-pull, "come here—go away," "I love you—I hate you" reactions which are the basis for the impossible binds.

As a rule, the more "romantic" the initial courtship mood, the more "perfect" the other person seems to be and the more "uncanny" the apparent mutuality, the greater the potential for crazy-making, double-bind communications, as the torrent of repressed aggression, assertiveness, turn-offs, denial of needs for dominance, power and control subsequently and in myriad indirect ways continuously contaminates the "loving" communication.

The sense of being off balance, the insecurity, the vague feeling of unreality, the pendulum swings between euphoria and despair, the sudden silences, the walking-on-eggs sensation, the constant reassuring and need for reassurance that the other one "really" loves you, the sudden unpredictable eruptions of rage, the tendency to premeditate and calculate ("Shall I call her again? I've called her three times in a row and she hasn't called me") and the fear of saying the wrong thing—all of which may characterize romantic interactions—are overt manifestations and outgrowths of this repressed aggression.

2) There is a basic masculine ambivalence about committed, monogamous relationships for the reasons previously explored in the chapter "Sex Distortions, Misinterpretations, Myths and Stereotypes About Men" (page 117).

This ambivalence toward commitment produces a tendency toward extremes in his reactions from day to day, going from euphoria and sentimentality to despair and rage as different responses are triggered. Consequently, he may be cursing one day the very thing he applauded the day before.

3) Few men and women have gone through the kind of individual development that has truly freed them to be self-aware, emotionally responsible people who are able to perceive themselves as the psychological captains of their ships and to a great extent create that which happens to them. Particularly in an intimate heterosexual relationship, there is a tendency to finger-point, to blame and to portray oneself as a disillusioned, betrayed and abused victim. Few relationships have the kind of foundation required for a comfortably transparent, self-caring attitude, personhood rather than gender-limited behavior and capacity for sensuality, which are required to keep a relationship playful, pleasurable, alive and in a state of growth.

Instead, the bottom-line security needs are the ones usually met, while the needs for growth and exploration are stifled and buried. An underlying cause, then, of impossible binds is the war between these security needs—to belong, to be loved and to "have someone"—and the frustrated growth needs, which are made up of a hunger to explore, to experience new relationships and to follow one's own rhythm and instincts without needing to get permission from the other. I believe these frustrated growth needs are in part responsible for the periodic flare-ups of rage which seem unconsciously designed to push the other person away, to create more space, to provide a justifiable rationalization ("It's your fault") for the desire to become autonomous for a period of time *without* permission.

Finally, in an age of liberation, predictable, rigid, prescribed role behaviors and reactions will be shaken loose and underlying emotions and responses will pour through. In men, the sameness in response and the narrow limits of emotionality and reaction are the result of role straitjackets which create "supposed to" and "should" orientations motivated by conformist impulses to act out appropriately the role of being a man. When people start to grow, to get in touch with feelings and to have the strength to reject archaic role harnesses, they inevitably experience the turbulence and ambivalence of free-traveling emotions and reactions. Their responses are now emerging organically, flexibly and fluidly from circumstances and experiences, rather than from role prescription.

Whenever role behavior and conformist pressure to live up to external images are in a process of release and reexamination, the people involved become pioneers in the uncharted territory of internal experience. They are becoming people first and roles second, which is a radical departure from the traditional emphasis on roles first and foremost and "damn the person inside the skin." While this transition to inner-directed response tends to be a frightening, upsetting and threatening process, it may also be the only legitimate soil for growth and development.

In summary, in an era of change for the alive, fluid person, there is a tripartite struggle between:

1) *Role-prescribed behavior*—the way a person is taught he "should" be;

2) *Individuality*—the pull of individual need and emotion, which is different from person to person;

3) *Visions of potential*—notions, fantasies or models of what might or could be.

An exclusive emphasis on any single one of these three is unbalanced and stifling. The role-bound person is rigid, predictable and boring. The totally inner-directed person becomes an offensive narcissist, and the one whose functioning is shaped entirely by visions of what might be lives in a dream-world that will isolate him from others.

The ultimate and ideal heterosexual relationship, freest of loaded messages, communications and impossible binds, is one in which both the man and the woman are fluid in behavior and are thus able to float between role-prescribed behaviors, inner motivations and visions of the possible in a conscious way that allows them to share their experience and work through those aspects and moments which create turbulence in a relationship.

DEALING WITH IMPOSSIBLE BINDS

As long as impossible binds and crazy-making communication are a built-in reality of male-female relationships, the inability to recognize and deal with them will result in intensification of self-hate, the perception of oneself as a victim and endless varieties of emotional problems, anxieties, frustration and despair over not being able to make a relationship fulfill its romantic promise and work the way one has been told it's supposed to work.

Surviving these communication hazards, therefore, requires:

1) Recognition of their omnipresent potential existence;

2) An awareness of the layers and levels in oneself that produce them;

3) An acceptance of their inevitability and a commitment to working them through when they arise, rather than fleeing toward a new utopia;

4) A constant emphasis on self-development and self-

awareness, because without such individual development relationships tend to become rigid and destructive.

The culture seems to encourage young, romantic, growth-stifling relationships and does not have the perspective required to teach younger people to avoid the traps. To an extent, of course, older generations are threatened by younger generations that seem freer and more sensual and who reject the traditional role harnesses. Obviously, the early acquisition of heavy burdens of responsibility, such as children, mortgages, insurance and so on, creates a cage which makes growth, exploration and risk taking extremely difficult, if not impossible.

The impact of impossible binds can be softened and dealt with in a nondestructive way if the relationship is composed of partners who:

1) Are committed to their own growth and willing and able to experience the anxieties and assume the risks inherent in the process;

2) Genuinely and realistically know, like and enjoy each other and have the trust capacity to encourage a mutual journey that is satisfying rather than self-denying.

Traditional relationships are often maintained by sacrifice, self-denial and selflessness, endurance and learning to put up with deprivation and hardship. This interpersonal masochism has been glorified by labeling it "maturity." However, too often "maturity" becomes little more than a mutual blocking of growth, expressiveness, transparency and joy.

In a psychologically enlightened world, relationships will be considered mature and constructive only as long as they create an optimum environment for growth, physical and psychological health, fluidity, openness and the kind of mutual enhancement that brings the people involved to a new and better place in the path of their development. Once a relationship becomes predictable, rigid and constricting, it becomes a psychological tomb and perhaps ought best to be abandoned.

In the context of a living, fluid relationship, "impossible binds" will be part of the soil for self-awareness and creative change. In the context of a rigid, predictable relationship, they are only another toxic and destructive element.

PART THREE

HE AND HER CHANGES

12. Who Is the Victim? Who Is the Oppressor?

> In fact, most of the male characters come off poorly in *The Thorn Birds*. A fairly typical sentence runs: "She eyed his flaccid penis, snorting with laughter." The ambitious men are silly and the steady ones are inconsequential. Meggie's eight brothers die or disappear into the woodwork. Women seem to live forever, while every hundred pages or so another man is burned alive or disemboweled by a wild boar or drowned or unsexed by gunshot wounds. None of this carnage is required by the plot. The males are punished because their punishment is what romantic fiction requires.[1]
>
> —From a review of
> *The Thorn Birds,* by
> Colleen McCullough
> (major best seller of 1977–78)

Much of the energy of the feminist movement is derived from rage over being a victim. The male-female dynamic is portrayed in the following way: He is the oppressor, victimizer, abuser, user, exploiter, chauvinist, sexist pig. She is the oppressed, victimized, abused, used, exploited, maligned, passive, blameless, helpless victim.

A major article published in the early days of the women's movement in one of America's largest and most widely read magazines illustrates this well. Various activist women articulated their perceptions of the male-female relationship. Martha Shelly, a poet, expressed a common attitude. She said, "The average man, including the average student male radical, wants a passive sex object–cum–domestic–cum–baby nurse to clean up after him while he does all the fun things and bosses her around—

while he plays either big-shot male executive or Che Guevara—*and he is my oppressor and my enemy.*"*[2] Radical activist Dana Densmore said, "No more us taking all the blame. No more us trying to imitate men and prove we are just as good. Frontal attack. It's all over now."[3]

There are other examples, Feminist Phyllis Chesler wrote a classic "victim" piece entitled "Men Drive Women Crazy." In it she attempted literally to prove just that.[4] And Kate Millett promulgated the idea that women were helpless because men controlled the basic mechanisms of society.[5]

A recent best-selling novel, *The Women's Room*, is written from a woman's perspective. The author, Marilyn French, has her heroine express an attitude frequently articulated by contemporary married women who are angry about their role. "She felt bought and paid for and it was all of a piece; the house, the furniture, she, all were his, it said so on some piece of paper."[6] In a recent interview, Marilyn French said, "All men are rapists and that's all they are."[7]

I personally noted an example of the extent to which such accusations can go during a panel discussion at the University of California, Los Angeles. The subject was human liberation. The speaker on behalf of women's liberation was an officer of the National Organization for Women (NOW). Part of her support for her contention that men exploited women was that women had traditionally been forced into having babies to satisfy the man's ego.

I was amazed to hear that. I thought of the beliefs most men, including myself, were brought up with: Women wanted to have children. Motherhood was their special form of fulfillment, just as jobs and careers were for men. It would be selfish, hostile and unmanly not to support a woman's desire for motherhood.

I thought of the many reluctant fathers whose wives had informed them they would leave them if they refused to father children. I also thought of many very young men, adolescent or barely older, whose personal growth was thwarted or retarded because of an unwanted, unexpected

* Italics not in original.

pregnancy. The woman concerned either refused to have an abortion or simply sentimentally expressed her desire to be a mother. The man got the message! It was his responsibility. He could not refuse to marry her and assume the appropriate, responsible roles of father and provider. Then there were the countless other men who fathered at an early age because they were busy building careers. They felt it was only fair to facilitate their wives' fulfillment by fathering a baby. Only a selfish man would deny her this, they had learned.

The notion of woman as victim is displayed in its extreme form in the catch phrase "Woman as Nigger." When one considers that blacks have lived through generations of rejection, hostility and humiliation, this comparison is ludicrous. Women have more often than not been placed on a pedestal and glorified for their birth-giving powers. These accorded them their special status: "ladies first." While it has become fashionable to reinterpret this phrase as a hidden, indirect put-down, its original, conscious meaning reflected men's belief in women's vulnerability and specialness. The history of the civilized world is replete with occurrences of men giving up careers, fortunes and kingdoms for the love of a woman, of men battling other men, often to the death, because of an insult to a woman's honor or because of competition for her love. Then they spent years afterward proving themselves worthy of her.

At its best, therefore, this depiction of the oppression and victimization of the woman by the malevolently motivated man is unbalanced, unfair and psychologically invalid. At its worst, it is harmful and destructive to the real potential in the man-woman relationship. It puts her self-righteously on the offensive. She walks her new road looking for implied put-downs and inequities, without a balancing emphasis on *her* contribution to the creation and perpetuation of these destructive gender games and on her responsibility in transforming them constructively. Any changes that result from such guilt-inducing accusations will only generate a kind of righteous hypocrisy.

As in the case of condemnation and guilt-making by religionists, the result is often repression and the hiding of the real self rather than genuine, meaningful growth. The man who buys this portrayal of himself as oppressor will thus be manipulated into repeatedly needing to prove he is not what she says he is.

In this regard men have been the victims of their own tendency to misperceive the woman and to dress her up in their fantasies. If indeed he kept her "powerless," it is most probably because he believed the often dirty, deceitful and difficult work of the outside world was beneath her and that only an inadequate man, willing to submit himself to hostile innuendo and direct put-downs from other men, would subject "his" woman to it unnecessarily. He has perceived her as fragile, easily hurt, possibly even destroyed by stress and insensitivity. Therefore it was his role to protect her. She was the keeper of the sanctuary, creator of their oasis—his place of retreat, pleasure and satisfaction away from the cold, harsh jungle. She was also the giver of life, and it was his role, the test of his manliness, to make and protect the best possible nest. Undoubtedly there were selfish reasons as well: She may have been his sole outlet for sexual satisfaction in a time when sex was not readily available, and he may have had concerns and anxieties about her being exposed to other men who might seduce her.

Until very recently, most men have responded to feminist accusations of chauvinism and oppression by passive or sometimes even direct and guilty agreement. Men so readily absorb guilt and responsibility because they are deeply woven into the fabric of the traditional man-woman relationship. He has learned that she is sensitive, giving, warm and loving ("sugar 'n spice 'n everything nice"). He is cold, selfish and a potentially brutish animal ("frogs 'n snails 'n puppy dog tails"). This perception emerges directly from the traditional *actor-reactor* interaction already described: The woman's role was a passive-submissive and therefore a non-responsible one, while the man initiated, structured and decided. Also, because he sees her as the physically weaker sex and as a woman like his mother, he views it as unchivalrous, unmanly behavior to place responsibility on her or to defend himself against her assertions and accusations with any kind of vigor. This would cut directly across his conditioned orientation. He validates his masculinity by protecting her. Consequently, even today, as she changes and emerges as a strong, autonomous person in her own right, he has difficulty perceiving this as real and responding appropriately. He is frozen in his protective pose, not out of a demeaning, oppressive motivation, but rather out of a tendency to see her according to his fantasies and needs.

The finger-pointing attitude, the accusations of oppressor-sexist-chauvinist, the blaming and victim posture used by some women deny their emergence as equally responsible people. It is the strategy of a child or a neurotic, manipulative irresponsible adult to attribute to others the failures and problems of life rather than to focus on one's own part in the creation of these problems.

As a therapist who often works with couples in marital distress, I have found that the least optimistic prognosis for significant, positive change is when one or both partners assumes a blaming attitude, while portraying himself or herself as an unfortunate, well-meaning and faultless victim. The point is that the assertion that men exploit women is as valid as the generalization that women manipulate men for marriage, security and money. For every chauvinist who "uses" women, there is a woman who uses wiles, coyness, helplessness and other "feminine" manipulations to gain her end and to goad him into proving himself the big man, the succeeder, the dominant, fearless, powerful protector. For every woman who is frigid because her man is insensitive and abrupt, there is a man who is abrupt and insensitive because his woman is frigid. For every woman who complains of being confined to kitchen and house, there is a man who is driven to exasperation by his wife's compulsive, annoying obsession with cleanliness and orderliness around the house. And for every man who patronizes prostitutes for the reason expressed by Jackie MacMillan of the *Feminist Alliance Against Rape* in Washington, D.C., which is that the "Johns" get their kicks from the feeling of power that comes from buying a woman and that the sex is often secondary,[8] there is the equivalent evaluation such as the one by a woman who was interviewed for a book on "Sex Objects" and who works in a massage parlor and takes "care of" men sexually. She said, "A man lying flat on his back, naked, on the verge of orgasm, looks ridiculously vulnerable and powerless; the masseuse has complete control. I think the women really get off on seeing men in that position."[9]

The following are examples of typical male life experiences. Who is in fact the victim here?

First, marriage. A man who wrote about a marriage that couldn't be saved stated:

> I went through the wedding mechanically, devoid of any emotion. I simply figured I was following a road that was meant for me to follow. But I was very conscious of Marie's emotions. She was euphoric, and I was happy to be able to produce that in her. She was very beautiful. Perhaps that gave me the happiness I needed. I thought maybe that was all I really was there for. . . .
>
> Our first baby was born. . . . It was a girl, and Marie was ecstatic. I felt her joy. I really did. It would have been hard not to. But I did not feel my own joy. There was a glow coming out of her, but I had the feeling that it had nothing to do with me, that anyone could have stood in my place. It seems to me that there was a game plan laid out long before I got there and I merely was pushed from spot to spot, like some checker on a board. Yes, I was happy I had a daughter, but I felt more of a numbness. Here I am. What am I doing here? I don't remember how I got into this spot, but I'm here, so I guess this is where I'm supposed to be.[10]

A divorced man talked about his experiences with women:

> Everybody is looking for a winner. They're impressed by position and status even if they're not being treated well. They evaluate a man by such things as his dress and his home.
>
> If you start saying you want freedom and space, they can't handle it. You can just tell that they wouldn't be there if you didn't have money. . . . It's really easy to get laid. Just go to a nice place dressed nice—everyone's looking for a well-off guy.

Regarding his job, he said that he really wanted success, but had found that it was a lot of responsibility and a lonely place to be. He felt that his woman (or any woman) wouldn't love him if he failed.

> Society preaches that you must be this or you must be that. Success has nothing to do with human qualities. I found that it was empty. I couldn't feel a damn thing emotionally. I was numb. Everything was in order, but nothing—no tears, no real happiness, no real sadness either. When you can't find anything to be sad about, that's *really* sad! I'm getting so I don't want to do anything. I'm emotionally upset by humanity. Not that I'm an angel, but it's discouraging to see that there's only one place you can go. Everyday I almost feel like vomiting.
>
> I've always had people crash on me, but I've never been able to crash on them. It scares the hell out of me. There's no one who cares enough. The only reason I'm here is to keep the whole damn thing up. I wonder why I can't sink. It's scary.

A Sunday-school teacher describes the way a father reacted to his son on the first day of class:

> A father brought his little boy into my room for Sunday school. The boy was quite small, only three years old. He didn't know me and was visibly frightened at the prospect of being left there. He was crying and clinging to his father. Normally I would have taken over in such a situation. I would have had the parent tell the child good-bye. Then I would have held and comforted him and assured him that his parent would return right after church.
>
> This father wasn't about to leave the child in my arms, though. He sat him on the piano stool and began to berate him for his crying. He spent several minutes demanding that the child not cry, that he act like a man. During this time, there was no touching or any type of comfort being given the child. He just sat there crying while the father carried on. Finally,

he slowed down his sobbing somewhat and the father then insisted that he shake hands good-bye.

A mother compares the behavior of her son and her daughter and the reactions of onlookers in an emergency-care situation:

> My daughter was three years old when she got her foot caught in the spokes of her sister's bicycle. Her foot was torn up and needed stitches. As the doctor was working, my daughter, who had to be held down by both myself and her father, screamed constantly. She was scared and it was painful, and she let us all know very clearly how she felt. She shouted at us very determinedly, "Stop that! You stop that stingy stuff!" And then she would yell that it hurt, over and over again. People in the other end of the clinic heard her and wondered what was wrong with the poor child. During the time the doctor was putting in the stitches, I stood at my daughter's head talking to her, trying to sympathize and reassure her that it would all be over soon. No one attempted to interfere with her reactions or mine.
>
> A few years later my son, who also happened to be three years old, fell and cut his arm on a piece of glass. It was apparent that he needed stitches, so I took him into emergency. I have never told him not to cry when he hurt himself, but he seems to have developed a need for restraint in spite of that. If I'm the only one present, he is fairly free with his emotions. But if others are present, he is not. In the emergency room, to the strangers, he appeared to be a very "brave boy." He was impassive. He held still when they probed for glass. He held still when he was given a shot. He didn't cry out at all. The people in attendance were very complimentary about this.
>
> But I could tell from the expression on his face that he was scared to death and was straining not to cry. I tried to let him know that I knew he was scared and that it was okay, that I would help him. I said something like, "This is really scary, isn't it? Jimmy, it hurts, doesn't it?" Right away I heard the

people around me saying things like, "Oh no, he's not afraid. It won't hurt! My, isn't he a nice husky boy?" I didn't argue with them but continued to hold tight to my son's hand and to provide what comfort I could.

We were soon finished and went home. I wanted to share my concern with my husband, that here was our son at such a young age already trying to squelch his feelings and act strong and tough. I began relating the sequence of events, and as I told of Jimmy's refusal to let his feelings show, my husband broke in and said, "Oh, I like that!" I could literally see him puff up to hear that his son had lived up to and had proven his inheritance. It seemed useless for me to go on. I just said, "Well, I don't," and dropped the subject. I knew then that I was kidding myself to think the pressure to deny feelings didn't exist in our family.

As women emulate increasingly the style and orientation of men, they may also expect to experience similar payoffs.

Thirty years ago men were twenty times as likely as women to get ulcers. Today the ratio is two to one.[11]

A recent study on suicide in California revealed that the suicide rate for women rose forty-two percent during the ten-year span from 1960 to 1970, while the male rate rose approximately fifteen percent. Nancy Allen, a suicide prevention expert at UCLA's Neuropsychiatric Institute, who prepared the study, interpreted the findings. "In precisely those arenas where liberated women are making the most progress the male-female suicide ratios move toward equality."[12]

In line with that, a report from the Medical College of Pennsylvania by Robert Steppacher, an assistant professor of psychiatry, and Judith Mausner, associate professor of community and preventative medicine, showed that among women professionals women psychologists commit suicide at a rate nearly three times that of women in the general population. Likewise, the rate for female physicians is three times the rate of women in general.[13] Perhaps these professional women are experiencing the stresses, conflicts and "pay-offs" that many success-oriented men do, namely, isolation and loneliness, emotional overcontrol, and constant conflict between professional ambition, success demands, and the fulfillment of personal needs.

The research firm of Yankelovich, Skelly and White, conducting a survey for the American Cancer Society, found that in 1969 only ten percent of teen-age girl smokers used a pack a day or more. By 1975 the rate had increased to thirty-nine percent. From ages eighteen to thirty-five the percentages of women who smoke more than a pack a day rose from nine to twenty-five percent.[14]

Between 1960 and 1972 the FBI Uniform Crime Reports show that arrests for serious crimes for women increased 256.2% as compared to 81.7% for men. In violent crimes such as murder and aggravated assault it rose 119.7%, and for teen-age girls it increased 388.3% as opposed to 203.2% for guys eighteen years old and under.[15]

The fantasy and hope that women in politics would have a humanizing impact and possibly generate a different perspective and mood is proving false. Instead, their performance is almost identical to the men. Comparing ten women members of the United States House of Representatives during the 91st Congress with thirty males of the same congress, Frieda L. Gehlen, a sociologist at the University of New Mexico, found that:

"Female legislators are no more conservative, independent or ineffective than their male colleagues, but neither is there clear evidence that they are significantly more liberal, dependent or effective. They emphasize the traditional female concern of health, education and welfare only to a small extent. This study lends little support to those who would like to argue that all will be well or ill with the world if women become our key political leaders."[16]

The blaming stance even permits wives to behave violently toward their husbands—to the point of committing homicide and attributing it righteously and exclusively to self-defense. This is a lethal variation on the theme of woman as victim, a rationalization that now more than ever in our culture demands serious and objective scrutiny. In 1976, for example, *for the first time in the history of Chicago, more women than men killed their spouses.*

"With more handguns available today, and women much more independent, it isn't surprising we're seeing more of this," said a police captain.[17]

The portrayal of the man as top-dog exploiter living a privileged existence and the woman as victim is a lopsided, black-and-white interpretation of the age-old gender dance. In its extreme form, it creates a paranoid atmosphere. As a closed system, the "victim's" perception allows for no new or conflicting information to alter his or her perception of the other person. While this orientation may temporarily succeed in intimidating the guilt-ridden other, it also widens the psychological gulf, rigidifies the interaction and creates an increasingly self-conscious, defensive and latently angry mood on the part of the habitually accused.

Women have as much to be legitimately enraged about as men. They have been deprived of their autonomy, their sexuality and their aggression by gender conditioning. But the price they have paid is no greater than for men, who have paid the price of masculinity with their emotions, expressiveness, capacity for intimacy, passivity, dependency, vulnerability and so on. To pull out the threads and determine who has done what to whom is futile, destructive, and probably impossible.

The woman who reacts with rage and fury at men for their alleged abuses reveals her lack of perspective and empathy. She is also not able to see beyond the surface to realize that men have been trapped in a powerful way, and that behind their chauvinism and sexism dwells a self-destructiveness, self-hate, isolation and rigidity. Be he the dominator, the wife abuser, even the rapist, more than anything else his behavior is a testimony to the most profound form of self-contempt and the rigid inability to change his behavior to a more self-caring style.

The woman who plays on the mono-theme of male chauvinism is exploiting a cultural fashion that at present sanctions such a biased perception. It apparently pays benefits with no immediate cost. But a more constructive orientation, presuming goodwill and a mutual desire to work through destructive gender roles, would be for both women and men to focus on the part of each in creating and perpetuating gender games, manipulations, deceptions, distortions and exploitations. This would probably be less exhilarating than the orientation which allows each person to see himself or herself as the maligned underdog combating a virulent oppressor. But it would generate a genuinely humanizing atmosphere which would allow both men and women to grow beyond destructive gender rigidities. And that is what feminists assert their ultimate motivation to be, anyway.

13. The Liberation Crunch: Getting the Worst of Both Worlds

Two men were dining in an expensive Manhattan restaurant with three women they had met that evening at the fashion-show opening of a new disco where admission had been by invitation only.

One of the men, Len Rockwell, was a vice-president of an entertainment agency. Bob Reynolds, the second man, was a young writer of fiction who had published two novels with fair success but paid his weekly bills primarily by writing commissioned magazine articles.

Of the three women, one was an attorney for an insurance corporation, another was a fashion editor for a popular women's magazine and the third, newly arrived in New York, had a job writing copy for an advertising agency. At the end of the meal—which included a drink before dinner and two bottles of wine—the waiter brought the check. He placed it by the two men. Rockwell was reaching for his wallet when Reynolds, sensitive to women's feelings about chauvinistic behavior in dating situations (having just recently researched an article on it for a singles magazine), casually said, "What would be the best way to divide up the check?"

There was an embarrassed silence. None of the women responded. Finally one woman said, seemingly on behalf of all three women, "We'll make it up to you later if we go somewhere for a drink." Rockwell, increasingly uncomfortable about what was going on, turned to Reynolds and said, "Let me get this one." He handed the waiter a credit card. The subject was quickly changed and the matter was never brought up again.

Harvey Gold, twenty-four, living in Los Angeles and working at a low-paying sales job in the garment center (having dropped out of a doctoral program in history), became infatuated with an attractive, outgoing young actress of twenty-three named Kathy. She had recently come to Los Angeles from a small town in Kansas, hoping to break into the film business.

Her impact on Harvey was instant and powerful. She had the natural, free, spontaneous and sensual quality he had always fantasized about finding in a woman. When he met her, he told himself that this was the woman he wanted to spend his life with.

Though he earned only $150 a week, he would regularly buy tickets to rock concerts that cost as much as thirty dollars apiece, would bring her little surprise gifts and on holiday weekends would take her to Palm Springs, San Diego and San Francisco. On occasions when she didn't feel well, Harvey would go to her apartment before and after work to bring her food and medicine and to run errands for her. It made him feel good to be protective of her and to let her know that she could depend on him. He wanted her to think of him as her best friend.

Secretly, however, he often felt hurt, resentful and insecure because Kathy rarely reciprocated by inviting him over for dinner, offering to help him clean his apartment or sew a button on a shirt she saw lying around waiting to be mended, which she knew he was less than competent in doing himself, and never bringing him any surprise gifts.

He never made an issue of any of this, afraid of seeming to be demanding, petty or, worse still, a "chauvinist pig." He knew from her enthusiastic support of feminism and her cutting remarks about the "sexist creeps" she met in the film business that she was very sensitive about the way men treated women. Also, she often quoted from articles she'd read in *Ms.* magazine, and in the car, while he was driving, she often sarcastically pointed out billboard advertisements that used sexist symbols to sell products.

Their relationship swung between euphoric highs and lows that were characterized by sudden, vicious interchanges. During one such fight, ignited by Kathy's forgetting to pick up concert tickets that were being held at a theater near the studio where she had acting classes, Harvey blurted out, "You don't really care about me, do you? I keep taking you to all of these concerts and expensive restaurants, and it hardly ever occurs to you to make me a meal or even a sandwich."

This comment enraged Kathy, who shot back, "I knew you'd bring that up someday. I was just waiting to hear that! You think you can buy my time and services with the few lousy dollars you spend on tickets or a meal? You spend that money for yourself, so you can feel like a big man. I never asked you to do it. But for me shopping and preparing dinner takes half a day."

When things quieted down, Harvey apologized for being so "demanding" after Kathy had suggested that they should consider breaking up if he thought she was so selfish, because she wasn't about to change to please any man.

Because Kathy turned him on sexually in a way no other woman ever had and he loved being with her, Harvey accepted the limits she set. He rationalized to himself, "You can't have everything. I can always go to a restaurant for a good meal, or to the cleaners to get a button sewed on, but a woman like Kathy is impossible to find."

The relationship continued until one of Kathy's beloved cats was found dead in the courtyard under the window ledge of her apartment. She had often told Harvey about the hostile remarks made by the building superintendent, an ex-merchant marine who had retired because of back injuries, regarding her three cats. He had unsuccessfully tried to get Kathy thrown out of the building because of them. Kathy suspected he might have been responsible for knocking her cat off the ledge while the cat was outside sleeping.

She asked Harvey to go with her and confront him, but Harvey refused. He had heard of the superintendent's explosive temper and paranoid personality, and he was frankly afraid. He confessed his fear honestly and told Kathy, "There's got to be a better way of dealing with this guy. Let's write a letter to the owner." At this Kathy began to cry and told Harvey she couldn't love or respect a man who was so "spineless" and "easily intimidated," and she wanted to end the relationship.

The wife of a forty-one-year-old physician who for ten years had quite contentedly played the role of the supportive "doctor's wife" suddenly transformed in her attitude. Almost overnight, with no obvious indications to her husband that it was coming, she told him she felt stifled and would not play the part of his "shadow" or "backstop," as she resentfully called it, anymore.

She asked him to move out, and soon thereafter she filed for divorce. On her behalf, her attorney asked for the house, custody of their children and alimony for eight years so that she could go back to school and become a counseling psychologist.

Because her husband typically worked a fifty- to sixty-hour week (which had been one of her chief complaints), and he knew he'd have to continue that pace now in order to support two households if she didn't come back, he did not contest the demands. Besides, he felt certain that she would eventually return and that there'd be a reconciliation. He moved into an apartment in a singles complex with a lawyer friend of his who had also recently separated from his wife. He considered this very temporary.

Less than a year later it became clear to him that his wife was not coming back. She had become emotionally involved with a younger man of twenty-nine who was a Ph.D. candidate in clinical psychology at the university where she was taking undergraduate work in psychology.

When her ex-husband found out about her affair and the fact that her lover often slept at the house overnight and that, according to the report of a neighbor, his ex-wife often prepared meals, paid for dates and bought gifts of clothing for her lover, he became enraged. He confronted her with this and threatened to stop all support payments. She responded to this threat by telling him that if he so much as missed even one payment, she would not let him see the children, and if he continued to withhold money, she would have her attorney press charges and have him put in jail. Furthermore, she told him if he harassed her in any way, she would get a court order stopping him from coming to the house at all. "I was ripped off of my identity for ten years playing the 'good doctor's wife,' and now that I'm enjoying myself and finding out who I really am you're not going to stop me," she told him.

The once demure "southern belle" wife of an investment counselor, always elegant and in the very best of taste in dress and manner, informed her wealthy husband that it was degrading for her to be asked to play hostess to his business friends and associates at their home. In the future, she informed him, she would no longer spend days arranging fancy dinners for those "materialistic boors." She told him that she found the constant discussion about stocks, bonds and real estate vile and would no longer be a party to it in any form. That meant she would not attend the numerous civic and "social" affairs they were invited to, which she found to be excruciatingly boring.

She told him that she would be spending her free time with people in the arts. "Business is your interest. You're turned on by it. I'm not. I'm interested in the theater, music and sculpture, so that's where I'm going to spend my time."

Michael and Roberta were high school sweethearts who married soon after graduation. Their relationship and the sexual excitement that were once so magnetizing deteriorated when Roberta decided to go back to college, and then to work for a graduate degree in speech and hearing. Meanwhile, Michael continued working the plumbing trade.

From year to year there was an almost direct correlation between her educational advancement and their marital strain.

Eight years after marriage, with two children in elementary school, they separated. Michael had a breakdown six months later after almost continuous drinking, and was admitted to a hospital.

Roberta told the psychologist who called her in after Michael had attempted suicide, "When I was about to take a job that had prestige and paid me almost as much the first year as it had taken him six years to earn, he began to say things that told me he felt angry and inadequate. I guess I picked up on that and couldn't respond to him sexually anymore, even though I tried. That made him feel even more inadequate. He blamed himself for not turning me on, even though I told him it wasn't his fault. Finally he wasn't even able to get an erection at all, and that's when he really fell apart. I had to leave him, or we both would have gone under. I couldn't stand to see him going from being a person who was so proud that nothing scared him to being somebody who seemed to be afraid of everything."

The twenty-eight-year-old wife of an electrician and mother of a six-year-old daughter told her husband she resented him for the pornographic films he'd been bringing home for them to watch during their marriage. Whereas she had once indicated to him that the porno turned her on, she now expressed the feeling that she had felt sexually exploited during all that time.

He had married her ten years before because she seemed to him to be the ideal woman. She loved homemaking, "desperately" wanted to be a mother and went all out to please him, even to the point where she went along with and seemed to enjoy his sexual whims and explorations, including the pornography, vibrators and experimentation with various exotic positions.

Soon after she told him never to bring home pornography again, she exploded in rage over the ways she said he had always expected her to cater to him. The list of tasks she now said she found demeaning included being responsible for his dry cleaning, laundering his shirts, preparing him a lunch to take to work and cleaning up after him. Then she dropped the big bomb. She told him she wanted a more open marital arrangement that would allow her to have her own friends and even date other men if the occasion arose.

The changes and demands at first enraged and then threatened her thirty-year-old husband, who worked in a business where he rarely had the opportunity to meet women, except for the few that sat around in the after-work bars, and they disgusted him. He pictured a life spent all alone if she left him, so he agreed to go along with her demands.

He began to do his own chores after work, packed his own lunch in the morning and even occasionally prepared his own dinner when his wife told him she'd be out late. He tried to develop a social life of his own, going out with the boys after work and trying to meet women, but found it boring and depressing. So while his wife explored her freedom, he found himself coming home each day after work.

He accepted what he knew was a painful and somewhat loveless existence, because he rationalized that the loneliness and the probable loss of his six-year-old child if the marriage broke up would be far more painful.

In most of these increasingly common situations the man found himself experiencing the dilemma, confusion and painful impact of being involved with a woman in the process of change while he himself had not yet been able to define his own new direction and respond in a self-caring way. Perhaps the rules and rhythm of the relationship were suddenly changed in midstream. Or he found himself in a situation where he was getting the worst of both worlds: He was still assuming the old responsibilities and pressures, being the strong man—protector—provider, but the woman he was involved with was no longer willing to play the roles that had provided him with the kinds of gratifications, satisfactions and securities that he had come to expect and depend on. In most instances he saw himself with no suitable alternatives or options. He was caught in the "liberation crunch," which means he still felt compelled to live up to the old model and pressures of the masculine role but without receiving the payoffs he had come to see as his reward for playing these roles. He was not only the "victim" of a woman who was behaving in hurtful ways, but also of his own rigidity, dependency, isolation and vulnerability which were now being clearly exposed. Consequently, he was not able to deal with the situation self-caringly and could only respond in helpless rage, or simple acceptance. Otherwise, he felt he would have to face the seemingly more painful experience of rejection and self-hate. In some cases, there were no apparent choices available to him at all as he found himself suddenly and inexplicably abandoned anyway.

The "liberation crunch" is occurring in endless variations everywhere today across the country, and it's not difficult to understand why so many men are threatened, traumatized and thrown into a state of desperation as they find themselves defensively clinging to a relationship that provides progressively diminishing payoffs. That is, while women begin to set new limits and write new rules—refusing to cater to the man any longer, rejecting the exclusive assumption of responsibility for household chores, insisting on establishing their own style and identity socially and in their careers, becoming sexually assertive and untying dependency binds—many of their men seem unable to relinquish their traditional role behaviors and ways of seeing and reacting to things. Consequently, the man continues functioning in the same style, still playing the old games by outdated rules, still feeling he must assume responsibility for being the performer, the provider, the protector and the stud. Since he has been portrayed as the guilty one, and labeled the male chauvinist exploiter and abuser of women, he now feels he must also be responsible for supporting the woman through her changes.

This situation often puts him in an increasingly untenable, unsatisfying and frustrating position. That is, he is still assuming onerous responsibilities and playing old roles without the usual payoffs, while his partner charts her new direction, increases her demands and throws off stereotypical role restrictions, informing him that he may no longer expect *anything* from her on the basis simply of her so-called obligations as a woman. While she has put him on notice that he should not count on her putting his needs ahead of her own and has made it clear that even the proverbial "barefoot and pregnant" is no guarantee that she'll harness herself, put up with anything stifling or even, for that matter, stay around, he still goes through his traditional posturings, trying to conform to the old masculine blueprints.

He finds himself unable to demand anything concrete in return, or to establish new limits and a balance that would afford him new payoffs and rewards to compensate for the loss of the old ones. Instead, because of his rigidity and the defensive essence of his masculinity, it seems impossible for him to shift gears and respond fluidly and self-caringly, and the price of being a "cardboard Goliath" becomes starkly apparent as he flails about trying to hold on and find some security and satisfaction in a relationship that has gone out of control and is increasingly frustrating and painful.

For most men involved with a woman who is throwing off the traditional feminine harnesses and restrictions, her liberation has meant nothing more than greater involvement with household chores, child care, and support for the woman in her new career and academic aspirations. In other words, it has only *added* to his pressures, responsibilities and burdens, and stretched him thinner, without providing any obvious benefits in terms of greater freedom, mobility, expressiveness, security and satisfaction, feminist rhetoric notwithstanding. What feminists describe as beneficial to the man in these changes is an ideal—a potential rather than the reality of his daily existence. For example, being forced into a more active participation as a father may be potentially rewarding. The fly in the ointment, however, is that he enters into new behaviors under compulsion rather than with any positive motivation of his own. He sees himself as without choice, and therefore changes to please her. There is probably no genuine, spontaneous pleasure even though he might tell himself there is.

In his anxiety over possible abandonment, his rigid self-definition, his lack of self-awareness and his inability to respond in self-caring fashion (by charting a new course that will enrich his existence, untie him from self-destructive response patterns and afford him new areas of satisfaction, pleasure and development) have become clear. He has instead defined his new role as accommodator to her changing rhythm. He is placating the energy of her new ambitions and the fury of her newly experienced resentments and demands, perhaps secretly marking time until she "comes to her senses" or falls on her face and gratefully resumes her time-honored womanly roles.

What would seem to be a glorious built-in opportunity for his growth and change also, were he fluid enough to take advantage of her new assertiveness, independence and overt sexuality, has instead become a nightmare characterized by fears of rejection and mounting frustration and paralysis. He is pinned by his own delusions of privilege and top-dogdom and his inability to shift directions.

He is trapped by his own unconscious defensiveness and corresponding inability to define himself as a person rather than a masculine thing. He has founded his identity and self-respect on his ability to perform, do his job, have his erection and assert his dominance. In the process he has isolated himself by making every other man his competitor and every woman an object and a witness to his exploits.

Faced now with a woman who no longer responds positively to his traditional style or, worse still, reviles him for it, he fears that to let go is to face identity annihilation. He has no recourse, therefore, but to accept, accommodate and adjust. As he does this, however, rather than pleasing her by giving her what she wants or what he thinks she wants, all too often he finds himself even less respected than before. To accommodate is to appear weak, guilt-ridden and pitiful, and ultimately to generate contempt in the other person. On some deeper level she may perceive correctly that his accommodation is motivated more by fear and rigidity than by love, goodwill or concern for her growth. Therefore, his accommodation rings false and repels her, even though on the surface she may respond with appreciation.

Listen to this comment from the authors of a recent book written to help women make their men more sensitive. Special attention should be paid by those men who equate their liberation in the eyes of the woman by their ability to show emotion and to cry. Say the writers:

> And so, somehow, you must decide how far you want to go in this journey toward sensitivity. An odd and troublesome little refrain we've heard again and again in our talks with some of the more futuristic social thinkers has to do with men crying. A man who feels free to weep when he hurts is taken to have achieved the ultimate in male improvements. "I want my man to get rid of all those macho trappings," a typical female dreamer might say. "I want him to feel he can cry in front of me without any sense of castration." We've talked pessimistically about this dream before, and now we ask you to consider it with cold honesty. Would you really want your man to weep frequently when things go wrong? Can you easily imagine him sniffling into a handkerchief, tears running down his cheeks? If the idea gives you trouble, then you already know something about yourself and him. You

know there are limits beyond which you don't want him to change.[1]

At present the composition of the "liberation crunch" is a woman in transition in a relationship with a traditional man. In this situation all of the options seem to be hers. It is up to her whether she chooses to play the part of the traditional or the liberated woman. Meanwhile, his behavior is a reaction and accommodation to *her* choice.

The man who in moments of honest reflection asks himself, "What is in all of this for me? What am I getting, and what can I expect in the future?" may find himself at a considerable loss to answer positively or optimistically. Her changes in combination with his rigidity have put him up against the wall. If he persists in his old ways, he stands accused of chauvinism and sexism. If he stretches himself to take on new responsibilities without making equal demands and throwing off parts of his traditional harness, he will only find himself overloaded and strained to the breaking point. If he lets go of the traditional masculine style completely, he may find to his terror that he is becoming invisible, unsexy and unworthy in the eyes of most women and even most other men, who turn away from a man who is without money, a job, status and power. The man who thinks he can avoid all of these dilemmas by finding and becoming involved with an "old-fashioned" woman is also placing himself in great potential jeopardy, as she may go into transition and change and alter the rules at any time, when her underlying rage over having to be passive and submissive is triggered into consciousness and overt rebellion.

Equally untenable and disorienting is being involved with a woman who knows what she doesn't want to do, but not what she does want to do. In such a relationship, for him to take a dominant role, for instance, is for him to stand accused of being sexist. To cease leading, however, may mean to see nothing happen at all. In a dating situation, for example, this may manifest as his deliberately avoiding chauvinistic behavior by seeking suggestions from the woman as to what to do for the evening, or waiting for her to initiate or structure a date, or even a conversation, and to be frustrated because little or nothing happens as she lapses into silence or passivity or quite honestly says that she doesn't really know what she wants to do that evening.

Another hazard of the "liberation crunch" is when he finds himself stretched in ways that entangle him in impossible binds. That is, while his woman partner may on the one hand vigorously assert her independence, she may at the same time resent him for not taking care of her. Or she may want power equalization and yet reject him if he is not more powerful than she. She may protest his macho style and his lack of emotional expressiveness and yet be repulsed by anything that smacks of his being effete, weak or overly emotional. She might protest his sexual aggressiveness that makes her feel exploited and like a "sex object" and yet not take the initiative and resist being sexually assertive herself. And while she protests the time and energy he puts into his career ambitions and his "masculine" interests such as sports, when he lets go of these masculine obsessions and begins to be readily available to her, she may find him boring, less attractive and too demanding of her time. The wife of a very busy attorney personified this bind when she cried to her husband that he seemed to have so little time for her, only to become exceedingly uncomfortable some months later when he began to talk about cutting down his work week to four days so that he could be at home more with her and the children. "I don't think I could stand your being around that much and watching me all the time," was her response.

The paradoxes and impossible binds for the male attempting to relate to a woman in transition in this "liberation crunch" were also well expressed and demonstrated by a twenty-two-year-old woman law student who was interviewed by one of my researchers on the question "What does the contemporary woman look for in a man?" The interviewee responded as follows:

> I want a man to be understanding, a good listener, a family-oriented person who is able to express himself and his affection and feelings. I want him to be compassionate, athletic and emotionally stable.
>
> I want him to be an all-around guy who plays many types of roles—father, worker, lover and so on.

> He has to be a flexible person in his reactions and outlook on people.
>
> If he earns less money it's O.K. But in a sense, I would not marry a man who made less money than me. For a marriage partner I want an achievement-oriented person, someone who is motivated to earn more money and be more successful.
>
> I would not want a "loser." If he's a loser, then he doesn't have self-confidence. That means there is a lack of motivation and concern and that turns me off.
>
> It doesn't bother me if he cries. I'd like him to be emotional because that would mean he is a very human person. But it would bother me if he was scared. I don't mind if he needs to make a decision and can't adequately judge and doesn't know the outcome if it's a really big consequence. But it's not O.K. for him to be whimpy. I also don't like a dependent man. I want him to be independent and confident in himself.

Along this line, the inherent contradictions and binds men find themselves in in trying to become less macho in their relationship with a woman were poignantly expressed in a letter written by a young man to a New York newspaper in response to an article that addressed itself to a question posed by a woman writer—whether women would be able to think of a non-macho man as sexy. The letter writer wrote:

> I am by nature a gentle and non-aggressive 27-year-old man who often finds women turned off sexually by my tenderness and non-macho view of the world. I have come to realize that for all their talk, a lot of women still want the hairy, sexy, war-mongering, aggressive machoman of their dreams. So after several fruitless years as a gentle poet-man, I now turn myself into a heavy machismo when I go out with a woman. It works. *I* open the doors, *I* order the food and drinks, *I* decide which movie or play we will see. I keep my shirt unbuttoned down past my nipples and wear a gold chain around my neck with a carved elephant tusk medallion, and if the relationship is not

working out, I make the first move and tell my companion that I'm sorry but we're through.

The sad thing about all this is that it *works*. After all those years of being naturally sensitive and gentle, and now I've got to turn myself inside out just to appear sexy. It's fun and it's nice, but I do wish I could just be myself again.[2]

AVOIDING THE "LIBERATION CRUNCH"

In the final analysis, the "liberation crunch" is not the result of women's anger or malevolence, but simply reflects masculine rigidity and the male's uncreative and reactive attitude toward the woman's changes. Trying to accommodate her new rhythm will only drive him crazy and unconsciously enrage him, just as her having been a *reactor* to him over the years created a pool of latent rage that finally erupted into the fury of feminism.

There is no psychologically constructive alternative for him except to develop a new blueprint for himself based on placing priority on his own growth into a self-caring, fluid, expressive person. To move in this direction he may require a support system composed of other men and caring women who will create for him the kind of supportive atmosphere that assures him that no matter what his growth involves and reveals, even if it threatens the status quo of his relationship with his woman partner as her changes threatened him, it is the only course he can self-caringly take.

Clinging to archaic models of masculine behavior will leave him a crumbled, anachronistic fool. Changing to accommodate to her changes will create rage in himself and contempt for him on her part. Changing to make himself a complete, expressive, transparent and emotionally in-tune, fluid person will give him a sense of well-being and self-care that will make it increasingly possible for there to be a genuinely caring relationship with the woman rather than one based on desperation, isolation and the desire for escape from her changes which are perceived as rejecting, intimidating and dangerous.

14. "Nothing I Do Pleases Her"; or, How to Recognize a No-Win Situation

Certainly one of the saddest manifestations of masculine vulnerability and rigidity can be seen by watching a man cling to a dying or already dead relationship. He hangs on desperately and tenaciously, despite the fact that he is getting little from the woman except indifference and rejection.

In fact, the relationship may have been deteriorating for a long time, and even he *himself* may have entertained thoughts of breaking free. Yet, when he is suddenly faced with the realization that his woman is involved with someone else or for other reasons is serious about leaving, his "love" for her and even his once flagging libido are reignited. In fact, there seems to be no more powerful aphrodisiac for a man than to be told by his woman that she wants out or is involved with somebody else. Perhaps the freedom created by a safe emotional distance and the excitement of the renewed challenge bring about a rebirth of his feelings of caring and sexual desire.

The same woman in whom he had lost interest, become bored with and turned off to is now a desperate obsession. Whereas earlier he may have thought her a ball and chain, once he is threatened with abandonment he perceives her as his lifeline and suddenly doesn't want anyone else but her.

Such was the situation for thirty-year-old David Rogers, a commercial photographer. He had been married to his wife, Terry, a shy, quiet, passive woman who had related to him in a subservient manner, for nine years. Intimidated by her minimal formal education, she would say very little at social gatherings, or even when she was alone with David. To her mind, he had all the answers, and was overpowering with them. Even when she disagreed with something or felt a conversation was boring or stupid, she said nothing.

Her husband never really noticed her moments of discomfort or resentment. He took it for granted that when she was unusually withdrawn that was just the way she was. In fact, he believed that's how most women were. He also accepted the fact that he would have to get his stimulation elsewhere, and he did, during his frequent trips out of town servicing clients who owned entertainment production companies.

His wife always remained at home, taking care of their two children. While she was forgetful about errands, often misunderstood his requests and got sick regularly, at least David knew she would be around to mind the house and children when he was busy working and playing. Evenings when he was home for dinner, conversation consisted mainly of his instructing her on better ways to do things and giving her lists of things to be taken care of the following day.

While he felt bored with the marriage, he rationalized that he couldn't leave. He had two children and a "good" wife who never questioned him about what he did during his trips out of town. He saw himself as having the best of both worlds.

He had become progressively uninterested in his wife as a person until one day she announced to him that she was moving out and that he could have the two children. She told him of an affair she was having. She said she was in love and would be taking an apartment in order to be free to be with her lover.

David became desperate. He begged her to stay, and told her he loved her no matter what she had done. Still, years of Terry's repressed anger came pouring out. She screamed at him about his indifference, the humiliation she felt when they were together with his friends and his treating her like a child and a "slave." She told him that she had known all along from the perfume smells in his suitcase that he had been having out-of-town affairs. She had said nothing to him only because she was afraid of him.

Now, however, she had had enough. She was leaving because she no longer felt anything for him. David cried and trembled in panic and guilt. He blamed himself for everything, apologized and promised her he would change. Anything she wanted he would do. He even called a psychologist—something he had always expressed cynicism about when he had heard that other couples were in therapy or marital counseling. When he repeatedly told her how he loved and needed her, she responded only with sarcastic disbelief. "You're just saying that because I'm finally doing what *I* want to do. But you're not going to stop me again."

The tables had turned completely. She moved in and out of the house several times over the following ten-month period, then finally left for good. The times when she returned, it was out of fear that she couldn't make it on her own because of financial problems. Each time, however, David accepted her back gratefully and hopefully. He grasped at any straw that suggested a possibility that they would get back together. During the times she returned to live with him, he even sat by quietly while she had lengthy telephone conversations with her boyfriend. David never stopped believing she would return to stay until she finally moved out of the city with her lover.

In another dramatic reversal, a forty-year-old, twice-divorced man who was a successful wholesaler of women's shoes came for consultation because he wanted to end a relationship with a woman he'd been living with for two years. According to him, no matter what he tried, he was not successful in getting her to leave. Since it was his apartment they lived in, he periodically packed all of her things in suitcases and boxes, offered her money for several months' rent and asked her to move out. She would become hysterical, at which point he would back off and let her stay.

When he came for consultation, he was at wit's end. "How can I get her out of my life?" he kept asking. At home he would insult her constantly, stay out late or all night and tell her about other women he'd been with. If she reacted negatively, he'd tell her to leave if she didn't like it.

One night he came home late and she wasn't there. At 3 A.M. she called to tell him she was at a girl friend's apartment and would not be returning. Within three days after that he proposed marriage, something she'd been asking for all along. She became suddenly the "most special woman" he'd ever known, as he now talked desperately to his therapist about strategies to get her back.

Whereas she had always called him at work—a habit toward which he reacted with annoyance—now *he* was calling *her* constantly at her place of employment, and *she* was putting *him* on hold and telling him that she was too busy to talk and would call him back later. While at first she had seemed somewhat receptive to his proposal of marriage, it now appeared that there was a lover in the picture with whom she was already seriously involved. In spite of this, he continued to pursue her with letters, gifts, phone calls, invitations and tearful pleas.

Many men in formerly traditional relationships with women they were sure of have experienced their recently liberated women going through profound changes. Often there were no other men involved. The message of feminism had connected, and they simply wanted to reclaim their autonomy.

Her previous attentiveness to every household detail became absentmindedness. Compulsive punctuality was transformed into a casual disregard for schedules. Her former reticence was replaced by aggressive pronouncements on assertiveness, freedom, "finding oneself" and "male chauvinism." The less involved the woman became, the more clinging her husband or lover became.

Often a man in this situation found himself caught in an impossible bind. The woman confronted him with complaints about his domination, preoccupation with success and sexist behavior. Many of the behaviors she castigated him for, however, were the same ones he thought had originally attracted her to him. If he tried to change to meet her demands and threats, while it may have temporarily placated her, she would be ultimately repulsed by his desperate hunger to please and his sudden willingness to give things up that she had been asking him to stop doing for years. He would be seen as weak and sniveling in her eyes. If he resisted change, she would reject him for his rigid chauvinism and "piggishness" and tell him they couldn't go on.

In many instances, I believe, a woman's transition into liberation comes after so much repressed anger has built up over the years that there is really no way to please her or to change in a way acceptable to her once these feelings are unleashed consciously. While it may appear that a re-alignment of the relationship is what she seeks, in reality the man may be facing a hurricane of these previously controlled and denied negative feelings, a force of emotion far beyond rational negotiation. Her feminist philosophy in these instances serves as the socially acceptable channel for this explosion of rage.

The man who fails to recognize this, who clings to the relationship in the belief and hope that the differences can be rationally negotiated and resolved, may find himself in for a prolonged period of humiliation and of being kept off balance as he grovels and gropes for the light at the end of the tunnel that never appears. Like a cowboy on a bucking bronco, he is hanging on for a little more time, but the end is inevitable.

Through all of this he continues to misread signals, to view things from a distorted perspective that allows him false hope. He is unable to see it for the hopeless situation it is, so he is stuck, unable to pick up the pieces and begin anew elsewhere. The false hope is apparently less painful than an acceptance of the reality.

Often such a man, involved with a woman who is going through profound changes, tries to accommodate by understanding and even supporting her feminist philosophy. Instead of pleasing his woman by doing this, however, he succeeds in alienating her even more. She reacts with suspicion and even contempt to these efforts, which she recognizes as being motivated by desperate fear rather than a genuine awareness, understanding and commitment to a non-sexist consciousness. The woman's resistance in these instances is, I believe, well founded. Only a masochistic, desperate and self-hating man could integrate without appropriate resistance all of the rage and guilt laid on him by an accusing feminist doctrine.

Contained in these turning points of change are important moments of truth. She is being united with her long repressed rage while he, in turn, is being reunited with his deeper vulnerability, dependency and the sham of his so-called control and dominance in the relationship.

The behavior of this man is also often an important illustration of the dangers of the masculine tendency to focus on intellectual or rational messages rather than the emotional and nonverbal aspects of communication. He takes what he hears from her literally. Consequently, while he is working at changing in the ways he hears she wants him to, she may be already in the process of replacing the relationship with other relationships that have become more important to her. However, he can't see or believe this. Instead, he is preoccupied with understanding her, figuring the situation out, developing strategies, adapting to the changes, coping with the rejection and hurt and trying to bring back to life something that is beyond reviving. Partially, he resists seeing the reality of her rejection because her pulling away puts him directly and painfully in touch with his lack of any other emotionally satisfying involvements or sources of support and comfort.

She, in turn, may be giving him just enough reinforcement to provide hope, probably motivated by ambivalence about her newly experienced power and her insecurities about her ability and capacity to make it on her own as well as the desire to let him down easy and not be unnecessarily hurtful. She therefore maintains some attachment to him and he uses this minimal involvement to fuel his illusions about the possibilities and potential of a reconciliation. He, however, cannot recognize that she is not interested in maintaining a relationship that no longer feels good to her. Consequently, he gratefully, hungrily and blindly holds on to anything that will feed his hope that things will again be as they were.

If he is the average working man in our society—not the professional person or the independent entrepreneur—he is *particularly* vulnerable to her shifts and changes and will be prone to accept all kinds of humiliation and buffeting in order to hang on to the illusion of hope. Contrary to the woman's belief about men's "privileged" position, his is largely a slave existence in which the opportunities to meet and form new and satisfying relationships with women are extremely limited. If his work involves heavy labor, he is probably surrounded primarily by men. The only women he might be able to meet are those who come to the bars he partonizes. In his mind, however, no woman worthy of an enduring relationship can be met there. Because of his extreme isolation from social environments where he can meet women, a situation which becomes particularly aggravated as he gets older, slower, more caught up in routine and responsibility and less able to communicate in the self-assured manner he will need to initiate relationships, his desperation will be especially acute. From his point of view, if he loses her, it may condemn him to a life of painful isolation in bars getting drunk. He is truly a trapped being.

Once the spiral of alienation from his woman is set in motion, if he doesn't know when to get out and begin some personal reconstruction, he may be irretrievably, seriously and self-destructively caught. Therefore, he must be able to recognize the signs of a no-win situation and not allow himself to be sucked into illusions he would like to believe are real but which, while giving him temporary hope, only make the eventual crash more painful. He is part of a disintegrating relationship because he couldn't read or deal accurately with the signs earlier on. Now he can't get out, because he fixates on each crumb of "hope" and denies the larger picture, which contains massive indications of indifference and rejection.

Over the years I have observed many such men trying to talk themselves into believing the unbelievable, ignoring the obvious and evading confrontations with the woman that would allow them to see the realities of the situation. Certain behaviors on the part of the woman, particularly when they are bunched together, are evidence, I believe, of the demise of the relationship, or, at best, the continued existence of a relationship contingent on the accommodating and self-degrading behavior of the man. The following are some of these signs and indications that I have compiled from working with many men in this situation. The man who resists recognition of them may be looking for love where it no longer is and seeing potential for renewal where the ground has been leached of all its nourishing elements.

SIGNS FOR RECOGNIZING A NO-WIN SITUATION

1) It's hard to pin her down to specifics of any kind—a date, plans for future meetings, how she really feels, what she thinks or what she's been doing. If you press the issue and demand specifics, she withdraws, tells you that you're smothering her and suggests that perhaps it would be best to end things completely. Out of fear, you back off and let *her* establish the rhythm and nature of the interaction.

2) She makes dates and shows up late, with ever-changing excuses, or she forgets to show up at all. Of course, you're always there on time. Occasionally, when she forgets, she may have forgotten so completely that if you never mentioned it, the broken date might have escaped her memory altogether. Clearly, she is not "there" for you, and you are no longer central in her consciousness.

3) She does not remember the nuances or subtleties of your preferences, your habit patterns and issues of importance to you, while you, on the other hand, seem to remember *every detail* of hers. Whether it be a food preference, a seating preference, a critical matter you are involved in and have told her about she seems oblivious. Your feelings are constantly being hurt by this, but if you tell her that, she responds with annoyance over your "spoiled," "little boy" expectations. "If you want me to remember, remind me. I have other things on my mind. Don't expect me to think of everything. I'm not your mother," might be her response.

4) On occasions when she tells you that she really cares about you or even that she loves you, you have a sense of unreality, a feeling that it's too good to be true and that the bubble will burst momentarily, which it almost always does.

Indeed, if in a romantic moment on the telephone she indicates this love, if you follow up her statement with a request to be with her right away or even very soon, she almost always has an excuse for why that would be impossible.

5) Frequently when you are with her, she seems distracted, preoccupied and resistant to being touched. Rather

than feeling welcomed when you come close, you sense that you're intruding on her, even though she may deny it. If you ask her why she seems so distant and cold, she tells you that it has nothing to do with you. It's just the mood she's in.

6) When the two of you are together, you feel that you're giving out all of the energy, and that, indeed, if you did not take responsibility for initiating and maintaining conversation or deciding on activities, little would be said or done because she is relating to you in a passive, detached, low-energy way.

7) When in a moment of extreme frustration and exasperation you say, "Maybe it would be better for us to stop seeing each other for a while," her response is calm, casual agreement. She might say, "Maybe we should. I don't like the fact that I bring this out in you. I obviously can't be what you want me to be, what you really seem to need." You then retract your threat.

8) There is no sense of continuity in the relationship. Each time you meet, it's almost like starting at square one. You feel no development of solidity or momentum, and after each time together, no matter how good it seemed, you sense that there might not be a next time.

9) You are obsessed with thinking about her. You rehearse conversations with her in your head and premeditate strategies for holding on to or interesting her. While nothing else seems important except being with her, you're often too insecure even to telephone her without your heart racing, while questioning whether you really should call or whether you're just making a nuisance of yourself and driving her away. You've lost your spontaneity and balance, and it's been replaced by premeditation, an overly deliberate scheming and manipulation born of insecurity.

10) You're constantly showing off to her, trying to prove yourself worthy in ways you don't ordinarily do—talking about how much money you just earned, how well you handled a situation, how successful you've been at work and so on. This reflects your very low self-esteem when in her company.

11) You catch her in little lies and distortions of the truth. If you confront her with this, she always succeeds in

evading admission and may even make *you* feel guilty for not showing more trust.

12) You're anxious around her, and certain self-destructive habits intensify. You find yourself constantly reaching for cigarettes or alcohol, sipping coffee, spilling drinks, clumsily bumping into things, dropping dishes, scraping your car in parking lots and in conversation frequently putting your foot in your mouth. You drive faster, stop exercising and become more belligerent with men who you think are coming on to her. All the things that in your more balanced periods you control and know better than to do you find yourself doing.

13) Like a child, you find yourself constantly asking everybody for advice, information and answers to help you deal with her. Underneath, the real message that you give off is that you're looking for reassurance and want people to tell you that everything will work out all right.

14) You focus on and magnify any little sign that allows you to tell yourself, "She wouldn't have said or done that if she wasn't planning to stay with the relationship." Your search for such indications and clues is insatiable.

15) Many parts of you emerge that you usually hold other people and even yourself in contempt for, such as possessiveness, clinging, suspicion, insecurity, jealousy, manipulation and the never-ending need to prove yourself in front of her. You withdraw energy from other relationships and from activities and pursuits that are important to you. You even feel uncomfortable and distrustful around male friends when she's around, because you think they're interested in her and that she might find them more attractive than you.

You think every man is interested in her. When you see her in conversation with other men, it generates anxiety and suspicion in you, because you suspect she's establishing a liaison. When you mention this to her, she becomes enraged, tells you you're being paranoid and that she resents your watching her.

16) You're constantly the one doing the apologizing. No matter what the conflict, you are left feeling at fault. She seldom acknowledges that she has done anything to create the problem or to hurt your feelings. The responsibility for problems always seems to be yours.

17) You give up things that are important to you—activities, friendships, work—to be with her at *her* convenience. You might even move to another city just to be with her, even though she wouldn't do the same for you. You are somehow always available and flexible in regard to getting together with her, while she is always having a hard time figuring out when she can fit you into her crowded schedule.

The meetings, therefore, always seem to be structured to accommodate *her* schedule and desire, not yours. You feel unable to change that, because you sense that her motivation to be with you is less than yours to be with her, and that if you pressure her in any way, she'll sever the relationship and you won't be able to see her at all.

18) You accept progressively more outrageous behavior on her part and self-degrading behavior on yours. You go along with things alien and humiliating to you to the point that you might even consider supporting her boyfriends if she wanted to have them move in with you and her. In short, you'll do and accept almost anything if you believe it will make the difference between holding and losing her.

19) While you're constantly thinking of little ways to please her—gifts to give, places to go, surprises and so on—she rarely, if ever, does the same for you.

20) She encourages you to take more freedom, do more things without her, even to see other women. However, you can't think of anything you want to do or anyone else you want to be with.

21) Sex, particularly "good sex," occurs only when *she* wants it. Even then you may get a sense that she's not really there with *you*. When you're turned on and she's not, you're left feeling like a demanding, lustful animal, the insensitive, "horny" one, and nothing you do can turn her on.

22) No matter what she does or says and no matter how objectionable her behavior, you put her on a pedestal and excuse her, thinking she's the most perfect, sensitive and incredible woman in the world. Obvious facts to the contrary are ignored or disregarded. *Clearly, you are addicted to your fantasy of her.*

23) You're terrified of doing *anything* to displease or anger her. The relationship feels so tenuous to you that

you feel anything negative could trigger her into leaving you. Indeed, arguments often lead to a threat from her that "we ought to end things completely right now. I don't want to hassle anymore." You apologize.

24) Many times when others are around, you feel as if you weren't there, or even that you're an intruder. Specifically, she may begin to talk to someone and forget to introduce you, or not include you in the conversation at all, leaving you standing there uncomfortably.

25) She doesn't call you or want you around when she's feeling bad, even though you tell her you'd like to be there for her. She tells you, instead, that she needs to be alone when she's blue or depressed.

26) She seems to say the very things that make you feel hurt or rejected. For example, you speak of love and she says she's not sure there is such a thing—that it's all really just immature dependency. When you speak of intimacy and relationships, she philosophizes about how people are afraid of freedom and don't know how to give each other space.

27) Your mood swings are volatile in relation to her. When she says something reassuring, you're elated and energetic. Desperation, loneliness, anxiety and apathy set in whenever she is cold or in any way seems to indicate a lack of interest in the relationship.

28) No matter how much you pursue clarification, you're never really sure of where you stand with her. When you ask her how she's feeling toward you, the answer is either evasive or an angry "Stop asking me!"

29) She is always surprising you. She telephones just when you've given up or even resigned yourself to never seeing her anymore. Then, when you think things are becoming more solid, she doesn't call when you expect her to or are sure she will. There's constant unpredictability that keeps you off balance.

30) You're obsessed with her during the day and are constantly struggling against the impulse to call her, to talk or to tell her that you love her. When you do, she often puts you on hold, tells you she's busy, just on the way out or talking to somebody, and asks you to call her back in a few hours. You don't want to ask her to call you back, because you sense that she won't, so you say yes.

When you do call her back, sometimes she's not even there.

31) She seems oblivious to your down moods. When you're hurting, she doesn't seem to notice your pain.

32) You're constantly having to explain what you *really* meant. Or you're interrogating her about the *real* meaning of something she said. Either way it's as if there is always some tension and distrust, a sense of walking on eggs that you'd like to avoid but can't seem to.

33) You rarely laugh around her spontaneously. Instead, discussions with her tend to be heavy, intellectual and grim in their intensity, as you are seemingly always and endlessly discussing and analyzing "our relationship."

34) She's always telling you she needs time, freedom and space to be alone, to collect herself and to think things over. She rations out the amount of time you can see her, and the amount of time seems to progressively decrease.

35) She considers your endless gropings for affection and reassurance to be infantile, and she tells you they make her uncomfortable.

36) Your intuition tells you that you're not central in her life, that she doesn't love you and that the relationship is doomed—and YOU'RE RIGHT! To fully accept this is very painful, but to continue to deny it will be self-destructive.

15. The Feminist Movement Can Save Your Life

It is both surprising and not surprising that the male would resist or even feel threatened by the emergence of the woman as a total person. *Were he self-aware and self-caring, however, he would not only welcome the emergence but would insist upon it while setting into motion equivalent life-preserving changes of his own.*

He has nothing to lose from feminism but his guilt and his fantasies of what women supposedly are. The guilt is a built-in inevitability because of the way he related to the traditional woman, struggling constantly to live up to the model of the ideal man, the dutiful and faithful husband, the responsible father, the successful career person and the sexual performer. In the process, he was always feeling himself falling short or in danger of doing so. When his life became more frustrating and painful than satisfying and pleasurable, and when he fantasized changing his life-style or the direction of his aspirations, he often found himself trapped. To leave or change or let go would mean to betray, inconvenience, hurt or let down those who counted on him, because in his mind *he* was ultimately responsible for everybody. He was strong. She was weak and dependent. He was unbreakable. She was fragile. He could take the stress and self-denial. She couldn't. His lot, therefore, was to suffer in silence and to take it like a man.

From a psychological perspective, in the traditional marital interaction he was daddy and his wife was the child. She expressed her femininity by being dependent and essentially unsexual except as an expression of "love" to him. Her love was as much a love born of need, a child's love, as anything else, and was based largely on her belief in his strength and protectiveness and not on him as a real person. She feared and avoided conflict and confrontation.

When it occurred, her response, because she was unable to assert herself directly, was usually a tearful, hurt one that subtly or directly laid the blame on him. As the "daddy," he saw it as his role and obligation to make the decisions, provide for everybody, take major responsibility for fighting the battles and so on.

Indeed, the closer his relationship came to being an "ideal marriage," the more it resembled this father-child model in its dynamics, and the more suffocating and destructive it had to become for him. However, from his masculine viewpoint there were no acceptable alternatives. To avoid or reject these roles and responsibilities would be to impugn his masculinity. Therefore, he went along with the program no matter what the price to himself. The guilt and self-hate for letting go or failing at these role demands were his constant shadow and chain, and in his imagination avoiding them far outweighed the possible benefits of any alternatives.

If men could see beyond feminist blaming and rage—rage that inevitably builds up in any party to a relationship who chronically assumes a passive-submissive role—the feminist movement could be regarded as simply a movement describing a new attitude. Primarily, it represents an insistence by women that they function as a whole people, rather than feminine gender stereotypes. They are saying, "We refuse to relate like children anymore."

By doing this, the woman is shattering the man's fantasy of her as the weak, ethereal creature, the balancing opposite to his self-perceived animallike, selfish and destructive nature. It is hard for him to believe her when she communicates to him that she is not who and what he thinks she is.

He has come to need this fantasy of her in order to justify his own rigid, destructive style. Though it alienated him from other men, he saw himself as doing his performing, competitive and often destructive dances primarily for her. It is indeed disorienting and painful to have one's system of rationalization and justification pulled away, for now he too is faced with the psychologically threatening task of having to become a whole person rather than remaining a gender stereotype.

The best part of the old-style, traditional, *actor-reactor*, man-woman relationship was the fantasy, the initial burst of elation, the sense of magic and salvation that occurred upon meeting and joining. It felt to him as if he had been rescued from isolation and meaninglessness. The moment-to-moment process of the relationship, however, as it evolved in this dominant-submissive, daddy–little girl, "macho warrior"–"earth mother" interaction had to transform it into an increasingly deadening and unsatisfying experience.

The feminists would have us believe that men's satisfaction in these traditional relationships was in the control they supposedly had. He was the authoritarian thriving on her dependency and helplessness and her "need" for him. However, his was the kind of "power" and "control" that a parent gets in knowing a child won't leave as long as the child is unable to function and survive autonomously in the outside world. In marriage it is an expensive, exhausting form of control, contingent on the woman's remaining a child and relating in childlike fashion. The price for this is that he is endlessly under pressure to perform and drained constantly by responsibility. It is the sick parent who is distressed by a child's growing into maturity and autonomy. The healthy parent welcomes the easing of burdens and the pleasure of relating to the child as a capable adult person.

There are aspects of the way in which feminine changes have taken place that caused some men to react with resistance and justifiably with a sense of threat. So often what has been portrayed and labeled "men's lib" in the media, which in the minds of many people is a counterpart to feminism, amounts to a harried man rushing home from work to help with household chores such as vacuuming, washing dishes and cleaning or baby care. While there is nothing inherently wrong in the man's sharing in these responsibilities, compare that image of liberation with that of a woman emerging as an independent, assertive, sexual person who is redefining her role and her life to meet her needs for growth. In other words, while women's liberation has been depicted as a joyful, energetic freeing up and casting off of sex stereotypes and the onerous responsibilities that accompany them, "men's lib" has been depicted as the *addition* of responsibilities and onerous tasks to an already laden and pressured life and little else. No wonder the average man has resisted and reacted defensively.

In other words, what has been commonly described as "men's lib" is not liberation at all, but merely accommodation to women's changes. *What this means is that once again he is playing daddy, only this time, unlike in the traditional relationship where he got nurturance and support, the payoffs are almost nonexistent.* Changing would simply allow him to hang on to the relationship a little longer.

Authentic liberation means assertion, freeing up, breaking through gender barriers and refusing to continue playing self-denying and self-destructive games. It does not mean accommodation. For the man's liberation to be defined in terms of being a reinforcement and support for the woman while she goes through her changes is for him to be once again placed in the role of "strong man." His first assertive step must therefore be to reject that role with the realization that she is strong in her own right—indeed, *stronger* than he in many ways—and to transfer the focus of his energy toward finding ways that allow him to free up his own life from lethal and non-gratifying patterns.

Feminism was not born of or propelled by accommodation, but rather by a rejection of accommodating attitudes. The liberated woman is refusing to play nursemaid, housekeeper or "earth mother" anymore. It is time for the man, therefore, to reject the role demands on him to play superman: the unneeding, fearless, unemotional, independent, all-around strong man. Liberation for him would mean a reentry into the world of playfulness, intimacy, trusting relationships, emotions and caring, and a priority on fulfillment of *his* needs and *his* growth.

Until now, for many men the message of feminism has simply been that he has been a "bad boy," who must stop being a chauvinist. Nowhere has he been clearly informed or figured out what feminism *could* mean to him, i.e., no longer having to take responsibility for the woman. Furthermore, he could now also expect from her as much as he gave to her. It is no longer necessary for him to be exclusively responsible for courting, paying, performing, providing and deferring. In short, he no longer needs to put her on a pedestal, to hide his true self from her and to behave like a drone buzzing around a queen bee.

Clearly, the woman's role *before* feminism was psychologically disastrous for him. Because she repressed her autonomy, the burden of responsibility and decision making was placed on him. He was under constant pressure to produce and to be right. Her dependency may have engulfed and smothered him, but he couldn't acknowledge it. That would have meant being unmanly. Because it made him feel guilty to reject responsibility for her well-being, he could have no other relationships that might detract from the commitment to "his" woman. Nor could he walk away from an unsatisfying job, because she counted on him. Whatever resentment he felt about all of this he had to repress or deny. To control these feelings, he behaved in an even more mechanical, detached way. This only brought him further criticism, as he was then attacked for not being sufficiently involved and human.

It was clearly a no-win situation. To be a man, he had to take on burdens that eventually overwhelmed and deadened him. If he rejected them, however, he felt guilty and considered that he was a failure. Alcoholism, television, work, cars and watching sports became his distraction and salvation. All were largely dehumanized activities. Often, too, he was chided for overindulging in them. So while her dependence on him may have given him a sense of "control," since he saw her as helpless and was therefore convinced that she would never leave him, from the psychological vantage point he paid a heavy price.

The woman *before* feminist emergence denied her sexuality. She was to be sexually expressive only to a point, which meant satisfying her husband, and only in response to the overtures he initiated. The combination of his lustfulness and her denial of her own sexual need transformed the sexual experience into a gift that she granted him. It gave her tremendous power, although at the cost of her potential pleasure. She could control him and grant him sexual gratification in return for his courting her handsomely, taking responsibility for her, marrying her, giving her what she wanted and so on.

Theirs was, therefore, the relationship of a sex-hungry man and a woman who was all-powerful because she didn't need what he seemed to need so badly. To get it he would pay as high a price as he was capable of. He did so with gratitude and fear that the prize might be withheld or withdrawn again at any time if he stopped performing successfully. In this respect, if he was married he was trapped. She could withhold sex and he could do nothing except humiliate himself by trying to seduce or otherwise persuade her. Once he had married, if he chose to "cheat" on her or leave her, the price was often the loss of most of what he had worked for.

That time was not so long ago. Until recently, most men made lifetime marriage commitments because they hungered for regular sex. Often they married while they were still unable to see the woman as a person beyond her vagina. Then, it was too late. After the wedding he often found himself again in the pathetic position of having to beg for the very thing he had paid so dearly for. Clearly, the dynamic couldn't have been uglier or more degrading for him. Although she many times gave him sex, it was with a passive unenthusiasm that turned it into a distasteful experience, and may even have caused him to become "dysfunctional" in response to the uninvolvement on her part. Then *he* would be flooded with feelings of inadequacy and terrifying doubts about his masculinity. In this old-time man-woman interaction the feminists are rejecting, the man was a source of security who was reinforced and rewarded with sex according to his success. *He married a sex object. She married a standard of living.*

The fantasy of the woman Madonna, someone who is sexually "pure," is also being rejected by the feminists. As a result, he need no longer feel himself to be the hungry animal lusting after a woman who grants him a gift of love because she does not *need* sex. Recent studies on female eroticism, in fact, caused researcher Julia R. Heiman to conclude, "When the smoke clears after the last battle of the sexes, I suspect we will find that men and women aren't as different as we thought—not in needs, not in desires, not in sexual response. Jong's fantasy of the 'zipless fuck' is, after all, what males have yearned for and joked about for years: a sexual encounter with literally no strings attached—neither physical ones, such as zippers or girdles, nor emotional ones, such as feelings of guilt and anxiety."

Heiman continues, "My research finds, indeed, that women like erotica as much as men do, that they are as turned on by sexual descriptions, that their fantasies are as vivid and self-arousing. . . . The experiment also tested the cultural assumption that women are slower to become aroused than men. It is possible that they are merely slower to *admit arousal*."*[1]

Using a series of erotic and romantic tapes, researcher Heiman wrote, "We found, first of all, that explicit sex, not romance, is what turns people on—women as well as men. . . . One erotic tape . . . was especially sexy to women, the female-initiated, female-centered story. . . . I was fascinated that both sexes preferred the female initiator."[2]

The woman before feminist emergence also denied her aggression. Consequently, she resisted dealing directly with conflict and fighting on her own behalf. If she saw herself as injured or neglected, or if she sensed her husband's resentment or anger, she responded with tears or demonstrations of having been hurt. She presented herself as sensitive, fragile, weak and easily injured. In contrast, he was portrayed as the insensitive and hurtful one. He was ultimately responsible and therefore had to apologize. Fights had to be his fault, because she did not release her anger or aggression directly. She simply reacted to him and gained her power and control by acting helpless and maligned.

She gained her power indirectly also by making him feel guilty. Or she developed a repertoire of symptoms such as "nervousness," worry and fear. If he "misbehaved" by coming home late, looking at another woman, forgetting a birthday, making a hurtful remark and so on, she punished him by withdrawl of affection. The conflict, the differences, the causes of the difficulty were rarely dealt with or worked through directly. Nothing could ever be resolved, therefore, and there was little he could do but feel guilty and accept her demands.

In other, more damaging ways the repression of ag-

* Italics not in original.

gression was destructive to males. It is my belief that the resentment and rage a wife felt toward her husband over being "controlled" and "exploited" she displaced onto her son, toward whom she would overreact with excessive discipline, control, defensive overprotection and a punitive blocking of his sexuality and aggression. She reacted to her son as she might have wished to react to her husband but could not. The result of this, I believe, may partially explain the astounding disproportionate rates of problems experienced by young boys in comparison to young girls. Autism, hyperkinesis and stuttering all show rates several hundred percent higher for boys. Childhood schizophrenia is almost 50 percent higher.

According to government statistics in the early 1970s, admission to state and county mental hospitals for behavior disorders for boys in the five- to nine-year-old group was sixteen times greater than for girls.[3] Boys outnumbered girls five to one in this age group for admission for adjustive reactions.[4]

For residency in state and county mental hospitals, boys outnumbered girls by approximately ten to one for behavior disorders, and five to one for adjustive reactions.[5]

Psychologists Janet Hyde and Benjamin Rosenberg recently explored the myth of the demure little girl. With a broad sampling of females of all ages who were asked if they considered themselves tomboys when they were growing up or, for the young girls, at present, over 60 percent said they either were or had been tomboys. These researchers found that "tomboyism is not so much abnormal as it is typical for girls." The image of the sweet, passive little girl sitting at home by her mother's side was, they concluded, a false stereotype.[6]

The woman before feminist emergence denied her assertiveness. When asked by the man what she wanted, what she liked or disliked, where she wanted to go and what she wanted to do, she frequently responded with a vague "It doesn't really matter," or "Whatever you want." She would go along with his choices but often react later with boredom or even resentment.

In the matter of sex, also, she rarely asserted herself. It was hard to determine what she really liked or disliked. She saw it as her job simply to please him. She waited for him to initiate and orchestrate the experience. Her resistances emerged as physical symptoms—headaches, fatigue, cramps and so on. Or she responded simply in lukewarm or passive fashion, which was also a powerful message of rejection. They were her indirect ways of saying the no she could not take conscious responsibility for.

Because she did not initiate sex or assert herself sexually, a "bad" sexual experience was blamed on *his* ignorance, insensitivity, poor timing and so on. In this regard he was caught in a bind. She would not clearly define her likes and dislikes, nor would she initiate sex. Consequently, he was groping in the dark, and when things went wrong, it was not possible to remedy them. She would not give him feedback or take responsibility and he could only blame himself.

Overall, with her autonomy, sexuality, aggression and assertiveness repressed or consciously hidden, he was living out a part of a gender nightmare which he believed he was supposed to enjoy. After all, he was the master, he was told. The moment-to-moment reality of the situation, however, had to be excruciatingly unsatisfying, crazy-making and boring. He knew something was wrong, but there seemed to be no workable clues or ways to change things. It was a situation beyond his control.

Feminism has been a trauma for some men only because they have reacted defensively, trying to accommodate to the woman while being castigated for being exploiters and chauvinists. These were accusations he could not see beyond. While she was busy defining her new role, he was busy trying to adjust to it rather than redefining his. While she reexamined and rejected aspects of her roles as wife and mother and passive-supportive figure, he was unable to challenge the preconceptions and presumptions of his roles as father, husband, active dominator and so on.

Perhaps the single most valuable contribution of feminism has been the way it has chipped away at men's fantasies about women. Today it is the destructive woman, consciously or unconsciously intent on controlling, manipulating and exploiting men, who feeds on his regressive, pathetic desire to see himself as the dominant superman. In return for these false ego strokes, he assumes responsibility for her. As a result, his emergence out of the gender nightmare is aborted, and he remains a posturing caricature.

This hostile attitude was well expressed by one woman who responded with the following comment to a survey on attitudes and experiences regarding the roles of men and women in our society. She wrote:

"[If men learn that women are superior] we'll be stuck with a lot of sniveling little boys clinging to our skirts. It's better to let them think they're king of the castle, lean and depend on them, and continue to control and manipulate them as we always have."[7]

A man is in jeopardy if he fails to realize that the "fragile," "passive" women of today is not "feminine" but repressed, and may well emerge as the angry woman of tomorrow who will turn the tables on him at a time when he may hardly be prepared or equipped to adapt to the changes. Such is the price of refusing to recognize what is.

The man who grasps the psychological meaning of feminism will be the man who can liberate himself from the destructive compulsion to perform and to assume all responsibility. He will be free to create a life-style that puts a focus on his own development as a person. This will mean an end to the all-consuming obsession with success, which has produced in him a defensive, distrustful stance toward the world such that all of his energies go toward protecting and proving himself. He will live not by the symbols of masculinity but by the measure of whether his life feels good and brings him in closer contact with himself and other people. Gone will be the days and the relationships that have drawn him into endless penis waving, muscle flexing and wallet flaunting in order to prove that he is worthy of love and respect.

Indeed, should the feminist movement falter, should the impetus toward female liberation be slowed by the regressive pull of old-time manipulative feminine role playing, men, out of the most self-caring of motives, must insist and facilitate woman's transition to the point where she relates and functions as a total person who is equally responsible, sexual, assertive and autonomous. The growth of men depends on the growth of women, and vice versa, in order for the sexes to experience the full potential of themselves and each other. To fall back into the sex-object, success-object way of relating may be a temporarily anxiety-reducing, even seemingly pleasant seduction because it is familiar ground, but the price will be the continuation of the destructive gender fantasy which perpetuates the annihilation of each other's full personhood.

PART FOUR

HE AND HIS CHANGES

16. Self-Destruction Is Masculine, Getting Better Is Feminine

It is a core factor in the tragic paradox of masculinity that the attitudes and patterns that break a man down are uniquely masculine, while the processes required to move him in the direction of reintegration and growth are feminine.

The traditional man does not come to therapy until he has reached an insurmountable crisis and exhausted all other remedies. He is usually in a state of desperation when he arrives for help and, understandably, he wants instant relief and concrete results. No matter that his crisis is merely an end point, a rupture caused by years and years of repression and unawareness.

After working with large numbers of men over a long period of time, one can predict with fair accuracy a man's initial response and the length of time he will remain in therapy. The more "macho" he is in his orientation, meaning that he is:

1) Strongly rational or problem-solving oriented;

2) Threatened by the acknowledgment of weakness, fear, vulnerability, the exposure of his inner life or the fact that he can't solve his problems himself;

3) Competitive toward other men and compulsively needing to prove himself superior and able to control and dominate situations while projecting an image of self-containment and strength;

4) Impatient and suspicious of any process that has no clear-cut path or timetable and promises no specific results;

5) Needing to project a totally masculine image while defensively denying anything in him that might be construed as "feminine" or "homosexual"; and

6) Fearful of depending on and trusting somebody else,

the quicker will his anxiety, resistance, resentment and overall defensiveness build, causing him to back away from the therapeutic process. In fact, if there were surgical procedures or drug therapies available that could bring women back to their terrified husbands or lovers, restore erections instantly or create success, most men would forever close themselves off from the exploration of their emotions and their life experience.

Typically, the more "macho" his orientation, the more resistant will he be and the more delicate will be the process required to bring him around to a commitment to the arduous and unpredictable process of growth.

A thirty-one-year-old bus driver came for psychotherapy because his twenty-nine-year-old wife had become involved with a fireman she had met while working as a hostess in an all-night coffee shop. She told her husband of her intention to move out and file for divorce proceedings, though financial insecurity was causing her to postpone an immediate move. After his initial shock he retaliated by dating several women and was impotent with each. His wife had always passively accommodated his most idiosyncratic sex fantasy or experiment, even though she found it distasteful, and so he had never had any potency problems with her. He had treated her like a sex object, never even aware of her growing resentment and lack of genuine responsiveness. His experiences with his dates, coupled with the prospect of losing the woman with whom he felt sexually secure, terrified him. So he came for psychotherapy.

He entered the office looking very depressed. He ruminated openly about suicide. He was filled with regret and self-hate over what he had put his wife through sexually. He described all the things he had done to try and get her back—threats of self-destruction, violence toward her boyfriend, withholding financial support and fighting for custody of their child. Nothing swayed her. He looked to his therapist for an "answer." After only forty minutes of the first session, when his therapist said he could offer no quick or easy solution, the patient stated, "I don't think I'm getting anything out of this. I knew I would be wasting my time," and he left.

In a similar instance, a man in his mid-thirties who had been abandoned by his wife six months before and had since been having difficulty getting erections came for therapy because he had found a woman he felt he might want to marry. He had not yet risked sexual involvement and came for therapy to prepare himself so that he'd be sure not to fail. He was afraid that if he couldn't perform, her image of him as a man would be destroyed and she would end the relationship. He was even concerned lest she somehow find out that he was seeking help. This would mean that he had "clay feet," and she would lose her romantic feelings. Further, he sought immediate assurance that his employer would never find out he was seeing a psychologist, because he was up for a promotion and feared he would be labeled "unstable."

He came, as many men do, looking for psychotherapeutic magic. He wanted his impotence "cured" as quickly as possible. He announced defensively that he knew many women who had gone to "shrinks," and he didn't see any real changes in them. However, he didn't know what else to do, so he would give it a try. He said, however, that he didn't want to waste time talking about his past or himself. He wanted a solution to his "sex problem."

When his therapist didn't immediately pursue a line of questioning focused on sex, he became antagonistic. He asked if the therapist performed hypnosis or could teach him fantasy imagery that he could use to stimulate himself when he was having trouble. When the therapist said he didn't feel that was the best solution the patient asked to be referred to a urologist. "Maybe I have a physical problem," he said.

A twenty-five-year-old man, a bank-management trainee, came for psychotherapy because his wife of two years was openly involved in an affair with a young attorney who lived directly across the courtyard in their apartment complex. His wife informed him that she needed a month to think things over and to decide what she should do and would be taking her own apartment. Her husband pleaded with her to give him a chance to change in order to get her back. When he asked her to be specific about what she didn't like about him, she told him that his temper was a major cause of her leaving.

He took her contention literally and came for therapy.

He announced with great urgency that he only had one month to change and wanted to know how to get rid of his temper. When his therapist asked him if his temper was a lifelong problem, he replied that he had always thought of himself as mild mannered until about a year ago. When his therapist responded that perhaps his temper was a reaction to something in the relationship, the patient retorted, "I don't like my temper, either. I think she's right. Just tell me what I can do about it." When his therapist told him that they'd have to explore his angry reactions in greater depth, the man asked for a tranquilizer prescription to hold him over in the meantime. He couldn't risk the possibility, he said, that it might take longer than a month to overcome *his* problem.

The bind faced by any therapist working with these men in their time of crisis is that by the time they come for help they often feel that the stakes are too high to engage in any time-consuming process. If the therapist accommodates the patient's urgency with some expedient procedure that might bring about a temporary change and a reduction in discomfort, the patient is likely to terminate. The usual comment is, "I think I can handle things from here. I feel much better." The hard job of growth and self-awareness has been aborted. If the therapeutic process is allowed to proceed at its usual and slower pace, the patient's anxiety, impatience and resistance often become so great that he leaves to seek out an alternate solution. Either way he never really learns about himself, and the problems are bound to recur.

A twenty-five-year-old marketing manager with one of America's largest computer corporations came for help because of the panicky feelings he experienced whenever he had to make a presentation at a staff meeting. He was intensely competitive, and was concerned that if he didn't overcome his problem quickly the other salesmen might soon be passing him in the climb up the corporate ladder.

Realizing the urgency of the situation (several important presentations were scheduled for the next few months), his therapist used the behavioral technique called systematic desensitization. This is a form of relaxation training and requires the patient to lie on the couch with his eyes closed as he pictures himself in the process of preparing for and giving his presentation.

Shortly after beginning his first session, the patient became noticeably tense. His therapist asked him what he was thinking, and he replied, "Nothing." After another twenty minutes of obvious discomfort and an inability to focus, the patient fearfully revealed his fantasy that the therapist might attack him violently and homosexually. Asked to explore this further, he began relating experiences with his father and early memories of being insulted, punished, hit and called a sissy when he performed poorly at a task. He related this to his experience during a sales presentation where he imagined his peers making fun of him if he made any mistakes or did not appear polished.

Had his therapy remained confined only to symptom relief, specifically the elimination of his "stage fright" or nervousness while making a presentation, the underlying dynamics that were the actual cause of his anxiety would never have been uncovered. He might have experienced temporary relief, but the problems caused by the deeper feelings would have intensified. Increasingly, his energies would have gone toward protecting himself against these anticipated assaults.

Because men define themselves by denying the existence of internal and emotional factors that threaten or contradict their masculine image, they will avoid an approach to their problems that is probing or psychological in nature. The idea that there is something inherent in their masculine orientation that might be a factor in creating their problems will provoke hostility and a defensive reaction.

At a talk I gave in a conservative business community in California, sponsored by a chapter of the American Association of University Women, many men were present who would not ordinarily have come to my lectures. They were there only because they traditionally accompanied their wives to this once-a-month meeting for married couples.

The majority of the men in attendance were between the ages of thirty and forty, and many were in the midst of developing their management and business careers. A half hour into my talk, the tension level in the room was unusually high as I elaborated on the subject of masculinity and the "hazards of being male." Several men were nervously shifting about in their seats, looking down at the floor or at me in obvious resentment. After the presentation was over, a conversation with the husband of one of the women who had arranged for my talk revealed his concern that one of the men would lose control and become physically assaultive. He had planned a strategy, as he stood in the back of the room, in the event that this happened.

The "macho" male, resistant to psychotherapeutic help, is often still unconsciously reacting to his painful and destructive relationship with his father, who had been rigid, punitive and emotionally withholding when he was a young boy. Entering therapy with a male therapist, who is seen as an authority figure, threatens to reproduce the father's hostile reaction to any exposure of the patient's inadequacy, fear or weakness.

A thirty-two-year-old man, a compulsively achievement-oriented accountant who was completing law school at night while holding down a full-time job, was ridden with anxiety and feelings of inadequacy. He described his relationship with his father this way: "My father never felt that I did anything right. He has never shown in any way that he cares for me. I never told him how I felt inside, because he would have gotten angry and thought I was weak."

In a more pathetic instance, a professional counselor who was a quadriplegic victim of the Vietnam war went for therapy because of severe strain in a relationship with a woman he hoped to marry. He sought out a female therapist because he said that he could never trust a man who might turn out to be like his father. "He was so cold, so violent. He never showed any feeling except violent anger, and if my brother or I showed any feelings at all he would beat us. He beat us into holding everything inside. I can't do that anymore. He'd never understand this."

There are numerous vicious circles that operate in the father-son relationship that perpetuate and intensify the emotional strangulation that takes place from generation to generation. A father who has incorporated as a positive value his own compulsive self-denial as he stoically takes on stifling and frustrating roles passes on his own emotional repression and self-punishing orientation to his son. He erupts in explosive defensiveness when his son displays any of the emotion he himself has expended much of his psychic energy to control and deny. He is much like the puritanical mother who reacts with extreme punitiveness to any overt expression of her daughter's sexuality, the impulses she has fought against and denied in herself.

The paradox of psychotherapy, one of society's approved ways of getting better emotionally, is that the process itself, if analyzed according to its dimensions, is essentially a feminine and unmasculine enterprise. Consequently, it throws a man up against the very things in himself that he fears most. It is understandable, therefore, that most men are inclined to ridicule the process of therapy and to view it as a rip-off, an expensive price to pay for a shoulder to cry on or a waste of time engaged in primarily by unstable women. The male view of it as a "feminine" activity makes sense when one recognizes that a person who enters therapy is consciously or unconsciously engaging in the following "feminine" or "unmasculine" behaviors:

1) Asking for help and acknowledging that one cannot do it by oneself. This is tantamount to crying uncle, and any man "worth his salt" will resist that to the very end.

2) Exposing one's weak side, one's helplessness, vulnerability, confusion and pain. Men have learned that to do this is foolhardy because it may lead to destruction. At best it will result in humiliation and rejection.

3) Depending on someone else for a sustained period of time. Dependency is acceptable only for women. The dependent male is a "sissy."

4) Acknowledging that one has emotions and that a rational, problem-solving, goal-oriented approach is not enough. To be emotional is to be feminine. Giving in to this unknown and threatening entity, in the man's mind, may lead to being overwhelmed and losing complete control.

5) Suspending the masculine desire for action, immediate answers and a concrete approach that will produce specific, rapid results.

6) Spending money on something that is intangible. Psychotherapy is a process that is nonmaterial. One can neither eat, wear, drive or play with it. In his mind, such frivolous spending is a wasteful, feminine extravagance.

7) Experiencing and working through the blocks to intimacy. The possible feelings of affection and warmth that might arise would be upsetting, particularly if the therapist is a man. Worse still is the prospect of any homosexual fantasies or desires arising in the process.

8) Confronting and suspending his competitive need to prove himself superior and to "defeat" his therapist. In that sense he had to give up his inclination to be "one up."

9) Recognition that life decisions and long-held cherished values may have been based on distorted and destructive premises and motivations. This is a particularly threatening realization for someone who has committed himself to the belief that he must always be right. In other words, by probing his inner experience he is confronted with the frightening possibility that the lie will be given to that which he has tenaciously clung to as being the correct and best way.

It is not surprising, therefore, that women have traditionally made up the bulk of most psychotherapists' practices. The reason for this is not the one feminists have put forth, namely, that women have more emotional problems and are vulnerable to more psychological distress. Rather, men have by and large unconsciously boycotted psychotherapy because it is essentially a "feminine" activity. The men who in the past have willingly gone into analysis or therapy are, I believe, primarily those whose gender identification is softer, less masculinely defensive, and allows for more of their "feminine" parts to be available and acceptable to them.

Masculine resistance to therapy is a tragedy more because of the implications than anything else. The efficacy of psychotherapy is still a matter of debate. However, the implied statements men make by resisting it are the crucial aspect. Quite simply, they are tactily indicating that asking for help, depending, giving up control, being emotional, acknowledging fear, weakness, vulnerability and so on are all unacceptable. The only masculinely appropriate alternative is to battle it out on one's own to the last vestiges of one's strength. There are *no* other non-implicating alternatives. Such is the nature, paradox and tragedy of the masculine attitude when it comes to change and growth.

17. Feed Yourself!

Ike was fifty-nine when his wife, Ruth, went into the hospital for the removal of a malignant brain tumor. The doctor leveled with him. "She may not live more than a year, and it's going to be a very, very difficult time. The chemotherapy will make her nauseous, weak and forgetful. She'll need a lot of your attention and help."

Ike was despairing when he related this to his ex-daughter-in-law, Sally, who called him after the surgery.

"I know why I left my husband," Sally said to a friend of hers while describing her conversation with Ike. "When he really sounded the most upset, it was about food. 'Who's going to prepare my meals? Ruth's the only one who knows how I need to have my food cooked.' I had to reassure him," Sally continued, "that he would still get fed properly and wouldn't starve. His son was the same way when we were married."

A forty-three-year-old woman was married to a cement worker who had the habit of behaving in a seductive way with other women in front of his wife. It never failed to enrage her, to the point where she would threaten divorce, even though this behavior had been going on for years.

Theirs was a traditional "earth mother"–"macho warrior" relationship from the start. When they were married, she was virginal, religious and passive-submissive in her reactions to him. She spent much of their first two years together designing menus and preparing special meals, in between keeping the house immaculate and the clothes cleaned and ironed. Her husband, Acker, would come home tired and often slightly high on alcohol and would sit in front of the television set with his dinner. Periodically he would call out, "Another beer, honey, please!" That constituted the bulk of his verbal communication.

From the first year of their marriage he had shown his resentment toward her by regularly finding fault with one of the dishes she prepared for dinner. He'd always leave some food on the plate, and then later complain that he was hungry. When he was really upset about the food, perhaps because it was over- or undercooked, he would go over to the pot on the stove and spit in it or feign vomiting.

Each day she woke early to prepare him a lunch to take to work. On the days she was angry with him because she had caught him staring at a woman or he had been particularly offensive in his reaction to something she had prepared for dinner, she would punish him by not preparing him a lunch. Not knowing how to prepare it himself, Acker went to work without any. His co-workers would tease him. "Sheila and you been fightin' again, huh, Acker? Why don't you start treating her right and you won't have to starve!"

It always embarrassed him to be lunchless, so by evening he was contrite. He knew that if he irritated her any more, there'd be no lunch the following day and he'd have to face the gibes of his co-workers again.

Julie, a thirty-year-old woman, also submissive in her response to her engineer husband, though very successful in her professional work as an economic analyst for a government agency, had married her husband ten years before.

Now, ten years later, she found herself in a sexless marriage, sleeping in a king-size bed with an invisible line down the center, demarcated by her husband. She was not to trespass it when they were in bed together unless he gave her permission.

Her strict Mormon upbringing had made an affair a frightening, out-of-the-question idea, until quite suddenly and unexpectedly she found herself with an adolescentlike crush on a co-worker, a recently divorced man her own age. She was overwhelmed with anxiety when, after a morning in bed with him at his apartment, he asked her to leave her husband and move in with him. She sought the help of a psychologist to deal with her guilt and confusion.

She related the details of her marital relationship. She

described the rigidity and emptiness of a life which revolved around her husband's six-day, twelve-hour-a-day workweek, with his Sundays spent tinkering with his boat or sports car.

The idea of leaving him, however, left her guilt-stricken. "I can't do it," she said. "He counts on me completely, and he'd be helpless if I left. I wake him in the morning and get him going. I put out his clothes for him and buy him new ones when he needs them. He doesn't know how to shop or cook or even do dishes. He'd be eating out of cans and wearing the same underwear until he'd have to throw it away if I wasn't there. I really think he might die without me," she said in guilty, anxious tones. "I just couldn't do that to him. He depends on me for everything."

A report on the plight of America's two million widowers, published in the *U.S. News & World Report,* indicated that American widowers have a much higher rate of mental breakdown, physical illness, alcoholism, suicide and accidents than do widows or married men.[1]

Helena Lopata, a professor of sociology and director of the Center for the Comparative Study of Social Roles at Loyola University, writing on widows and widowers, described how the division of labor in the family has meant that husbands become totally dependent on their wives for most activities pertaining to the home, and even for their own maintenance, except for a few "male" tasks. In addition, the woman has been assigned, or has taken upon herself, the function of maintaining the couple's social interactions, not only with her family and other couples, but even with her husband's family.[2]

Many widowers are incapable of adequate self-maintenance. They go to pieces when their wives die, as they find they can't turn on a gas range, operate a washing machine or even buy their own food or clothing. They also tend to become socially isolated, because they don't know how to maintain social relationships outside of work without their wives to act as intermediaries. For some, even making a personal telephone call becomes a terrifying experience.

The phenomenon of helplessness, which is plainly visible

among widowers, also exists among many married men. Their relationship to their wives becomes progressively more regressive, the man transforming into a demanding child and the wife emerging as the mothering figure, the feeder and the wiper.

The blossoming of this deadening, draining dependency often occurs early in the relationship. One desperate twenty-four-year-old man had a wife of two years who was restless, busy liberating herself and putting increasing emotional distance between herself and him. In a moment of despair when he thought he might lose her altogether, he told her, "You give me life. Without you I don't really enjoy anything."

It was obvious why his wife, in the interest of self-preservation, began secretly dating other men. In two years' time the relationship had gone from being a very erotic, spontaneous one with frequent weekend trips to one in which weekends were spent in their newly purchased home, with him doing yard work, making repairs around the house and working on his car. Sex occurred on a predictable, twice-a-week schedule, often during commercial breaks on television.

They rarely saw other couples unless she initiated it, which she did with decreasing frequency, because he always looked so bored when they went out. His wife could see the tomb she was being enclosed in. She was only surprised that he couldn't see it the same way. She couldn't understand how he could claim to be happy. It didn't please her to hear that *she* was his happiness and that *she* was his best companion. Without her, he'd tell her, all that would remain for him would be barhopping with co-workers, shooting darts, getting drunk and trying to pick up a woman in order to get laid. "I already have the best," he'd tell her, thinking she'd be flattered. Her reaction, however, was resentment and revulsion at his childlike dependency and predictability.

Once most men become deeply involved with a woman, they steadily abandon their own tastes and sensibilities and progressively relate to her as a mothering figure in charge of feeding, clothes selection and home decoration. Worse even than little boys, who at least choose their own friends and create their own social life, these men tend to turn the responsibility for social arrangements over to their wives. Then, after resisting sharing in these decisions, they passively endure what she plans, all the while complaining of boredom.

Eventually this social withdrawal extends to a resistance even to making phone calls, whether to members of his own family or a "friend" or to make a doctor's appointment. Sending off gifts, thank-you cards and birthday greetings also gets assigned to her. At best he signs the card, and often only after repeated urging.

In a regressive social withdrawal, he becomes practically phobic about initiating or involving himself in any social experience by himself, except perhaps for going to a sporting event or to a bar for a drink. (Many men won't even do that.)

He is setting the stage for extreme vulnerability and isolation should his relationship with his wife change or end. It is a dramatic reversal from their courtship days, when he felt that decisions as to where to go and what to do were his responsibility. Once the relationship has taken on a permanence, however, he regresses to this passive, detached state. Some men even begin to believe that they would starve, walk around in filthy, tattered clothing, stare all alone at television in a dirt-infested room after nursing a beer in a seedy bar if it were not for her.

It took one man almost three years after his marriage had ended to realize that he disliked most of the clothing he'd been wearing, which had been selected by his wife at *his* urging. He also found his household furnishings, most of which his wife had originally picked out, uncomfortable. During the course of his marriage he had come to believe, as many married men do, that his taste and judgment in these matters were crude and even embarrassing. Perhaps it started when he picked out a shirt or suggested an upholstery fabric or some artifact or painting. His wife's reaction may have communicated to him that he lacked taste and that he was lucky to have her, because in this regard she could save him from himself. He accepted her reaction as truth, because it jibed with his own image of himself as an aesthetic clod. He stopped trying to develop his own tastes, to the point where he really had no conscious opinions on these matters. After a while he didn't trust his judgment and he didn't really know what he liked.

In so doing, he had given up a large part of his self and his potential. Many of these areas of responsibility—food preparation, decorating, social planning, clothes selection, even parenting—had been defined to him as feminine when he was growing up. A "real man" would be suspect if he showed great interest or sensitivity in these areas.

A less conscious reason for turning over these matters to the woman was that it created a basis for communication. It gave them a way of connecting. Not to give her these responsibilities might push them toward the very threatening realization that they had little in common, little to say to each other or to share and enjoy together. Without this structure they would have to relate person to person as one would expect to do in a friendship, rather than as mother to child. Indeed, many who choose each other for marital partners or for living together (because he sees in her "earth mother" qualities and she sees in him qualities of protectiveness and dominance and a source of security) would not be compatible enough to choose each other as friends. That is, they do not truly enjoy each other's company as play companions. To look closely at all of that is a frightening prospect. It is easier to polarize and behave in rigid, gender-defined ways.

Growth is blocked, then, because growth requires relating as person to person rather than by prescribed roles. To move in that direction might reveal that there was nothing to fill the vacuum. In addition, once he has invested his primitive dependency needs in her and feels simultaneously compelled to affirm his masculinity, he cannot risk jeopardizing the balance of the relationship, lest his perceived source of life be withdrawn. His unconscious resistances to change, therefore, become very powerful. The man who scorns "men's lib" or is glad his wife is not a feminist may be merely hiding his own dependency needs, revealing his fear of change and possible abandonment and the loss of the precious breast.

The relationship in these instances becomes progressively less sensual and playful. Its focus gradually moves to the kitchen and the dining room. She feeds and he eats. To prove her love, she prepares special "goodies" at mealtime and encourages him to eat several helpings. To demonstrate his acceptance of her love, he eats even when he's not hungry or doesn't really like what she has prepared. In restaurants she regularly shovels food from her plate onto his, or leaves some of her food for him to finish. It is interesting to note how rarely one sees the reverse—the man pushing food onto the woman's plate—unless it involves a special dessert treat. Then, in a temporary role transformation, he becomes "daddy," giving his "little girl" a fatherly token of love.

When he's angry with her, he rejects or insults her food or precipitates a fight at the dining table and stalks away. When she's angry with him—if she's bold enough—she won't prepare anything at all, or will simply throw something together haphazardly, serve it late, over- or undercook it. That becomes her way of punishing him.

Even when the mood in the house seems to be pleasant, he may suddenly be transformed into an angry child when he comes home in the evening and dinner is late, or if he asks for something from the refrigerator, which he could easily get himself, and she doesn't immediately meet his demand or, worse still, tells him to get it himself. Each minute that he waits for the food seems to him like an hour, because it is unconsciously translated to mean rejection. Each request becomes a test of her love. The greater his underlying insecurity, the more frequently the testing occurs.

Often she prepares meals even though she's too tired and doesn't really want to, simply because she is afraid to upset him. Even illness may not be a satisfactory excuse for warding off his resentful response to not being fed. After all, his mother always managed to have food on the table, sick or not. If his wife "really" loved him, she'd find a way also.

He eats the meals she prepares for him even though he may not be hungry, because not to do so would mean symbolically to reject her love, aggress upon her, hurt her "fragile" feelings, upset the "earth mother"–macho interaction or possibly turn her off to the preparation of meals in the future. He can't afford to get her angry or have her remain angry too long, any more than a child could live with that in his mother.

Without the rituals around food there might be little other ongoing basis for verbal communication. The oft-repeated feminist contention that men have controlled women by keeping them in the kitchen could be looked at in the opposite way. That is, women have controlled men by reinforcing the processes that caused the men to feel that they could not survive—or could barely survive—without the women there to prepare the food.

Feeding him, together with all the other mothering activities she performs, becomes the major basis for the traditional relationship. Even though he may be less physically active than she on a daily basis, he usually eats much more than she. Again, this is a replay of his early childhood experience. Mother was always too busy feeding others to eat herself. She was the food preparer and server. Her son was constantly pulling at her for an extra something to eat. When she provided it, he relaxed and felt loved. When she didn't, he felt hurt, tense and angry. Part of being a "good boy" was also being a "good eater," the one who never left anything on his plate.

The obsession with dieting which is so common in these marriages can also be seen as having some of its roots in this interaction. When food is the major basis for sharing and communicating, weight problems and an obsession with eating become inevitable. The huge market for diet books is thus created.

Diet and an obsession with calories and weight become a never-ending, insoluble problem, because the eating rituals are critically needed to sustain the interaction. Such couples cannot afford to downplay or eliminate the eating focus for too long a time. Going out to eat, discussing what will be eaten or was just eaten, preparing special things to eat, are too important to the maintenance of the relationship. Like the couple who are having "sex problems" because of a lack of genuine interest, passion, playfulness and pleasure in each other but are afraid to deal with these feelings and therefore intellectualize and abstract this "problem" by attributing it to physiological ignorance or faulty techniques and proceed to buy books to study up on the subject of sex, the "earth mother"–macho couple become involved in an endless pursuit of the perfect or magic diet. It can never be found, because each new diet must eventually be undermined in order to preserve the relationship.

If the overweight man looks to the woman to help him with his dieting, an impossible bind is created which will subvert his best intentions to lose weight permanently. Since her way of showing love has been to feed him, and eating has been his way of accepting her love and feeling loved, dieting throws this interaction off balance and the relationship into a crisis if the diet lasts too long.

Socially, he becomes progressively more withdrawn as he responds mechanically to her announcements about what they'll do or whom they'll see on the weekend. As part of his masculine posture, he will groan and complain, while she plays out her mother role and chides and warns him to be civil and to try and make an effort to be friendly. He welcomes this unconsciously, because by himself he would have no social life and no friends. Her social arrangements, despite his complaints, save him from confronting the total emptiness of his interpersonal life.

The social life of his own creation at best involves talking to his next-door male neighbor, discussing the latest in gardening equipment or automobile maintenance. Nothing really intimate is shared, and "He's a nice guy" becomes the extent to which these men can describe each other. Often even these truncated relationships break down when one of the men becomes disappointed, bored, angry or sees the other as just "an asshole!" or a "jerk!"

All this was perhaps viable *before* feminism. Today, however, women are owning their feelings of resentment. This is the inevitable result of having played passive-submissive-receptive "earth mother" and being drained by his little-boy demandingness, his pouting when food was late or not prepared to his liking or a sock misplaced, at the same time his once frantic sexual appetite turned into mechanical, perfunctory, even grim efforts at lovemaking. She is actively making changes, refusing to play some old roles and sometimes abandoning the relationship altogether.

The result of having given up these significant parts of himself confronts him. He doesn't want to live, or is afraid to live without her as a feeder, a buffer against people and an all-around protective, caring figure. On his own he finds he is only a compulsive work machine. He has lost so much of himself that he can only envision a life of loneliness, canned food, dirty underwear and an unkept apartment.

This primitively dependent way in which many men tend to relate to the woman in their life is *the* invisible obstacle, *the* single most powerful block to their growth. It will abort any significant, genuine, self-caring change in the man. The rapid and powerful movement toward growth and change by many women during the last fifteen years came about because female dependency on the male did not have the kind of primitive tenacity that the male's has on the female.

Her dependency need for him existed primarily to the extent that the economic marketplace appeared to her to be an intimidating battleground. The nature of her need, however, was not the primitive one of being fed, cleaned, dressed, provided with human contact and so on. For many women the unfamiliar economic world was even an attractive one in its way, an area of masculine privilege that she wanted to participate in.

For most men, however, the woman *is* perceived as a lifeline. It is not surprising, therefore, that the abandoned man often becomes deeply depressed, even suicidal or violent toward the man he blames for taking "his" woman away. "I don't want to live without her anyway," was the way one man expressed it after mutilating a man who was having an affair with his ex-wife.

It is also not surprising that so many women today are initiating the breakup of these relationships. It is a self-preservative response designed to protect them from having their lifeblood drained by the man's tendency to fixate on them as a mothering figure. The woman has become exhausted playing the ever-flowing breast. If she is anything but a masochist or a frightened manipulator holding on to him as a meal ticket, she must inevitably reject him for her survival's sake.

Samuel Wallace, an associate professor of sociology at the University of Tennessee, in his book *After Suicide,* interviewed in depth twelve women who had been widowed by suicide. The thread that tied together the narratives of these women was that their husbands were men who had a never-ending need for care. These women originally had a seemingly equal need to provide that care. Their lives revolved around this care-giving, with increasing isolation and the exclusion of others as the marital relationship became more intense. The man's dependency progressively dominated the whole marital life space.

Wallace states that at first these women continued to live with their husbands. "They threatened, they complained, and they suffered, but they slept in the same house and usually in the same bed. They lost their friends, their neighbors, their families, their children, their financial and emotional resources and still they continued to care."[3]

Then something happened which caused seven of these women to reverse their pattern and to break from their men in what Wallace describes as a "social dying." It preceded the eventual suicide.

This study by Wallace is particularly significant, I believe, because it is only an exaggeration of the state of most marriages in which the woman is cast in the role of "care-giver," at first appearing to thrive on it but ultimately being engulfed and drained by the demanding dependency and the increasing isolation from outside influences. When she finally becomes overwhelmed and makes a break for freedom, he is flooded by terror and depression and behaves desperately and self-destructively.

The possibility of alienating or offending her with his changes, his movement toward liberation and away from stereotypical masculine role playing is an intimidating and powerful obstacle to his growth. He is much like the young child who is fearful of expressing his anger or independence directly toward his parents for fear that they will reject him and he will be left to starve.

He is caught in yet another impossible bind. To change in a way that might result in rejection is threatening because it might lead to abandonment. To change in a way that meets her demands will not really deal with the important issues of his life, and while he might temporarily appease or please her, she may be ultimately alienated and repelled when she sees through his façade of "goodwill" and recognizes its underlying motive, which is the fear of losing his lifeline. Not to change at all is also to risk losing her.

Until he can find the resources within himself and among others, both men and women, to nurture and sustain him through transition periods which may upset the balance of the relationship he is in, he will lose *whatever* direction he goes, because he is pinned by his primitive dependency. In this light it is understandable that many contemporary women are resisting intimacy with men altogether. Their choice too often seems to be between a rigidly masculine sexist who is controlling and unemotional in his attitude and an accommodating male who is changing for fear of rejection and abandonment.

To remedy this difficult situation there must first be a male awareness and understanding that the primitive fixation on one woman for his nurturance is psychologically destructive and a dangerous, untenable choice. Then he must begin the hard work of bringing himself up again.

First, he must experience the anger and fear that underlie the dependency grip that is strangling him. While the woman is *not* to blame for his fixation—since her psychologically controlling role is as unconscious and automatic as his reaction—the resentment is nevertheless there and must be experienced directly. Just as the woman needed to experience her anger and rage initially in order to free herself from her narrow role, he needs to experience his. However, to experience these feelings, including the intense need, the fear of loss and the anger, is deeply threatening to him, because it contradicts everything he has learned to cherish as part of his masculine image. Still, growth, I believe, will be aborted without it.

Once this is experienced and worked through, he must avoid the temptation of a repetition of investing his total self in one woman while systematically cutting himself off from all other intimate ties. Instead, he must establish a new relationship rhythm, working through the defenses that block him from getting close to more than one person at a time. Typically, competitiveness, fear of vulnerability and homosexual anxiety have kept him away from closeness to other men, while various forms of sexual games have blocked him from having friendships with women. Intimate ties with caring people of both sexes must be nourished and nurtured if he is to have the safety and security required to emerge as a person rather than as a gender stereotype.

Next, he will have to reown all of the basic survival skills and aesthetic sensibility that he has traditionally believed belonged to the woman or thought he was incapable of handling. Feeding himself is the symbol of these changes, because food has been the primitive glue that kept him fixed to the regressive and destructive "earth mother" relationship. A non–"earth mother"–macho relationship will be based on the pleasure of each other's friendship rather than on being taken care of in childlike fashion. He will come to her to expand himself as a person rather than to be mothered.

To be fed by her, to eat at certain prescribed ritualistic times, to feel angered when meals are late, to be fearful of not eating because doing so might upset her, to see himself as incapable of choosing and preparing exactly what he wants to eat by himself when he wants to eat it will be viewed by the free men as humiliating and self-destructive. Therefore, while the pleasure of sharing in the preparation of food with her can still be retained, he will self-caringly reject a relationship in which the woman's basic and primary posture toward him is one of feeding and taking care of him. It brings out the worst in both of them as he becomes increasingly a demanding, clinging, insatiable and guilt-ridden boy, while she assumes the part of the long-suffering, all-giving "earth mother."

Feeding himself will also be a symbolic launching place for freeing himself from other forms of childlike dependency. Most important, he will need to choose and maintain his own relationships, whether she shares in them or not. Choosing only individuals that both he and she are comfortable with tends to reduce the level of these relationships to the lowest, least threatening and unstimulating common denominator.

Further, the tendency of the man to relate to his woman intimate as the sole close relationship, and to lay on her the responsibility of being the social director who decides what they will do and with whom, systematically thwarts and blocks the development of his own social sensibilities and makes him self-destructively vulnerable. Should the relationship with his woman ever be in jeopardy, he will tend to accommodate and cling, rather than move in a self-caring direction, because to lose her is also to witness the collapse of his social world.

Along with the "feed yourself" attitude will come the rediscovery and reclaiming of his own taste in clothing and grooming styles. To give these up is tacitly to affirm that his judgment is inferior and that she knows best. There will be much pleasure in exploring and learning what feels and looks good to him.

He would also need to discover what makes his environment feel good. A Los Angeles psychologist recently described the experience of selecting and decorating his own place to live. "It is like exploring a larger part of something of me I have never explored before; I have always lived with the assumption, one I grew up with, that as a man I wouldn't understand how to make a place 'feel at home.' Now I am making the decisions, exploring what *I* want, trying to find what feels comfortable. I don't think these things can be classified as female, but I think that is how many men perceive them. I have admired men who seem to have more of a feeling for doing these kinds of things."[4]

Once he has resumed all of the basic dimensions of self-care, feeding himself in his own rhythm, selecting and caring for his clothing, creating his own environment, selecting and maintaining his own relationships regardless of whether the woman in his life shares or approves, he can then relate to his woman on a basis that can produce the highest form of the male-female relationship. They can become playmates who assume the burdens and responsibilities for life equally, who come to each other not out of the motivation of regressive dependency and the inability to survive separately, but out of the drive to enhance their lives, to be exposed to new dimensions of experience, to be challenged and stimulated, and without feelings on his part that he needs to cling to her for his life's sake, to feel responsible for her or frightened of alienating her. In short, they will come together to facilitate each other's movement toward a spontaneous, authentic, playful, expansive and exploratory attitude toward life, rather than the rigid, serious, isolated and conservative attitude that describes the posture of the "earth mother" and the "macho," the nurturer and the demanding child who is seeking to be fed both literally and symbolically.

18. The Recovery of Male Sexuality: From "Serious Sex" to "Playful Sex"

Of the impossible binds that ensnare and ultimately paralyze and destroy the male by confronting him with paradoxical and insoluble dilemmas, perhaps the cruelest is the area of "sex." I put quotation marks around the word "sex" because I believe that the traditional way the word has been used is misleading, psychologically erroneous, damaging and in many ways crazy. Consider these statements and questions:

"How's your SEX LIFE?"

"I don't like SEX."

"Do you have less of a SEX DRIVE than he/she does?"

"What is the normal number of times a week to have SEX?"

"Sometimes I'm too tired to have SEX."

"How do you feel about SEX?"

These create, then reinforce and perpetuate a depersonalized, split-off orientation toward this experience. The implication underlying these usages is, "There's ME, and then there's my SEX LIFE." My "sex life" and "sexual functioning" have a life of their own.

The language used to describe sexuality and the nature of most discussions about this subject continually perpetuate this orientation. A man who is sexually involved with a woman might acknowledge, if he stopped long enough to look at it honestly, that he was bored with her conversation, did not particularly find attractive the sound of her voice, her smell, the look or motion of her body, nor did her touch even feel good to him. *Yet that same man would feel threatened, anxious and defensive if he were not sexually aroused by and able to perform with that woman according to the standards he had established for himself or accepted as being masculine.*

He might even allow himself to stand accused of being an inadequate lover or, worse still, labeled impotent if he were to have erection "problems." In effect, he has separated his sexual response from his emotional, sensual and sensory experience. He expects to perform sexually in spite of himself. Even though the separate components of attraction are missing, he feels he must maintain high levels of sexual excitement and performance.

The way men have continued to function sexually with this orientation is by depersonalizing the experience. They are not having sex with someone they are tuned in to and aware of as a person. Rather, they are "having sex" with a "thing," "making love" to an "object," and there is no genuine awareness of their own or the woman's internal experience. In fact, this may very well be necessary. Were they suddenly and totally aware of their real emotions and sensibilities in the here and now toward their partner, they might experience severe disruptions.

"Having sex" with their woman, therefore, becomes much like masturbation. The woman as a person does not really exist. Rather, she is an orifice, a challenge and a proving ground. Indeed, many women complain that they are simply receptacles for the depositing of the man's semen and feel that they could easily be interchanged with other women. The language of the men confirms the truth of this. For example, they might say, "When the lights are off all women are the same," and describe a woman as "a piece of ass."

Because he is not tuned in to her as a person, he may also delude himself into believing that his "sex life" with a particular woman is "great," even though she herself might not be enjoying it at all but refrains from telling him to avoid conflict or to "protect his ego."

Before the female sexual awakening of recent years, men were able to maintain their sexual illusions and delusions and a depersonalized orientation in which they saw the woman as an object because, indeed, many women colluded with this and allowed themselves to be seen and used that way too—as objects for the man's pleasure. Partially, this was the result of their conditioned inhibitions, resistances and distaste, which caused them to distance themselves from the experience, and partially they were bartering their bodies for support and security. The man and the woman were, indeed, "having sex" rather than having each other.

It was not a genuinely human sexual experience for her, or for him. The only times he might be jolted into an awareness of her as a person with feelings and sensibilities were when she would protest during sex, "You're hurting me!" or "Not so hard!" This might occur as he tried to penetrate her while she was still unlubricated and he did not know or care that she was not ready. The overall dehumanization between the man and the woman was often expressed in nonverbal ways by the fact that after the initial romantic phase they rarely kissed or made direct eye contact while making love.

Today he is confronted with a new and intimidating dilemma. Many women will no longer collude with the man's denial of their personhood. They are refusing to pretend satisfaction and to serve merely as a sexual outlet for him. This has placed him in a crisis situation for which he is unprepared, because he must now relate to her as a person and not a thing, and he is not ready for this.

The conflicts and dilemmas this presents are anxiety-provoking. Will he continue to function as a performing machine, only now with a new and more demanding program which requires him to perform according to more elaborate prescriptions involving mastering the specifics of her body, accommodating her likes and dislikes and bringing her to orgasm? This often translates into meeting her needs rather than his own. Or will he be able and/or willing to risk becoming a person himself, insisting on the right to his own individual rhythm and the honest expression of his responses, sensibilities, resistances and emotions? In this case, he will surely become an erratic performer, sometimes "better," sometimes "worse," but always changing according to his varying inner states and reactions. He will be sometimes erect, sometimes not; sometimes aggressively lusting, sometimes passive; sometimes affectionate, sometimes cold; sometimes fast, sometime slow. Will he be able to be all of these without fear, guilt, apology or a sense that his masculinity is in jeopardy?

Because many men still don't or can't experience or

express their humanness, yet feel pressured to become ever more skillful performers, some are turning off to "sex," particularly within sustained relationships, and are withdrawing into self-protective detachment or humiliating themselves with lies and the kinds of evasions that have previously been part of the woman's avoidance repertoire—"I'm tired," "I don't feel well," "I'm preoccupied with things at work" and so on.

Male backlash by means of such passive resistance, withdrawal and lack of interest is already under way. Popular and professional articles are describing the decline in male interest in "sex." I believe it has nothing to do with "sex." It does, however, have everything to do with the fact that he is confronted with impossible binds: the combination of extremely demanding expectations and standards he has been taught are attainable if he is man enough, with a psychological conditioning which makes these expectations and standards impossible to attain. Therefore, like the schizophrenic child who withdraws because he is confronted with unresolvable, damned-if-you-do, damned-if-you-don't binds, he walls himself in, assuming the stance of nonparticipation and non-emotional involvement.

A new breed of negative permission-giving psychologist-writers is predictably emerging, telling men that it is all right for them not to desire sex at all. The following quote is from a recent book on male sexuality by a psychologist who for five years headed the men's program and was co-director of clinical training of the Human Sexuality Program at the University of California, San Francisco.

> Sex is not the most important thing in the world and it is not necessarily good for you. Only the individual can decide how and where sex should fit into his life, if at all.[1]

SEXUAL ROOTS

Rather than retreating and giving up one of the most joyful and pleasurable ways a self-aware, healthy and spontaneous man and woman can play with and enjoy each other, we need to examine the binds and processes that have produced the destruction of the male's sexual humanness. To do this we must examine the roots of male conditioning and sexual attitudes and transform them, releasing men from their grip and creating a new set of attitudes, perceptions and ways for him to experience himself.

The major reason sexuality has become a decreasing source of anxiety-free pleasure for traditionally conditioned men is that the elements that make sexual intimacy pleasurable, satisfying and comfortable have been systematically extinguished in him through the processes of his early conditioning.

1) Sensuality: Parents rock, hug, caress, stroke, cuddle, lick and engage in body play with little girls. Fathers especially, but often even mothers, fear that to indulge their sons in this way beyond an early age is to risk turning them into sissies and homosexuals. Therefore, boys respond negatively to such behavior, and the young boy who desires and seeks out this kind of interaction becomes suspect and arouses the concern and anxiety of his parents.

As an adult lover, however, sensuality is expected of him. But the early repression of his sensuality dwarfs his capacity for such physical sexual play. After the initial romantic phase of the relationship, in fact, it is not uncommon for husband and wife or lovers to "have sex" with a bare minimum of sensual touching.

The impossible bind here is simply that the very sensuality that is repressed in him as a boy, that would have defined him as a sissy, is both demanded of him by his adult woman partner and required in order for *him* to enjoy *himself* fully and playfully.

2) Emotionality: The capacity for accurate recognition and communication of feelings is a prerequisite for good sexual relatedness. Like sensuality, however, emotions are repressed and largely forbidden to him as a growing boy. Sensitive boys are seen as girlish or sissies. Free expression of his emotions as a boy puts his maculinity in doubt.

As an adult lover, however, he is told he must express his emotions, which often he cannot recognize or communicate, and be sensitive to and able to read correctly his woman's emotions. His inability to do so makes the sexual experience a limited and mechanical one, and causes him to both depersonalize his partner and, at the same time, be an unknown quantity to her.

The impossible bind here is that getting in touch with and expressing emotions threaten his masculinity. To remain in a state of repression, however, is to continue to function mechanically and without an awareness of the emotional reality of the interaction with his partner.

3) Expression of needs: He learns as a boy that the less need he acknowledges and the more self-contained and independent he is, the more masculine he is. The words "I need" become two of the most difficult and threatening for a man to say. When he does have needs, he tends to deny them.

As an adult lover, his inability to acknowledge and communicate needs makes him a silent partner who accumulates considerable hidden anger and frustration because he feels misunderstood and insensitively responded to. He expects his needs to be read without his having to acknowledge or express them. When they aren't, he becomes resentful. At the same time his partner becomes confused and put off by his childish reactions to hurts she never knew she perpetrated.

The impossible bind here is that to express these needs is to feel unmasculine. Not to express them is to remain frustrated and unknown and to build a considerable amount of hidden anger.

4) Aggression toward women: Early in his conditioning as a young man he is taught to see the female as fragile, emotional, vulnerable and easily hurt. Especially if he loves her, therefore, he will tend to feel protective of her.

As an adult lover, this repression of his aggression toward her places him in impossible binds. It will make it very difficult for him to be honest about his resistances and his dislikes and even to say no to sex. He will also be unable to express his negative reactions to the ways she touches him, smells, sucks, makes love and so on for fear he will hurt her feelings and possibly injure her emotionally. In general, he fears that to be assertive in any of these ways may destroy her, cause her to withdraw or to reject him.

Furthermore, his own defensive overreaction to his aggression will cause him to be overly self-conscious and inhibited in bed, treating her like a fragile flower and going to extremes in order to be gentle and sensitive. He may even reserve his more spontaneous, aggressive, "animalistic" impulses and reactions for encounters with prostitutes or for affairs where he feels sufficiently free and detached to be himself.

The impossible bind here is that aggression toward the woman makes him feel guilty and fearful of losing her love, while suppressing this part of himself makes him an inhibited, dishonest lover.

5) Passivity: Because passivity is feminine, he loses his capacity to lie back, do nothing, allow himself to be made love to, give up control and the need to dominate, be the receiver and periodically turn the lead over to his partner, and thereby share the responsibility for the success and rhythm of the sexual encounter.

Worse still, the need to control and dominate eventually turns the sexual experience into a job. When the experience is unsatisfactory, unless he can blame it on fatigue, illness or *her* lack of interest, he has no way of escaping the conclusion that a complaint or failure is his fault.

The impossible bind is that he cannot let go of his need to control and dominate because it threatens his masculinity, yet holding on to it eliminates the possibility of having a flowing experience, one in which he can move easily and comfortably between active and passive behavior.

In summary, his early conditioning has severely impaired or destroyed most of what is required for sustained pleasure in the area of sexual involvement in a relationship. The one motivator acquired from his early conditioning that does allow him sexual excitement is challenge. Consequently, if he meets resistance from the woman, if she is a new partner, if she communicates unavailability or, in a longer-range relationship, if she manages to keep him off balance and uncertain as to whether he might lose her to someone else, he may very well retain a high level of excitement. But in a relationship where challenge is not present, there are no techniques, no words of wisdom, no magic elixirs that can make "sex" a genuinely pleasurable form of play in a sustained, caring, person-to-person relationship, short of reclaiming these lost capacities, sensibilities and awarenesses.

"SERIOUS SEX" vs. "PLAYFUL SEX"

His compulsion to perform and the repression of his humanness and personhood have resulted in his being involved in what I term "serious sex." "Serious sex" I define as sex which is goal oriented, laden with imperatives, "shoulds," standards, evaluations, performance pressures, measurement and so on. It is this orientation to sex that inevitably produces "sex problems," which are accompanied by the onus of ugly medical diagnostic labels.

In "serious sex" one or both partners are working hard *at* "sex" rather than playing pleasurably. It is depersonalized and discussed with the terminology that suggests that "sex" has a life of its own ("I like sex," "I'm good at sex," "I'm getting tired of sex," "Sex is good (bad) for you," "I don't feel like having sex right now" and so on).

Its terminology is depersonalized because it has become an experience which is separated from the self and from an awareness and acceptance of the continual changes in a person-to-person relationship. In "serious sex," static, mechanical compulsion replaces fluid human interaction. It results in the man examining his "sex life" with questions that characteristically begin with the word "How":

1) How often?
2) How long?
3) How many (orgasms)?
4) How was "it"?
5) How to do "it"?

Symptoms inevitably arise in "serious sex" when the realities of the relationship do not coincide with the external standards. That is, by turning "sex" into a separate entity, an experience with a life of its own, replete with externally imposed measurements and expectations, "sex" will inevitably be thought of in terms of "good" or "bad," "healthy" or "sick," and the man will see himself as "functional" or "dysfunctional." His penis will be seen as "working" or "not working." Whenever he fails to live up to the expectations and standards which he has set for himself, he will view himself and will also be seen as having a "sex problem." His inclination will then be to do something about "it," to overcome "it," to remedy "it." As soon as possible he will want to "fix the penis" in order to regain his masculine self-esteem.

If he remains in the relationship with the woman with whom he has a "problem" and never successfully "fixes it," never rises to the standards of performance he was using to measure himself, his self-confidence as a man may be forever crippled. He will be pathetically grateful if he is still accepted and seen as worthy of "love" by the woman in spite of "his problem." His self-hate will lead him to constantly anticipate rejection and he will have to face the repeated humiliation of experiencing, explaining and trying to cope with and overcome "his failures."

In his search for a "cure" he may initially pursue magical solutions such as special diets, vitamins, prayer, concentration, exercise, autosuggestion, fantasy and so on. If these fail to "help," he may turn to a physician for hormone injections, pills, hypnosis and occasionally even new and bizarre surgical remedies, such as plastic implants.

The recovery of his capacity and potential for sexual pleasure will therefore require a movement away from the "serious sex" orientation toward the one of "playful sex." In the absence of neurotic or other kinds of emotional problems, the questions he might ask himself in order to recover his personhood and break the stranglehold of "serious sex" while entering the realm of "playful sex" would be in the nature of:

1) Are my senses turned on to my partner? Does her smell please me or do I need her to perfume and deodorize herself in order to come comfortably close to her?

2) Do I find the look, motion, rhythm and grace of her attractive? In other words, does it please and delight me to watch her as she moves?

3) Do I enjoy the taste of her and the flavor of her body as I kiss, lick or suck her?

4) Do I enjoy listening to her speak and am I stimulated by the conversations we have? Specifically, does the timbre and quality of her voice please me? When she talks, do I find myself readily and enjoyably concentrating and listening to her? Do I focus in on and feel good about what she says and the way her words convey her perception of people, situations, experiences and life? Or do I find myself getting bored with her conversation, does my mind wander when she talks to me and do I resent her outlook and way of seeing things?

5) Do I enjoy touching her and being touched by her? Does my body experience a relaxation, comfort, openness and responsiveness when we make physical contact? Do I enjoy the feel of her skin when her body is next to mine and the touch of her hands as she caresses me? When she strokes and hugs me, does my body delightedly pull toward her or do I find myself avoiding her, tensing up, touching her as little as possible and pulling away from her when she reaches out and touches me?

6) Do I feel playful around her, free to be myself regardless of whether I have an erection? Or is sexual involvement with her a deliberate and serious business in which my major focus is on techniques, timing, "right" places to touch, erections and so on?

7) When I sleep beside her, do I find myself turning away from her and avoiding contact, or do I seek out the closeness of her body?

8) When we're making love, do I comfortably and effortlessly delight in the foreplay or do I want to get right into the act of intercourse? During intercourse, do I enjoy staying inside her and maintaining that contact as long as comfortably possible for both of us? Or is my primary mo-

tive and emphasis ejaculation? Do I tend to come quickly and do I have to make great and deliberate efforts to avoid ejaculation because my honest desire is to come and then to pull out and break contact? Or is it easy to control myself because I feel comfortable and close to her?

9) After I ejaculate, do I find myself wanting to turn away, withdraw and go to sleep? Or do I still enjoy the closeness, the hugging and the feel of her body next to mine after the orgasm?

10) Do I feel expressive, open, readily and trustingly transparent, comfortably able to be fully and honestly myself and able to share my internal reactions and responses with her spontaneously, be they positive or negative, strong or helpless, confident or frightened, affectionate or angry? Or do I find myself guarding and censoring what I say and withholding important reactions?

11) Do I feel I must always be strong, dominant, unafraid, in control of myself and unneeding in any way in order to retain her love? Or do I feel that I can be vulnerable around her, sometimes weak and a failure, confident that it will not affect her love and respect for me? In a larger sense, do I feel that she is seeing me as a person rather than as a symbol—specifically, a provider—protector—performer—security blanket?

12) Does she relate to me in an open, assertive way, or is she basically passive-submissive-receptive toward me so that it is difficult for me to see or understand what it is that she really likes or dislikes, feels, thinks and wants?

13) Can I comfortably confront her with things I don't like, expressing my anger and resistance honestly, confident that I will not be made to feel like a "heavy" or a bad guy for being honest? And do my negative expressions incite her to destructive forms of retaliation and punishment such as pulling away and turning cold?

When I share negative reactions, does she assert herself in return, engaging me actively in conflict resolution in order to work things out constructively? Or does she react in a way designed to communicate that I am guilty of being destructive and insensitive by becoming tearful, falling apart and accusing me of being hostile?

In other words, does our relationship tolerate negative interchanges and will she stay in there with me and fight things out in a constructive way until matters are comfortably resolved for both of us, or does she have a tendency to lay the blame on my shoulders?

14) When she confronts me and gives me negative feedback, is it in the spirit of closeness and to enhance intimacy, or do I experience it as motivated by an underlying desire to hurt, humiliate, control or triumph in the relationship?

15) Do I feel that she really sees me as I am and loves me for that, or do I feel she or both of us need to play out a fantasy, create images for each other and be unreal in order to keep the "love" going?

16) In general, do I find joy and pleasure in being next to her and am I readily playful with her? In simple terms, does she make me feel good about myself, my life and the experience of living, and do I do the same for her?

The primary motivation and pleasure in "playful sex" is the nearness of the other person. There is only minimal concern or focus on erections, orgasms, techniques and timing. It is the *process* of being close, not the end point of sexual tension relief that is the primary goal.

This is not to suggest that in short-term relationships or non-emotionally involved encounters sexual interaction cannot be pleasurable. However, sex motivated primarily by tension release ("horniness"), flights from loneliness, curiosity, challenge, the desire to please or the need for reassurance that one is lovable or attractive is more or less a depersonalized experience and it is usually not of great significance who one's partner is. It is particularly important, therefore, not to measure, evaluate or define oneself in terms of one's performance and responses in these kinds of sexual experiences.

"Playful sex" will be ever changing and reflective of the relationship and mood changes of the people involved. At different times it may be accompanied by sadness, silliness or seriousness, exploration, confrontation, reminiscence, reflection on feelings and so on. The act of intercourse itself will occur with a minimum of deliberate intention. "Sex" itself will never be evaluated or measured except as it reflects the state of the relationship and the way the partners are feeling toward each other.

In "playful sex" there is nothing to prove. There is no emphasis on techniques or premeditated positions. When the "sex" is "bad," the *relationship* rather than the performance of the sex act will be examined with a view to improvement.

In the best of "playful sex" one discovers who one is and what one's sensual and playful potential is. It is, I believe, a part of the highest form of male-female interaction. It is physical play between two people who accept, love and trust each other. As opposed to "serious sex," in which there is deliberate effort, self-consciousness and a censoring of feeling and fantasy, "playful sex" is expressive, flowing and easy.

The tragedy in the past is that many men have measured their masculinity and attached their sense of self-esteem and self-worth to their performance in "serious sex." They expected to be great performers, to reach and maintain certain levels and standards *regardless* of their feeling toward the woman. When the "sex" was poor, when they were "impotent" or ejaculated "prematurely," they accused themselves of inadequacy, rather than focusing on how their response reflected their feelings and the state of the relationship.

Undoubtedly, "playful sex" and the capacity to function on that level require a man to be self-aware and capable of expressiveness, because in "playful sex" he *is* his sexual response, and the limits and potential of the experience are *his* limits and reflect the extent to which he is a person in touch with and capable of feelings, sensual responsiveness and so on. Such a man will not be controlled by externally imposed standards which pressure him to function at a certain level. He will recognize those standards as erroneous and destructive to himself.

Nor will he expect himself to be a good performer simply because he married the "right woman," or is involved with a woman *everyone else* tells him is "perfect" for him. In the past many men became involved with the "right woman," who earned him the plaudits of the world because of her looks, education, background, financial standing and so on, but he may have found his own personhood atrophied and his emotions numbed by this interpersonally forced and emotionally dishonest interaction. There were the instances in which he functioned within the orientation of "serious sex." He was making love with a woman who fitted an intellectual model of the person he felt he "should" be with. He married on the basis of this, and when his emotions and his body resisted, he struggled to deny and overcome his responses, labeled himself negatively in the language of a medical diagnosis and tried to overcome and "correct" his deeply rooted resistance by describing it as a "problem."

This orientation, so typical of most men's relationships, created the basis of much of the sexual agony men have experienced in the past. They navigated in response to external pressure, and tried to live up to the appropriate masculine image: the standards, rules and expectations established by social pressure. Consequently, they had to constantly deny their real responses and remain in a relationship where the bond was fragile or even nonexistent. Eventually they were destroyed by the numbness, or the situation exploded in their faces and ended, as so many of these relationships do, in cold hate.

The liberation of male consciousness in the "sexual" area will mean trusting his responses. The only negative self-evaluations he will make of himself will be self-chastisement for the compromising and denial of his sensibilities: his resistance to recognizing the real nature of the relationship and to assuming responsibility for becoming a self-aware person whose intimate relationships could be governed by a desire to be with a partner toward whom he moved easily and delightedly, and where the relationship was playful and the hunger was to know and be known.

The man who lives in the self-caring consciousness of "playful sex" will never again measure his performance harshly or allow himself to be labeled diagnostically. He will respect and delight in the awareness and full communication of his body's responses, recognizing them as one of the truest expressions of himself.

19. To the Woman Who Asks, "What Can I Do to Help?" (Will She Be There to Hold the Net?)

While many relationships begin with the fantasy of the man as the protective partner and the woman as the weaker and vulnerable one, a turnaround in this interaction often takes place. Sometimes it occurs almost immediately after the relationship takes on a permanence and commitment. In this reversal the dynamic becomes one of woman helping man. *She* becomes the tower of strength, the stable element in the relationship, and *she* is now busy trying to help *him* straighten out his life—be it the overcoming of a drinking problem, regaining a lost erection, learning to relax and minimize stress, watching his diet, recuperating from a major illness or weathering a job crisis. He becomes the leaner and she seems now to be holding him up.

Such is the condition increasingly emerging as a result of the newly evolving relationships between a woman in the process of liberation and growth and a man who is threatened, confused and flailing fearfully about, trying to cope with, adjust to and perhaps even change in rhythm with her changes. As she becomes more of a complete person—assertive, sexual, autonomous—he is revealed to be *anything but* the strong, protective partner she might have originally imagined him to be. In fact, the more she lets go of some of her feminine poses, needing him less and less for all of those reasons she needed him originally when she was still committed to playing the dependent, submissive and vulnerable role, the more she can begin to see him for who and what he really is. Rather than being strong, he can be seen as rigidly tied to narrow behavior patterns, out of touch with his emotions, activity-driven, interpersonally blind and naïve, hooked on obviously body-destructive behavior patterns designed to numb and keep him going, hardly the stud he was once touted as being and, more than anything else, threatened by change.

Thus, many caring and well-meaning women, aware of their own need to change and to grow, while still wanting to maintain their relationship with their man and perceptively sensitive to the self-destructiveness and impasses reached by him, are now asking a new variation of the old woman-helping-man-to-cope theme, namely, "How can I help him to change—to become a more liberated, satisfied, fulfilled, relaxed person?" It is an important question indeed, and its ramifications and unconscious implications demand clarification lest old traps cloaked in new, well-meaning liberation disguises are fallen into anew.

The processes and meanings of the word "help" from a psychological perspective are complex and laden with myriad motives, often the least of which are genuinely loving and caring ones. Helpers need their helpees, and often become as committed to the maintenance of the interaction and thus the problems and illness of their helpees as the helpees themselves.

The link between the helper and the helpee is a psychologically complex one, particularly in the area of emotional problems. Being a "helper" allows one to remove the focus from oneself—for example, the wife who is "helping" her husband with "his" impotence or the woman who despairs because she had married three times and each time had the "misfortune" to marry an alcoholic whom she "tried" to help and failed. It was easier to focus on solving "his" drinking problem than on her attraction to and the gratification she received from repeated involvements with such self-destructive men, and the ways her behavior might have reinforced their patterns.

Likewise, the woman who seeks to "help" her husband or lover to change in a given way, seeing that as her benevolent role, is more than likely also going to be consciously or unconsciously committed to controlling the limits of his changes. It would only be natural that she would not want him to change to the point where he realized that he no longer needed her. Or that his relationship with her was a manifestation of his problem and therefore it would be best for him to get out. Nor would she want him to become so self-caring that he began to indulge his interest in other people, women and men alike, to the point that he would spend increasingly less time with her, nor so in touch that he became aware of *his* anger over playing certain of his required roles in which she had an investment, such as the dutiful, responsible, monogamous, predictable lover-husband, provider and strong man—roles often born of the feeling of guilt and the compulsion to prove oneself masculine. Once he was self-aware and self-caring, he might refuse evermore to assume those roles as he became increasingly more individualistic, unpredictable and resistant to such lifeless, compulsive, ritualistic behavior.

The very orientation of woman "helping" man, in its traditional meaning, may no longer be viable in an era of change, growth and liberation. In fact, the helping pose may always have been a potentially or actually contaminated and psychologically loaded one. Surely it is a charged one in the context of male-female intimacy, because each has a powerful stake in the kinds of changes that will take place in the other, namely, that the changes should be comfortable, attractive and enhancing to the status quo. Alas, the changes that men may have to go through may prove not at all to be the kind that an involved woman would approve of or be happy with, just as her liberation changes were/are often disorienting and painful for him.

The common stereotype of a "new" man is one who can cry and hug his son. However, for too long being a socialized man has meant being a well-oiled, predictable, compulsive, controlled performer-machine. He blocked out and denied a host of emotions and impulses in himself in order to fit "comfortably" into harness and to play out the accepted and approved masculine image. The man who becomes suddenly and genuinely self-aware would have to confront and deal with the long denied responses, with the boredom, stultification, numbness and meaninglessness of his programmed life. He might have to experience suppressed rage over the ways he had denied himself, such as by reporting dutifully home each day, refraining from and feeling guilty about joyful, unabashed sensual responses to attractive women, cutting himself off from close relationships with men and from a transparent orientation that says, "This is who I am and this is how I feel!" All of these have long been repressed and denied because of unconscious guilt, mother transferences to his wife, the belief that it was his role to be all-responsible and self-denying and that anything short of this would bring vile inferences and castigations about his acceptability as a man and as a person.

The traditional model of woman-helping-man would also reinforce in more subtle ways the already guilt-ridden, "earth mother"–fixated orientation of the male. Behind the "helping" posture there may very well lie a one-upmanship, sometimes blatant though usually subtle almost to the point of invisibility. The "helper" is righteous, selfless and deserves gratitude and love from the helpee.

Likewise, the helping attitude within the context of a relationship takes the heat and focus off the "helper" in terms of how he or she partially creates and perpetuates the very problems he or she seeks to "help" and places the blame and focus squarely on the helpee.

Parents of a disturbed child, for example, often see and present themselves as eager and willing to do anything to help the child. At the same time, they tend to unconsciously resist focusing on the family dynamics and the processes within their own relationship that have created the "problem child" and his or her illness. Thus, they would gladly and responsibly feed the child medicines, maintain therapeutic reward and punishment schedules, change the child's school, give the child special attention, alter the diet and so on. Gladly would they act out the behaviors that reinforce their required self-perceptions of being good parents, which keep them in the good light of "helping." But they would at all costs avoid a helping process that requires the really painful and hard work of examining the destructive processes in the family, such as their own double binds on the child, nonacknowledgment of their resistances and resentment toward the child, each other and the role of parenting, plus all of the other fearful and hidden, often unconscious emotions and motivations that would expose the deeper roots of the "problem."

Furthermore, in regard to the notion of "helping," it is my belief that interpersonal problems are created and changed primarily by the "being" rather than the "doing" of the people involved. In fact, those who are the most destructive psychologically, I believe, are the fine interpersonal technicians, those who have the "doing" down to perfection but in combination with an underlying emotional "being" that runs contrary to the "doing."

For example, the parents of a schizophrenic boy had raised him according to sophisticated parent-effectiveness techniques. They always said and did the "correct" and appropriate thing. However, this only obscured and made the communication more destructive, because their body messages and unconscious nonverbal cues constantly telegraphed their underlying resentment and resistance over having to give up time and energy to a son they didn't, on a deeper level, really want. They had him originally for narcissistic reasons, to enhance their image in society and to solidify their relationship, but resented his intrusion on the satisfaction of their own pleasures. Every response of theirs was therefore unconsciously replete with "come here—go away" characteristics. The child would have been emotionally healthier had he received straight-out rejection messages. He might have grown up angry toward the world but he wouldn't have become schizophrenic. He would have known who his enemies were and would have learned to react accordingly and appropriately.

"Helpers" are indirectly saying, "It's really basically your problem, and I'll help *you* with it." In light of the traditional male-female, *actor-reactor* orientation, this only reinforces the end product of the same interaction that results in the man's assuming responsibility and operating with a guilt reflex to the woman in the first place. Consequently, when she sets out to "help" *him* with *his* problem, she only reinforces his "guilty boy" orientation and his fantasy perceptions of the selflessness, altruism, givingness and wonderfulness of the "earth mother."

Another question arises. Will the woman be there to hold the net if he genuinely lets go of the things in him she protests against so vigorously, namely, his power-dominance-success-unemotional-autonomous-performing orientation? In that sense the feminist attitude, while it is freeing women, may also trap them in a paradox at the same time. For while the woman liberates herself, the standard by which she evaluates men may become tighter instead of looser. Rather than appreciating men on a broader, more humanistic basis, the newly assertive, successful, autonomous woman often wants a man who is a success symbol first and a person second. She rationalizes her expectations by saying, "It's not that I have anything against blue-collar workers or men of less education or money. It's just that I don't find them stimulating enough. They're defensive and lack confidence because I'm doing better than they are. I prefer the man who knows who he is and feels good about himself and that seems to be primarily the successful ones." As Gail Sheehy said in a recent interview, "Weak men are not in great demand."[1]

A successful, educated feminist confessed that when her lover, whom she lived with, happened to be sick, she could accept his being in bed for a day or two, but longer than that she found herself becoming increasingly uncomfortable and impatient at his being ill, to the point where she'd be thinking, "Enough's enough. Don't act like a helpless baby."

The paradox produced by raising the woman's expectations rather than broadening them as she becomes "liberated" will increasingly become a problem. Despite oft-heard allegations that things are not "really" improving for women in concrete ways, a recent research study on the changing status of American women in the 1970s indicated that between 1970 and 1974 alone the number of women in college increased by 30 percent while the number of men increased by 12 percent. In 1971 women earned 42 percent of all B.A. degrees and 40 percent of all M.A.s. The proportion of women enrolled in professional schools for law, medicine, architecture and engineering has risen steadily since 1960. For instance, of the total enrollment in law schools, women accounted for 4 percent in 1960, 12 percent in 1972 and 19 percent in 1974. The same trend is seen in enrollments in medical schools, in which women represented 6 percent of the total in 1960, 13 percent in 1972 and 18 percent in 1974.[2]

The question that will arise is simply whether the women who want to "help" men will still find them attractive and be able to love and relate to them when their education, power, money and success symbols are less than hers. If men have been reluctant to let go of the success style of masculine validation, it is as much out of an unconscious fear and awareness that without the success symbols they (the men) would only become progressively more invisible, unlovable and sexually unattractive. They are caught in a double-bind—castigated on the one hand for their power and success orientation and rejected when they don't have them because, as Gail Sheehy pointed out in the same interview, "powerful men are an aphrodisiac for women."[3]

John Dean, in his autobiography *Blind Ambition*, echoed this assessment from a territory and perspective where men observe the impact of power all too clearly. He wrote:

> Maureen went home to California, and I resolved to conquer as many new women as time and power would grant. Henry Kissinger once remarked on power's properties as an aphrodisiac and I found it true.[4]

A major Los Angeles newspaper ran a feature article about a group of men who had fallen on hard occupational times and were experiencing unemployment with little success or hope of getting a new job because of age or a drying up of work in their specialty areas. The common note sounded among them was that with unemployment came shame, invisibility and rejection. Some of the men would even hide the fact that they were at home during the day while their wives were working. They kept their cars locked in the garage, did not answer the phone or the door and kept the window shades drawn. The wife of an engineer whose husband was unemployed for several months reported:

> Normally the phone rings all the time. As soon as word got out, it stopped. One girl left a note on the front porch saying she couldn't reach me. We were here. . . . It's gotten so they don't ask about Gil. Just the kids. It's like I don't have a husband.

The man's son had even asked his mother, "Does this mean Daddy's a bum?" His wife admitted being disturbed by her husband's constant "escape" reading, as she termed it. Also, she told her nine-year-old daughter to keep it quiet that Dad was unemployed.[5] Similarly depressing themes were sounded by the various other men who were unemployed. They were filled with self-loathing and a sense that others looked down on them as if they had committed some heinous act.

The woman who would truly help a man would do so best by working on her own growth. First, by becoming a complete person rather than a gender caricature—assertive, autonomous, sexual and expressive of her aggressive feelings—she would soon find it intolerably painful and boring to become involved or remain with a compulsive, macho-fixated male. She would inevitably find herself drifting away, thereby fomenting a crisis for any man who cared about or had been in a relationship with her. Indeed, in light of the psychologically shut down and rigid state of most men, the only hope for their ever changing, or even just looking at themselves objectively, would be as a result of a powerful crisis that would raise their anxiety to a level where they would be forced to reach out for help or sink and lose the relationship and find themselves completely isolated.

Most women overlook their own unconscious commitment to and benefits from the man's macho style. Particularly if the woman has been raised and conditioned in the traditional feminine mold, her whole tendency will probably be to attach herself to a male who will repeatedly seek to validate himself by the ways in which he can provide for and prove himself to her. Any letting go on his part would demand a balancing assertiveness and strength on her part or else she would feel her own security to be threatened and would have a strong tendency to encourage him back toward regressive masculine-role posturing.

Again, what some women want when they say they want a man to change, to become liberated, is the best of both worlds. They would like him to continue to provide the spinoff benefits of his macho compulsive style while *also* becoming the new, sensual, sensitive, emotional, vulnerable, transparent man. One perceptive, sensitive woman in her early thirties, twice married, examined her own motives in this regard:

> It is one thing to ask a man not to step on people, not to define himself by how viciously and quickly he climbs the success ladder and acquires things. It's another to cancel the charge accounts so that he can play guitar and sing to the children. It would be rather ironic if we one day found ourselves being threatened by men's lib.
>
> Men may have been initially responsible some time in history for the beginnings of this problem, but women have long since learned to be a part of it—have acquiesced and even helped to perpetuate the stereotype. I was just as guilty of "seeing" a man in this way as the man himself was (tough, macho). I wanted a man who was sensitive and in touch, but *in addition to,* not instead of the other.
>
> The question comes to my mind, and I really have to work with it—can I promise that I am mature enough, loving enough, spiritual enough, to let him be as real as he can be even if the neighbors think he's lazy or weird. Maybe his fears aren't so funny—maybe they are more accurate than we women choose to believe.
>
> The woman blows the whole thing if she is somehow implicitly agreeing that, "Yes, men *are* in danger of not being 'male,' of not being respected and loved if they let their emotions go free." If we tell him he can go this far, but no farther, we have done nothing as far as I'm concerned.
>
> I think I could handle such a change and be glad for it. I sure don't underestimate the necessary readjustment though. I'm also very aware that it took three committed relationships, two marriages and once living together, lying in bleeding pieces behind me, for me to get this far.

A woman who wants to "help" a man in his growth and change first needs to recognize how she feeds into, perpetuates and reinforces his tendencies to be driven and dominant and how she disdains and emotionally turns away from the man who is softer, less predictable, more egalitarian and humanistic and generally less concerned about power and success. Then she needs to recognize and alter the consciousness that has taught her to find and attach herself to the man of highest status available to her. Therefore, the best thing she can do to "help" in this regard is to grow to the point where a man is evaluated as a friend-companion-playmate rather than as a provider–protector–success symbol. Without doing that, her liberation becomes an oppressive, destructive treachery that only binds the man who is rigidly caught even further.

QUESTIONS TO ASK

Women who want to be constructive in their relationships with a man in need of, on the verge of, or in the process of change need to ask themselves the following questions:

1) To what extent do I play traditional feminine games and give off messages that indicate my desire to be taken care of, paid for, courted, protected and freed of the need to make decisions?

2) To what extent do I want it both ways—to get the benefits of my liberation when it suits me while retaining the old-time feminine prerogatives when they serve my purposes?

3) To what extent am I drawn to a man because of his status and success symbols, and would I be able to get equally as involved emotionally with a man who made less money, had less education and a lower occupational status than myself?

4) To what extent do I feel that a man owes it to me to take care of me because I have been exploited, have denied myself, was "forced to put up with things" and was held back by men and "society" and gave more than the man did, and am therefore a victim deserving of reparations?

Once clarifying for herself the extent to which she feeds into and perpetuates the destructive gender interactions, a woman would facilitate the growth of a man most if she herself would:

1) Realize that in any relationship with a man she has made a choice to be with him and therefore probably has a stake in his retaining major parts of his style.

2) Refuse to collude with or accommodate to his needs by suppressing her own identity, assertiveness, aggression and sexuality to boost his ego.

3) Acknowledge and own up to the fact that she enjoys some of the fruits of his compulsive, success-driven, power-oriented, dominant behavior and might therefore subconsciously sabotage his attempts to let go of them.

4) Not be afraid to upset the balance of the relationship and therefore precipitate a crisis. For most men, growth will not occur without a crisis that literally forces introspection and self-awareness on them.

5) Acknowledge and own up to the ways she would not want him to change for her own selfish motives because these changes might jeopardize her role in his life. Owning up would at least prevent the communication of double-bind messages that say, "I really want you to change but please don't do it in a way that would threaten my position in this relationship."

6) Tell the truth about her boredom, her sexual responses, even her manipulations so that he can get to know her as she knows herself rather than as he would like to believe she is.

7) Make it clear to him that she is not fragile and easily hurt by his being real, does not want to be taken care of and is quite capable of protecting herself and fighting on her own behalf.

8) Initiate and structure dates, experiences and sex on a level equal to what she expects from him, accepting the fact that he will not always respond with great enthusiasm to her just as she would not to him were she being real.

9) Maintain her own activities, network of friends and schedules that are separate and for herself and assume that he, as a self-caring person, will do likewise. At the same time, she would refuse to play the role of social director by taking responsibility for their social calendar.

10) Never fake anything socially, sexually or by playing "earth mother" roles. Further, she will not fake inter-

est in or accompany him on activities that essentially bore her and where she doesn't want to be present. Likewise, she will tell him she doesn't want him to participate in activities when he is lacking in genuine interest and enthusiasm.

11) Make it clear that his inability or refusal to be transparent and honest out of an alleged motivation to keep the peace or be protective is a turn-off to her.

12) Avoid doing or being anything in the relationship that, if the relationship ended or he in some way rejected her, would cause her to feel martyred, exploited and manipulated.

20. The Emerging Male

> All of my life I been like a doubled up fist . . . Poundin' smashin', drivin',—now I'm going to loosen these doubled up hands and touch things *easy* with them . . .[1]
>
> —"Big Daddy,"
> *Cat on a Hot Tin Roof,*
> Tennessee Williams

In this age of gender redefinition we are all psychological pioneers. The new directions are uncharted and fraught with the anxieties and pain involved in cutting loose from familiar rituals and predictable responses.

The tendency in times of interpersonal crisis and drastic change is to wish for a return to the known, often in a mood of distorted nostalgic sentimentality. It resembles the phenomenon of the homesick college student who yearns to go back home and remembers it as the warm, safe place it never was.

In fact, we have been witnessing recently the flareup of numerous regressive women's groups advocating that women return to traditional, stereotypical role playing. Undoubtedly, there are many threatened men who would also like to see this happen.

The security of the familiar, even at the price of stagnation, is, in its way, seductive and one major reason why so many people never change their life-style, life pattern or primary relationships, no matter how unsatisfying or painful they are.

One need look no further than the vulnerable, even pathetic stance of most middle-aged and older men to recognize that their human potential has been seriously aborted because their conditioning process has cheated them of so much. The rewards for playing out these assigned roles were interpersonal isolation, emotional repression, rigidity, premature physical deterioration and an increasing sense of futility and cynicism. Only the man's ego defensiveness and the fear of acknowledging the lies he has lived by keep him functioning in so self-destructive a manner.

Aside from its polemical distortions and unfair stereotyping, the women's movement is a profoundly important and freeing one for the male. Books such as this one would probably have found no home and might even have been ridiculed had it not been for the climate of change generated by the women's movement. For men now to stand by without engaging in an equally profound examination and redefinition of their roles would attest to the fact that the masculine defense structure is so rigid and deeply embedded that there is no hope for its alteration and revitalization.

Without a drastic recasting of his role and an equally dramatic change in his consciousness, things can only get worse for him. Specifically, women have already begun filling up the hallowed territories of performance men previously used for defining themselves, and there have been few or no compensations or expansions for him.

His old behaviors with the new woman will not bring him any satisfaction or comfort. The supports of the past, the ones that allowed him to maintain, perpetuate and justify his behavior, are being steadily removed, and he is left exposed as fragile and brittle. He survives by feeding mainly on himself, and precious little nourishment remains within him. He must, for his life's sake, begin to move *past* his age-old orientation of living a life which conforms to external role pressures.

When I am asked about my own motivations for changing, my response is that the alternative of *not* changing seems far worse and more frightening. Mine is not idealistic rebellion or personal sacrifice. From my point of view it is a matter of survival. I do not want to pay the price I see extracted from most of the men around me.

I offer the following basic directions as tone setters and guideposts for men to help them develop a process and rhythm that will break through and beyond their embedded patterns and reflexes. They are, I believe, to be approached in slow motion and with constant questioning and examination. It is not just a matter of the simple development of some cognitive solutions. Intelligent awareness can help define a vision, but the movement toward it will require his total person.

GUIDEPOSTS

1. *Recognize and resist responding to words of sexist masculine intimidation.*

Over the years, the vocabulary of masculinity has become laden with words that menace the male and have the symbolic power to trigger reactions that are self-destructive, because of a deeply rooted tendency in the man to do whatever will allow him to avoid their implications.

These words are often used in wholesale fashion. They are intimidating partially because they cover, in loose and general ways, a wide variety of responses that are actually quite different from each other. Under the spell of masculine intimidation, these labels get reduced to a similar narrow meaning which blocks the man's capacity to see and come to grips with his inner experience: something which would allow him to act on the basis of long-range better sense and the instinct for survival rather than immediate compulsion. To avoid these labels, he settles for the momentary reduction of anxiety. Among these words of sexist intimidation, the following are some of the most powerful motivators.

"Coward": How many men have needlessly placed themselves in jeopardy, been injured or killed because they responded to challenges or threats to their masculinity when little or nothing was at stake except to avoid the label "coward"? In many of these instances, the healthy response would have been to *flee* rather than to *fight,* or simply to refuse to participate.

So too have the words "afraid of" bullied him and made it difficult for him to take the long view. He would assume a responsibility, accept a challenge, put up with an onerous situation, endure an unsatisfactory relationship just to prove that he wasn't *afraid* to do it; that he didn't "chicken out." This made it impossible for him to understand and learn from the important messages his acknowledged fear would have provided.

"Failure": Men are living in an era when they are confronting proliferating and hazardous double-binds. On the one hand, it is suggested to them that success and winning are not the all-important things in life. At the same time, words such as "loser" and "failure" are still applied in derogatory fashion to men who do not effectively compete in the prescribed ways.

Even among the seemingly enlightened segments of the population, subtle evaluations that categorize men in this way are constantly being made. The message is usually indirect—for example, when a successful and powerful man is viewed as charismatic, dynamic, interesting, exciting and so on, while the man who is not is described as "boring," "negative," "drab," "uninteresting," "depressing," and the like.

Even the question "What does he do?" when asked as the source of primary interest in discussing a man has that same undertone. Certain kinds of work imply a positive image and give a man allure. Others immediately fix him with a negative stereotype.

The insidious and pervasive power of such labeling forces men into narrow, repetitive ruts and channels so that they can preserve their image of being a "success" and avoid the alternative negative labels.

"Immature" and "irresponsible": Men in our society often take on overwhelming and debilitating responsibilities at a very early age and burn out prematurely in the cause of proving themselves to be mature and responsible.

A man who marries, fathers, makes a permanent career choice and in general launches for himself a life of "service" and self-denial in his twenties is congratulated by society and defined as a responsible, mature person. In fact, he may actually be a child masquerading as the responsible man. Canny women involved with such men see the immature being that hides behind their socially applauded veneer.

That men in their twenties, who are just beginning to test the waters of their lives, are reinforced for putting themselves firmly in harness at this young age seems particularly destructive. The words "immature" and "irresponsible" are often used indiscriminately to describe any man who moves at a slower pace and chooses to remain uncommitted to a specific life-style for a longer period of time.

Part of the process of freeing the male will be to encourage him to express his playful, emotional and exploratory sides. In the past this would have exposed him to negative reactions. It is within these dimensions, however, that we can see whether we live in an environment whose survival would be threatened if men were to stop fitting themselves into harness and develop a life-style of greater self-care.

"*Lazy*": The equating of a slower-paced style with nonproductivity and laziness is a psychological trap that results in premature physical deterioration. Part of proving one's manliness is to maintain a high level of activity and reduce to as little as possible one's passive inclinations. A man who naps in the afternoon or sleeps late in the morning is suspect.

The free man will need to come up with a new formula and to recognize that some passivity does not necessarily equal "laziness" or unmanliness. He will need to recognize and respect his fatigue and his resistance to activity and to give them equal play so that he can avoid being a driven, perpetual-motion machine. Learning to turn off the inner accusing voice that labels him "lazy" or something equally negative when he lies back will be a major breakthrough.

"*Impotent*": This sexist label of intimidation is also loosely and destructively applied to define myriad responses and motivations. The first time they fail to get an erection, many men think of themselves in the negative context of "I was impotent with her," or "I couldn't get it up." The underlying implication is of sexual failure or of a shadow on their masculinity.

In general, the word "impotent" serves no useful purpose and is clearly sexist because it implies a standard of acceptable masculine sexual performance that makes a man abnormal if he can't live up to it.

The diagnostic quality of this word is also devastating. Men who are labeled "impotent" are also inevitably subjected to self-hate and to pity from others. The word "impotent" clearly needs to be rejected, and those who apply it should be confronted with its sexist bias.

Even if a man has a serious, chronic "problem" with his erections, to apply the word "impotence" to him is still destructive, because its effect is to pressure him to "overcome" "his problem" as soon as possible—at whatever cost to his personality. The process of becoming aware of the meaning of his responses is put under great pressure. He wants his erection back and in top functioning condition as soon as possible so he will no longer be labeled "impotent."

Likewise, other labels for male sexual problems, such as "premature ejaculation" and even "sexual dysfunction," are often sexist and I believe destructive in their connotations. Self-caring men would not apply such labels to themselves, nor would they tolerate their being applied by others.

"Latent homosexual": These words have had a particularly devastating impact on men in terms of blocking the development of affectionate, warm, caring experiences between them. A man who finds himself responding to another man with loving and sensual feelings, unless he has a strongly rooted sexual identity and equally strong self-esteem, tends to be flooded with anxiety and self-doubt. "Maybe I'm a latent homosexual," he tells himself.

Most men, to ensure that they will not be suspect, therefore keep a deliberate and self-protective distance from other men and do so with a defensive, isolating rigidity that loudly signals the message "Don't touch me."

If the words "latent homosexual" imply the potential for an affectionate and sensual response toward a man, practically all men could be considered "latent homosexuals." It is only that most men have rigid and powerful defenses against this tendency that allows them to masquerade as being "totally masculine."

Very simply, all males who have been raised in our culture and who have had women as their primary nurturing and identification figures are "latent homosexuals," in that they have a strong feminine imprint and potential. Their powerful reaction against closeness with men is psychologically defensive; a phobia protecting them against this very threatening interest and desire.

Except in limited instances, the label "latent homosexual," as it is so loosely applied, is a term of sexist intimidation. Warmth, affection, physical touching in a gentle, caring way and attention paid to the needs and feelings of a man all fall under the hostile, intimidating rubic of this label. This is particularly unfortunate and destructive because it sets up such powerful barriers to supportive, loving friendships among men, which are absolutely imperative if he is ever to free himself from his dangerous emotional isolation and his inordinate and debilitating dependency on "his" woman.

"Woman hater": The nature of the traditional male-female relationship is such that women's passive-submissive posture results in the development of unconscious anger and rage toward the man she inevitably comes to resent being controlled and used by. All traditionally conditioned women are therefore potential or latent "man haters."

Likewise the pressure on the traditionally conditioned man to:

1) Constantly prove himself;

2) Repress his needs and emotions;

3) Take responsibility which results in feeling guilty;

4) Be granted sex on a limited and controlled basis subject to his "good behavior";

5) Thwart his own impulses to be playful, spontaneous and expressive in order to live up to the image of the mature husband and father;

6) Experience and yet have to deny intense dependency and therefore vulnerability in relation to the woman in his life;

7) Be unable to express and deal directly with his

resistance, boredom, conflict, resentment and so on in the relationship;

8) Put himself second,

all build up underlying currents of anger and resentment. All traditionally conditioned men are therefore potential or latent "woman haters."

It has, however, been fashionable and tolerable for women to express this anger directly toward men without becoming suspect, because women are perceived as the "victims" and the exploited and "used" ones. The male, who has been considered "top dog," has been given no such justification for anger and therefore his feelings toward women must be hidden and denied. If it is openly expressed, he becomes sexually and psychologically suspect and open to derogatory labeling.

In a repressed, polite, ritualized society where male-female resistance, resentment, anger and so on are not readily surfaced and dealt with unless they can be well justified and tied to an obvious external cause ("You were late"; "You looked at another woman [man]"), significant amounts of hostility build up. The traditionally conditioned woman avoids both anger and conflict, while the male sees his role as being protector of the female and feels himself to be the "heavy" if he initiates an argument or fight.

Consequently, anger in these relationships is always lurking underneath and searching for an outlet or acceptable channel. In the meantime, it surfaces in numerous indirect ways, such as detachment, indifference, boredom, insensitivity, lack of sexual responsiveness, forgetfulness, guilt-making, manipulation and sundry psychological and emotional symptoms. The extremely romantic, never-fighting couple usually have the most fragile, potentially explosive relationship because conflict is never surfaced, dealt with and resolved directly.

Today, women's consciousness raising has provided acceptable channels for the expression of female anger and rage, while men's anger still tends to remain dormant. Potentially, male anger toward women is just as great as women's toward men. However, the controls against its expression are still extremely rigid and powerful. The chivalrous protectiveness many men exhibit toward women, even when the women don't desire it, and the common male perception of women as very fragile are, I believe, part of the defense structure by which the man denies and defends against these angry feelings.

It is both interesting and significant that, while most men would deny having anger and hostility toward women, many women perceive men as having tremendous anger, to the point where some of them fear most men and see them as potential rapists. The important point is simply that anger in men toward women exists just as powerfully as in the opposite case, and the label "woman hater" as a form of accusation is one other term of sexist intimidation that tends to incite his guilt and block him from experiencing and dealing with a real part of his internal experience.

If men are to grow beyond their present rigid positions, they must experience, openly acknowledge and come to terms with their anger toward women, just as women have toward men. The man with no experienced and acknowledged anger toward women is a repressed individual just as the woman who denies any anger toward men would be. This kind of repression often produces unexpectedly cruel and cold behavior in an intimate relationship, so that the person who persistently denies anger may suddenly abandon the relationship, get involved in a secret affair, become detached, all the while denying any negative motivation.

In the long run, women will find men who *do* experience and express their anger toward women openly and directly easier and more satisfying and comfortable to relate to and be with than "Mr. Nice Guy," and potentially capable of significantly more intimacy and love.

"Chauvinist pig": It has been acceptable and fashionable in the last decade to keep men psychologically on the defensive through the intimidation of accusing labels such as "oppressor" and "chauvinist pig." This has played directly into the large potential for guilt in men toward women. Consequently, the sexist ways women behave toward men and the ways women reinforce male sexist behavior have not been focused on and dealt with. In the meantime, many men are finding themselves self-conscious, unsure

and somewhat paralyzed in their responses toward women lest they be accused of saying or doing something sexist.

Male acceptance of such derogatory labels clouds his understanding of what it is that he is reacting to and why. Such accusations can also be self-serving on the part of women, who may use them to keep a man off balance, accommodating and bending over backwards to prove that he is *not* sexist.

The vocabulary is rife with many other words of masculine intimidation that need to be rooted out and exposed for their toxic impact.

2. *Cultivate buddyships.*

It is my belief that well-founded and self-caring, meaningful change and growth for men can only happen if they develop same-sex support systems that would lighten their dependency on women and would also allow them to go through whatever changes they need to go through without fear of alienating their sole source of intimacy.

The one factor more than any other that has facilitated the changes in women's consciousness in fairly rapid and smooth fashion is their ability to take and give support and comfort to each other and to get enough satisfaction from these relationships to compensate for the periods when their relationships with men were in crisis or entirely absent. Because of a sense of mutual support, women did not feel the need to ask for men's permission to change, nor did they fear alienating the man or incurring his disapproval if they risked change.

Likewise, unless men can go through their changes without the terror of losing their woman's love, any change will be contingent on and limited by her approval. In addition, a caring, loving buddyship relationship in a time of unpredictable and volatile heterosexual relationships can provide roots and sources of pleasure, warmth and comfort. The most exciting and dramatic potential in the cultivation of a buddyship orientation is the reduction and softening of the defensive, guarded, detached and competitive posture most men have toward each other.

3. *Avoid the "earth mother" and embrace the woman-person.*

The surgeon general should caution that regardless of how inviting and seemingly satisfying the "earth mother" seems to be in her submissive, adoring, Madonna-like giving posture, she is ultimately extremely dangerous to the man's psychological health. The "earth mother" reinforces his self-destructive, regressive tendencies to dominate, control, prove himself, perform and take major responsibility while also feeling himself in competition with other men for "his" sexual property. The rewards he gets for playing this role are illusory because the "earth mother" will reinforce his tendencies to feel guilty for everything while she herself develops strong latent anger which may emerge as sudden rebellion, raging explosions, unexpected abandonment of the relationship or an endless catalogue of psychosomatic and psychological symptoms.

Above and beyond everything else, intimacy with an "earth mother" is boring, stagnant and devoid of surprise or spontaneity. It is true that a relationship with a woman-person who relates as an equal, responds according to her needs and rhythms, surfaces and negotiates conflict, expresses her anger directly, shares in decision making and the expenses, initiates activities and is a friend and partner as well as a lover and nurturer might prove temporarily threatening because she will not go along passively and submissively with things and will therefore upset the man's long-time orientation of controlling these relationships. However, the growth and freeing aspects of being with a woman-person, relieving the man of the need to put himself second, to feel chronically guilty and responsible when problems arise—as well as providing the freedom for him to concentrate on loosening and expanding the boundaries of his consciousness—more than compensate.

"Earth mother" is destructive to a man's growth. An aware, self-caring man will avoid such a relationship just as an aware woman-person will not involve herself in the destructiveness of a relationship with a sexist-macho male who chronically needs to dominate, control and deny emotions and needs.

4. *Reintegrate your feminine side and revel in the pleasure of experiencing and giving expression to these denied parts of your personality.*

A courterpart to assertion training for women ought to be passivity training for men. As women have been integrating their masculine side, men need to integrate their feminine side in order to move beyond the present liberation crunch. In other words, men must take the benefits of women's growth and not just stretch their capacities thin to handle more stress and responsibility.

Specifically, as women integrate their previously repressed assertiveness, autonomy, sexuality, anger and aggression, men need to reclaim emotions, dependency needs, passivity, fluidity, playfulness, sensuality, vulnerability and resistance to always assuming responsibility. Men too need to become balanced people.

If all that the growth and change in women's consciousness will mean for men is an adaptation to her expanded identity, he will be locking himself into an unbearable position. Women's liberation must not be allowed to mean for men accommodation to her new image. Rather, it must herald the opportunity for men to become fully human themselves, and in the process, like her, reconstruct or even abandon relationships where their changes and growth are not accepted, nurtured and cherished.

5. *Postpone binding commitments.*

The powerful external pressures on the man as a young, growing person, I believe, make it necessary for him to take a number of adult years to establish and develop an autonomous, inner-directed focus on who he is and what he wants.

The traditional male harness has meant the early and often premature establishment of career, marriage and family, which gave the man the appearance of maturity but actually made genuine self-development very difficult, because he was constantly struggling to deal with external pressures. Just as women are realizing and rebelling against their traditional role harnesses, men need now to recognize and alter their self-damaging orientation of assuming and striving to live up to the inordinate demands and pressures laid on them early in life.

6. *Recognize and acknowledge emotions as critical guides to reality.*

The masculine orientation to emotions has characteristically been to perceive them as an interference, threat or challenge which he needed to learn to control and transcend. Consequently, men have given up one of the truest indices for self-understanding and the accurate perception of their relationships. It is perhaps the most harmful aspect of male conditioning that emotions have been made synonymous with femininity and that men have thus been deprived of access to their humanness. Identification and acceptance of fear, affection, resentment, boredom, resistance, longing, sadness, hurt, frustration and so on are crucial to men's development as full people.

7. *Be your own child.*

It is axiomatic that fathers attempt to compensate for personal frustrations and unrealized fantasies through their sons. Fathering a son can be seen as a symbolic passing of the baton, a way of saying, "Here, you fulfill the dreams that I couldn't."

It is perhaps time for men to father themselves, to become their own children and to give themselves what they never got; in effect to undo some of the destructiveness of their own parental conditioning. It will make him that much better a father to his own children later on, as he will father for the *pleasure* of the process and not as a way of acting out his own unfulfilled desires. The effective father therefore will not be the man who works at the role but comes to it fully conscious and fulfilled himself.

8. *Change yourself first!*

It is very much a part of the masculine orientation to want to change the world at the same time or before he works at changing himself. Fortunately, the important changes required for male growth and emergence are intimate and can be effected with great benefit to himself *even if nobody else* changes The development of a buddyship relationship; experiencing and acknowledging emotions; accepting and recognizing his sexual response as an honest expression of himself without making negative judgments; enhancing his capacity for sensuality; developing relationships with women who take equal responsibility and relate as friends and partners; altering self-destructive body habits; giving play to passivity, dependency, vulnerability and fear; postponing intimate commitments; and disengaging from the stranglehold of the obsession with success or fear of failure, can all be worked at and reached without having to change the world in the process. While it produces changes in his life-style, new energies will also be released that make him more productive and his life more fulfilling than it ever was when he was driven by the compulsions of a rigid masculine orientation.

9. *Remember that "masculine" and "feminine" are conditioned phenomena and therefore always in the process of redefinition and change.*

Gender definitions are always transitional. The model of what a man or woman "should be" changes from year to year. Being a "hero" at a heavy personal cost, proving oneself just for the sake of proving when it is detrimental to oneself, is to trade foolishly for temporary approval or adulation. The important thing is to separate the necessary and meaningful challenges from the mindless, compulsive activities one engages in from day to day to allay the anxiety and concern over how it will fit one's gender image and look in other people's eyes.

10. *Support and insist on the continued emergence and growth of women.*

The addictive power of traditional femininity in its ability to stimulate fantasy is so great that few men can withstand its pull. Regressive women's movements that encourage women to resume traditional feminine role playing are highly destructive to the man. The genuine woman-hero is the one who risks relating as a fully and honestly participating, equal and responsible person. It is time for men to see through the webs woven by the femme fatale and old-time female manipulators, who play on men's emotions, learn to push the correct buttons and therefore draw the major attention and interest from most men.

11. *Ask for help.*

It is in the masculine orientation not to ask for help, to go it alone, to seek quick, unambiguous answers and to reject any approach that is not clear-cut and obvious in its logic.

In matters of the emotions and psychological processes, only charlatans hold out the promise of rapid, dramatic change. Defenses cause a person to see himself and reality as he wishes. Change is difficult because it requires bringing back into awareness and integration disowned and threatening parts of oneself.

The ability to ask for help is important in allowing oneself to accept support. It is equally important as a symbol of one's capacity to recognize that the problems and issues are often too complex and overwhelming to negotiate by oneself.

Help can come from many sources, not necessarily professional. The important part is being able to acknowledge one's confusion enough to say, "I need help."

12. *Custom-make your life.*

Look around and ask yourself if on a personal and interpersonal level it still makes sense to live up to old models. Technologically we are living in a highly sophisticated space age, while on the level of human interaction most of our expectations and value systems are ages old and anachronistic.

We are all pioneers in this era of loosening and changing gender definitions to fit human needs rather than to reinforce masculine and feminine stereotypes. It is both an exciting and a threatening time. There will be periods when the changes seem to be too painful, even impossible. The solace I choose in those moments is to ask myself,

"Do I want to repeat the cycles, fit the patterns and play the games that seem to have been played by others from time immemorial? Do they feel good, and do they yield what they're supposed to?" That, I believe, is enough of a spur to maintain momentum in those threatening moments when wresting oneself free from very powerful, very established and very debilitating sexual role models seems like an impossible challenge.

References

CHAPTER 1

1. Mark Strand, "About a Man," *New Yorker*, October 10, 1977, p. 44.

2. Bureau of the Census, *1970 Census of Population. Vol. 1: Characteristics of the Population: United States Summary*, pp. 1–259. Bureau of the Census, *Current Population Reports: Population Estimates and Projections*, February 1975, tables 2, 3, 4.

3. Aaron Latham, "My Lost Generation," *New York*, November 19, 1973, pp. 53–56.

4. Barry Farrell, "The Power Politician behind the Badge," *New West*, December 19, 1977, p. 30.

5. Sandra Lipsitz Bem, "Androgeny vs. the Right Little Lives of Fluffy Women and Chesty Men," *Psychology Today*, September 1975, pp. 58–62.

6. *The Way of Life according to Lao-tzu*, Witter Bynner, trans. (New York: Capricorn Books, 1962), p. 73.

CHAPTER 2

1. *Time*, April 25, 1977, p. 67.

2. *Los Angeles Times*, April 27, 1976.

3. *Newsweek*, July 4, 1976, pp. 30–31.

4. Michael J. Kaufman and Joseph Popper, "Pee Wee Pill Poppers," *Sport*, December 1976, pp. 16–25.

5. George Simpson, "College Football's B.M.O.C. Crisis," *Sport*, November 1976, pp. 19–30.

6. Eileen Brennan "Epitaph for a Dead Mercenary," *People*, August 23, 1976, pp. 18–20.

7. "Abe Maslow—1908–1970," *Psychology Today*, August 1970, p. 16.

8. *Time*, November 22, 1976, p. 61.

9. *Los Angeles Times*, January 15, 1976.

CHAPTER 3

1. *Newsweek*, December 27, 1976, p. 59.

2. George E. Vaillant, M.D., and Charles C. McArthur, "Natural History of Male Psychologic Health. I. The Adult Life Cycle from 18 to 50," *Seminars in Psychiatry*, vol. 4, no. 4 (November 1972), pp. 415–27.

CHAPTER 4

1. Richard M. Coffman and Larry J. Pinter (U.S. Air Force Academy), "The Sex Ratio of Post-industrial America," p. 5. (This paper was presented at the Western Social Science Association Annual Meeting at Tempe, Arizona, April 28–May 1, 1976).

2. "Life Expectancy Statistics in U. S. Take Sudden Jump," *Los Angeles Times*, July 25, 1977, Part I, p. 2.

3. David C. Glass, "Stress, Competition and Heart Attacks," *Psychology Today*, December 1976, p. 57.

4. William Shakespeare, *Macbeth* (Cambridge, Massachusetts: Houghton Mifflin Company, 1931), Joseph Quincy Adams, ed., Act II, Scene II, p. 36.

5. Simpson, George, "College Football's B.M.O.C. Crisis: Battered & Maimed on Campus," *Sport*, November 1976, p. 30.

6. Christing McKee, M.D., Billie F. Corder, Thomas Harzlip, M.D., "Psychiatrist's Responses to Sexual Bias in Pharmaceutical Advertising," *American Journal of Psychiatry*, vol. 131, no. 11 (November 1974), pp. 1273–1275.

7. Rose Dosti, "Shedding Light on Diet and Athletics," *Los Angeles Times*, July 7, 1977, Part VI, p. 1.

8. "Latest in Health and Medicine," *U.S. News & World Report*, Vol. 82, No. 2, January 17, 1977, p. 69.

9. *Los Angeles Times*, April 30, 1978, Part I, p. 18.

10. Erik Eckholm and Frank Record, "Worldwatch Paper 9: The Two Faces of Malnutrition," December 1976, p. 46.

11. Quote taken from the film *Men's Lives* filmed by Will Roberts and Josh Hanig, *New Day Films*, Franklin Lakes, New Jersey, 1975.

CHAPTER 5

1. John Le Carré, *The Honourable Schoolboy* (New York: Alfred A. Knopf, Inc., 1977), p. 533.

2. Gail Sheehy, "The Life of the Most Powerful Woman in New York," *New York*, December 10, 1973, p. 51.

3. Ibid., p. 57.

4. David C. McClelland and David H. Burnham, "Power-Driven Managers: Good Guys Make Bum Bosses," *Psychology Today*, vol. 9, no. 7, December 1975, p. 69.

5. Jack Horn, "Good Guys Make Unchallenging Bosses," *Psychology Today*, vol. 9, no. 3, August 1975, p. 55.

6. David C. McClelland, *Power: The Inner Experience* (New York: Halsted Press, 1976), p. 276.

7. *The Collected Works of Henrik Ibsen, Volume III, An Enemy of the People, The Wild Duck* (New York: Charles Scribner's Sons, 1913), pp. 187–188.

CHAPTER 6

1. Louis I. Dublin, *Suicide—A Sociological and Statistical Study* (New York: Ronald Press, 1963), p. 41.

2. Kate Frankenthal, "Suicidal Differences of the Sexes," *Proceedings of the Sixth International Conference for Suicide Prevention* (Ann Arbor, Mich.: Edwards, 1972), p. 182.

3. Robert E. Litman, M.D., "The Prevention of Suicide," *Current Psychiatric Therapies*, vol. 6 (1966), p. 271.

4. Harry Levinson, "On Executive Suicide," *Harvard Business Review*, vol. 53, no. 4 (July-August 1975), p. 118.

5. David Lester, Ph.D., "Suicide Behavior in Men and Women," *Mental Hygiene*, vol. 53, no. 3 (July 1969), p. 340.

6. Warren Breed, "Occupational Mobility and Suicide among White Males," *American Sociological Review*, vol. 28, no. 2 (April 1963), pp. 179–88.

7. *Los Angeles Times*, September 4, 1977.

8. Don D. Jackson, "Suicide," *Scientific American*, November 1954, pp. 88–92, 94, 96.

9. H. Goldberg and R. T. Lewis, *Money Madness: The Psychology of Saving, Spending, Loving, and Hating Money* (New York: Morrow, 1978), pp. 126–58.

CHAPTER 7

1. Jules Feiffer, *Village Voice*, December 12, 1977.

CHAPTER 8

1. Ashley Montagu, *The Natural Superiority of Women*, rev. ed. (New York: Collier, 1974), pp. 181, 182, 183.

2. Lester Gelb, "Masculinity—Femininity: A Study in Imposed Inequality," *Psychoanalysis and Women: Contributions*

to New Theory and Therapy, Jean Baker Miller, M.D., ed. (New York: Brunner/Mazel, 1973), pp. 369–77.

3. Joseph Epstein, *Divorced in America* (New York: Dutton, 1974), p. 206.

4. David G. Winter, Abigail J. Stewart and David C. McClelland, "Husband's Motives and Wife's Career Level," *Journal of Personality and Social Psychology,* vol. 35, no. 3 (March 1977), pp. 159–66.

CHAPTER 9

1. Robert Frost, "The Hill Wife," from *Complete Poems of Robert Frost* (New York: Holt, Rinehart & Winston, 1949), p. 162.

2. Evelyn P. Stevens, "Marianismo: The Other Face of Machismo in Latin America," in *Female and Male in Latin America: Essays,* Ann Pescatello, ed. (Pittsburgh: University of Pittsburgh Press, 1973), p. 91.

3. Rogelio Diaz-Guerrero, "Neurosis and the Mexican Family Structure," *American Journal of Psychiatry,* vol. 112, no. 6 (December 1955), pp. 411–17; "Adolescence in Mexico: Some Cultural, Psychological and Psychiatric Aspects," *International Mental Health Research Newsletter,* vol. 12, no. 4 (Winter 1970), pp. 1, 10–13.

4. Stevens, loc. cit., p. 95.

5. J. Mayone Stycos, *Family and Fertility in Puerto Rico* (New York: Columbia University Press, 1955), pp. 136–42, 158; Theodore B. Brameld, *The Remaking of a Culture* (New York: Harper, 1959), pp. 107–8.

6. José B. Adolph, "La emancipacion masculina en Lima," *Mundo Nuevo,* April 1970, pp. 39–41.

7. Salvador Reyes Nevares, "El machismo en Mexico," *Mundo Nuevo,* April 1970, pp. 14–19.

8. *Los Angeles Times,* June 10, 1977.

9. Carroll, Smith and Rosenberg, "The Hysterical Woman: Sex Roles and Role Conflict in 19th-Century America," *Social Research,* vol. 39, no. 4 (Winter 1972), pp. 652–78.

10. David H. Stoker, Louis A. Zurcher, and Wayne Fox, "Women in Psychotherapy: A Cross-Cultural Comparison," *International Journal of Social Psychiatry,* vol. 15 (1969), pp. 5–22.

11. *Los Angeles Times,* September 9, 1976.

12. Robert S. Weiss, "The Emotional Impact of Marital Separation," *Journal of Social Issues,* vol. 32, no. 1 (Winter 1976), p. 135.

13. Ibid., p. 143.
14. Carol A. Brown, Roslyn Feldberg, Elizabeth M. Fox and Janet Kohen, "Divorce: Chance of a New Lifetime," *Journal of Social Issues,* vol. 32, no. 1 (Winter 1976), p. 129.
15. Ibid., p. 126.
16. Ibid., p. 129.
17. Ibid.
18. Ibid.
19. Ibid,
20. Weiss, loc. cit., p. 137.
21. *Los Angeles Times,* September 9, 1976.

CHAPTER 10

1. Helen Singer Kaplan, "Friction and Fantasy: No-Nonsense Therapy for Six Sexual Malfunctions," *Psychology Today,* October 1974, p. 80.
2. Leonard R. Derogatis, John K. Meyer and Bridget W. Gallant, "Distinctions between Male and Female Invested Partners in Sexual Disorders," *American Journal of Psychiatry,* vol. 134, no. 4 (April 1977), pp. 385–90.
3. Reproductive Biology Research Foundation, Seminar on Human Sexuality, December 5–6, 1977, Los Angeles, Calif.
4. Gloria Steinem, "Is Child Pornography . . . ABOUT SEX?", *Ms.,* August 1977, pp. 43–44.
5. Susan Brownmiller, *Against Our Will: Men, Women and Rape* (New York: Simon & Schuster, 1975), p. 290.
6. Ibid.
7. Ibid., p. 294.
8. Dick Hobson, "Survivor's Notes from the Sexual Revolution," *Los Angeles Magazine,* April 1977, p. 107.
9. Terri Schultz, "Getting It On," *Penthouse,* April 1974, p. 46.
10. Warren Mintz, "The Male Sexual Cycle," *Humanist,* vol. 36, no. 6 (November-December 1976), p. 11.
11. Mary Harrington Hall, "A Conversation with Masters & Johnson and Mary Harrington Hall," *Psychology Today,* July 1969, p. 55.
12. Schultz, loc. cit.
13. Herb Goldberg, *The Hazards of Being Male* (New York: Signet, 1977), p. 22.

CHAPTER 11

1. Karen Durbin, "How to Spot a Liberated Man," *Mademoiselle,* April 1973, pp. 172–73.

CHAPTER 12

1. *Time,* May 9, 1977, p. 85.

2. *Time,* August 31, 1970, p. 16.

3. Ibid.

4. Phyllis Chesler, "Men Drive Women Crazy," *Psychology Today,* July 1971, pp. 18–98.

5. *Time,* August 31, 1970, p. 16.

6. Marilyn French, *The Women's Room* (New York: Summit Books, 1977), p. 161.

7. *People,* February 20, 1978, p. 33.

8. Jackie MacMillan, "Rape and Prostitution," *Victomology,* Vol. 1, No. 3. Fall 1976, pp. 414–420.

9. Eric Kroll, "Testimony," *Sex Objects* (New Hampshire, Addison House, 1977). New York. Printed in U.S.A. by Foremost Lithographers, Providence, R.I.

10. Herb Goro, "Portrait of a Marriage That Couldn't Be Saved," *New York,* September 18, 1972, pp. 31–42.

11. Meredith P. Smith, M.D., "Decline in Duodenal Ulcer Surgery," *Journal of the American Medical Association,* Vol. 237, No. 10, March 7, 1977, pp. 987–988.

12. Nancy Allen, "Suicide in California 1960–1970," State of California Department of Public Health, 1973, pp. 6 and 10.

13. Robert C. Steppacher and Judith S. Mausner, "Suicide in Professionals: A Study of Male and Female Psychologists," *American Journal of Epidemiology,* Vol. 98, No. 6, December 1973, pp. 436–445. (Published by Johns Hopkins University.)

14. "Cigarette Smoking Among Teen-agers and Young Women," published by the National Cancer Institute in cooperation with the American Cancer Society, p. 5 ([NIH] 77–1203). U.S. Dept. of Health, Education and Welfare, National Institutes of Health. Note: The findings reported in this pamphlet are part of an extensive research project on smoking among teen-agers and young women conducted in 1975 for the American Cancer Society by Yankelovich, Skelly and White, Inc.

11. " 'Gentler Sex' Turns to Guns, Knives, Bombs," *Los Angeles Times,* September 2, 1974, Part I-B, p. 6.

16. Frieda L. Gehlen, "Legislative Role Performance of Female Legislators," *Sex Roles,* February 1977, Vol. 3, No. 1, p. 1018.

17. *Los Angeles Times,* September 8, 1977.

CHAPTER 13

1. Diane and Dick O'Connor, *How to Make Your Man More Sensitive* (New York: E. P. Dutton & Co., Inc., 1975), p. 175.

2. David Bond, "Letters," *Village Voice,* April 12, 1976, p. 3.

CHAPTER 15

1. Julia R. Heiman, "The Physiology of Erotica: Women's Sexual Arousal," *Psychology Today,* April 1975, p. 91.

2. Ibid., p. 93.

3. "Ratio of Male to Female Admissions to State and County Mental Hospitals by Age for Behavior Disorders and Adjustive Reactions, U.S., 1973," *National Institute of Mental Health Statistical Note* 115, Table 3, pp. 10–13.

4. Ibid.

5. "Ratio of Male to Female Residency in State and County Mental Hospitals by Age for Behavior Disorders and Adjustive Reactions, U.S., 1973," *National Institute of Mental Health Statistical Note* 115, Table 3, pp. 10–13.

6. Janet S. Hyde and B. G. Rosenberg, "Tomboyism: Implications for Theories of Female Development"; paper presented at the Western Psychological Association Convention, San Francisco, Calif., April 1974.

7. Carol Tavris, "Woman & Man," *Psychology Today,* March 1972, p. 58.

CHAPTER 17

1. *U.S. News & World Report,* April 15, 1974, pp. 59–60.

2. Helena Lopata, "Widows and Widowers," *Humanist,* vol. 37, no. 5 (September-October 1977), pp. 25–28.

3. Samuel Wallace, *After Suicide* (New York: Wiley, 1973), p. 78.

4. *Los Angeles Times,* August 29, 1976.

CHAPTER 18

1. Bernie Zilbergeld, *Male Sexuality: A Guide to Sexual Fulfillment* (Boston: Little, Brown, 1978), p. 56.

CHAPTER 19

1. Martin L. Gross, "Conversation with an Author: Gail Sheehy, author of *Passages,* on 'Crises of Adult Life,'" *Book Digest,* August 1977, p. 32.

2. Roxann A. and Sheldon Van Dusen and Eleanor Bernert, "The Changing Status of American Women: A Life Cycle Perspective," *American Psychologist,* vol. 31, no. 2 (February 1976), pp. 106–16.

3. Gross, loc. cit.

4. John Dean, *Blind Ambition* (New York: Simon & Schuster, 1976), p. 127.

5. *Los Angeles Times,* February 26, 1978.

CHAPTER 20

1. Tennessee Williams, "Cat on a Hot Tin Roof," *Best American Plays,* Fourth Series 1951-1957, Gassner, John ed. (New York: Crown Publishers, 1958), Act 2, p. 60.

Index

ABOUT THE AUTHOR

Herb Goldberg received his Ph.D. in clinical psychology from Adelphi University. He has been on the faculty of California State University since 1965, where he is presently Professor of Psychology. In addition, he has had a private practice with individuals, couples and families for over ten years and conducts workshops across the country. He is a contributor to numerous professional publications and the author of several books, including the best-selling THE HAZARDS OF BEING MALE, available in a Signet edition.